MIDNIGHT'S KISS

DONNA GRANT

St. Martin's Paperbacks

MIDNIGHT'S KISS

For information address St. Martin's Press, 175 Fifth Avenue, New York, NY 10010.

ISBN: 978-1-250-01726-0

Printed in the United States of America

St. Martin's Paperbacks edition / June 2013

St. Martin's Paperbacks are published by St. Martin's Press, 175 Fifth Avenue, New York, NY 10010.

10 9 8 7 6 5 4 3 2 1

For Melissa Bradley, the best assistant! Extraordinary planner, mutual shoe-lover, and treasured friend.

ACKNOWLEDGMENTS

As always, my thanks go first to my fabulous editor, Monique Patterson. I'm fortunate to be working with such a wonderful person, and talented editor. Thank you for suggestions, insight, and spot-on ideas.

To everyone at St. Martin's who helped get this book ready, thank you.

To my amazing agent, Louise Fury. So glad to be on Team Fury!

A special note to my shout-worthy street team, Donna's Dolls, who circle the globe. Y'all rock!

To my kiddos, parents, and brother—A writer makes sacrifices, but so does the writer's family. Thanks for picking up the slack, knowing when I'm in deadline that I might not remember conversations, and for not minding having to repeat things.

To my amazing hubby, Steve. I couldn't do any of this without your support and encouragement. You have always known how to make me feel like the most special person in the world. The very first time I met you, you made me laugh. Eighteen years later and you're still making me laugh. I love you, Sexy!

CHAPTER ONE

Things had changed.

And not exactly for the better.

Arran MacCarrick stared at the chessboard with unseeing eyes. He was 646 years old, and today he felt every day of those years.

A great sadness weighed upon him. Not for himself, but for his friends. It warred with the restlessness that urged him to do *something*.

The need for battle, to work his body into a frenzy as he unleashed the powers within him from his god, Memphaea. The yearning for something to do kept him awake at night—and on edge through the day. He searched for anything—and everything—to occupy his thoughts and body. If only for a little while.

Camdyn said he needed a woman. Arran inwardly snorted. The last thing he needed was a woman to get in his way and make him fret about her mortality.

A woman.

"No' likely," he murmured.

An unwanted memory of his sister filled his thoughts. She had been a bright, shining star in his world. A free spirit who saw only good. Her future was supposed to have been filled with love and laughter.

Instead, Deirdre had found him. Shelley, his sweet sister, had tried to help him. In return, she was torn to pieces before his very eyes.

He hadn't been a Warrior then, hadn't had the power to stop the wyrran. But even now with that power running just beneath his skin, he knew he was better off without any hindrances.

Are you really?

He glanced up from the chessboard to see Lucan and Cara walk hand in hand up the stairs, whispered words of lovers passing between them.

Unbidden, the lonely nights assaulted him. While the others laughed and talked with their women, he sat in his room alone, staring at the telly without paying attention to whatever movie someone had given him to watch.

Arran might know he was better alone, but he would admit—only to himself—that he envied what the other Warriors had with their women. The smiles, the touches, the secret looks.

It was those women, formidable Druids all, who had helped shape every Warrior in the castle. The Druids were strong, independent, and fierce. Perfect matches for the immortal Highland Warriors they had claimed.

Arran and the others of MacLeod Castle had killed two of the most evil Druids who had ever walked the earth, and they lost friends in the process.

It had taken centuries to end the reign of evil. After defeating such threats, happiness should have followed.

But Fate wasn't always so kind.

Arran remembered his partner as he looked up to find Aiden staring at him impatiently. Arran was moving his knight on the chessboard when Larena burst into the great hall, followed closely by her husband, Fallon MacLeod.

"Check," Arran said as he folded his arms on the table and tried to pretend he didn't hear Fallon and Larena as their year-old argument started up again.

Aiden MacLeod snorted and drummed his fingers on the table. "Uncle Fallon and Aunt Larena are at it again," he mumbled, his fingers alighting on top of his queen.

Arran looked at Aiden, one of only two children brought into a world of magic and Druids. Aiden was the son of Marcail, a powerful Druid, and Quinn MacLeod, one of three brothers both Highlanders and Warriors.

With a nudge of his foot against Aiden's, Arran said, "Make your move, lad."

Aiden's green eyes flashed confidently. "I bested you last week. I can do it again."

"Doona get cocky," Arran warned, though a smile had pulled up the corners of his lips. They teased Aiden as being just a lad, but he'd come into manhood just as stubborn, intelligent, and headstrong as any of the MacLeods.

"I'm tired of waiting!" Larena shouted. "It's past time, Fallon, and you know it. We've sacrificed centuries! I want a family. I want to hold my own children."

Arran could no longer ignore the couple. He found his gaze shifting to his leader and Larena. All the men at the castle, save for Aiden, were Warriors—Highlanders with primeval gods locked inside them.

They had enhanced senses, incredible speed and strength, as well as individual powers given to them by their god. Each of them deadly in their own right.

Larena was the only female Warrior in a castle full of women who were Druids. The Druids often said the stones of the castle seemed to hum with magic. It was no wonder, Arran thought, with Warriors and Druids occupying the massive structure for over seven centuries.

"Larena," Fallon said wearily as he wiped a hand down his face.

"No," she interrupted him, anger making her voice quiver. "Don't try to tell me it'll be all right, because it isn't all right."

Larena walked away, leaving Fallon staring after her. Arran glanced to his left to a room off to the side that had been converted into a media room. There Hayden, Galen, and Logan watched Fallon silently, waiting to see what would happen.

The people who lived at MacLeod Castle were family. They weren't bound by blood—they were bound by fate. Arran took a deep breath and thought how each of them had walked a path that had converged at the castle.

Even during their darkest hours, the love between them, the laughter, and the determination held the group together. For the past year, tensions had grown. And patience was wearing thin.

All because of a spell that could bind the gods inside them once more.

Aiden silently rose from the table and strode from the great hall as Fallon's shoulders slumped. Arran knew his leader needed a large glass of scotch, but Fallon had turned away from any kind of liquor long ago.

Instead, Arran grabbed Aiden's untouched mug of coffee and walked to Fallon. Fallon took it without a word, his face lined with concern and dread.

"You know she's no' going anywhere," Arran said.

Fallon and Larena's love was too strong for anything to tear it apart.

Fallon sipped the coffee. "She's hurting, and I can no' make it better. I've tried. I'd give her the moon and stars if I could."

"So, I guess this means the lead we had on the spell was another dead end?"

Fallon nodded.

Arran grimaced. The spell to bind their gods wasn't much of a concern for him, but for the other ten Warriors who were married, it was all they focused on.

It was only through Isla's powerful Druid magic of hiding MacLeod Castle from the world and keeping the Druids within her shield from aging that the mortals had lived as long as they had.

Aiden, Quinn's son, had been born four hundred years before, and with special magic allowed to age until his twenty-fifth year. The Druids had also taken precautions through the centuries by a potion that would prevent them becoming with child. No one wanted to bring children into the war that had raged.

It worked until last year, when Camdyn and his wife, Saffron, had found themselves surprised, expectant parents.

"Larena saw Emma," Fallon said into the silence. "It's always worse for Larena afterwards."

Larena wasn't the only one affected by the birth of little Emma. Camdyn and Saffron were still on MacLeod land, but they were building their home outside Isla's shield. With the threat of both Declan and Deirdre gone, everyone felt safe enough to leave the shield.

Camdyn and Saffron had left the castle, mainly because of their child. Aiden was gone more than he was at the castle—and with the tensions so high, it was no wonder.

"We all thought to have found the spell by now," Fallon continued.

"And to have your own child."

Fallon drew in a long, deep breath. "We waited centuries until the evil had been eradicated, and now that it has, we can no' find the spell."

The spell had been written on a scroll and hidden in Edinburgh Castle, but it, along with three shipments of magical items, had been taken from Edinburgh to London centuries ago. Two of those three shipments arrived in London. The other was lost.

"We've searched London, and even Buckingham Palace. It's no' there," Arran said.

"It's no longer a scroll, but nothing we've come across exhibits any magic."

"Could it be cloaked somehow?"

Fallon lifted a shoulder in a shrug. "I doona have an answer."

Arran might not care if his god was bound or not at the moment, but he knew his fellow brethren were suffering as much as Fallon. He was one of four Warriors who wasn't mated, so if he could do something, he would.

"We need to follow the path."

Fallon's brow furrowed as he looked at Arran. "What?"

"The journal you found at Edinburgh Castle, it said that there were three shipments. One by water, two by land. We know that one by land didna make it to London. Since nothing has been found in London regarding the scroll—"

"Then we assume it was in the shipment of other items that was lost," Fallon finished. A ghost of a smile appearing. "I like your thinking."

"I was just coming to propose the exact same thing," Ian said as he descended the stairs into the great hall. His light brown hair was left long and loose, brushing against his shoulders.

Arran wasn't startled to hear that someone else had his idea. It was just a matter of time before one of them had thought of something. The fact that it was Ian was a surprise. Especially since it was Logan's wife, Gwynn, who could do wonders on a computer.

Arran smiled, thinking of the computer and how he, Ian, Logan, Camdyn, and Ramsey had struggled to come to terms with the modern world after they had been jumped forward in time from 1603.

"Did Gwynn find something?" Arran asked.

There was a gleam in Ian's eyes as he said, "Actually, I did. I've learned a thing or two from her."

He and Ian shared a smile. Only someone who had time-traveled could understand the complexities and differences of the world they had known and the modern one they had been in for over a year.

"Impressive," Arran said.

He and Ian weren't just united by their leap forward in time. They had been held in Deirdre's mountain, Cairn Toul, for years as she tried to break them to her will so they would serve only her.

It's what happened to most Warriors. The gods were too insistent, too powerful when they were first unbound. It took a certain kind of man to be able to come back from that and learn to control the god himself.

Arran considered himself one of the lucky few. But then

again, he'd have found a way to take his own head before he ever did the bidding of evil.

Ian and Arran had escaped alongside Quinn. It had never entered Arran's mind not to join the MacLeods in their fight against Deirdre.

"What did you find, Ian?" Fallon asked, jerking Arran out of his thoughts.

Ian stuffed his hands in the front pocket of his low-slung jeans, causing his dark red tee to stretch tight over his muscular shoulders. "We doona know the exact route that was taken from Edinburgh to London, but we were able to discover the course of the other land-bound shipment."

"And?" Arran prompted when Ian hesitated.

Ian's lips flattened. "The other shipment went the fastest, quickest way."

"Bloody hell," Fallon muttered.

Arran folded his arms over his chest. "Which means the one we're looking for went the long way round."

"Precisely," Ian said with a nod. "I've been poring over maps all morning long, and I've narrowed it down to four possible routes."

"Hold on," said a female voice from the floor above.

A moment later, and Dani's head of long silvery blond hair popped into view as she hurried down the stairs with a bunch of papers in her hand. She cast a smile at them and said, "I discovered something interesting in the news that was very near one of the routes."

"What was so noteworthy?" Fallon asked.

Dani waited until she was beside Ian before she answered. "A dig. An archeology dig, to be exact. They happen all over the UK, and they always make headlines. I've put a tag on them, so when something's posted, I get an alert in my e-mail. When I got this one, I did some more poking."

She paused and licked her lips. "I tried making some calls, but I was blocked every time. Even with Gwynn's talents on the computer, we found nothing. So . . . I did what anyone who knows a megamillionaire would do."

"You talked to Saffron," Arran said with a grin. Not only was Saffron a Seer, but she was also connected to people all over the world through her business and charity work. If anyone could get information, it was her. Or her money.

Dani nodded. "Thanks to Saffron and her connections, I think I know where we can begin to look."

"Where?" Fallon asked, his attention focused for the first time since the conversation began.

"Southwest of Glasgow. They've been at the dig site for almost two months now."

Before Fallon could even put out a request for someone to go check it out, Arran said, "I'll go."

Ian didn't seem fazed that he had spoken up, but Fallon raised a dark brow.

Arran rocked back on his heels. He had to get out of the castle and do something before he went crazy. Besides, none of the others would want to leave their women. "Everyone is . . . occupied besides me."

"We could ask Phelan or Charon to check it out," Dani said.

Arran bit back a growl. He might have forgiven Charon for spying on them while locked in Cairn Toul, but that didn't mean Arran wanted him to take over his mission. "Why bother Charon? And Phelan, who the hell knows where he is? He disappears the same as Malcolm."

As soon as the words were out of his mouth, Arran regretted them. Though all the men were Warriors, Malcolm was different. Four hundred years ago, he'd been a mortal helping his cousin, Larena, hide from Deirdre.

He was attacked on Deirdre's command and left for dead. Malcolm had been brought to the castle, and Sonya, with her healing magic, did all she could. It saved his life, but it didn't heal his scars or fix his right arm so that he could use it.

It wasn't much later before Deirdre found Malcolm and unlocked his god. She used Larena against Malcolm in order to keep Malcolm doing her bidding. But it had been Malcolm who betrayed Deirdre at the end, helping them to end her once and for all.

But Malcolm's scars went much deeper than his skin. They went to his very soul, and nothing could heal them now. Only time would aid in tempering the past.

Arran cleared his throat. "Regardless, I'll go. I can only best Aiden in chess so many times. With no wyrran to battle, and no evil to kill, I need something to do."

"No evil to kill," Dani said with a look at Ian. "That sounds wonderful."

Ian wrapped his arm around her and brought her against him for a kiss. "It's music to my ears. I never thought I'd see the day that Deirdre was no longer alive. And then to have also ended Declan. It's almost too good to be true."

Arran looked away. It *was* too good to be true. If there was one thing he'd learned, it was that the evil Deirdre and Declan had been wasn't going to give up so easily.

They'd had a reprieve. But how much longer could that last?

"Find me the spell," Fallon told Arran. "Please."

Arran glanced at Ian and Dani. They had been together for only a short time, as had Logan and Gwynn, and Ramsey and Tara, but Arran knew they all wanted normal lives.

To have children.

To grow old and die with their wives.

Camdyn had almost succeeded in pushing Saffron away because he'd been married before. It was watching his first wife die that had confirmed to Camdyn he was better off alone.

But, as Quinn was often heard saying, love finds a way.

Arran had been given a home—and hope—with the Mac-Leods. He owed every man and woman there a debt, one that a single mission couldn't come close to repaying.

"I'll find it," he vowed to Fallon. "I'll follow every lead. I'll do whatever it takes."

"Even steal?" Ian asked.

Arran didn't hesitate in his nod. "*Whatever* it takes."

Dani held out a large manila packet. "I thought one of you might be going, so I had Saffron pull some strings. You'll be working at the dig as a volunteer."

"I willna have to sneak around?" he asked, a little peeved that he couldn't use his Warrior skills.

"No," Dani said, her voice flat. "There's no need. You'll be able to look at everything they find as well as help in the dig. If you find something, being a Warrior, you should be able to take it easily enough."

Arran was eagerly looking forward to the task.

"But," Dani said hurriedly, "remember, you're working under Saffron's company. She's helping to supply the funding for this dig, which is how we were able to get so much information."

Ian rolled his eyes. "Is there anything Saffron is no' involved in?"

"Not really," Dani said. Then she turned back to Arran. "In other words, if something happens, they'll look to Saffron and her company, so we need to make sure that doesn't happen."

"If it does, I'll ensure another company is at fault," Arran said.

"Good. You can leave in the morning. They're expecting you tomorrow afternoon," Dani said.

Arran just smiled. "I'll be leaving now. It takes only a few hours to reach Glasgow. I can be there by eight or nine this evening. That way I can have a look around before everyone starts working tomorrow."

"A fine idea." Fallon walked to the kitchen, where the keys to the vehicles were kept. He tossed a set to Arran and said, "Take the Range Rover. It'll do better where you're going than the Porsche."

Arran pocketed the keys and hurried to pack a bag. His blood pumped with the need for something more exciting than sitting around playing chess.

There was only so much training a Warrior could do before his god demanded battle. And death.

Arran might not have evil to kill, but he had a spell to find. It was just what he needed.

CHAPTER
TWO

27 miles south of Muirkirk, Scotland

Arran parked the Range Rover and looked through the windshield at the chaos before him. A sizzle of magic rushed over him. He was definitely in the right place.

The magic was ancient and . . . potent. It made him smile, but that smile froze when a different feel of magic swarmed him. It left him breathing hard, need filling him until he could see nothing, feel nothing but the exquisite magic.

A Druid.

There was a Druid at the site. And he was going to find the Druid as soon as he could. The only thing that kept him from searching immediately was that the magic wasn't evil.

Saffron had told him the excavation site was run by Dr. Ronnie Reid, who was a premier archeologist and one of the best ever to come out of the field.

Arran had also been warned that Dr. Reid ran a tight operation, so he'd have to be careful while he searched for any clues to the missing spell and the Druid he'd just felt.

Not that Arran was concerned about this Dr. Reid. He would put himself in the good graces of the man, and make sure Reid saw Arran was a good worker. Once that was established, then Reid would leave him alone. Thereby giving Arran the time he needed to look around.

He sighed. He'd thought this mission would be a quick one, but as he watched the dozens of people moving back and forth from the different dig sites, hauling away dirt while others were prone on the ground, dusting possible finds with what looked like paintbrushes, Arran realized this was going to be anything but simple.

In all likelihood, he'd be here several weeks. Mayhap months.

Not that he was upset about it. With no more evil to fight, Arran was bored. It wasn't that he wanted evil around, it was just that the god inside him craved battle, yearned for bloodshed.

Demanded death.

What better way to appease his god than by battling evil?

Arran clenched his jaw. There would be no clashes at the dig site, which meant he would have to find another way to work off some of the pent-up energy he felt thrumming through his body.

Exerting his muscles with physical labor was just the thing.

Arran opened the door and got out of the Range Rover. The wind howled across the land, slamming into him just as the magic had done, and a glance at the evening sky showed that rain was on the way.

He closed his door and quickly opened the back passenger door to grab his duffel and backpack. Saffron had assured him that lodgings would be made available. In a way, Arran was hoping there wasn't anything. It had been a very long time since he'd slept under the stars as he'd used to do four hundred years ago.

After adjusting the bags on his shoulders, he closed the door and looked at the site once more. The magic was beckoning to him, the sensual feel of it like kindling on a fire.

Desire pumped, scorching and burning, through him as his gaze scanned the area. With every breath, a yearning he'd never felt before filled him and grew until it consumed him, engulfed him.

Devoured him.

Where was the Druid? There was hunger such as he'd never borne. Every bone in his body urged him to find the Druid posthaste. It had to be the Druid who was causing such . . . desire.

The need was pulling him under, dragging him down a chasm of craving so dark and deep, there would be no coming back from it. If he didn't do something soon, he would be lost.

He searched his mind for anything to hold on to, and that's when he thought of MacLeod Castle. That was all it took for him to gain the upper hand on the desire raging within him.

Arran ground his teeth together. The Druid would have to wait. Right now, he had to meet Dr. Reid and learn as much about the man as he could.

The summer sky was still light despite it being past eight in the evening. It wouldn't get truly dark until well after midnight, yet lights standing tall around the dig had already been turned on.

"Here we go," Arran said, and started toward the site, the feel of magic growing with each step he took.

He'd barely gotten ten steps in before he was dodging people who assumed he'd get out of the way. Since there was a possibility they were carrying ancient magical items, they were right.

But still, a low growl sounded deep within his throat.

He was a Warrior, a man used to being feared. It didn't sit well that he was dismissed so easily.

Arran walked over to a man with thin, windblown white-blond hair and glasses he kept shoving up his hawklike nose. The man was bony, his shoulders already hunching forward despite him being as young as his mid-thirties, if Arran guessed right.

"Excuse me," Arran said as he reached him.

For several moments, Arran was ignored. The man glanced up from the clipboard in his hand as he scribbled something on the papers with his pencil. Arran raised a brow when the man seemed to look right through him.

Then, a double take later, the man took a step back, his blue eyes wide as he shoved his glasses up on his nose. "Dude. How long have you been standing there?" he demanded, his American accent thick, and his voice deeper than Arran had imagined would come out of someone so willowy.

"Longer than I'd like," Arran replied, giving just enough inflection in his voice to tell the man his irritation was rising.

"Oh. Yeah. Sorry 'bout that. I tend to get involved with my work. I'm Andy Simmons, the site manager."

"Arran MacCarrick," he said, and held out his hand.

Andy shook it with a grip that was much stronger than Arran would have guessed. "You arrived earlier than expected. I was just told a few hours ago that you'd be helping out."

"I was eager to get started," Arran said with a smile.

"We're glad to have you. Anyone connected to Ms. Fletcher . . . er . . . Mrs. MacKenna, is a friend of ours. Sorry. I'm still getting used to the fact that Saffron is married."

"Aye. To a verra good friend of mine. Saffron knows how interested I am in the history of my land, and when she told me about the dig, I wasna about to let the opportunity pass." Arran wondered if he'd layered on the lie a little too thick, but Andy just nodded as if he understood.

"You either love archeology or you don't." Andy shoved his glasses higher on his nose and jabbed the pencil behind his ear. "Everyone seems to think it'll be like *Indiana Jones*."

Arran just chuckled along with Andy, since he had no idea what Andy was referring to. "Can you point me to Dr. Ronnie Reid? I'd like to get acquainted."

There was a loud pop followed by static and someone's disembodied voice yelling Andy's name. Andy jumped and reached for the walkie-talkie strapped to his waist.

"Dr. Reid is there." Andy pointed over his shoulder before he clicked the walkie-talkie and began a conversation as he strode away.

Summarily dismissed, Arran let his gaze wander the site. Since he didn't know what Dr. Reid looked like, he began to look for someone who appeared to be in charge.

His gaze paused when he found himself looking at the

nicest bum he'd seen in a long time. The woman wore tight, faded jeans that looked well worn, as if they were her favorite. The denim hugged her slim hips and long legs.

The wind paused, allowing the back of her tan jacket to fall into place, instantly hiding her backside from his view. Arran frowned. He liked what he'd seen. A lot. With one look, his blood was already burning for more than just a glance at her, churning with barely restrained desire.

That mixed with the Druid magic that was pushing the limits of his control only added to his hunger. He got another eyeful of the woman's backside and smiled in approval. He'd always appreciated a nice body when he saw one, and this woman had a particularly superb figure.

Just before he looked away, the man beside the woman caught his attention. The older white man had a full beard more gray than black. A wide-brimmed, olive-colored hat rested upon his head to shield his eyes from the sun. He was speaking while the woman nodded her head of wheat-colored hair pulled back in a low, loose bun.

And just like that, Arran found his eyes locked on the woman once more. His fingers longed to run down the length of her slender neck before delving into the strands of her hair, pulling her slowly toward him until her lips were parted, begging for his kiss.

He swallowed and adjusted his jeans around his swollen cock. With great self-control, he looked away from the beauty and focused on the older gentleman again until his desire was in check.

Arran knew he'd found Dr. Reid. Without hesitation, he walked to the duo. His curiosity about what the woman looked like caused him to change course so that he came up from her right side instead of from behind her.

His gaze slid over her at his leisure. Her face was a golden bronze from her time outdoors. Her boots were muddied and as well worn as her jeans, proving she didn't mind getting dirty.

The long-sleeve plaid shirt he glimpsed under her jacket was tucked into her jeans and showed off her full breasts.

But it was the gold chain with the trinity knot dangling just above her cleavage that intrigued him.

It wasn't just any piece of jewelry. It was ancient, and Arran would bet his immortality that she had unearthed it herself on some dig.

Where, he'd like to know.

There was another crackle of magic, and for an instant Arran thought it might have come from the woman.

The magic was *mie* magic, or good magic. The *mies* were the ones who used the magic nature gave them to heal and to help things grow. They were the ones who had counseled the leaders of the clans, the ones who had educated the young.

Had he felt *drough* magic, black magic, he would have sought the source immediately and ended it. Because *droughs* were evil. They gave their souls to Satan in order to use black magic.

The feel of their magic was cloying, sickening—whereas the feel of *mie* magic was calming to a Warrior.

As far as he knew, only Warriors could sense or feel the magic of the Druids. It had saved his brethren more times than he wanted to count.

The woman glanced at him, her hazel eyes barely giving him a second's notice as she went back to her conversation. But with that quick look, the color of her eyes would be embedded in his memory forever.

Arran slowed his steps. Her heart-shaped face was angled a bit to the left. High cheekbones and a smooth complexion without a hint of makeup gave her an earthy, natural look he found appealing. The only thing that marred her face was a small scar on her chin.

Her full lips were a dusky pink that quickened his blood as he imagined them opening for his kisses and whispering his name. The clear, vibrant hazel eyes were by far her best feature. They were large, and every emotion could be detected in their rich depths.

Arran smiled. It was too bad he didn't have time to pursue the woman, because he loved a good challenge, and that's exactly what she'd be.

He gave her bum another look, inwardly smiling at how his hand itched to smooth over such nice curves. Anyone who stirred him as much as she deserved attention. Hours and hours of attention. Perhaps after he found the spell, he could turn his time to her.

A strand of her wheat-colored hair was pulled out of her bun by the ever-present wind and tangled in her long eyelashes. Long, slim fingers reached up and patiently extradited it again and again. Arran would bet his case of Dreagan Scotch hidden in his room that it was a motion she did every day and no longer noticed.

He was upon them now, and he hated that his perusal of the woman had come to an end. Arran wanted to know her name. He wanted to see her smile, hear her laugh, and listen to her scream his name as he brought her to climax.

His balls tightened as he imagined loosing her bun and allowing her hair to fall free as he removed her clothing one piece at a time until she was bare before him and he could feast his eyes upon her beauty.

Being this close to her made his blood run like molten lava in his veins. He craved a touch of her, yearned to hold her. Longed to claim her.

Months with just the two of them. Touching, kissing. Loving. Sheltered and wrapped in their desire.

He reached toward her, the need to touch her overwhelming, crushing. Just before he made contact, Arran dropped his hand, silently cursing himself for allowing his passion to rule him. But damn if he didn't want to give in and see where it took him.

"Dr. Reid," Arran said to the older man as he realized he'd been staring at the woman too long.

Except it wasn't the man who answered, "Yes?"

Arran glanced at the woman to his left and narrowed his eyes. He jerked his gaze back to the man. "Ronnie Reid?"

There was a long-suffering sigh before he heard, "Right here, imbecile," to his left.

Arran's eyes slowly turned to the woman. "You?"

"Yes," she said with a roll of her eyes. "Why is everyone so surprised?"

"Maybe because you use 'Ronnie' as your name, lass."

The older man chuckled, but kept quiet when Ronnie sent him a withering glare.

"Listen, I don't know who you are, but let's get this straight once and for all. I'm Dr. Veronica Reid, also known as Ronnie."

"There's no need to get riled, lass," Arran said to calm her, but he loved the fire he saw within her. By the way her hazel eyes blazed, he knew he'd said the wrong thing.

"No need, huh?" Ronnie asked, her American-accented voice getting higher the more irritated she became. "How would you like everyone questioning who you were?"

"Ronnie," the older man said as he tried—and failed—to hide his smile. "Give the poor bloke a break. He can't know you've had a bad day."

Ronnie closed her eyes and took a deep breath. When she looked at Arran again, her anger had evaporated. "Forgive me. As Pete so wisely stated, you can't know about the day I've had. I had no right to get riled, as you put it."

"No harm done. I'm Arran MacCarrick."

She winced when she heard his name. "Saffron said you were coming. I know first impressions are important, Mr. MacCarrick, but I hope you'll forget mine."

Arran had no such plans, but he didn't tell her that. Besides, he liked what he'd seen. Maybe too much. The fact that she was Dr. Reid definitely put the brakes on any kind of flirting he might have thought of doing, however, his cock be damned.

Flirting might be out, but he was there to know all there was about Ronnie and what she was on the verge of discovering. He had to get close to her.

Yes. Verra close.

How he was going to do that and not give in to the need to pull her against him and taste her delectable pink lips, he had no idea. But he'd have to think, and quickly.

"Doona fash yourself about it, Dr. Reid."

"Please," she said as she held out her hand. "Call me Ronnie. Any friend of Saffron's is a friend of mine."

Arran took her small, thin hand in his. Something electric passed between them with that one, simple touch. And just like that, the passion erupted out of control, and was directed right at Ronnie.

His body heated, his balls tightened again. All the desire he'd been pushing aside roared to life, urging him, driving him to pull her in his arms and taste her lips. She had the appearance of a calm, collected person, but Arran could see the passion simmering just beneath the surface, waiting to be released.

The slight widening of her eyes let him know she'd felt it, too. He wanted to press her, to make her acknowledge what was between them.

He wanted to see the desire in her eyes, feel her warm flesh beneath his hands. A tremor went through her hand, and Arran found himself tugging her to him. For just a moment she leaned into him. His gaze lowered to her lips. Nothing mattered but sampling her kisses.

She hastily looked away. But not before he saw lust darken her hazel eyes.

Arran bit back his smile at the last minute. As soon as he was alone, he was going to call Saffron and let her know her little jest about keeping secret Ronnie's identity as a female hadn't been funny.

He'd wondered why she had intentionally left out what Ronnie looked like. At first he thought Saffron was just preoccupied with the baby, but now he knew the real cause.

Yet, for all the reasons he was irritated with Saffron, Arran was more than pleased with what he saw of Ronnie. He wanted her. Nay, *want* was too weak of a word. He *hungered* for Ronnie, ached to feel her soft body against him.

Her wheat-colored hair and hazel eyes stood out against the dark bronze of her skin. Almond-shaped eyes, pert nose, amazing lips . . . there wasn't anything about Ronnie that wasn't feminine and altogether too alluring.

She was the kind of woman who would look good dressed

in a formal gown, or as she was with jeans, shirt, and coat dusted with dirt and mud.

She was the kind of woman Arran liked. The kind he'd never been able to find.

The irony didn't go unnoticed.

"Call me Arran, please."

For long moments they simply stared into each other's eyes. He knew she felt the desire, knew by the way her pulse quickened at her throat that he affected her.

"I'm Pete Thornton."

Arran reluctantly released Ronnie's hand and shook Pete's. It took everything he could not to growl at Pete for interrupting them. Instead, he forced a smile. "How do you factor in this dig?"

Pete looked at Ronnie and they both laughed, but it was Pete who answered. "I was Ronnie's professor at Stanford. She had a love for archeology I'd never seen before. And her knack for finding things is unparalleled."

"Is that so?" Arran grew more intrigued about Ronnie Reid the more he discovered about her. There was magic here. Could it be from the magical artifacts lost long ago, the pendant Ronnie wore, or Ronnie herself?

Arran couldn't wait to find out.

"Enough, Pete," Ronnie said with a shy smile. "You know sometimes we get lucky in our digs, and sometimes we don't."

"Ah, but you're luckier than most."

"Come, I'll show you to your tent," Ronnie said to Arran.

He wasn't fooled. She had cut Pete off before he could say more about how she found her artifacts. "Verra intriguing," he murmured to himself.

With a wave to Pete, Arran followed her as they walked across the area roped off by the government; the rope border allowed them to dig but also kept others out.

Thousands of conversations, shouts, the sound of shovels plunging into the ground, and even the ring of hammers striking rocks filled the air.

As if reading his mind, Ronnie smiled. "No one ever realizes how loud the sites can be."

"Aye. I wasna expecting this. The noise, nor the sheer amount of people."

"We could use about a dozen more. So this is your first archeological dig?"

"It is. I willna be a hindrance, though."

Arran didn't miss the way she looked him up and down once they reached the set of tents that stood in a semicircle in front of dozens of caravans.

"No, I don't expect you will. Why my dig, though?"

"It's my country. I want to see what the past holds."

She gave a small nod of acceptance. "This is your tent. You'll be sharing with Pete for a few nights before he returns to the States for business."

Arran ducked into the tent through the zippered opening. He saw two cots, one on either side of the small tent. It wasn't optimal, since he'd have to share, but it could have been worse.

"This will do fine," he said over his shoulder before he tossed his two bags on the cot that was freshly made.

Ronnie tried not to look at his ass, she really did. But she'd never seen a man fill out a pair of jeans the way Arran Mac-Carrick did.

And it wasn't just his jeans. From his wide shoulders and muscular chest to the way that torso narrowed to jeans resting low on slim hips and encasing long legs, he fascinated her. Ronnie would bet that beneath that black tee were abs so defined, she'd be able to count each of them.

In one word, he was yummy.

He was the embodiment of tall, dark, and handsome. It was his smile, the one that said he knew secrets of the flesh she could only imagine. A smile that beckoned her to throw caution to the wind and let her body lead.

But she'd already made that mistake once. One tall, dark, and handsome man was enough for a lifetime. It didn't matter that Arran exuded a sexual magnetism she found herself inexplicably drawn to. He had charisma and confidence in spades.

Add that to a tight, muscular body a blind woman could drool over, and Ronnie knew she was in trouble with a capital *T*. Arran flashed that smile and stared at her as if he could look deep into her soul and uncover her wildest dreams and desires.

For a moment, she almost let him.

For a moment, she could see herself with him. Naked. Limbs entwined, breaths harsh and uneven, skin slick with sweat, and desire ruling her, leading her.

Ronnie couldn't dislodge the image now that she'd conjured it. And felt it. Her body throbbed, as if it yearned to be touched. By Arran.

Her heart thudded in her chest as she fought against the pull of his body. It would be so easy to give in and let her passion and his virility dictate everything.

The newest member of her team was friendly enough, but she didn't miss the way his gaze moved around the site, as if trying to study everything without being seen.

Saffron had funded many of Ronnie's digs, so she wasn't about to tell her no when Saffron asked if a friend could help on the site. Yet now Ronnie had the urge to call Saffron and learn all she could about Arran.

It wasn't just his rugged good looks that set her off kilter. It was the gleam in his golden eyes, the way he stood, as if he were ready for battle.

Which was silly, because there was nothing to fight.

Ronnie chuckled to herself.

"What is it?" Arran asked when he straightened.

She shook her head and grinned. "Every time I come to Scotland, I find myself thinking I'll see men with swords strapped to them, ready for battle."

He didn't laugh as she expected. Instead, he gazed at her with his amazing golden eyes, an intensity about him that made it difficult for her to draw breath.

Dark brows slashed between eyes and a high forehead. A wealth of hair so dark brown that it almost appeared black was kept long with a hint of a wave and hung past his shoulders. He had impossibly long, thick eyelashes, and the dark stubble on his chiseled cheeks and square jaw only added to his attraction.

Then there were his wide lips that were fuller than a man's ought to be. They made her think of tangled limbs, of long, sensual kisses where she'd forget everything but the man touching her.

As a total package, Arran was the kind of man who turned heads wherever he went. Women wanted him, and men wanted to be him.

Ronnie knew what came with having a man like Arran around. Every instinct told her to have him leave, but she needed extra hands around. And she couldn't refuse Saffron's request.

Not to mention she couldn't ignore the yearning of her body, no matter how hard she tried. Her heart had been racing, her blood ablaze through her veins since he had walked up. His easy, devil-may-care attitude and stark enticement couldn't be disregarded, no matter how much she tried to do just that.

She pulled her jacket tighter in an effort to shield her aching nipples. They'd grown hard at the first inflection of his deep, velvety voice. His Scots brogue low and thick. Just hearing him talk made goose bumps rise along her arms.

Odd how none of the other Scots caused the same reaction.

"You're no' off the mark," he finally said, drawing her out of her thoughts. "My land has seen countless battles as men fought to rule us."

"You speak as if you've lived here from the beginning of time."

He shrugged. "Maybe I have in a past life."

Ronnie normally dismissed such inane sayings, but somehow, she believed it when Arran said it. Maybe not that he'd lived another life, but that he was much more than he appeared to be.

He was dangerous. Of that she was sure.

Dangerous to her psyche. Dangerous to her capacity to forget him as she had done so many other men.

He was captivating, charismatic, and entirely too interesting.

"Why do I get the feeling, lass, that you doona want me here?" Arran asked.

"Because men like you—"

"Men like me?" he interrupted, one dark brow raised as if he didn't like being compared to other men.

And she had to admit, Arran MacCarrick really couldn't be compared to anyone else.

"Yes, good-looking men who come to the digs distract the women. They flirt and get involved instead of focusing on the dig. People can get injured, artifacts lost, broken, or even stolen, and any number of things when people aren't concentrating on their tasks."

"So, you think I'm handsome," he said with a crooked grin.

Ronnie sighed and rolled her eyes, trying her damnedest not to feel the flutter of her stomach at his smile. She had the urge to return his smile, but she had learned her lesson long ago with such daring, gorgeous men.

"What I think is beside the point. You're here because Saffron requested it. I know her. If you're her friend, I just want to ask that you remember that when the women begin to take notice of you."

His smile disappeared and his gaze narrowed. "I know my duty. You willna have a problem with me sniffing around any of the women. I can no' help if they come to me, but I give you my word, I'll dissuade them."

This Ronnie hadn't expected. "Uh . . . thank you."

"I'm many things, Ronnie, but I wouldna think of compromising this dig or you."

She shifted from foot to foot, feeling like an ass for saying all those things to him. "I just needed you to understand."

"And I do, lass. Doona fret over it. My hide is thicker than most, so it'll take more than your honest words to rile me."

"I'd almost like to see that," she said with a grin. As soon as the words were out, she wasn't sure where they had come from. Ronnie cleared her throat. "Why don't you take the rest of the evening to look around? We're wrapping things up for the night, and Andy and Pete are around if you need anything. First thing in the morning, I'll give you your duties."

"Sounds good. Only, you might want to think of covering that," Arran said as he pointed to the twelve-foot-by-four-foot section of newly excavated soil. "There's about to be a downpour."

"They said not until sometime tomorrow."

"Scottish weather is as fickle as I've seen. You can no' trust what weathermen say. You must learn to read the weather yourself, lass."

Ronnie looked at the section. They'd dug just four inches, but already they had found bits of broken pottery. After three years in Scotland, she knew how changeable the weather was. If it rained, there was no telling what would get washed away. And she knew something was there, waiting to be discovered.

Yet covering it now would put them behind schedule.

The other six sections they had been digging on for over a month were already covered to shield 90 percent of the rain.

Ronnie glanced at the sky before she looked at the new section. There was something important underneath all that dirt. She knew it in her soul.

She *felt* it.

It wasn't something she told anyone, but that same feeling was what led her to so many finds on her past digs. Her . . . gift . . . was what made her famous, but it was a secret she would have to take to the grave. There wasn't a soul she could trust with such knowledge.

"Andy!" she called. "Cover the new section ASAP. Rain is coming!"

Andy gave a nod, and instantly the diggers moved while others hurried to cover the section. Ronnie was surprised when Arran rushed to help.

So surprised that it took her a moment before she followed suit. As they all struggled with the bright blue tarp, the wind howled around them, trying its best to jerk the canvas out of their hands.

It wasn't until the tarp was staked securely in the ground that Ronnie looked up. And found golden eyes watching her, assessing her. The pull she'd felt earlier tugged her toward him.

She kept her feet rooted to the spot somehow, but there was no denying she wanted Arran. His kisses, his touch, his . . . body.

A heartbeat later, the first fat raindrop landed on her cheek. Before she could gain her feet, the heavens unleashed a rainstorm like none she had ever seen.

While everyone rushed to get out of the driving rain, Ronnie checked the stakes one more time before she moved on to the next section and the tentlike structures that had been erected over the freshly dug sites.

The rain soaked through her jeans, but her jacket, which was waterproof, helped to keep her upper body mostly dry. The way the wind lashed, the jacket couldn't stop all of it.

And the droplets running down her face and head into the neck of her shirt were quickly drenching her.

As she checked one of the ropes of the structures covering a dig, another came loose of its knot and began to flap wildly in the wind.

Ronnie jumped for it, but it seemed to go higher, as if teasing her. Suddenly, a shadow loomed behind her as a large hand grabbed the rope.

She jerked around to find Arran. He blinked the rain out of his eyes, and with a nod, knelt to retie the rope. She didn't watch him or the way the wet tee clung to his back so his muscles moved and bunched as he worked.

At least she tried not to.

It was difficult when he so big. She wasn't a tiny person, but he made her feel that way.

She stepped back to put some distance between them when she tripped over one of the stakes. Her arms flailed wildly as she tried to keep her balance.

Suddenly, she was yanked against a rock-hard chest,

looking up into Arran's hooded eyes. One of his arms wrapped tightly around her while his other hand was splayed on her lower back, holding her against him.

Ronnie instinctively grabbed hold of him, the thick muscles beneath his wet shirt were warm and solid, his body unmovable, rigid. She blinked through the rain to find his face inches from hers. That tug she'd felt earlier reeled her in quickly, promptly.

Decisively.

His gaze dropped to her mouth, and her stomach fell to her feet as she found her lips parted, waiting expectantly for his kiss.

Her heart raced when she felt the hard ridge of his arousal against her stomach. Heat flooded between her legs, and her knees grew weak.

His arm tightened a fraction while his head lowered those last few inches. There was no way she could deny the kiss she knew was coming. And she didn't want to.

His lids lifted so that golden eyes stared at her, desire blazing for all to see. He pulled back a little, as if containing himself. "You need to be more careful, lass."

He said *lass* as an endearment, soft and beckoning. It took a moment before Ronnie could release him because she didn't trust her legs to hold her up. When she did, he gave her a slight nod and went back to tying down the tarps.

She didn't know what she was more disappointed in— not getting his kiss, or having to relinquish her hold on him. She'd just thought his body amazing. Then she'd touched him, handled those wonderful muscles and felt his heat.

With both of them checking the rest of the structures, Ronnie was done in half the time, which was good, since her mind was full of Arran and the need still coursing through her. She motioned him to follow her as she ran to her tent, her boots splashing water with each step.

It wasn't until she was inside her shelter and turned to watch him dip his wet head and step inside that she wondered what could have made her invite him in? Especially after their near kiss.

She had given in. He was the one who had kept it together. Maybe that's why she felt safe enough with him. He wanted her. The evidence was there for her to see in the way his wet jeans molded to his thick erection, but he wouldn't carry through with it.

No matter how handsome he was, dangerous was dangerous. Despite how much she argued with herself, she was intrigued by Arran.

It was a precarious and perilous game she played, but she was confident she wouldn't make the same mistakes of her past.

That was, until Arran's golden eyes fastened on her, then dropped to her breasts, which were outlined by her impossibly wet shirt and tank.

CHAPTER
THREE

Ronnie could have covered herself with her jacket. She could have turned away.

Instead, she stood completely still, as if daring him to touch her, to kiss her. To take everything that she was too afraid to offer herself.

The desire she saw in Arran's eyes held her transfixed, captivated. A spark of hunger so raw, so visceral flashed in his depths that her breath caught, locked in her chest.

She was seized, held. Captured. All by the look of need in his golden eyes. When she dragged in a ragged breath, Ronnie could feel her body melting toward him.

Arran was like a force field pulling her, tugging her. She knew she should turn away, or at the very least pretend she hadn't seen his reaction. But she couldn't. It was as if the world stopped for a few seconds, and it was only the two of them.

He was the first to look away, and Ronnie didn't want to evaluate how upset she was at that.

With the fortitude that had gotten her through life, she shrugged out of her jacket and slung it over the chair to dry. She then turned her back to Arran and wiped strands of wet hair from her face. At least her bun had held.

"Thank you for the help," she said when she was able to find her voice.

"I did what anyone would've."

"If they'd been there," she said, and looked over her shoulder at him.

He stood to the side, his gaze on something outside through the opening in her tent as he lifted the flap a few inches to peer through it.

Ronnie thought she'd pegged Arran as soon as she saw him, but even in the little time she'd spent with him, she realized she had been woefully wrong.

With his attention diverted, Ronnie peeled off her wet button-down and tank before hastily pulling on one of her old Stanford sweatshirts.

Arran kept his gaze focused outside, but inside the tent he was aware of Ronnie's every move. From the sound of the wet material leaving her body to her quick inhale as the cool air hit her bare skin. Somehow he managed to keep from looking at her while she changed shirts, which had been a feat in itself.

He'd gotten a glimpse of her breasts as her shirt clung to them. They weren't small or large. They were a perfect handful.

And how he yearned to see them bared, to watch while her nipples grew rigid as he teased and suckled them.

Arran knew he was attracted to Ronnie, he just hadn't realized how great that attraction was until he'd held her.

Felt her.

Touched her.

He knew the sensation of her body against him now. He'd embraced her, knew her softness, and longed for more. So very much more. How close he'd been to kissing her. She'd wanted it, would have accepted it.

For his part, he couldn't remember feeling such need to kiss a woman before. It had surprised him enough that it made him pause. Now he regretted that hesitation.

Ronnie wanted to keep him at a safe distance, because of her own desires that she obviously didn't trust. He'd been there less than an hour, and already his cock ached to be buried inside her, to feel her wet clingy heat as he filled her.

Arran clenched his teeth. What the hell was wrong with him? Ever since he'd arrived at the dig site and the magic touched him, he'd been on edge, a strange sensation running through him that he hadn't felt before.

It wasn't *drough* magic. That he knew.

He'd spent the last year in constant company with Druids, so why would the magic be affecting him now? The only explanation was that it was ancient magic he was feeling.

Whatever it was, he needed to get a hold of himself. Hastily. Ronnie had already told him she didn't want him fooling around, and since all he wanted to do was toss her onto the cot and cover her body with his, it was getting damned problematic.

Now he wished he'd brought another Warrior with him. This was supposed to be a simple mission. Arran should have known it would be anything but.

"Why don't you tell me why you're really here?"

Ronnie's voice, cool and to the point, tugged his head around to her. Whatever desire had been in her hazel eyes before was banked. "What are you talking about?"

"My foster father was a detective in our local police department. I know that alert look you have, the one that says you notice everything and everyone. Now, stop jerking me around and tell me what you're really doing here."

Arran liked her forthright attitude. He studied her for a moment, noticing the faded lettering on her sweatshirt and the way locks of hair fell from the bun to hang alongside her face. He wondered how long her hair was, and if it was as silky as it appeared.

He imagined it falling around him as she leaned over him, slowly lowering herself on him. His hand fisted as he thought of sliding his hands through her hair and winding it around his fingers.

"I'm here to help with the dig. I'm interested in it, and

that's the truth. Aye, I notice things. It's what I do. It's part of me and no' something I can change."

"Men like you don't just show up for no reason."

"That's the second time today you've said 'men like me.' Do I frighten you, lass?"

She lifted her chin and stuffed her fingers in the front pockets of her jeans. "There isn't much in this life I can't handle."

"That I believe." He couldn't stop the grin that followed.

Ronnie had spunk. It was obvious by the way she kept referring to men that something had happened in her past. Did it have something to do with her father? A past lover? Possibly a husband?

Arran didn't know, but he wanted to find out. He didn't like being compared to others, especially when no one else could rival a Warrior.

He glanced at the gold chain that fell hidden beneath her sweatshirt. "Where did you get the pendant?"

"On a dig three years ago in Northern Scotland." She pulled out the pendant and ran her fingers along the knot work. "It's exquisite, isn't it? I find it amazing that they could create such works of art so long ago that our craftsmen today can barely replicate."

"The Celts were an amazing people."

"I've always been fascinated with them," she said with a small grin, her gaze still on the pendant.

"What did your American studies tell you about my ancestors?"

Her eyes lifted to his then. "Not nearly as much as I know is out there. I've done my fair share of research, and I always come away feeling as if a huge chunk of the Celts' history has been left out."

"Maybe because they didna want others to know?"

She snorted. "They were a proud people. You know that. Can you imagine them not wanting to tell the world who they were?"

Arran shrugged and folded his arms over his chest. "What

if I told you I could answer all your questions about the Celts?"

He didn't know why he offered. He couldn't tell her. It would be dangerous for anyone other than a Druid or a Warrior to know of a Warrior's existence. And the Celts were linked with Warriors.

"Sure," she said, and made a sound in the back of her throat. "I've had that same offer before and was told some nonsense about magic and Rome and warriors."

Arran jerked, his full attention on the woman before him. His arms fell to his side and he took a step toward Ronnie. "Who told you this?"

"A volunteer on the dig three years ago. He was an elderly man that made sure everyone had something to drink and eat. When I found the pendant, he asked me if I wanted to know the story of the Celts. Having no idea I was going to be given a line of bullshit, I said yes."

Arran took a deep breath to keep calm. "What is the man's name? Where is he?"

"What does it matter?" she asked, her voice lowering with suspicion. "It was just a story."

"Ronnie, I need to know who this man is."

She searched his gaze for a moment before she said, "He died a month later at the site. He fell and hit his head on a rock. He was dead instantly."

The story of the Druids, of Rome and the Warriors' creation wasn't one that anyone other than a Druid or a Warrior would know. Who was this man who had told Ronnie the story?

"What was the man's name?" Arran asked.

Ronnie's brow rose. "What does it matter? He's dead."

"Please, Ronnie."

"Tell me why."

"Damn, you're a stubborn one," Arran said in exasperation as he glanced away and tried to find a plausible reason he could give her.

She merely smiled and shrugged. "As anyone who knows

me will attest. Now, tell me why it's so important. Why are the ramblings of an old man of interest? . . ." Her voice died as realization fell over her face. "Unless his story was true," she finished.

Arran had to think quickly. Ronnie's mind was sharp, but he wasn't sure how much she knew, nor how much the old man had gotten right.

"We Scots are a wee protective of the stories bandied around. Magic has long been associated with this land. Some believe in it and will seek to do whatever they can to find it."

"For what purpose?" she asked.

"To destroy it. Or worse, to use it to their advantage."

Her head cocked to the side. "Do you believe in magic?"

"If you'd seen the things I've seen, Dr. Reid, you wouldna be asking me that."

She laughed, the sound so musical and beautiful that it caused him to smile in return. "That was a good response, but not an answer."

"It was most certainly an answer. You just have to know how to decipher a Scot's words."

"You like toying with me, don't you?"

"I like this banter," he replied honestly. He also liked watching the emotions flash through her lovely hazel eyes. "Most of my friends are married, and while we do spar verbally on occasion, it's nice to be able to do it with someone as intelligent and fetching as you."

"Oh, and now a compliment," she said as she looked at the ground. "I don't get much of those. Thank you."

"I doona say things I doona mean. Remember that. The man's name?"

"I'll give it when you tell me why it's so important."

"I did, lass."

She rolled her eyes. "You gave me a line of shit. I deal in truths, Arran. Remember *that*."

The conversation was halted as Arran's cell phone rang, and then Andy came into the tent.

"Until tomorrow," Arran said, and ducked out into the

rain before he changed his mind and ignored the call from Fallon.

Ronnie stared at the opening long after Arran had departed. Andy was speaking, but she didn't register anything he was saying.

In her mind, she was replaying her and Arran's entire conversation. He was witty and charming. A rogue of the first order. And one she should keep away from.

But she knew she wouldn't.

It had been so long since her body had ruled her, and it felt good—right, even. Being in Arran's arms made her remember what it was like to feel breathless need racing through her.

Except with Arran, that breathless need was magnified tenfold. It frightened her, this all-consuming need she felt to be in his arms, to know the sexual promise she saw in his gaze.

To give herself to a man such as him.

If it was just attraction she might be able to fight that, but the pull went deeper, as if an invisible bond kept dragging her toward Arran.

As if their destinies were intertwined.

The thought chilled her.

A future that involved anyone but herself would only end in tragedy. She had to keep herself apart if she wanted to find the relic she searched for.

It was too important to forget. Too important for her to dally, even with a man as charming and sexy as Arran Mac-Carrick.

CHAPTER
FOUR

Arran answered his phone with a terse, "Aye?"

"I gather you're there?" Fallon asked.

Arran sighed and quickly ducked into his tent. He was drenched, but his blood was on fire because of one woman—Ronnie Reid.

"Aye," he answered.

"What's going on? I hear something in your voice."

Arran wiped the water from his eyes as he stood in the middle of the tent. "Nothing I can no' handle, Fallon."

"This mission is important. If I need to send another Warrior—"

"It's a damned woman, all right," he replied tightly. "That's all that's wrong with me. No need to send anyone."

There was silence for a heartbeat before Fallon laughed. "You had me worried. Who is this woman?"

"Ronnie Reid."

"The archeologist running the dig?"

"The verra one."

"You're buggered, mate."

"And I know it." Arran decided to turn the subject away from him. "There's magic here. I felt it as soon as I drove up."

"Do you think it's the spell?"

Arran peered out the tent's entrance. The rain had sent everyone scurrying away. It would be a perfect time for him to have a look around. "It could be, or it could just be the remainder of the magical artifacts sent from Edinburgh. Ronnie has a necklace that's ancient Celt. That could be part of the source."

"There's something else."

"It's probably nothing."

"Arran," Fallon said, his voice low. "I can be there in a blink. Doona lie to me."

He squeezed his eyes closed because he hadn't wanted to share the next part yet, at least not until he knew for sure. "There's a Druid here. And before you get all excited, I've no' found them yet. This entire area hums with magic. I'm having difficulty with the sheer amount of it."

"But you felt something?"

"Aye. And it wasna *drough* magic."

Arran could hear Fallon tapping his finger on the table through the phone. He waited as Fallon thought through everything.

And even though Arran's gaze should be on the dig site, he found it going to Ronnie's tent. The light was on, and he was able to see her and Pete's silhouettes in the darkening night.

"Tread carefully," Fallon said.

Arran knew he was talking about the mission, but Arran was thinking of Ronnie. "That was decided before I left."

"Aye, but we didna know what to expect. I think you'll learn more there on your own, but I willna jeopardize anything. At the first hint of trouble, I'm sending in Charon or Malcolm."

"It willna come to that," Arran said, and ended the conversation.

He stuffed the phone into his bag and stepped into the rain once more. It was a dousing rain, a storm that would last for several hours.

Though Arran wouldn't chance lifting any of the tarps to peer inside, he could scout the area to know where the best places for him to sneak in or out would be.

The area was larger than Arran first realized. There was

much that had been sectioned off that apparently Ronnie
wanted to dig, but they hadn't even broken ground there.

He looked to the newest section of earth that had been
dug. That seemed to be the place she was most interested in.
Still, Arran made a mental note of where the others were.

The clouds of the storm had darkened the sky, but it was
light enough that he could be seen, so Arran walked to his
SUV to make it appear as if he'd forgotten something.

After digging in the back for a moment, he shut the hatch
and then leaned against the vehicle. The rain had never
bothered him. He always found it odd that people in this
modern world he now found himself in scurried out of it as
if the rain would harm them in some way.

In his eyes, the rain washed away the filth that littered the
world. And the world needed more rain.

He made two rounds of the entire dig site, making sure
no one saw him. With the storm, it was easy, since everyone
stayed in their tents or caravans.

With his patrol over, Arran slowly headed back to his
tent. He couldn't help but glance over at Ronnie's. She was
alone now, and for a second, Arran thought about going back
to her to see if he could get the name of the old man.

Or a kiss.

But Ronnie would want to know why he needed the name.
Arran couldn't exactly tell her the truth, though she'd nearly
pieced it all together.

It was necessary for him to stay at the dig, and if she
delved into the old man's story and discovered Arran was a
Warrior, he doubted she'd allow him to remain at the site.

Arran kept walking until he was in his own tent. He
straightened and shook his head vigorously to rid himself of
the water.

"I think I should've stayed outside. I'd be drier."

Arran jerked his gaze up to find Pete sitting on his cot
and covered in droplets of water. "Apologies. I didna know
you'd returned."

"I'd thought to have dinner with Ronnie, but her mind is
elsewhere."

Arran removed his shirt and dug into his bag for a fresh pair of jeans. Once he'd changed and laid out his sodden clothes and boots to dry, he sank onto his bed and bent a knee to put his bare foot on the cot.

He let an arm rest across his knee as he studied Pete, who was busy flipping through a book by the light of the lantern on the table between them. His male vanity was glad to hear his near kiss with Ronnie had addled her as it had him.

"Ronnie is a determined woman," Pete said into the silence. He looked up from his book, his eyes pinning Arran.

"I've noticed."

"This is her life, and she doesn't let anything interfere with it. If you have any ideas of seducing her—"

"That's no' why I'm here," Arran interrupted him before Pete could continue. "I'm here for the dig, no' to find a woman."

Pete grunted and flipped a few more pages. "Just keep what I said in mind. Ronnie is capable of taking care of herself."

"Yet you feel the need to protect her."

"Yes. Ronnie is . . . special," Pete said. He closed the book and set it beside him as he turned to sit on the side of the cot. Then he rested his forearms on his legs and clasped his hands together. "I like you, Arran, and I saw the way you looked at her before you knew who she was."

"She's a verra beautiful woman. I'm a man who appreciates such beauty."

Pete smiled and looked out of the tent. "She has no idea of her attractiveness, which is part of her allure. Men mistake her noninterest as being coy."

Arran wasn't sure why Pete was telling him all this. To warn him off, yes, but there was something else there as well.

"Do you often help her on her digs?"

Pete chuckled and looked at him. "No. Ronnie has long since been on her own. She likes having me drop by, but it's just as a friend not a professor. She's the one teaching me now."

"But you help her," Arran urged.

"In a way. I help set up the parties to maintain the donations so she can continue her work. Archeology is an expensive business."

Arran nodded. "Which is why Ronnie is friends with Saffron."

"Ah, yes, Miss Fletcher who has become Mrs. Mac-Kenna. Saffron's company has been a supporter, beginning with donations by her father. Even when Saffron seemed to disappear, the money was still sent to Ronnie to continue her digs."

"With Saffron's donations, why do you need more?"

Pete threw back his head and let out a full-bodied laugh. He ran a hand down his face before he reached beneath his cot to a bag and pulled out a flask. He unscrewed the lid and tilted back the flask for a hearty drink.

"No thanks," Arran said when Pete offered him a drink.

Pete took another drink, then screwed the cap back on. "Saffron's donations are large, but it doesn't cover everything. It does allow us not to have to ask for quite so much from others, however."

"I see." And Arran did see. Pete had moved on from the actual digging to keeping Ronnie digging.

"I think you'll fit in nicely here." Pete turned and lay back on the bed. He threw an arm over his eyes and grunted. "If only this damned place would get dark when it was supposed to."

"Where will Ronnie go after this dig?"

Pete shrugged. "This is her third year in Britain, and it looks like she has no intentions of leaving. I keep trying to get her back to Egypt, but she's determined to remain here. I have no idea what it is about this land that keeps her finding things."

"What's wrong with that?"

"Nothing." Pete lifted his arm and looked at Arran a moment. "There is more history in Egypt is all I'm saying."

Arran didn't respond as Pete's arm once more covered his eyes.

"The National Trust of Britain is sure happy to have her, though."

"Meaning?" Arran asked with a frown.

"Meaning that she gives all her finds to them."

"All?"

"Oh, she'll keep something small every now and again, like the necklace she wears."

"I thought part of being an archeologist is giving the finds to the government."

"It is."

But there was something in Pete's voice that made Arran wary. "I suspect the government demands the finds in exchange for digging on their land."

"Yep. It's the way it's always been. Archeologists do all the work, and get a little of the praise. Long after the artifacts are placed in a museum, the ones who found them are forgotten."

Arran relaxed at his words. He'd thought for a moment that Pete had been motivated by money, but now Arran understood the tone that had been in his voice.

"How does Ronnie feel about it?" Arran asked.

"She doesn't seem to care. For her, it's just part of who she is."

Arran let the silence grow after Pete finished talking. There was much about Ronnie that Arran had learned, and he'd yet to find anything he didn't like.

An image of her tall, lithe body standing in her tent with her shirts soaked and clinging to her skin flashed in Arran's mind. His damned cock began to harden when he remembered holding her.

He tried to push it aside, but it was too late. His body heated, instantly ready and needy. If he felt such an overwhelming need for her now, what would it be like if he ever kissed her?

It can no' happen.

But he wanted it to. Desperately.

All it took to wash away those thoughts was Fallon and Larena, and the other couples at MacLeod Castle who wanted to bind the gods and have a normal life.

As if they could live normally. They'd spent hundreds of

years as immortals, as Warriors who had powers of their own. For Arran, he was able to control ice and snow.

It came second nature to him. Did he want to live where he couldn't use that power? Did he want a life where he couldn't see in the dark as a Warrior did, or hear as a Warrior did?

To have the speed and strength of his god taken away from him?

He didn't, but this wasn't about him. This was about his friends.

Arran told himself he didn't have to have his god bound, but in the back of his mind he worried that once that spell was out there, anyone could bind his god.

Anyone.

Was that a chance he wanted to take?

What if evil returned? Because it would. Eventually. What would happen to the world if the Warriors weren't there to stop the evil?

Arran didn't want to find out.

CHAPTER
FIVE

Ronnie sighed as she sat up from her cot and yawned. She hadn't been able to sleep last night. Every time she closed her eyes, she saw golden ones staring back at her.

Even awake Arran haunted her mind. She couldn't stop thinking of how at ease he'd been. Until she'd mentioned the old Celtic story.

The predator she sensed in him had woken at that moment. It was such a part of him that he probably hadn't even realized he'd leaned toward her, his body seeming to bow up as if waiting for a fight.

And for just an instant, she could have sworn his eyes flashed . . . white.

It proved how exhausted she was that her mind played tricks on her.

"Eyes flashing white. Yeah. Like that actually happens," Ronnie mumbled as she swung her legs over the side of the cot and rose.

The storm had stopped only a few hours before, but that wasn't going to halt the dig. She splashed water on her face and dressed in another pair of jeans and a thicker button-down. She was brushing out her hair when she heard Arran's voice.

That deep, smooth voice sent chills racing over her skin. He laughed, and she wondered who he was talking to. And then, his voice faded away. She hated that she was disappointed in not hearing more of him.

"Get a grip," she said as she glared at her reflection in the small mirror. "He's a guy. There's no time for that."

Not that there ever was time.

Ronnie pulled her hair back into a ponytail, then twisted the long strands around and around before wrapping the hair into a bun. She stuck three bobby pins in her hair to hold it and then reached for her jacket as she rose.

As soon as she walked out of her tent, Andy was waiting for her.

"Hey, Ronnie," he said, and looked at his clipboard. "I'm happy to say that all the tarps held last night through the storm. Looks like we had very little damage. A little rain got in some sites, but not all."

"How about the newest one?"

"Nope. All clean," he answered with a smile.

She nodded and made her way to the tent that was set up with food. "Just what I wanted to hear. What other news?"

"I've sent our newest volunteer to help dig today. Since he's rather strong, he'll be doing some heavy lifting."

Ronnie paused in pouring her coffee and looked at Andy. "You put him with me?"

"You said yesterday you wanted to concentrate on this new section, and that means getting deeper than the four inches we got yesterday."

"He could destroy any finds."

Andy shook his head. "I don't think so. He seems capable, and I've got others watching to make sure he doesn't."

"Fine," Ronnie said with a sigh. She grabbed a croissant and a few strawberries and headed out of the tent.

Andy was right on her heels. "I thought you liked Arran. If it's an issue, I'll move him somewhere else."

"No, it's fine." It wasn't, but if she had Andy move Arran, then it would alert Pete and Arran that she had an issue with him.

That she wanted to avoid.

When she reached the site, the tarp had been removed

and Arran stood leaning on a shovel, laughing at something one of the other guys said.

He'd taken off his shirt, revealing an amazing amount of exposed muscle all the way to the very low waist of his dark jeans. Dirt and sweat already coated his chest.

He was raw masculinity, dominant and commanding. Compelling. Without even trying, he drew every eye to him—including her own.

Her breathing grew erratic, her blood heating until her skin was damp from the visceral, innate desire just being near him brought her.

Even his smile, which he directed at someone else, caused her stomach to flutter. She licked her lips and let her gaze slide slowly down his wide chest, seeing the power and strength in every corded muscle.

Her eyes paused when she reached the waist of his low-hung jeans, just giving her a glimpse of that sexy V of sinew that disappeared into his pants.

She knew the feel of his arousal, the hardness, the length. Her mouth went dry as she thought of it against her. It had haunted her dreams. But in those dreams, she had rocked against him, not stood there like an idiot, waiting for him to do something.

Ronnie swallowed and mentally shook herself. She had to stay away from Arran. He was temptation in its purest form.

"I thought he just got here. What did he do, fall in the dirt?" she asked, not trying to hide her irritation.

Andy chuckled and tucked his pencil behind his ear. "Actually, he's been working for about two hours now."

She turned her surprised gaze from Arran to Andy. "Are you serious?"

"Yeah. He was awake when I got up, and then he helped me remove all the tarps. He wanted to get to work right away. The next thing I knew, everyone else was getting up."

Ronnie looked back at Arran to find his gaze on her. He gave a slight nod of his head as if he knew she was talking about him, and then turned his attention to his new friends.

Damn, but she didn't want to notice him.

A look around showed she wasn't the only one. All the women were ogling him, which she couldn't blame them for. A hunk of a man like Arran couldn't—*wouldn't*—be ignored.

Just when she thought she was going to have to tell him to put on his shirt and go somewhere else, he said something to the men and began digging again.

A second later, everyone else got back to work as well. Even the women gawking at him.

"I've always heard there were people who were natural leaders," Andy leaned close and whispered. "I'd never seen it before today. Arran doesn't even have to say anything. They just follow him."

"They're working, that's what matters." But Ronnie was just as amazed—and awed—as Andy.

She'd never seen someone command attention the way Arran did. It wasn't just his good looks and muscles, it was his manners and demeanor.

It was as if everyone recognized him as a leader and gave him the position.

Ronnie walked around the section they were digging, inspecting things as she did. She could feel the artifacts below the dirt. Their song was only one she could hear. It led her to them each and every time. This time, the song was stronger, more urgent. Ronnie had never felt such urgency from an artifact before, and it made her wonder what could be hidden beneath all the tons of dirt and rock.

She was so deep in thought, listening to the song from the artifact that she didn't realize she had stopped behind Arran until he turned to her.

"Did I do something wrong?"

"Actually, no," she said, and turned her mind from the sweet song. "I hear you've been working for a few hours."

He shrugged and leaned a hand on the shovel. "I was awake and eager to get started."

"As you know, the days are really long this time of year. I like to take advantage of that."

His smile was slow as it spread. "Aye, lass. And you'll

come to learn we Highlanders doona mind hard work. Or long hours. We have natural endurance we use every chance we get."

His voice had a teasing lilt to it, but she saw the seriousness in his golden eyes as well as the sexual undertone. And how she loved his brogue. She could listen to it all day.

"It appears all your muscles are going to be needed throughout the day. I just don't want you wasting them too soon."

"Doona worry. I doona tire easily."

She nodded and walked away before she did something really stupid like reach up to touch his muscles again. Or kiss him. When all she wanted to do was keep talking to him, to get close and feel the heat radiating off him. Ronnie hated herself for it, too.

The morning soon turned into noon, but she hardly noticed. She drank when a bottle of water was put in her hand, but she rarely looked up from her work.

Unless she heard Arran's voice.

His was the only thing that could break into the growing song that occupied her mind. There were artifacts all over the land, but the ones in the area where she dug were important.

It's the only reason they would be so loud and insistent. At least that's what she told herself. There had been relics before who had been almost as loud and been extremely important.

What would she find this time? An ancient sword? Maybe a hidden burial chamber? She loved to guess and see if she was right when she finally did unearth it.

She just hoped it wasn't another mass grave like the one she'd found two years ago that dated back to the Saxon invasion. There had been over thirty bodies in that grave, all of them women and children. It was those times she remembered that the UK had seen many bloody wars.

The sound of Arran's voice pulled her gaze to him once more. A couple of times he'd come to her side and helped her move a large rock, but he kept his distance. Ronnie was thankful and angry about it all at the same time.

She finally called for lunch at half past noon. When she stood, she saw just how much progress they'd made.

"Wow," Andy said as he came up beside her. "We've never dug a section so quick."

"No," she said, but she knew a large part was owed to Arran.

"We've done five times as much this morning as we did yesterday alone."

Ronnie glanced at the other sections. "What's the update on section three?"

"We found nothing until about thirty minutes ago, and then we found an arm bone."

"Human?"

Andy nodded. He hated to find remains, but it was something they ran across frequently.

"Any other parts of the skeleton?" she asked.

"Possibly. I'll let you know as soon as something is found. In section two, there's been nothing."

"Hmm. Keep digging the rest of the day. There might be something under all that dirt yet."

"A bowl matching the one dating back to Rome would be nice," Andy said as he walked away.

Ronnie drained the rest of her water. When she turned to make her way to the food tent, it was to find Arran blocking her path.

"They made you a sandwich," he said, and held out a wrapped package.

She took it and a bag of chips. "Thanks." Though she knew she shouldn't, she found herself saying, "Why don't you eat with me?"

He gave a nod and followed her to her tent. Inside, Ronnie sank onto her narrow cot and let Arran have the chair. They ate in silence for a few minutes before she couldn't hold it in any longer.

"What do you think of your first day so far? Want to return home?"

Arran chuckled, his gaze locked on her, and finished swallowing his food. "Nay. I'm enjoying it immensely. I'm used to a lot of activity, and over the past few months, there hasna been much to do. This is just what I needed."

"And you're getting everyone to work, and work hard. How did you do that?"

He shrugged. "I didna do anything."

"Where do you live in Scotland?"

He put down his sandwich and said around his food, "The Highlands, of course."

"Of course," she said. But she saw the look of pride and satisfaction that came over him when he spoke of the Highlands.

"Do you have a family?"

"What's the sudden interest in my life?" he asked, though a grin played at the edges of his lips.

It was her turn to shrug. "I'm just curious to know one of Saffron's friends. I've known Saffron awhile. She's spoken of her husband and new baby a lot, and every once in a while she'll mention something about her husband's friends. You'd be one of those, right?"

"Aye."

"I get the feeling you all do something important. What do you work for, MI5 or MI6? Scotland Yard, maybe?"

Arran shook his head, a half grin pulling up one side of his lips. "Nay, nothing like that. No' sure why she thinks we're important."

"She said it was you all who found her."

It didn't go unnoticed how still Arran got at her words. "Aye," he finally said. "What did she tell you?"

"Only that. The papers made light of her disappearance, but I saw in her face that there was much more to it. Three years is a long time to be gone. I'm so glad you all found her."

"Us as well."

Ronnie smiled and cracked a chip in two with her finger. "I also gather that you all are a rather tight-knit group."

"You could say that."

"So you can't tell me, because you do work for the government, right?"

He leaned forward and peered at her. "Why does it matter?"

"I don't know," she lied. She couldn't exactly tell him she wanted to know all there was about him because she couldn't stop thinking about dragging him into bed with her. "I just like to figure people out, and there is so much about you that doesn't fit together nicely like everyone else."

"It makes me more interesting."

That it did. "Listen, I know Saffron knows you, but . . . I don't."

"And you're leery," he finished for her. "I'm just here to work."

It was time to get to the heart of things. "Things have been stolen from me in the past. I like to know the people working for me, whether they're being paid or not. Saffron gave me her word you were a good man. Can I trust that? Should I trust that?"

"Saffron is no' a liar. That's the first thing you should know," Arran said softly. "Second, I doona claim to be a good man, but if I give you my word on something, it's my bond. I'll work as long and as hard as you ask of me, and I give my vow I willna steal anything."

"Thank you." It was just what she'd been looking to hear, but she hadn't expected to believe it in every fiber of her body.

Whoever Arran MacCarrick was, he was becoming more and more dangerous to her sanity. Too bad she needed him so desperately for the dig.

CHAPTER
SIX

Arran tossed aside another shovelful of dirt and wondered why the hell he promised Ronnie he wouldn't steal when he had sworn to Fallon he would if it came down to it.

What a bloody damned mess he'd gotten himself into.

His family came first, and that's what everyone at Mac-Leod Castle was. But it didn't explain his need to comfort Ronnie, or vow he wasn't going to steal.

There had been something in her voice when she spoke of thefts. Once he'd heard that, he found himself giving a promise before he realized it.

There wasn't much he could do until he found the spell, and then he'd have to do his damnedest to convince Ronnie to let him have it.

"No' going to happen," he mumbled.

"What?" a woman beside him asked.

Arran shook his head and shoved the shovel into the ground. Memphaea, his god, wasn't exactly content, but he had calmed tremendously since Arran arrived at the dig site. At least now Arran didn't have to worry about his god pushing for his need for blood and death, not with the way Arran was working his body.

His muscles strained, and he pushed himself harder. It felt good to be doing something physical. For too long he'd sat in the castle idle. That wouldn't happen again.

Magic washed over him, strong and forceful, taking his breath as it did. It was so powerful, it caused him to take a step back.

He stared at the ground, trying to see through the dirt to what was beneath. There was something under the ground, something that had been buried a very long time.

If it was the cargo of magical items lost as it traveled from Edinburgh to London, then there was no telling what they would unearth.

There were things that could potentially harm someone. Or something that, in the wrong hands, could bring about war. None of the Warriors or Druids knew exactly what was in the shipment. Anything could be under the dirt.

Anything.

Arran glanced up and saw Ronnie staring at the ground intently. He narrowed his gaze at her. She cocked her head to the side, as if listening. Her lids began to lower, and then suddenly she was digging faster.

In that instant, Arran knew. Ronnie was the Druid he'd felt. As soon as he realized it, he felt her magic. It pulsed over him stronger than any of the other magic around. It swarmed him, submerging him in the delightful magic that was Ronnie's alone. He took a step back from the force of it, his body tensing from the effects of her magic.

He'd wanted her before. Now . . . he *needed* her.

His body was on fire, and only she could quench the flames. Their gazes clashed when she suddenly looked up. Worry clouded her hazel eyes for a moment. Then she seemed to accept . . . what? That he was watching her? That he wanted to push her back and take her right there in the dirt in front of everyone, to claim her as his own?

There was no way she could know he'd guessed she was a Druid or that her power was unearthing artifacts. He'd bet most of what she uncovered were magical relics as well.

Everyone thought she was one of the best archeologists because she was lucky in where she excavated, but Arran knew the truth now. It was no wonder she didn't like it when Pete tried to brag.

"Forget it," said a man beside him.

Arran turned his head at the sound of the Irish accent. "Forget what?"

"Her. Dr. Reid. Every mon here has tried to get her attention. I don't think she likes men."

Arran recalled how she'd looked at him, the flare of interest in her hazel gaze had been unmistakable. "Maybe she just hasna found the right man to show interest in."

Irish snorted. "Not likely, mate. She's a cold one. Her only interest is what's in the ground."

Arran turned his gaze back to Ronnie to find her kneeling and bent over, looking at something in the ground. Cold? Ronnie was anything but cold. She was passion and fire, and with the right man, she would glow with it.

He'd like to see if he could bring out her passion, and maybe once he found the spell, Arran would take up the challenge. He wanted to find the spell soon, because he wasn't sure how long he could retain control over the unbendable need that pushed him.

With a shake of his head, he went back to shoveling to work off some of the frustration of his body. Dirt covered his jeans, and he'd long ago given up his shirt. Sweat ran down his back. The sounds of boots stepping in squishy earth along with the scrape of spades scooping and tossing dirt filled the air.

To anyone who looked, he was concentrating on his job. In truth, Arran was focused on Ronnie. There were many conversations, but Arran blocked them all out. All except for Ronnie's. With his enhanced hearing, he was able to pick her voice out of so many.

Just by listening to her, he found she was precise in her management of the dig, and took no quarter from anyone. She worked harder than those paid and the volunteers.

And her excitement when an artifact was found made him smile. She truly loved what she did. Even if she did use her magic to do it.

Hours faded away while Arran continued to dig and push the others to keep working. By the time the bell for supper was rung, it was clear whatever they were uncovering was large.

What it was was another matter entirely. Everyone speculated, but no one had any idea. Even the way Ronnie looked at the rocks that clearly formed some type of roof had her stumped.

Arran wanted to keep working, but his strength and endurance were beginning to look conspicuous. He slammed the tip of the shovel into the ground and stepped out of the dig site to call it a day.

No matter how hard he tried, he couldn't keep his eyes from Ronnie. He heard her voice before he found her inspecting another section. Section two, and one that everyone said wouldn't yield anything worthwhile.

Yet Ronnie kept having them dig.

While everyone made for the food tent, Arran went to wash the dirt and sweat off. The bucket of water waiting for him in the tent wasn't nearly enough. He'd prefer a nice long swim in a loch. There was one near. Near enough to visit.

As tempting as that was, Arran pushed aside the swim for another time. He stripped out of his dirty jeans and scooped the water in his hands and over his body.

When he'd gotten all the dirt and sweat off, he ducked his head in the bucket and scrubbed his fingers along his scalp. Only then did he lift his head from the water and towel off.

He pulled out a pair of cargo pants and a plain white tee that he put on. After raking his hands through his hair and scratching his jaw, which was in need of a shave, he put his boots back on and headed for the food.

"You're late," Andy said when he saw Arran walk into the food tent.

Arran shrugged. "Aye, but clean."

Andy laughed and reached for another shepherd's pie. "The food isn't all that great, but it's food. Tomorrow some of the volunteers are heading into the nearby town to stay at the hotel for hot showers and hot food."

"You have no' truly experienced Scotland unless you sleep beneath the stars and hunt for your own food."

"Ah . . . yeah. I think I'll pass on truly experiencing Scotland, then, dude. I wouldn't know the first thing about where to hunt for food, much less what to do with it after I caught it."

"*If* you caught it," Arran said, trying his best to keep the smile from showing.

Andy grew pale and pushed his glasses up his nose. "Have I mentioned I hate the sight of blood? This is why archeology suits me. Everything is already dead. Bones I can handle. Blood? Yeah, not so much."

"So I guess I shouldna come to you if I get cut?"

Andy rolled his eyes. "Dude, you were just joking with me! I should've known. Ronnie says I take everything too serious."

He walked away, leaving Arran chuckling after him. He liked Andy. Arran grabbed a shepherd's pie, a roll, two apples, and a beer. There was a huge tub of bottled beer stuck in ice off to the side, and everyone had taken at least one.

Arran sat with other volunteers. Even though he'd been in this modern world a year and had learned much, he still found the people interesting to listen to. Especially when they came from different countries.

Many at the site were Brits, but there was also an equal number of Americans. There was the odd Irishman, Frenchman, and even a German or two.

Arran was content to listen to them talk of their homes, their lives, and mundane things. He tried to keep in the background, but all too soon they noticed him and pulled him into the conversations.

He hated having to lie, but in order to keep who he was, and his family, secret, lying was essential. A good liar mixed in as much of the truth as he could.

It had soon become common knowledge that he was friends with Saffron, and everyone wanted to know about her and what had happened when she disappeared for those three years.

Arran quickly diverted those questions by asking some of his own. He was always amazed at how people wanted to talk about themselves, given the chance. And he made sure they had those chances often.

It was well past ten when he rose from the table and made for his tent. Yet, as he stood in the night air, he found he wasn't tired.

His gaze went to Ronnie's tent. The light was on but dim, and he saw no movement inside. Arran started walking toward her tent, even when he knew it was a bad idea.

"Ronnie," he called as he reached the tent.

When there was no answer, he poked his head inside and found her lying on her stomach on her cot, her feet and one arm hanging off the side.

For long minutes, Arran simply looked at her sleeping. Her bun that she tied her hair in every day was hanging loose. It would take the smallest touch to knock it free so he could see her hair in all its glory.

But he didn't touch her. The light from her lamp cast her face in a golden glow, and it was then he saw the dark circles under her eyes.

"She does this," Andy whispered as he came up beside Arran.

Arran raised a brow in question.

"She works herself into exhaustion. Tomorrow she'll wake refreshed and ready. She might go a few nights without sleep because of something involving the dig, and then she collapses."

"You look out for her," Arran said.

Andy shrugged, his thin hair blowing in the breeze. "She took me as her assistant when no one else would. She's taught me so much."

"You're loyal. Everyone needs someone like that."

"She's loyal to me as well," Andy said. "No matter what, she keeps bringing me on these digs as her site manager. She's even allowed me to take the credit on my finds."

Arran nodded and turned his attention back to Ronnie. "She can no' sleep like that. She'll wake with a crick in her neck."

"What are you going to do?" Andy hastily asked.

Arran grinned at him. "Doona fash yourself, lad. Her virtue is safe with me."

"Yeah, right. I see how you look at her," Andy said, and set aside the clipboard on Ronnie's chair. "I'll get her boots. Just turn her over when I'm done."

Arran waited while Andy made quick work of removing Ronnie's boots, and then it was time to touch her. He hesitated for a minute because he wanted to feel her skin again, but at the same time, he knew it wasn't a good idea.

"Arran?"

He glanced at Andy. "Doona tell her it was me."

"Why?"

"I doona think she cares for me much."

When Andy didn't immediately respond, Arran glared at him.

"Okay," Andy said, and held up his hands in surrender. "I'll be sure to leave your name out."

Arran took a deep breath and rolled Ronnie into his arms. He cradled her against him, the shock of her warmth and softness causing him to still instantly.

Blood pounded in his ears and his balls tightened as all the blood pooled in his cock. Just from the exquisite, amazing feel of her. Arran's fingers squeezed her as the sudden need to hold her against him forever filled him. She sighed and rested her head against his chest.

That simple movement touched something deep within him. And caused his desire to soar until he shook with the force of it.

It took everything Arran had to lower Ronnie back onto the cot. He'd never been so grateful to have someone watching him as he did at that moment.

Arran pulled the blanket over Ronnie and straightened. He gave her one last look before turning off her lamp and walking out of the tent.

"Arran?" Andy called.

But he couldn't answer. He needed a run. Anything to calm the need consuming him.

Instead of running off as he wanted, Arran went into his tent and pretended to sleep.

CHAPTER
SEVEN

The box was small. The wood was smooth and dark, un-blemished and seamless except for the line around the top where the curved lid opened.

Veronica.

Her name was whispered in the musical notes that sounded whenever her abilities were used. She could feel the box beneath the ground, sense it inciting her to find it.

If her name hadn't been whispered, it would have been as every other artifact she'd gone looking for. Yet she felt fear now.

Every instinct she had cautioned her, but she couldn't listen. The box wanted her.

She was driven to find it. She'd known when she reached Muirkirk there was something special waiting to be found. Soon she would move aside the dirt separating her from the relic. She would hold the box in her hands. And she would open it.

Ronnie smiled. She placed her hands over the ground and felt the box below her. Its song was so loud, there were times it was all she could hear. It was begging her to release it, to let the sun shine upon it once more.

It was meant to be out in the world, not hidden away and forgotten. Its beauty was simple, its artwork meant to be marveled. She, along with all the others, would do just that.

But first, she would be the one to hold it and drink in its beauty.

Ronnie could hardly contain her excitement. Her hands itched to open the lid and see what was inside. The box, and whatever was inside, was hers. It wouldn't go to a museum. This one she would keep for herself.

Excitement coursed through Ronnie. The box's music grew louder, her name more insistent.

"Soon," she whispered. "I'm coming for you soon."

She began to move away the dirt with her bare hands when something caught her attention out of the corner of her eye. Ronnie shifted her gaze and found Arran staring. He was shaking his head, his golden eyes full of apprehension.

And then his eyes shifted to white.

Ronnie gasped and sat up, her breathing harsh and loud. She looked around the tent as her mind realized she was no longer dreaming.

She lifted her hands and saw they were coated with dirt as if she had been digging. With her bare hands. Ronnie worked the dirt from beneath her fingernails and tried to calm her racing heart.

It was true the song of the box was stronger than any she had ever encountered. And up until that dream, she hadn't even known it was a box that called to her.

Then again, she'd never had a dream about an artifact she was digging up either.

She ran a hand through her hair and closed her eyes. Her lips parted so she could breathe through her mouth while she tried to remember that dreams weren't real.

It was a surprise that she'd had such a vivid dream of the box and the relentless need she had to find it. But what caused her stomach to fall to her feet was that Arran had been in her dream.

Was the desire she tried desperately to ignore spilling over into her dreams? It had to be. Her body wanted Arran with an intensity that shook her to her very core. That had to be the reason.

The only reason.

"Please let it be the only reason," she prayed.

Ronnie threw back the covers and rose from the bed. She stared down at herself still fully dressed and tried to remember the night before.

She'd been beyond exhausted. She recalled that part. Past that was all a blur.

"Oh, good. You're awake."

She turned at Andy's voice as he came into her tent. Her stomach let out a loud growl at the smell of biscuits, which Andy promptly handed to her.

"I figured you'd be hungry since you passed out last night," he said with a smile.

Ronnie sighed and sank into her chair to eat the biscuits and drink the large mug of coffee. "Again? I knew I was tired, but I didn't think I was that tired. I normally don't take off my boots either."

When Andy looked away so he didn't have to meet her eyes, she set down her coffee and cocked her head at her friend. "Andy? What happened?"

"He asked me not to tell you."

A sick feeling began in her stomach. "Who?"

"Arran. He found you asleep. I took off your shoes, and he turned you over and covered you with the blanket."

Ronnie looked at her cot. Arran had found her and helped her. He'd held her. She'd been in his arms, felt his hard body and the strength of his muscles once more, and she hadn't even been awake to enjoy it? She felt cheated and angry that she hadn't been able to touch him again at her leisure.

"Probably for the better," she mumbled.

"What?" Andy asked.

She shook her head. "Nothing. I won't tell him you told me."

"Good," Andy said with a sigh. "He's a likable fellow, but I get the feeling he's not someone you want to piss off. I suspect he'd be a bad enemy to have."

Ronnie recalled how easy he shifted from casual to "battle-ready," as she'd come to think of it. It was as if he was primed for combat and just waiting for the right word or gesture. A Highland warrior of old, she inwardly mused.

Yes, she could see that. Arran, with his long hair, roguish smile, and the old soul she glimpsed in his eyes could very well have stood on the slopes of the Highlands hundreds of years ago in a kilt, sword in hand while an army stood at his back, waiting for him to give the word to go into battle.

"A true Highlander," she whispered.

"What?" Andy asked with a small frown.

Ronnie shrugged and took a bite of the large, buttery biscuit. "Nothing."

It wasn't like the biscuits she was used to in the States. These were bigger and better. Different for sure, but fast becoming a favorite.

"He's, ah, he started early again."

Somehow Andy's words didn't surprise her. Nor did she have to ask whom he was referring to. Arran. Since he came to the site, he'd become a force to be reckoned with. She couldn't look anywhere and not see or hear him.

Ronnie's body tingled just thinking of his hands on her again. If she'd been awake, would she have been brave enough to kiss him, to test the waters of passion she'd shied away from for so long?

Arran kept her from concentrating on the dig. With him being so near, her thoughts turned to his strong arms, hard body, large hands, and gold eyes. She remembered his hard body, and the stark hunger she'd seen reflected in his gaze.

She shivered just thinking about it. No one had ever looked at her as Arran had. The offer was there in his gaze, in the way he held her. All she had to do was give in.

If she did, if she dared such a thing, she knew being with him would be glorious, but he'd likely leave her in such a mess that she might never function again. Arran was that strong, that appealing.

That captivating.

He was sex and need, temptation and desire all rolled into one package. And she wanted him. The compulsion to lean into him, to run her hand along his muscles and open her lips for him was so strong, she had to fight not to do just that when he was near.

"Ronnie?"

She blinked and looked up at Andy. They'd been speaking of Arran. But what about him? Oh, yes, his working early. "As long as he doesn't mess anything up, I don't care."

"No chance of that. He woke me up and had me stay with him just to make sure he did everything right."

For some reason, that made Ronnie smile. Then she realized Arran wasn't doing it because he knew how much the site meant to her. He did it because that's what he was supposed to do.

The smile quickly died, but not the excitement she couldn't dispel at seeing him again. God, what was wrong with her? He was just one guy. One guy who had rocked her back on her heels since he'd walked into her life.

How in the hell was she going to survive weeks with him around? The bite of biscuit went down awkwardly and landed heavily in her stomach.

Weeks. With a hot Scot walking around, looking at her as if he were stripping off her clothes. It was never going to work.

"I'll be out shortly," Ronnie said as she got to her feet.

Andy left the tent and Ronnie zipped the opening to keep anyone else from venturing in. She ate the rest of her breakfast, and then sipped her coffee as her thoughts turned back to the dream. Anything to get her mind off Arran and what she'd like him to do to her.

There was no doubt she was close to the box. She'd sensed ancient artifacts before, but there was something different about this box. Why did it want her? Was it because it knew she could sense it? That had to be it.

She couldn't wait to discover what was inside it. Was it jewels? Gold? Or something even more precious?

When her coffee was finished, Ronnie got ready for the day. She shivered against the cold water used to wash up and the cool summer air.

She'd gotten more used to the weather than when she first arrived in Scotland, but there were times she missed the tropic-like heat of Atlanta.

The summers could be oppressive they were so hot and humid, but when she'd been raised in that kind of weather, it was going to take more than a few years to get accustomed to the dampness and cold of Scotland.

Ronnie unzipped the tent and stepped outside. Only to find her gaze riveted on Arran. He was shirtless again. All his wonderful muscles fully on display as he bent at the waist and dumped a bottle of water over the back of his head.

He straightened, throwing back his dark brown hair that looked nearly black when wet. He shook his head, sending droplets of water everywhere.

She watched water trickle down his face to his chest, and then zigzag through the valleys of his muscle to disappear in the waist of his cargos.

Ronnie tried to swallow, but her mouth was too dry.

When she lifted her gaze, it was to discover Arran staring at her. His golden eyes seemed to pierce right to her soul. There was an invitation there, as well as desire. Ronnie yanked her gaze away and found other women watching Arran.

Her only consolation was that he'd been looking at her.

"There you are," Pete said as he walked up. "I've been looking for you."

"What is it?" Anything to steer her thoughts away from Arran and his irresistible body. And amazing eyes.

Pete frowned a moment before he said, "The next fund-raiser is just days away."

"Damn. I'd forgotten."

"You always do," he said with a laugh.

Ronnie blew out a breath. She hated the fund-raisers. They were a necessity, but it was time away from her digs. "Where is it at, again?"

"Edinburgh. I'd tried to get it moved to Glasgow since it'd be closer, but no such luck, kid."

She shrugged. "It'll be fine."

"Have you thought about taking a date to this one?"

"No." And then she paused. After the last one, where the men wouldn't leave her alone, she'd vowed not to go alone again. "On second thought, I'll take Andy."

Pete laughed and then quickly coughed to cover it. "Sorry, Ronnie, but be serious. No man will think Andy is your date. He's too much like a brother to pull that off effectively."

She really hated when Pete was right. "Then you come as my date."

"You're sweet to even mention me, but that won't work either. You're going to need an actual date, kid, if you don't want to spend the time fending off the men."

"I know, but where in the world would I find a date on such short notice?"

As soon as the words were out of her mouth, Arran's laugh sounded. She found herself looking at him again. Her gaze was always drawn to him, as if he were the flame and she the moth.

Her hands curled as she recalled being yanked against his hard body while her hands grabbed a hold of his wide shoulders. It was only then that she realized Arran must have moved with the quickness of lightning to catch her before she fell over while he'd been tying the tarp.

"He'd do," Pete said.

"No," Ronnie said with a firm shake of her head. It was the fact that she wanted Arran to take her that made him so wrong. "Someone else."

"There are plenty of men here who would like the honor of a date with you. Just pick one."

"And then I'd have to come back and work with them. Besides, I don't want to lead any of them on. They'll think it's more than what it is."

Pete shrugged. "Then I suppose you go alone."

Ronnie bit her lip and looked at Arran again. She could ask him. He's the only one she'd even consider taking with her. And he'd certainly keep the others away from her. She wondered how he'd look in a tux. He was probably one of those men who looked good in everything.

And out of everything.

She inwardly groaned as she caught another look of his arm and chest muscles when he lifted a large rock. His stomach muscles tensed, making his abs look like a washboard before he tossed the rock aside.

Clothes would hide all those wonderful muscles, she said to herself.

But she knew Arran couldn't go with her. He might be the only one who she wanted to go, but he was also the only one who made her remember what it was to want to be touched by a man, to want to have him kiss her.

To feel the desire rush through her body. To crave strong arms holding her.

It was too risky. Much too risky. Especially after Max.

Ronnie didn't allow the memories of Max to surface. Instead, she threw herself into the dig. She inspected the progress of the new section, and was amazed to find Arran and the others had done a good job. That wasn't always the case with volunteers.

She got down on her stomach and reached for the large brush that looked like a paintbrush, and then gently brushed away the debris around a stone nearest her.

When more of the stone grew visible, she began to dig away additional dirt, going deeper until soon four stones were visible.

"They make an arch."

She melted at the sound of Arran's voice. He was beside her, his presence all around her. The air around her grew thick and hot.

"Yes," she managed to say, and prayed he didn't know the breathless sound of her voice was because of him.

"An entrance," they said in unison.

Ronnie looked over her shoulder at him, and they shared a smile.

"An entrance to what?" she asked.

"Knowing the Celts, it's most likely a burial mound. I know you've run across them before, but you want to be careful with these."

His caution didn't rile her as she expected. Instead, she took his warning to heart. Maybe it was the sincerity and worry in his eyes. Maybe it was just his proximity. Or it could be the dream she'd had that morning, where he'd been shaking his head at her as she dug.

"It's just a burial mound," someone said.

Arran's head slowly lifted, his gaze narrowed. "Some chambers are no' meant to be opened. Ever."

A tingle of foreboding shot down Ronnie's back. For a moment it was eerily quiet through the entire site, and then someone laughed nervously.

"Did the Celts put in curses like the Egyptians?" an American asked.

Arran's body didn't move a muscle, but she felt the anger begin to rise in him. She had to defuse the situation quickly.

"Curses or not, if it's a burial chamber, we treat it with respect. Is everyone clear on that?" she asked as she got to her feet.

She looked down to find Arran still on one knee, both hands on the ground. His gaze was on the stones and his body tense, primed. But for what?

Ronnie squatted beside him. "What is it?"

"I know you willna believe me, but I doona think you should dig further."

She laughed. "If I don't, someone else will. The stones have been seen."

Golden eyes turned to her. They were filled with uneasiness and agitation. "Tread carefully here, lass. I doona think what you find in there will be good."

She thought of her feelings she got when a relic was near. Was Arran the same? Did he sense something? "Tell me why."

"Nothing I say will stop you," he said, and got to his feet. He raked a hand quickly through the dark strands of his hair. "But if you go inside, promise you'll take me with you."

"I'm not scared of finding bones, Arran."

"You may find more than that."

CHAPTER
EIGHT

Wallace Mansion

Jason Wallace rocked back on his heels, his hands behind his back, as he surveyed the new drapes that had just been hung in his office.

"What do you think, sir?"

Jason glanced at his servant. Servant. Harry had been the leader of a small neighborhood gang that had bullied Jason from the time he'd been a young lad. Until Jason changed all that with his inheritance money.

"I think they'll do," Jason said, and walked to his desk.

Harry followed slowly, a slight limp after the beating he'd taken. "Sir, your . . . guests . . . are waiting for you."

"Why didna you tell me earlier?" he demanded.

"I did. You didna want to be bothered."

"Next time bother me. Now," Jason said as he started out of his office, "are they waiting for me below?"

"Aye, sir."

Jason walked through his home, a home he had re-created from the burnt shards left by his cousin Declan Wallace. Declan had been raised with the family money, whereas Jason had worried where every meal would come from. There were many meals he did miss because there had been no money.

Declan had never had to work for anything in life, but Jason had from his very first breath. It's what made rebuilding the family estate so sweet.

He'd been a little confused at the rooms belowground, especially the part that looked suspiciously like a dungeon. But Jason had even reconstructed those precisely as they'd been.

Including the hidden door beneath the stairs that led to the basement. Jason opened that door now and quietly closed it behind him before going down the narrow stairs.

Even now he recalled how he'd used a hammer to knock down a half-burnt wall and found a safe within. It had taken all Jason's skills as a picklock to open the safe, but he'd been aptly rewarded when he did so. There had been money, but it was the red leather journal within that had been the real treasure.

Jason smiled as he found his guests waiting for him. The dungeon had been a surprise the first time he'd seen it, but so had the second office he found.

If only he'd known sooner that magic ran in the family. But better late than never, he always said.

"Welcome," Jason said as he stopped before the six men and women waiting for him. "What news do you have for me?"

The woman nearest him rose and smiled as she came to stand beside him. Her ruby red lips beckoned, as did her kohl-lined eyes. She put a long red nail against him and let it slowly graze his shoulders through the blazer as she walked behind him until she stood on his left side.

"Oh, we've news," she whispered in a husky tone that always made him hard and ready.

There was something about a woman with black magic that never failed to turn Jason on. Mindy, with her black hair and eyes, had been his favorite since he first saw her almost a year ago.

"Tell me," he urged.

"One of the Warriors at MacLeod Castle left."

Jason's excitement waned. "So? They come and go often."

"True, but none have left to be a part of an archeological dig."

That got his attention. He shifted his gaze from Mindy to the two men off to the side. "What do you know of Charon, Phelan, and Malcolm?"

"Malcolm is hiding," said the tallest of them, Dale. He was a big brute of a man with a shaved head and a goatee that made him look even more sinister.

Jason leaned against the wall and glared. "You are Warriors. You should be able to find him."

"Charon still thinks his wee village is safe," said the red-headed Warrior with a cold smile.

"That will soon change," Jason said. He was eager for his plans to begin, and it was almost time. He'd planned everything out carefully. All the information he needed on the Warriors and Druids had been found in that red leather book.

And he'd used it to perfection.

Much had happened since he inherited the Wallace fortune. He might have taken his time rebuilding the estate, but he hadn't wasted any in learning about the black magic that ran through his family's veins.

He'd dived headfirst into that world and seized all that was his. It had taken some doing to create the Warriors, and even more in helping them control their god. Jason wanted them to kill, but he wanted to be the one ruling them.

If creating and controlling the Warriors had been trouble, it was nothing compared to finding *droughs*. Sorting the true Druids from the fake had been easy enough.

But now everything Declan had planned and penned in the pages of the red book, Jason had set in motion. Declan had failed and been bested by the MacLeods.

Oh, there was no proof it was the MacLeods, but if not them, then who else could have killed his cousin?

It was time for revenge. It was time for . . . payback.

"Aisley," Jason called to his cousin. A beauty with a flaw-less complexion and long legs, her midnight hair pulled back in a ponytail, and her dark eyes remained anywhere but on him. "What news do you have?"

She kept her head turned away and her arms crossed over her chest as she leaned her hips against his desk. "No more *mies* have gone to the MacLeods, nor have any been located."

"They're out there, just as we were. We need to make sure we end them before they get to the MacLeods," Jason warned.

He smiled as he heard a roar from the dungeon area. "It willna be too much longer before my next Warriors can join us. We have the advantage right now. The MacLeods have no idea we're here or that I'm amassing an army."

"When do we strike?" Mindy asked, excitement burning in her black eyes. Her red lips were lifted in a knowing grin.

Jason took her hand and kissed the top of it. "Soon, my darling. Verra soon. I want to know about this archeological dig and why a Warrior is there. If the MacLeods sent him, there's a reason. Find it."

"Maybe they're just bored."

Jason swung his head to Aisley and narrowed his eyes. "Are you bored, cousin? Maybe I should give you more to do."

Aisley straightened, her hands clenching at her sides. "I've got quite enough. Cousin."

"I'm no' so sure."

She looked away. "All I'm saying is that maybe this Warrior just wanted to get away from the castle for a bit. Family can be . . . stifling."

Jason smiled as he walked to her. Aisley's history was complicated, or at least that's what she called it. Jason called it perfect for his uses.

Aisley had many uses, though she didn't know of them. There were things about her Jason kept to himself, things that would be used to his benefit in the future. But she had to stay with him. He'd thought he'd made that point clear, but maybe it needed to be made again.

He took his cousin's hand in his and patted it. He leaned close and whispered in her ear, "You've no' seen stifling, Aisley. No' yet. I can give it to you though."

"I see." Her large brown eyes stared at a place in the wall.

"I thought you might." Jason dropped her hand and turned to Mindy. "Take Aisley and go to the dig site. I want everything you know on this Warrior."

Mindy smiled and rubbed her hands together.

But Aisley said, "It's a bad idea."

"Did I no' just go over this with you?" Jason ground out angrily.

Aisley rolled her eyes. "Think. You're the mastermind. Warriors can feel Druid magic. He'll be able to tell the difference between a *mie* and *drough*. Do you really want this Warrior to know there are two *droughs* there?"

"Ugh. As much as I hate to say it, she's got a point," Mindy said with a pout of her red lips.

Jason hated when he made a mistake. He hated it even more when it was pointed out to him. Despite that, Aisley had helped him from alerting the MacLeods.

"Fine." He turned to the two Warriors. "Go. Watch the Warrior, but doona let him know you're there. Stay hidden and out of sight."

With a jerk of his head, he sent everyone out. As Aisley began to walk past him, he grasped her arm.

"Oh, no. No' you."

When the door shut behind the last Druid, Aisley jerked her arm out of his hold, her lip peeled back in a sneer. "Aye, I know. I spoke out of turn."

"You wanted this, remember? You wanted control of your life. I gave it to you!"

"Oh, yes, you've given me a fine life!" Her chest heaved and her eyes glared daggers.

Jason smiled as his anger evaporated. "Everything has a price. You know that better than most."

"I don't need to be reminded of what I've done, Jason. I'm here. I do what you ask, and I've saved your ass more times than I can remember. I don't need you breathing down my neck and trying to put me in my place."

"But that's exactly what you need." He took a step toward

her, backing her against the wall. "You never knew your place, no' before. You will by the time I'm done with you."

Aisley watched him walk out of the basement. How she hated him. If she could get away with it, she'd plunge a knife through his heart.

She closed her eyes and gripped the wall. The scar on her left side was six months old, but it still hurt. Just as she could still feel the blade slicing into her skin slowly, relentlessly.

That had been Jason's response when she'd tried to leave. He'd told her it was just a taste of what he'd do to her if she even thought of leaving him again.

Aisley held out her hand in front of her. The black magic within her was like another entity. She could sense it flowing through her and gradually taking her soul.

This was her life. It was the one she had chosen. For better or worse, she needed to make the most of it.

"Before Hell claims me."

CHAPTER
NINE

Two days later, and Arran traded in his shovel and put his strength to use. The digging now consisted of small spades and other tools he couldn't care less about.

He and a few others carted the extra dirt away from the site. It wasn't exactly a fun job, but it continued to maintain his activity as well as keep him near Ronnie.

Which in itself was torture.

She had no idea of her allure. The way her jeans molded to her ass, the way her shirt stretched across her breasts as she reached for something. Or the way she would smile in abandon and happiness as she dug in the earth.

All of it was pure, exquisite, amazing agony. He couldn't look his fill of her. And at night when he tried to sleep, all he saw was her. Her smile, her hazel eyes, her wheat-colored hair that teased him with its length.

He dreamed of the different ways he would make love to her, teasing her body until she screamed his name as she peaked, her hands clutching him, urging him over her.

What was worse was that he had no effect on her. It would have helped his ego had he caught her staring at him a few times, but as he'd been warned—she had one love, and that was archeology.

Thankfully, Pete had left the day before to finalize some-thing in Edinburgh. He'd told Arran about it, but Arran hadn't been listening. He'd caught a glimpse of Ronnie through the tent flap and had been watching her.

He was always watching her.

Watching and wanting. He'd never felt such suffering before. His body blazed with need, and the only way he could keep himself from finding Ronnie and claiming her lips was to work himself as hard as he could. And even that was never enough.

Not after touching her, holding her . . . feeling her feminine curves and beckoning softness.

He put to memory every little move, laugh, and smile she had. Every time she smoothed back a strand of hair behind her ear, every time she bent to look at Andy's clipboard, every time she searched the site, eagerly hoping to find something. She was an astonishing woman.

What Deirdre had done to him when she unbound his god had been horrifying. But what Ronnie was doing to him, unintentional though it was, cut him even deeper.

Arran didn't want to desire her. He didn't want to feel the unquenchable hunger when she was near.

But damned if he knew how to stop it.

There were other, willing, women, but he'd given his word to Ronnie not to distract the others. If only he'd known what he'd be going through now, he would've reconsidered that promise.

Arran stood in his tent after another long day and groaned as he heard Ronnie's sweet voice. His control was holding on by a thread, a very thin thread that was about to snap.

He grabbed a change of clothes and exited the tent. He'd barely reached the parked vehicles when Andy ran up to him.

"Arran? Dude, you're not, like, leaving or anything? Are you? We need you."

"Nay."

Andy's tall body tripped and ran to catch back up with Arran's long strides. Arran knew he was being rude, but he had to get away, to get a better leash on the desire and the hunger hounding him.

He'd never experienced anything so clear or intense before. The yearning, the need continued to grow, never abating. It was driving him mad. If he didn't get away now, he'd find Ronnie and kiss her.

And then God help them both. One taste, and he knew he'd be done for.

"Where are you going?" Andy asked breathlessly as he jogged to keep up.

"For a swim."

"A swim? The closest loch is a mile away."

"I'll be here in the morn."

Thankfully, Andy drew to a halt and let Arran continue on his own. When he was far enough away from camp so the others wouldn't see him, he broke into a run.

If he wanted, he could use the speed his god gave him and be at the loch in a matter of seconds, but Arran was content to continue to exert his body.

He slowed to a walk when the loch came into view. Arran drew in a breath and simply stared at the sight before him. When he reached the loch, he squatted at the water's edge. Many had built homes around the water. It seemed like only yesterday that this loch had been largely left alone. There hadn't been any docks or boats tied up, bobbing languidly.

There hadn't been restaurants and homes lining the coast centuries ago. Or roads where the sound of cars could be heard even through the line of trees. It wasn't that he hated this modern time, just that he missed how things once were.

Arran kicked off his boots and shed his pants before he dived into the water. The cove was secluded, affording him the privacy he desperately needed at the moment.

Anything was likely to set him off, he was in such a state. One wrong look, one wrong word, and his desire could turn into a rage. He was that close to the edge.

Arran couldn't remember being so torn since his god was first unbound. The fury and anger simmered the longer his passion went unquenched.

He surfaced and shook his head. The water was cool and dark in the evening sky. The sky was still light, giving off a golden hue upon the clouds.

It could be a magical night. He could picture Ronnie in the water with him. He could even picture her smiling before he pulled her into his arms for a kiss.

"Shite," he grumbled at his fantasy.

Arran dived under again and swam beneath the surface, hoping his need would ease even a little.

Ronnie shut off her car and got out. She leaned against the door and looked across the clear, smooth water of the loch. When Andy told her where Arran had gone, she hadn't believed it.

She still didn't believe it, but at least Arran's Range Rover was still parked at the site.

A local told her of this isolated cove in the loch, and Ronnie thought it was where Arran might have gone. But it looked like she'd guessed wrong.

She was getting back in her car when she noticed the discarded boots and jeans in a pile by the shore. Ronnie softly closed her car door and walked to the clothes.

They were definitely Arran's. She'd been trying to ignore those jeans that had conformed to his ass all day. And had failed. Miserably.

Ignoring Arran proved impossible. He was everywhere. Always willing to help, always there when she needed someone. And everyone liked him. The women, of course, but even the men wanted to be his friend.

People were continually calling out his name. She could hear his voice no matter where she was on the site, and it had come to a point that when she didn't hear him, she searched for him.

Now, she'd come out to the loch. Why? She knew better than to be alone with him. She tended to forget everything when he was near, and she was definitely tempting herself this night.

Particularly when he put her so off-kilter. He made her think of long, hot nights, of pleasure, and of passion so intense, she'd never forget a moment in his arms.

Her gaze scanned the water. The only movement was the

water itself. She couldn't help her disappointment. Though she knew she needed to keep her distance, she wanted to see him.

Ronnie put her hands on her hips and sighed. "Timing, as they say, is everything. Maybe it's for the better. I just might give in to him."

She was about to return to her car when a head broke the surface. Her lungs seized as she recognized Arran's long, dark hair slicked to his head. He laughed, the sound carrying over the water and slamming against her.

Ronnie's feet were glued to the ground as she watched him tread water. His long, muscular arms spread the water as he turned and began to swim toward her.

She knew the moment he saw her because his easy stroke faltered. He dived beneath the water again, and she looked around with her heart hammering in her chest. Did she leave? Or did she tempt herself and stay?

Stay.

She dropped her hands from her hips and bit her lip as indecision warred. Before she could make a choice, Arran broke the water again, this time close enough she could see his golden eyes.

"How did you find me?"

Ronnie shrugged, hating the nervousness that ran rampant through her. "I asked a local if there was a spot on the loch nearby that was private. He sent me here."

"Why did you come?"

She swallowed and looked away. There was a hard edge to his voice she wasn't used to. It should've given her pause, but all she could think about was that the only thing stopping her from seeing him in all his wonderful glory was the water. "Andy thought you might be leaving."

"I told him I was no'."

"Yeah. Look, I just wanted to make sure you were all right. You obviously want to be alone. I'll see you back at the site."

She turned and had taken two steps to the car when he said, "Ronnie."

She kept her back to him and licked her lips. His voice had been rough, clipped. It was a side of Arran she hadn't seen before. What else did he keep hidden?

"I doona mean to sound so . . . harsh. I just . . . it's just that . . . I needed a cold swim."

"Like I said, it's all right." She wanted to turn and look at him, wanted to gaze into his golden eyes. She wanted to see every wonderful muscle. "I didn't mean to interrupt."

"You didna."

She knew that for the lie it was, but she was happy he'd said it anyway. "I'm glad you're okay. You've become quite the asset at the site. I don't want to lose you."

"The water feels good. Join me."

Ronnie was so surprised at the change of topic that she turned around. His hair was slicked back away from his face. He stood still in the shallow water where it covered him from the waist down.

He appeared like a statue, but she could feel the heat of his gaze as it held her.

"The last thing I thought to bring with me to Scotland was a swimsuit."

"Who said anything about wearing a swimsuit?"

The deep resonance of his voice sent a tremor through her, firing her blood until she had to clench her legs together. And just like that, the fire took her. A fire that only he seemed able to enflame.

He was offering her the very thing she'd only imagined in her fantasies. No sane woman would turn away a man like Arran.

"The water will soothe you," he urged.

She shifted weight from one foot to the other as her gaze took in the beads of water dotting his shoulders and abdomen. Her hands itched to run over all his muscles, down his chest and over his washboard abs.

Her legs grew weak just thinking about it. She moved so that she was leaning back against the hood of her car. It wasn't wise for her to be so taken with a guy. She had to keep her head, to stay in charge. Of everything.

It scared her how much she wanted to feel his arms around her, wanted to know the sensation of his lips moving over hers. It's as if Max had never happened, that she hadn't learned a valuable lesson.

Arran erased the pain of the past. He promised new memories, pleasure and ecstasy for as long as she wanted them. And did she ever want them.

He was right there before her, waiting.

"What are you doing out here? Really."

His brow furrowed at her question, but his gaze never left hers. "I'm no' sure you'd like the truth."

"I want the truth."

"You."

Her stomach fluttered. When she was able to pull in a breath, it was uneven and her chest was heaving. Her breasts swelled, her nipples ached. A hunger, deep and insistent, rose within her. A hunger for Arran MacCarrick that she knew would never leave.

All she wanted was Arran. His hands, his mouth, his body. There wasn't a part of him she didn't want to touch and kiss and put to memory.

"I needed the closest thing to a cold shower I could get."

Ronnie was glad the car was holding her, because she was sure her legs would have crumpled otherwise. No words would come, not that she knew what to say in response to his admission.

"I see you were no' expecting me to say that."

"No," she said with a shake of her head. "I had no idea."

"Liar." He chuckled and lowered himself in the water so that only his head showed. "Join me, Ronnie."

God how she wanted to walk into that water and go right up to him and kiss him. She wanted to thread her fingers into his dark hair and stare deep into his eyes.

But the past kept her on land, kept her from taking a chance. Damn Max for ruining this.

"I don't think I can."

He nodded and then stood up so quickly, the water splashed around him. It wasn't until he began to walk toward her that Ronnie found her body trembling from need, need of him.

The water kept getting lower and lower on his body with each step he took. It revealed the chiseled abs she'd come to know. It also bared his trim hips and the line of dark hair that traveled from his navel downward.

With his golden eyes locked on her and unmistakably filled with a deep, dark hunger, he looked like some mythical Highlander determined to claim her.

And God help her, but her heart beat faster because of it.

Her lips parted when the water lowered to show his thick, hard arousal and his legs corded with muscles. He kept walking straight to her.

Ronnie hated that he stopped just short of touching her. He leaned his hands against the hood on either side of her so that his lips were breaths from hers, water dripping from his body onto hers.

"I figured you for the adventurous sort," he said as his gaze raked over her face. "What a pity."

And then he was gone.

Ronnie blinked, angry that—once again—she'd been too timid to see what would happen if she gave in to Arran Mac-Carrick.

All she'd had to do was lean up and put her lips on his. He'd been waiting for it. He even told her he'd come for a cold swim because of his desire for her.

But she'd chickened out as she always did.

She expected to see him on the road or somewhere close, putting on his clothes, but he was gone. As were his clothes. It was like they just vanished.

Ronnie straightened and looked around the area. "Arran. Arran!"

No matter how many times she called, he didn't answer and she didn't find him. After several minutes, she gave up and got in her car.

"Damn," she said, and slammed her hands on the steering wheel. "I'm such a coward. I want him and what he's offering. Why can't I take it? What's wrong with me?"

She put her head on the wheel and simply sat there, hating herself for allowing the past to rule her. It was all because of Max, all because she'd been naïve and foolish.

Pete had warned her that what Max had done would jeopardize any future happiness. She'd laughed Pete off, but it seemed he was right.

Ronnie tried to remember the last time she'd had a date, a real date. The last time someone had asked her out had been just a few months after she broke things off with Max.

She'd declined the date, and the next several following that. Then she'd dived into work so that she hadn't realized it had been over two years since she'd had a date of any kind.

With a sigh she lifted her head and looked at the water. What would it have been like to swim with Arran? What would it have felt like to forget about the past and give in to the attraction?

What would it have been like to kiss him?

Ronnie angrily wiped at a tear that dared to fall. Then she did as she'd always done. She gave herself that minute to wallow in guilt and regret, then she shoved it aside and looked ahead.

It was the only course she had. Look ahead. Always look ahead.

She fastened her seat belt and started the car. As she drove away, she was determined never to think of the loch and Arran walking from the water again. Never to think of the way her body reacted to his mere presence or what could have been.

CHAPTER
TEN

Arran watched Ronnie drive away. Only then did he release the breath he'd been holding. He wasn't sure how he hadn't hauled her against him and plundered her mouth as he'd wanted to do from the first moment he'd seen her. Several times he'd nearly come out of his hiding spot when she called his name.

She'd wanted to come into the water. It'd been there on her face. But something had stopped her. What was it?

And why did he care so damn much?

He dressed as the sizzle of her magic began to fade when her car drove away. He'd felt her magic while he was under-water, but to break the surface and see her standing there had brought all the ardor he'd worked so hard to cool back in an instant.

If he could forget the burning need long enough to talk to her about Druids, he might learn more about her. But damn if he could get his body under control. Yet, he was going to have to—and soon. He'd seen the way she'd looked at the arches. Whether it was a burial mound or something else she was uncovering, he didn't like the feel of it.

And it seemed to be taking her. It was the way she looked at it that bothered him the most. The last thing he wanted was to confront her with being a Druid, but since he hadn't been alone with her, he was fast losing time.

He'd had that opportunity a few minutes ago, and he'd blown it. All because of his damned cock.

His phone rang at that moment. "Shit," he murmured, and jerked the phone out of his back pocket. Then he let loose another string of curses when he saw Saffron's name.

"You've got some explaining to do," he said by way of answering, since she'd refused to take his calls.

"Hello to you as well," Saffron said, a smile in her voice. "I thought you might like my little trick. Many people think Ronnie is a man based on her name."

"That's a natural deduction. And you could've answered my calls before about this. Why are you really calling?"

When she didn't immediately answer, he grew instantly alert. Saffron was a Seer. They were rare in the Druid world, so rare that she'd been kidnapped by Declan Wallace in order to use her magic.

It had been Camdyn, her husband, who released her from her imprisonment. Those were three years Saffron never spoke of.

"Saffron," Arran said softly. "Did you have some sort of vision?"

There was a long sigh through the phone. "Yes."

Arran squeezed his eyes closed because he knew whom the vision was about. "Ronnie."

"Yes," Saffron said again.

"What did you see?"

"Not nearly enough. I'm sorry. All I know is that she's scared. Really scared, Arran. The kind of scared like I was when Camdyn found me in Declan's dungeon."

Arran's gut clenched painfully. He struck a tree with his fist. "Fuck."

"I wanted to call you first. Camdyn went to the castle to tell the others. Fallon will want to send another Warrior, and maybe that's wise."

"Nay," Arran said forcefully. He didn't want to share Ronnie with anyone. "I can do this."

"I don't know what's going to happen to her. It could be

an accident at the site, or it could be a mugging in the city, a wreck while she's driving. It could be anything."

"A wreck," he repeated, and jerked his head up to where the taillights of Ronnie's car had disappeared. "I'll call you back."

Arran was running before the last word left his mouth. He didn't hold back this time. Memphaea wanted to be released, and with the dread pounding through him, he was barely able to keep his god clamped down.

Using all his speed, Arran hurdled parked cars and boulders. He didn't follow the road, but instead took a straight path until he saw Ronnie's taillights.

He began to slow until he saw a car turn the curve toward her. The tire blew at that moment, causing the car to swerve in Ronnie's lane.

"Ronnie!" Arran shouted as he pumped his legs harder to reach her.

It was going to be a head-on collision. The cars were too close to each other, and it was happening too fast.

"Turn the damn wheel, Ronnie!" Arran shouted, knowing it wouldn't do any good since she couldn't hear him.

But somehow, she did jerk the wheel at the last second. The car slammed into her passenger side. The squeal of tires and the smell of burnt rubber along with the crunch of metal would stay in his memory forever.

The cars were still rocking from their collision when he reached her. He threw open her door, halting his true strength so he didn't rip it off, to find her gripping the wheel so tightly, her fingers were white.

"Ronnie?" he asked softly, hesitantly. "Ronnie, lass. I need you to look at me. Look at me," he said louder when she didn't move.

Her startled, fear-filled hazel eyes turned to him. "Arran?"

"Aye. Are you hurt?"

"I . . . I don't know."

He did a once-over, but didn't see any blood besides a cut on her hand from the broken passenger window. "Stay here. I'll be right back."

Arran rushed to the other car, and after determining they were also all right, he ran back to Ronnie. She hadn't moved. Blood ran from the cut between her two knuckles, where a small piece of glass had embedded itself in her hand.

He took her face in his hands and made her look at him again. "Ronnie, did you hit your head?"

Her eyes were a bit dazed as she tried to shake her head no, but a wince quickly stopped her.

"Damn," Arran muttered.

He pried one of her hands from the wheel and felt how ice-cold it was. Shock. He rubbed her hand to help warm her before he gently took her other hand.

Arran carefully held her injured hand in his. "I've got to get the glass out."

"Glass," Ronnie repeated. Then she looked at her hand and nodded. "Yes. Please get it out."

"Turn your head."

He waited until she looked away before he looked at the glass. His fingers were too big to try to grab it without hurting her. The only option he had was to use his claws.

"Keep your eyes closed," he warned.

A ghost of a smile pulled at her lips. "Blood doesn't bother me."

"Well, you looking makes me nervous, and I doona want to hurt you."

"Okay."

He watched as white claws extended from his fingers. Arran was just reaching for the glass when she inhaled.

"I'm glad you're here, Arran."

He used that second to pull the glass free and toss it away. "Me, too. It's all over."

"Is my car dead?"

"Nay," he said with a chuckle, his claws now gone. "You'll need a new window and some bodywork, but the car should continue to drive."

It took longer than Arran liked to get information exchanged regarding the wreck. Once that was done, he cleared the passenger seat of glass and moved Ronnie over.

He was in the process of driving back to the site when his phone rang again. Somehow he wasn't surprised to see it was Saffron.

"It's over," he said.

"What do you mean?" Saffron asked.

Arran glanced at Ronnie to find her eyes closed. "There was a wreck. Ronnie is all right."

"I'm glad to hear it," Saffron said after a brief pause. "But I don't think that's what my vision was. Terror, Arran. True, heart-pounding *terror*."

He clenched his jaw. The only thing that would cause Ronnie to feel any of that was the evil they'd been fighting for centuries. An evil that was now gone.

"That's over," he ground out.

Saffron made a sound at the back of her throat. "Is it?"

"It's been a year."

"I know. Let me talk to Ronnie."

Arran held the phone out to Ronnie. "It's Saffron," he said when she looked at the phone.

He drove along the narrow winding roads, pretending he couldn't hear Saffron's voice through the phone asking how Ronnie was. Arran kept his gaze forward as he feigned not hearing the tremor in Ronnie's voice as she responded.

The conversation ended quickly, and when Ronnie handed him the phone, he felt her hand shake. He tossed the phone into the cup holder and wrapped his fingers around hers.

He gave her a reassuring smile, and to his relief, she didn't pull away.

"I've only ever been in one other accident," she said. "It was during college, and I was driving home. I had a friend in the car with me, and we were talking as I drove through the parking lot of the university. A car suddenly backed out right into me. Very little damage, but it scared the shit out of me."

"The unexpected always frightens. That's nothing to be ashamed of."

She looked at their clasped hands. "I suppose."

All too soon they arrived back at the dig site. Arran got

out of the car and hurried to the other side to help Ronnie. She'd already opened her door and was stepping out by the time he got to her.

Most everyone had already found their tents for the night, so there was no one to see them arrive. Arran waited until she was out before he closed the door.

He walked her back to her tent, and though he didn't want to leave her, there was no excuse to stay. His hands itched to hold her again and make sure she was really all right. Mortal life could be extinguished so quickly, too quickly. It left him cold just thinking about it.

"Thank you. For being there."

Arran shrugged. "You wouldna have been there had I no' gone to the loch."

"This wasn't your fault."

"Nor was it yours. Accidents happen."

She smiled and sat on her cot. "I can't even see where the glass was in my hand."

"It was small." He swallowed and glanced around. They were alone. He could ask her now about being a Druid, but the dazed looked in her eyes told him he wouldn't get any information out of her. He'd have to wait again. "Get some rest. I'll see you in the morning."

Arran left before he did something crazy like take her in his arms and kiss her until they were both senseless. The fear that had rushed through him when he witnessed the wreck left him cold.

Even after knowing Ronnie was safe, he couldn't shake the knowledge that at any time she could be taken. It could have happened that night, had she not turned the wheel.

Now he realized how each of the Warriors felt about their mortal wives. And why they had all chosen to stay beneath the magical shield at the castle.

Arran lay down on his cot and stared at the top of his tent. The accident replayed in his mind again and again. The crunch of the gravel, the squeal of the tires.

Despite knowing Ronnie's accident would haunt him for some time, it was Saffron's words that kept him awake.

The evil was gone. Arran had watched first Deirdre and then Declan be destroyed. They were gone, wiped off the face of the earth.

But they had killed Deirdre once before and she'd lived. Is that what had happened with Declan?

Arran rubbed the heels of his hands against his eyes. He then sat up and reached for his phone. For several minutes he considered calling one of the Warriors.

Before he could decide which one, his phone rang. He saw Ramsey's name pop up. The Warrior was also half Druid. He'd been the one to end Declan.

"Ramsey," Arran answered the phone.

"Saffron and Camdyn just left. She told us what happened."

"Is that all she told you?"

Ramsey paused. "She said the evil may no' be dead as we thought."

"You were the only one inside Declan's mansion. Is he gone?"

Ramsey chuckled, the sound filled with humor and satisfaction. "Oh, aye. Declan is gone."

"We thought that of Deirdre as well."

"True enough." Ramsey sighed. "We've lived a year thinking everything was gone. That's a year someone could've put things in motion."

"We'd have known. Wouldn't we?"

"I'd like to think so. Saffron has had no visions regarding Declan."

Arran rubbed his chin as he thought. "Aye, but we were no' looking for anything either, were we? We assumed the evil was well and truly vanished."

"As my lovely wife keeps reminding me, there can no' be good without evil. Tara should know, since her entire family is *droughs*. Has anything out of the ordinary happened there?"

"Besides the wreck? Nay. Nothing. There's magic everywhere. I've no doubt the magical items we're searching for are here."

Ramsey grunted. "What kind of magic? *Drough*? *Mie*? Fallon said you didna say."

"Because it's difficult. I doona sense *drough*."

"But," Ramsey urged.

"But . . . I sense lots of ancient magic. And *mie* magic."

"Does it involve any one person?"

"Aye."

"Ronnie," Ramsey answered. "You've spent more time with her since Fallon last spoke with you. Have you spoken with her about it?"

"No' yet. Things . . . keep getting in the way."

"Ah. You want her."

Arran braced his elbows on his legs. "I can barely think with the need, Ramsey. Her magic is—"

"Special," he finished.

"Aye. It's *mie,* but it feels different from any of the *mies* I've felt before."

"You shouldna be there alone."

He smiled at Ramsey's statement. "I'm a Warrior, my friend. I can take care of myself."

"There's no doubt about that. But as I learned while I was keeping Tara safe, it's always better to have someone watching your back while you're focused on someone else."

"Maybe."

Ramsey laughed softly. "I hear Dr. Reid is verra pretty."

"She's damned beautiful. And untouchable."

"Why have you no' seduced her?"

Arran closed his eyes. "It's . . . complicated."

"Interesting. Verra interesting."

"Meaning?" Arran asked.

"Never mind. We'll look into Declan, but I swear to you he's dead."

"That's what we all said about Deirdre," Arran said before he ended the call.

He tossed the phone aside and lay back on his pillow, one arm under his head.

Somehow he had to get Ronnie alone tomorrow morning and talk to her. It wasn't going to be easy with Andy hovering or the site calling to her, but Arran had to know how much she knew of Druids.

He wasn't worried that she might be working with evil. There wasn't a hint of it in her magic, but what he was worried about was her absorption to her current dig. If what he searched for was in there, he had to know before Ronnie saw it.

Or he was really going to have a problem on his hands.

CHAPTER
ELEVEN

Ronnie looked up from her spot on the ground to find Arran to her left. He was never far. It should have bothered her. It would have bothered her before.

But after the car accident, she liked having him near. She liked it entirely too much.

Whereas before the accident, he'd kept her off-kilter and desire smoldering beneath her skin, now he added a new element—safety.

There were only two other men who had ever inspired that sense of comfort in her—Pete and Andy. Never would she have thought Arran would be put in the same category as Pete and Andy, but there was no denying it.

When she'd woken that morning after another night full of dreams involving the box and more that involved Arran making love to her, she found just how bad the damage was to her car. How it had been drivable, she didn't know. She'd had Andy call someone to tow it away to get it fixed.

She'd woken at five, and had been going ever since. Several times, Arran asked to speak to her alone, but there was always something that came up that needed her urgent attention.

She didn't want to keep putting him off, but she couldn't help it. Whatever he wanted, she would make sure to have some time alone to hear what he had to say. As long as it wasn't him telling her he was leaving.

The thought made her stomach sour. Ronnie looked back at the ground. She needed to concentrate on her work, not the all-too-hunky guy who happened to save her life and bring forth desire she thought to never have.

She smiled. Well, saying he saved her life was a bit dramatic, but that's what it felt like. He'd been calm and collected while he saw to everything. Ronnie hadn't been able to think past the part that she'd been in a wreck.

Arran had not only seen to her but the other driver as well. He'd then gotten her back to the site and to her tent.

Ronnie couldn't remember the last time she'd had someone help her in such a way. She was used to doing everything on her own. It had become a habit, since she was raised in a foster home with five other kids.

Not that her foster parents had been bad people. They had been normal, and treated her kindly. But they both worked and had other kids to take care of.

Ronnie had learned that if she wanted anything done, she was going to have to be the one to do it. To have someone like Arran come to her aid and not expect anything in return was refreshing. It also didn't help the attraction she felt.

Another glance showed that, as usual, Arran was surrounded. It must be his infectious smile or his easygoing nature. But she'd seen another part of him that he kept carefully guarded when he was around others.

She'd seen the predatory side, the part of him that was ready for whatever life threw him. A side that wouldn't go down without a fight.

His golden eyes met hers, and for a moment she held his gaze before she looked away. Why did he hide that other part of him? She liked that part, which she didn't understand.

She frowned as she continued to dig around the stone. She'd never been one who appreciated the muscular alpha guys. Until Arran. There was no doubt he was an alpha. Everyone else seemed to recognize it as well, which was why they flocked to him.

But why did she?

It was the attraction. At least that's what she told herself.

"Need some help?"

The words were said in a low, seductive tone that sent chills racing over her skin and her heart to beat double time. *Arran*.

"I thought you already had a job to do," Ronnie said as she continued to dig.

"I've done it. You look like you could use a hand."

She did the wrong thing and looked at him. His golden eyes ensnared her, entranced her. Charmed her. Everything about Arran pulled at her, urged her to get closer to him.

Ronnie swallowed and rubbed some dirt from his cheek shadowed with whiskers.

"I didna shave," he said with a frown. He rubbed at his jaw a moment. "I forgot."

"It's a good look for you. Not that you need any help."

Was she flirting? Flirting! What the hell was wrong with her?

A lopsided grin stole across Arran's lips. "Is that so?"

"You know it is. Look around you. Every woman here can't keep her eyes off you."

"Every woman but one."

The smile was gone from his lips, and there was a serious thread to his words. He meant her, she knew, and for the life of her, she didn't know how to respond.

"How is your hand?" he asked.

Ronnie was grateful for the change of subject. "It's a little sore where the glass penetrated the skin. Other than my neck being tender from the impact, I'm fine."

"Good."

He didn't move away, and his gaze didn't shift. He was so close she could see the dark ring of gold around his eyes and a bead of sweat as it ran down the side of his cheek. Her gaze dropped to his mouth.

His lips were wide and firm. No smile turned up the sides now, no sweet words made her heart race. Yet it didn't dampen the fire he'd ignited.

It was only the sounds of the site that kept her from making a fool of herself and leaning in to kiss him. But oh, how she wanted to. His lips looked too damn good not to kiss. She looked up in time to see his gaze drop to her mouth, and she barely suppressed a groan.

Her nipples pebbled painfully. Her entire body ached to be closer to him, to have him touch her. Ronnie didn't know how, but she was certain he would be an exceptional lover.

To have a man take care of her, even if it was for a few hours, sounded too good to be true. It all hinged on her allowing him close.

Someone shouted her name. Twice. No longer could she ignore those around her.

Ronnie cleared her throat and looked away. "Thank you again for helping me last night."

"Has anything odd happened recently? Any people hanging around you doona recognize?"

She jerked her head to him. "Why?"

"Just curious." He shrugged while his gaze swept the scene around them.

"There's been nothing."

"Let me know if there is."

"Just as soon as you tell me why.

His nostrils flared in agitation. "Saffron said there might be people thinking to harm you."

Ronnie chuckled and shook her head. "There are always those out there who think that history should stay in the ground. It doesn't matter what country I'm in, there are people who want to harm me for digging into their pasts. I tend to think it's because they fear what I'm going to find."

"Or want what you're finding." He leaned close. "It's a threat Saffron felt I needed to know, which means you need to take it seriously, Ronnie. Keep your eyes open."

"Is this what you wanted to talk to me about?"

He gave a quick shake of his head. "Nay. That really does need to be private. But I'd like to make that talk happen soon."

By the way he spoke, she knew this "talk" wasn't going to be about the attraction between them. Her heart pounded as she realized how often he watched her. Did he know her secret? Had he worked out that she used her abilities to find the relics?

"There's no need to be frightened of me," Arran hastily said. "I'm your friend, Ronnie. I want to help you, protect you. There are . . . things . . . about me that could help. If you'll let me."

He rose and walked away before she could respond. For long moments she stared after him, his words reverberating in her head. He knew. He knew her secret.

But what could he have that could help her? It was a question only he could answer, and one she would demand as soon as she knew exactly what he thought he knew of her.

The rest of the afternoon Ronnie would glance up every now and again while she worked. Arran was always near, but she also looked around her as he'd asked. She didn't know what she was looking for. Despite her focus shifting constantly, they were able to make a good bit of headway around the arch.

It appeared Arran had been right, and it was a doorway of some kind. There was still so much dirt blocking their way, and every time they moved some, more would suddenly fall and fill in the spot.

Wooden barriers that resembled small fences were made and put into place. Still, the dirt fell through the cracks of the barriers and slowed their progress considerably.

Ronnie wasn't ready to stop work when the dinner bell tolled, but she was the only one. She sat back as the others readily put away their tools and walked to the food tent.

Lines of exhaustion were clear on their faces. She'd pushed them all hard, but even that hadn't gotten her what she wanted. Which was the entire arch visible to her so she could see what it was.

She planned to continue working when Andy was suddenly beside her, pulling her by her arm to stand up. He dragged her toward the food tent while he filled her in on the other sections around the camp.

It was only right before she walked into the tent that she spotted Arran striding around the perimeter of the site.

Arran made a third round of the site, looking at every parked car and camper. Nothing seemed out of the ordinary, but Saffron's visions were never wrong.

Events could change and thereby render her visions mute, but if she'd been right and Ronnie was terrified, then Arran doubted the events could change enough to prevent that.

There was a slight stir in the air and he turned to find Fallon behind him. "Bloody hell," he ground out. "Anyone could've seen you."

Fallon grinned. "Ah, but they didna. How are things?"

"The usual. I've yet to find anything."

"Us either. The same bad people that seem to populate the world with murders, rapes, and such, but nothing that would suggest *droughs*."

Arran crossed his arms over his chest. "They're out there. Just as the *mies* are."

"Aye, but where? If someone was taking Declan's place, I think we'd have heard something by now."

"I'm no' so sure. It could be they're waiting for something."

"Like what?"

Arran looked at the spot Ronnie had been digging. Almost half the arch could be seen now. "Maybe they're waiting to see what Ronnie finds."

"Shite," Fallon said, and raked a hand through his dark hair. His green eyes glittered with anger. "I'd thought we were finished with such evil. I want to give Larena the babe she craves so desperately."

Arran dropped his arms to his sides. He hated the spot Fallon and the others were in. He didn't want to bind his god as they did, but he understood their need to make their mates happy.

"Tell me of Ronnie."

Arran raised a brow at Fallon. "I'm sure Saffron told you

all there is to know. And knowing Gwynn with her computer skills, she was able to pull up Ronnie's entire past."

"Aye," Fallon said with a nod. "But I want your take on her."

"She's stubborn. Talented. Beautiful. There's a wee bit of pride in her as well, but it's understandable, being as good as she is in her field. Though she's that good because it's her magic leading her to the artifacts. She's good to her people, both paid and volunteers. She's also verra private and keeps men at arm's length. I think it has to do with her past."

"It does."

Arran glanced at the food tent, where he'd last seen her. He wanted to know her past. It would help him get closer to her, to know what paths to take and which ones to steer clear of.

"Her parents died when she was only four," Fallon said. "There were no relatives to take her in, so she went into the foster system in Arizona. A couple with five other foster children took her in and raised her."

Arran nodded as he listened to Fallon. "There was a man she was involved with, was there no'?"

"Aye. A man named Max Drummond."

"He broke her heart." Arran turned his gaze back to Fallon. It wasn't a wild guess. It would explain her hesitation to give in to her desires. "What did he do to her?"

"He lied in order to get close so he could steal the relics she was finding and sell them on the black market."

Arran closed his eyes at the realization that there were parallels between him and Max. They both got close to Ronnie for something she was digging for.

But whereas Max had done it purely for the money, Arran was doing it for his friends. Though he didn't like lying to her. He planned to tell her all of it when he spoke to her about her magic.

He hoped she wouldn't be too angry with him, but in all likelihood, she'd kick him off the site. How he wished Max was in front of him so he could put his fist into his face for what he'd done to Ronnie.

Now Arran understood why she was so hesitant to give in to the attraction between them. He'd have to work harder to earn her trust. He hadn't expected it or wanted it, but he cared about Ronnie.

As soon as the thought went through his mind, it felt as if he'd been kicked in the stomach by a horse. He did care for Ronnie.

Shite.

When he opened his eyes, it was to find Fallon staring at him curiously. "What? Ronnie is a good person who didna deserve such treatment."

"Hmm."

"What happened to this Max Drummond?"

Fallon shrugged. "He disappeared before authorities could find him."

"Did Gwynn find anything about him through the computer?"

"Nothing."

"What about Saffron? Any visions? Have Cara, Dani, Marcail, or any of the other Druids been able to use their magic to find him?"

"It's like he never existed."

Arran fisted his hands. "I doona like the sound of that."

"Neither did I, which is why I called Charon. He's using his network of men to see what they can discover."

Arran hated that they still relied on Charon. He'd forgiven the Warrior for spying all those decades, but it didn't mean Arran had to like the guy.

Fallon shifted his shoulders, and Arran smiled.

"You feel the magic of this place." He wasn't posing a question, and Fallon nodded in response.

"You were no' lying when you said it was overpowering. This is definitely the spot for the items sent from Edinburgh, then."

"At least we hope," Arran added. "Ronnie is close to finding something, I think. She unearthed a stone arch in the ground."

"Is that where the magic is coming from?"

Arran shrugged. "It's difficult to pinpoint the location. I feel the magic wherever I walk around the site. The arch does give me pause, though."

"Is it a burial tomb?"

"I think so."

Fallon's lips flattened. "Be careful. I'll call when I hear from Charon."

And just like that, Fallon was gone. Arran might have gotten the power to control ice and snow, but Fallon's was teleporting. It came in handy often.

He took a deep breath and turned to the food tent. He wanted to see Ronnie, not because he had something to tell her, but just because he needed to see her hazel eyes, wheat-colored hair, and smile.

He needed her beside him.

CHAPTER
TWELVE

Ronnie tossed and turned on her cot. Usually it never bothered her that the damn thing was so narrow, but tonight she couldn't shut her brain off enough to get some sleep.

It was Arran. And it was the site.

She sat up and swung her legs over the side of the bed. Her fingers itched to be back in the dirt, scraping it away from the stones of the arch.

The song was so loud, she couldn't shut it off. It kept calling to her, summoning her to it. The problem was, she could no longer wait. Morning seemed like an eternity away. She had to get to the box right then.

Only a few times since she'd become an archeologist had the need taken her so. One time had been when she found the trinity knot pendant.

What would be in the ground this time? What priceless relic was in the box hidden for hundreds of years, forgotten until she had located it?

Ronnie sighed and gave up forgetting about the site. The only way for her to find any kind of peace was to go dig.

She wound her hair into a bun and slipped back into her boots. The summer nights in Scotland only helped her. It was almost midnight and it was still light outside.

Since she didn't know how long she'd be working, she

found a light and kept it beside her so she could turn it on when it got dark.

It would have been better to keep the light on its stand, but it might wake others, and she'd rather be alone.

As soon as her fingers touched the dirt, she smiled. It calmed her in ways nothing else ever could. Except maybe Arran.

"Enough," she whispered to herself as she thought of his golden eyes and heart-stopping smile.

The first time she'd taken a geology class and the professor had them dig in search of rocks, she knew what she wanted to do with her life.

While she dug around the stones, she thought of the next fund-raiser. She couldn't go alone again. It was exhausting, trying to fend off the men. Not that she was a great beauty, but they seemed intrigued by what she did. Interested enough to keep pursuing her long after the party was over.

It had become a problem. She hated the things anyway. The thought of begging for money to continue her work irked her. She made a little money off the things she found, but it wasn't enough to support her digs.

Since Pete had ruled himself and Andy out, there was no one else for her to choose from.

Arran.

"No," she murmured.

She couldn't ask him. She wouldn't ask him.

First, because she knew he'd most likely say yes. Second, because she was inexplicably drawn to him and couldn't say no for much longer. If she was put in close proximity with Arran for any amount of time, there was no telling what she'd do.

She found herself smiling at that. It wasn't like she was ever the one who had taken control in a relationship. Yet, with Arran, she didn't want to wait for him to kiss her. *She* wanted to kiss *him*.

So unlike her. But then again, she hadn't been herself since he arrived.

Ronnie shook her head and continued to dig around the stones of the arch. She was prone on the ground, stretched as far as her arms would allow her. She continued like that, working slowly and methodically around the stones until she had removed another four inches of dirt the entire four feet across the arch.

She sat back on her heels and surveyed the arch. In order to get any more work done, she'd have to climb down to where the barriers were holding back the sides of earth from crumbling on top of the arch again.

"Damn," she said, and looked around the site.

Everyone was in their tents and campers, asleep. The few hours where the darkness crept across the sky had come without her even knowing it.

Still, Ronnie wasn't tired. She wanted to keep working. Even if only for another hour.

She set her watch to countdown from an hour and jumped to where the barriers were. Ronnie stayed still for a few seconds to see if the barriers would hold.

On her knees, she could just see over the top of the ground, so even if the barriers gave way, she had plenty of time to get out before she was injured.

With that resolved, Ronnie went to work.

Arran was on his stomach, one arm hanging over the side of the cot when he jerked awake. He was instantly on alert. His god bellowed, welcoming a battle, but nothing moved.

He'd long gotten used to sleeping in his pants in case there was an emergency. Arran sat up and put his feet on the ground.

Arran sat with his eyes closed and allowed the heightened senses of his god to determine what had wrenched him out of his sleep. He was unsure how long he sat there before he heard the unmistakable sound of someone digging.

It was slight and soft, but it was there.

Arran walked out of his tent and found a light shining upon the section with the arch. He barely had time to register that it was Ronnie's wheat-colored head he saw when he heard the ground shift.

There was no time to call out, nothing to do but get to her. Arran used his speed to cross the distance from the tents to the section just as there was a loud crack that reached him.

He slid across the ground, the claws of his right hand extended and digging into the ground as he went off the side just as the earth fell out from beneath Ronnie.

Arran snagged her arm as her screech reached him. He dug in his claws to hold him in place as Ronnie's other hand came up to grasp his hand.

"Don't let me fall," she said softly.

There were no hysterics, no screaming with his Ronnie. But he saw the fear reflected in her hazel depths. "Never," he said.

He could easily get them up over the side, but then she'd want to know how he did it. Arran wasn't ready to explain his immortality, his powers, or the fact that he was a Warrior.

Nor could he continue to allow her to hang suspended over a hole in the earth.

"I'm going to swing you up," he said.

She nodded her head jerkily. Arran didn't waste any time after that. He quickly swung her side to side with enough force to get back on solid ground.

Once he released her, he heard her gasp before she landed. Arran put his bare feet against the earth and used his legs and arms to jump himself onto land.

He landed with his knees bent and his hands on the ground. When he lifted his head, it was to find Ronnie looking at him as she lay on her side and propped up on her elbow.

"Are you hurt?" he asked, and hurried to her.

He knelt beside her and smoothed back her hair from her face. Somehow the damned bun still held and he wanted to rip the pins out so he could feel the tresses run over his fingers.

Arran tilted her head first one way and then the other, looking for scrapes or bruises. He inspected her hands before he pushed up the sleeves of her shirt and looked at her arms.

"I'm fine," she said shakily.

Her words halted him. This wasn't the woman he'd come to know. Even after the accident the night before when she'd been in shock, her voice had been strong.

He cupped her face and made her look him in the eyes. "You're safe now."

She blinked slowly, her pupils dilated so he could barely see the hazel of her eyes. "Arran."

He found himself leaning toward her tempting lips, his body urging him to taste her, savor her.

Claim her.

Somehow her hands moved so that she gripped his arms as if he were the only thing anchoring her to this world.

Arran moved slowly, the need urgent and consuming. He saw her eyelids flutter shut and her lips part on a sigh. Never had he wanted a woman's kiss more.

Never had he craved a woman more.

But that hunger caught him off guard. He didn't place his lips on hers as he closed the distance. He brushed his nose against hers, her lips not a breath away.

Arran could stand no more of the torture. He closed his eyes and, with a groan, kissed her.

Her lips were soft, pliant, and sweeter than any wine. He tried to keep things slow, but that one taste enflamed his desire to new, unparalleled heights.

All he could feel, hear, and taste was Ronnie.

At the first parting of her lips, he slipped his tongue inside and found hers. He moaned again when she not just accepted him, but kissed him in return.

He could sense her desire, and it burned, scorched . . . seared.

Arran wrapped his arms around her, pulling her tight against him as he deepened the kiss. Her nails dug into his back, a soft moan reaching him.

He was contemplating taking her right there in full view of anyone who might be looking. That's when he knew he had to pull back.

It went against everything inside him, but somehow he

ended the kiss and placed his forehead on hers. She was breathing just as hard as he. He wasn't ready to release her, and by the way she clung to him, neither was she.

All Arran knew was that with one taste, nothing and no one would do after Ronnie. Somehow, someway he had to have her.

With one kiss she had gotten in his blood.

With one kiss she had found his soul.

CHAPTER
THIRTEEN

Ronnie touched her lips. It had been several hours since Arran saved her, kissed her . . . and left her. Well, he really hadn't left. He was in his tent, but that's not where she wanted him.

She wanted him with her. Holding her. Caressing her. Stroking her.

His kiss had been all she'd hoped and feared. He'd stolen her breath and stirred flames of desire that now blazed within her, fiercely and hotly.

After such a scorching kiss that awakened something inside her, she hadn't been ready for it to end. It had taken her longer than she wanted to admit to emerge from her daze of the kiss to realize Arran had taken her to her tent.

Even then she couldn't think past the need coursing through her to comprehend that he was gone before she'd even uttered one word.

Ronnie had stumbled to her feet and rushed to the entrance to make sure Arran wasn't leaving the site. She'd sighed, and then walked back to her cot once she'd seen him enter his tent.

"Oh, God."

She was in so much trouble. She'd known, instinctively, that Arran wasn't going to be good for her. He was the type of man she'd make a fool out of herself over. The type that she'd set aside everything, even her own work, just to be with.

At one time she'd believed Max to be that man, but always her work had come before him. Always. It wasn't the case with Arran, and that was after only one damned kiss!

Ronnie fell back on the cot and let out a long sigh. One kiss. One soul-stirring, exciting, moving, amazing kiss. A kiss she'd waited her entire life to receive.

A kiss she thought she'd never get.

A kiss she'd never forget.

She should be at the dig, looking at why the ground had given out beneath her, but all Ronnie could think about was the kiss.

Her eyes closed as she remembered how his hands had held her gently, but firmly. How he'd made sure she was un-harmed before his golden gaze had darkened and his head lowered to hers.

Those wonderful lips of his had been soft and insistent, tender and unrelenting. He'd claimed her lips with the skill-fulness and talent of a man who knew not just how to kiss, but how to turn a woman inside out.

She'd forgotten her own damned name. "How does that happen?" she asked herself.

"Ronnie!" Andy shouted as he burst into her tent. "There's a collapsed part of the dig at section four."

"I know," Ronnie said and rose up on her elbows. "I was there when it happened."

Andy frowned. "Are you hurt?"

"No. Arran caught me before I fell."

"It's a good thing, too. It must be a twenty-foot drop to the bottom."

Ronnie sat up, her mind thinking back to when Arran caught her. She'd been so wrapped up in the kiss, she forgot all about her near death experience.

"Twenty feet," she murmured.

She mentally put herself back at the site. She'd been

digging, wondering what lay beneath her feet when the ground had lurched. A scream had lodged in her throat, but there had been no time to make a sound.

And then someone took her arm.

"Arran."

"What?" Andy asked.

Ronnie ignored him as she thought back to when she looked up to find Arran holding her. What had he been gripping to keep him anchored? She'd never been so scared before, but he'd been calm.

Almost too calm.

He hadn't called out for assistance in getting her up. In fact, he'd swung her up himself. She knew how strong he was by seeing his muscles, but how many men could catch her and then swing her up without help? How many men could make it look easy and without breaking a sweat?

None.

She'd been so grateful to be back on solid ground that it had taken her a minute to look up, but when she did, Arran had been there. How had he gotten up so quickly?

Ronnie stood and pushed past Andy as she stalked to the section. A memory that was blurry, stirred. She wasn't sure if what she remembered was correct, since she'd been so frightened, and then aroused to the point of forgetting everything else around her.

With her heart pounding, she kept her eyes on the ground until she found them. Five marks slashed into the ground about three feet from where she'd fallen.

The marks ended at the edge and grew deeper, as if someone had held on there.

Ronnie stretched her fingers out and placed them where the marks were. The slashes were thin and went at least two inches into the ground.

What could make that kind of mark?

"Something wrong?"

She froze at Arran's deep voice. Slowly she lifted her head to find him standing in front of her. "How did you save me?"

"Luck."

He always had an answer for everything, Ronnie realized. She stood and looked at the portion of earth that was now gone. A good four feet from the arch had fallen through.

"And these marks?" she asked, and pointed to the ones she'd been looking at.

"My fingers as I dug them into the ground for something to hold on to."

There was part truth to his words, but not the entire truth. She nodded, allowing him to assume that she believed him. There was a connection between the marks, Arran, and the ease with which he'd saved her.

She just couldn't put her finger on it yet.

"Ronnie, look," Andy said as he peered over where the earth had given way.

She squatted beside him and looked to where he pointed. "I don't believe it. The door to the arch is revealed."

"And barred shut," Arran pointed out from her other side.

The wooden planks over the door didn't deter Ronnie. "The wood has been underground for God only knows how long. They'll be easy to break."

"Aye, but should you break them?"

She turned to look at Arran and noticed the way his jaw was clenched and a muscle ticced. "What aren't you telling me?"

"You know as much as I do. I'm simply stating the obvious. How many burial mounds have you come across that had the door barred?"

She swallowed and shrugged. "None."

"My point." He looked at the door again and frowned. "The door is larger than most I've seen. And it's barricaded. Asking you no' to go in would be like asking the sun no' to shine."

Ronnie smiled tightly. "That's right. So don't bother."

"Then let me ask you no' to go inside without me."

Her smile dropped as she stared at him. "Why?"

For several seconds he seemed to try to find the right words. Then he said, "Because I may be the only one who can help if something . . . bad happens."

"Who are you?" she demanded, her patience wearing thin. "You wanted to tell me, so tell me now."

He glanced away and licked his lips. "I'm here to help. I have experience with unsavory things happening within burial mounds. If this is a burial mound," he muttered as he looked at the door again.

"What else could it be? You're the one who first suggested that's what it was."

"Because I thought it was. Now, I'm no' so sure. Just as you know there's something in there. You've been hunting for it."

She stilled, her blood turning cold at his words. "What do you mean?" Her voice was low, her words barely whispered.

"You know what I mean." There was no anger or disgust in his words, just simple truth. "I know you use magic, Ronnie. I can feel your magic. You doona have to hide being a Druid with me."

"Druid?" She frowned. Where did he get off thinking she was a Druid? But more important, how did he know she used her abilities?

The way he looked at her, as if he understood her, seemed to release the note that had been sitting in her chest for years.

"Aye, lass. A Druid. I thought you knew."

Ronnie looked down at the structure she'd just excavated. Was it magic she used? Was that what her abilities really were? And did that make her a Druid, as Arran suggested.

"Um, Ronnie," Andy broke into the conversation. "About section two. They've been digging for weeks now. There's nothing there."

"Give it one more day, Andy. I'll reevaluate the situation tomorrow."

"Don't forget you leave the day after for Edinburgh."

"Shit." She'd forgotten the party. Again.

"It's been on your schedule for six months now. You made me add in an extra day in the city so you could find a dress and get your hair done."

Like she needed to be reminded how awful her hair was. She cut her eyes to Andy and glared at him.

"Sorry," he murmured, and pushed his glasses up on his nose.

"No, it's fine. It's lack of sleep that has me snapping." Ronnie glanced over to discover Arran staring at her.

He waited until Andy walked away before he asked, "You know there is nothing in section two. Why keep digging there?"

She exhaled and took the biggest leap of faith she'd ever made in her entire life. She told him the truth. "I have to. If I always find something wherever I dig, people begin to question me."

"So you make sure to dig in places where there is nothing."

"Yes." Her hands were shaking from divulging that piece of information.

To her surprise, Arran placed a hand atop hers. "I'll never repeat your secret."

"And your secret?" she prompted.

"What makes you think I have one?"

She shrugged, liking the feel of him touching her. Now, if only he'd kiss her again. "You said you could feel my magic. I gather there is more you aren't telling me."

"Did you know you were a Druid?"

"No."

"Then once I tell you all you need to know of the Druids, I'll share my secret."

His hand squeezed hers before he stood and walked away, leaving Ronnie's mind so full of questions that it dimmed the song of the artifacts.

Arran held the rope that slowly lowered Ronnie down into the earth. He hadn't wanted her to go. He'd have begged had it helped, but he'd seen that stubborn set of her chin and knew it was pointless. At least she'd taken Andy down with her.

He allowed slack in the rope once she reached bottom so she could walk around. It took her and Andy about thirty minutes before they yelled up that others could come down.

Arran kept a hold of Ronnie's rope so he could pull her out as quickly as possible if something happened. He had a bad feeling every time he looked at the arch. There was something inside the structure that needed to stay inside. The magic he felt wasn't tainted with evil, at least none that he could sense. But that didn't mean anything should come out of the structure.

Whoever had constructed the arched building had made sure of sealing it with boards crisscrossing over the door. If these were the items taken from Edinburgh on their way to London, then something must have happened here that stopped the shipment and had others build the structure around the items.

And it wasn't just built around the items, but dug into the earth and then buried. Why?

"To keep it locked away from the world."

"What?" the man beside him asked.

Arran shook his head and flexed his hand. He needed Ronnie away from the arch immediately. But with ten other archeological students making their way down to her, that wasn't going to happen anytime soon.

The best Arran could do was keep an eye on her.

That's exactly what he did. Every hour she was down in the ground was like an eternity. He hadn't given her a choice about skipping lunch either. She'd managed to scarf down the sandwich in record time and get back in the ground.

The longer she spent down there, and the longer Arran stared at the arch and door, the more he knew it shouldn't be opened. He had one more day probably to convince her not to open it before they cleared the dirt and debris out of the way so Ronnie could get to the door.

At the end of the day, Arran made sure Ronnie was safely away from the section before he set up watch and began to call MacLeod Castle to fill them in on what was going on—when he felt Ronnie's magic.

"I thought you were resting," he said without looking up from his hands.

There was a sigh before she came to stand beside him. "I couldn't sleep. I'm too excited about the find. Besides, you have some information about Druids that I want."

"I'm no' sure this is the time for that conversation."

Her brows rose as she faced him. "We're going to make time. You can't tell me I'm a Druid and just leave it at that. I need answers, Arran."

He stared into her hazel depths and nodded. "Aye, lass, that you do. It's no' something you want people to overhear, however."

"They're exhausted and staying away from me for fear that I'll put them back to work. It's the perfect time."

"All right," he said, and put away his phone. "Long ago—"

"Ronnie!" Andy shouted. "Ronnie! Pete's on your phone. He says it's important!"

Arran watched her debate whether to take the call or not. "The story can wait. Go see what Pete needs."

"I'll be back," she promised before she stalked away.

Arran watched the sway of her hips, remembering all too well the taste of her. The kiss had kept him away, the desire making him ache.

He couldn't have stopped from kissing her if the fate of the world had depended upon him. He was amazed that he held off as long as he had, but she'd nearly died. That, apparently, was the catalyst that sent him over the edge.

After he'd ensured she wasn't injured, his body simply refused to do anything other than take her in his arms. Even now, it was difficult to keep his hands from her.

At that moment his phone rang and Broc's name popped up on the screen. "Broc."

"Arran. I'm calling because of Sonya."

Arran squeezed his eyes shut. Sonya's magic as a Druid wasn't just the ability to heal. She was also able to communicate with the trees. That magic had saved her life. "The trees."

Broc sighed. "Aye. They speak of something terrible coming."

"Did they say what? Is it another evil?"

"That's the thing," Broc said angrily. "They didna specify. Sonya is no' the only one hearing things. Gwynn is as well."

"Shit," Arran said.

Gwynn, another Druid and wife to Logan, had magic that let her hear and speak to the wind.

"The wind is telling Gwynn the same thing."

"Not exactly," Gwynn's voice could be heard in the background.

Broc grunted. "Wait, Gwynn."

"No," she said.

After a moment of struggle where Arran could hear Logan and Sonya telling Broc to hand the phone to Gwynn, silence filled the other end of the phone.

"Arran?" Gwynn said.

"I'm here."

"Sorry, but what Broc said isn't exactly true. Y'all don't always hear what we're saying. You Warriors think you know everything," she said in exasperation.

"Now, Gwynn," Logan said in the background.

Arran grinned at Gwynn's Texas accent and Logan's plaintive urging.

"It's true," she said. "Anyway, what Broc told you about Sonya is fact. What I heard was a bit different. You know the wind and trees don't always tell us what we need to know. The wind is adamant that . . ."

Her voice faded to nothing. Arran punched his leg in frustration, but kept his voice even as he said, "Gwynn? Tell me."

"I think it's about the dig site. The wind is speaking so fast, I can barely understand it, but I did hear your name. And Ronnie's."

"That isna good."

"No. Listen, I think y'all need to get out of there."

Arran chuckled as he watched Ronnie leave the food tent and hurry to Andy's caravan with the phone still at her ear.

"As much as I agree with you, I doona think that's going to happen. Ronnie is . . . well, she's tenacious. She's no' leaving without seeing what's inside the damned door."

"What door?"

"I was just about to call Ian to see if he and Dani had found anything more about the magical items taken from Edinburgh."

Gwynn sighed loudly. "I've been on the computer constantly looking at this with the others helping out, but that was so long ago, Arran. I'm not sure they would've added something like that to any records."

"I know it's a long shot, but keep a lookout."

"Wait," Gwynn said.

Arran could hear the phone being passed again, and this time it was Logan who was on the other end. "What's going on there?"

Arran ran a hand down his face. "I'm no' sure. I doona want to scare anyone needlessly—"

"What is it?" Logan interrupted. "Your instincts as a Warrior are good. Trust them."

"I've a bad feeling, Logan. A verra bad feeling about what Ronnie is excavating."

"Which is?"

"All we can see now is stones that make an arch over a door. Fallon felt the magic surrounding this place just as I did. It's ancient magic."

"So a burial mound, then? You'd best talk to Broc and Sonya about that, since they've explored many of them."

"I thought it was a burial mound, but I'm no' so sure."

Logan grunted low. "What do you think it is?"

"Something bad. The problem is, it appears that whoever constructed this no' only did it belowground and covered it up, but they barred the door with several crisscrossing boards."

"They wanted people kept out."

"Or whatever is inside kept inside."

"Shite."

Arran's lips flattened. "Exactly."

"You shouldna be there alone. If there is something in that structure . . . Wait. How big is it?"

"I've no idea. Only the arch and about half a meter of the ceiling have been revealed."

Logan was silent for a moment. "I didna agree with Fallon sending you alone. We've lost Duncan. I doona want to lose another of us."

Arran hated to think of Duncan. He'd been Ian's twin, and a close ally while Arran was locked in Deirdre's mountain.

When Deirdre had killed Duncan, they'd nearly lost Ian in the process. Nothing had been the same since Duncan's death. As Warriors, they might be immortal, but take their heads and you took their life.

"I know Ronnie is going to Edinburgh for a few days soon. Maybe Saffron could meet her there and keep her distracted so I can see what's behind the door."

"Nay," Logan said. "So *we* can see what's behind that door. You are no' doing it alone."

Arran hung up the phone and smiled. He'd wanted to get away from the castle, but now that he'd been gone, he missed the others. The laughter, the fights, the movie nights, the sparring, and the meals.

Mealtime was always so loud and chaotic. But it was special. Arran hadn't appreciated until then how much it meant to him.

If there was danger, he didn't want any of his friends there to possibly get hurt. He'd take care of it all.

Or die trying.

CHAPTER
FOURTEEN

Ronnie lay in her tent and thought of Arran. Nights were the hardest. He haunted her dreams. His kiss made her long for things she once thought she'd never want. And somehow Arran and her dreams of the mystery box interwove until she couldn't think of one without the other.

The one thing she could count on to help her forget about Arran and things that could never be was the dig. She'd had the boards taken off the doors after dinner. Arran, of course, had been one of the men who did the job.

The muscle tightening in his jaw told her in no uncertain terms that he wasn't happy about it. She stood by his side as he pulled one board off at a time.

It wasn't until it was over that she realized how tense Arran had been. Almost as if he had expected something to happen.

"Doona go inside," he'd begged her softly so that no one else could hear.

Ronnie planned to do just that, but something in Arran's eyes gave her pause. What was one more day? It had seemed simple enough at the time, but now, in the dead of night, she couldn't stop thinking about it.

The box wanted out. It wanted her to find it, to open it. And it couldn't wait one more day.

She flopped onto her back on her cot and blew out a breath. She'd gone out to the dig by herself already and nearly died. Did she really want to chance that again?

And if the box was there and she found it with everyone else, she'd have to give it to the government. The only way to know for sure was to go by herself. That way if the box was there, she could hide it. No one need ever know what she'd found.

Ronnie rose from her bed and hurried to dress while the ever-present song beckoned her. Even as she dressed, she knew she was doing the wrong thing, but the box was important. She felt it in her bones, deep in her soul. Somehow that box belonged to her. There was no way she'd give it over to anyone.

Anyone.

Knowing that, she had only one choice. She had to get inside the chamber.

Ronnie grabbed a flashlight and stepped out of her tent to look around. There wasn't a soul in sight. It was almost 1 A.M., and the sky was just beginning to darken. Everything had been left at the dig so she easily got harnessed and lowered herself into the hole.

It was dark and scary, now that she was in the ground alone. Swallowing a lump of unease, she turned on the flashlight. She unclipped her harness from the rope and faced the wooden door that Arran had been staring at.

The door itself was nondescript. The only thing that made it stand out was that it was well over twelve feet high and carved to fit perfectly in the arch of stones.

Ronnie walked to the door and turned the beam of light onto a stone she'd seen Arran inspecting earlier. She couldn't see anything, but that didn't mean nothing was there. She'd learned that she couldn't chance overlooking anything.

She picked up a handful of dirt and rubbed it onto the rock. To her amazement, she saw a trinity knot carved into the sandstone.

Why it hadn't show up before, she wasn't sure—nor did it matter. Ronnie quickly began to rub the dirt into other stones around the door and found even more Celtic symbols. Each different, and each invisible to the naked eye.

She stepped back and looked at the door again. "What is it about you that makes Arran leery?"

And makes me want inside so desperately?

After a deep, calming breath, she placed her hand on the door. There were no handles, nothing that suggested how she might open the door. Before she could even try, something zinged through her fingers and ran all along her body.

And then the door began to swing open on its own.

"Oh, shit."

Ronnie jumped back and stumbled over the rope. She landed hard on her butt, catching herself with the hand not holding the flashlight.

A gust of stale air rushed out of the chamber and right at her, causing her to choke and cough repeatedly. Ronnie had to turn her head away and cover her mouth until the dust mixed with the air had settled enough that she could see into the chamber.

The song swelled and then fell silent. She licked her lips and peered into the chamber, tilting her head first one way, then the other. The beams of the flashlight showed the chamber was twice the size she had guessed it to be.

Silence filled the area, and when she climbed to her feet, the stillness seemed louder than normal. She took a tentative step toward the entrance and shone her light all around the door, looking for booby traps of any kind.

Only when she was sure it was safe, did she step into the chamber. It was a rectangle with sides longer than front and back.

Ronnie shivered as the dampness of the chamber settled over her. She almost thought she felt a thread of . . . evil. But surely it was just her imagination and all those horror movies she loved to watch alone.

It was almost as if she were intruding someplace she had no business being. Her skin tingled unpleasantly, and the sensation caused her to shift her shoulders to try to make it go away.

In all her years as an archeologist, and all the places she'd dug, nothing had ever taken her aback like this place.

Ronnie squared her shoulders after a brief pause where she considered getting Arran. She proceeded farther into the chamber. And Arran's words of warning echoed through her mind.

She expected to find a body, as in any burial chamber, except there was none. Instead there were tables that lined the walls and ran down the middle of the chamber, where artifacts were scattered.

Ronnie went to each one, looking at it. Some were nothing more than a piece of rock or stone with a Celtic inscription or drawing. One piece was a ring. Another a dagger.

She wanted to touch each one, but she held back. As she walked each table, shining her light upon each piece, she was mentally cataloging everything.

Her mind, however, went blank when she came upon a stone tablet the size of a laptop that was broken in half diagonally. The pieces were set beside each other, the cracked edges not fully touching.

The writing was Gaelic, the knotwork etched with painstaking precision. She bent low over the table and tried to piece together any of her scattered knowledge of Gaelic to read what it said.

"'The one with unused—'" She shook her head. "No. Not unused—untapped, maybe. That's it. 'The one with untapped magic will . . .'" She pursed her lips and racked her brain to make out the next few lines. "'Will free those trapped by—' By what?" she said angrily.

Ronnie licked her lips and looked at the writing again. "'Will free those . . . trapped by the ones who came before.'"

She stopped and looked at the tablet again. The lines were written not as a letter, but as a prophecy.

"Shit," she murmured. She looked at the tablet with new eyes.

"'The one with untapped magic will free those trapped by the ones who came before.'

"'She,'" she said with a tremor she couldn't keep out

of her voice, "'will unknowingly bring about destruction and . . . death.'"

A chill of foreboding raced down her spine. That prophecy had probably been locked away for thousands of years. It meant nothing.

Didn't it?

Ronnie made herself walk away from it, yet the words she had read aloud repeated again and again in her mind

Until she came to the box.

"I found you," she whispered excitedly as the song began again. It was sweet, soft now, lulling even. It soothed her and erased all her worries.

Ronnie couldn't believe her eyes. It was the same box she saw in her dreams. Small but curious. It had the arched lid as well.

She set the flashlight beside the box so the light would shine on it and she could have both hands to hold it. Carefully she lifted the box in her hands and grinned.

She lovingly ran her hands over the plain wooden box. After having been so curious to know what was inside it, she now found she was a little hesitant to open it.

What could be so important that it was in such a small box? And why did it matter that she have it?

Ronnie fell to her knees on the dirt floor and set the box back on the table as more of the unpleasant tingling prickled her skin. Arran had warned her not to come in here alone. He hadn't been his laughing, cheerful self since she'd fallen through the ground.

The way he looked at the doorway had been almost as if he were sizing it up, like he was trying to determine what was inside.

She had no doubt he'd be pissed if he knew she was in here alone. Ronnie knew better than to open such a find by herself. It was reckless and stupid, but she'd found the box. That's what was important.

And it didn't mean she had to open the box right now. She could take it to her tent so she could open it whenever she wanted.

It seemed the right thing to do, and it would get her out of the dark, eerie chamber. Ronnie picked up the box, but before she could get to her feet, a strange sensation overtook her.

It was oppressive, overwhelming.

Insistent.

Suddenly she had to know what was in the box. If felt as if it was life or death if she didn't open it and look inside. Right that minute.

With shaky hands, she flipped the small metal latch and cracked open the lid.

CHAPTER
FIFTEEN

Arran came awake and jumped to his feet with a low, rumbling growl. His god was bellowing inside him, and that's when he felt the ancient, powerful magic blast from the section they'd been excavating.

He surged from his tent and ran to the section. Without a second's hesitation, he jumped over the side to land in front of the door and arch.

Only to find the door open.

His god was demanding he release him, insisting he fight. But Arran held back. He walked to the doorway and halted as he looked inside. It only took a moment for him to spot the light from a flashlight.

And then he saw Ronnie.

The strange pale dust swirling around her was coming from a box she held, and the magic arising from the dust felt . . . wrong. Very wrong.

Arran entered the chamber when the dust materialized into a mass of creatures unlike anything he'd ever seen. There had been nothing in his time as a Warrior that gave him pause. Until that moment.

The beings were tall and emaciated, as if someone had stretched their skin tightly over their bones so they looked like the bones would punch through at any moment. Long, stringy white hair fell in their elongated faces. Their eyes were solid black and their skin the color of ash.

They looked like death. And Arran comprehended that's what they'd bring.

The creature closest to him snarled, showing fangs even longer than the ones Arran had in his Warrior form. The magic he'd felt earlier only intensified, and there was no mistaking the evil now.

He had no choice but to release his Warrior. In an instant, claws sprang from his fingers, fangs filled his mouth, and his skin turned the white of his god.

Then they rushed him.

Arran used his long claws to slash the creatures. Whereas such a cut would have killed others, it did nothing but anger these new monsters.

Their regeneration was almost instantaneous. Arran knew he was in trouble, but he wasn't going to go down without a fight. In true Highlander fashion.

He released a loud roar from deep within his chest. With speed and skill, he began to move rapidly, cutting and slashing every creature that surrounded him. Something began to sting his skin. It burned like acid fire, and soon it had him on his knees.

The creatures were smiling as they closed in around him. Arran wasn't ready to die. Who would protect Ronnie when he was gone? Once more he lashed out with his claws, but it wasn't the effort he'd wanted.

The nearest creature caught his arm, its smile widening. Alarm swept through Arran. But it was too late to wish he had another Warrior with him.

Instead of cutting him, the damned thing bit him. Arran threw back his head and bellowed at the feel of fangs on his skin. But it did no good. The others soon began to feed off him as well.

He could feel the blood draining from his body, weakening him more effectively than whatever was burning his skin. Through the mass of bony gray bodies, he spied Ronnie. She was backed against a wall while one of the creatures stood over her.

"Nay!" Arran thundered. He turned to his god and sought Memphaea's strength, his power. His rage.

When it gathered inside him like a great ball of energy, he threw the creatures off him.

The monsters were immortal, and if there was one thing he knew, it was how to kill an immortal. Beheading. He stopped cutting at their chests and went for their necks.

He killed two before they realized what was happening. Then three more fell. They began fighting to restrain him, and in his weakened condition, they should've been able to stop him.

But there was Ronnie. She was all he could think about, she was all that kept him on his feet and fighting. He had to reach her, to get her to safety before the beasts harmed her.

Tears coursed down her face as she stared up at the monster in fear. Arran reached the being in front of Ronnie and swiped his claws through the bastard's neck.

Dimly, he heard Ronnie scream as the creature's head fell off its body and rolled on the ground. Arran grabbed the monster nearest him and wrapped his hands around its head. With a jerk and a yank, he pulled the creature's head off.

When he turned to continue fighting, he found the others gone. Arran felt himself begin to fall and moved one foot forward to keep his balance. He looked down at his body to see it riddled with bite marks and the blood of the monsters. It was then he grasped that it was their blood that burned his skin.

The chamber began to spin, and no matter how hard he tried to keep his feet, his legs gave out. Arran fell to his knees hard, his body working double to keep breathing.

A sound behind him—half cry, half moan—caught him right before he fell facedown.

Ronnie.

Arran knew his skin was still white, and no matter how

hard he tried to tamp down his god, it didn't work. He was in too much pain and too weak to have much command. The only good thing was that his god was also weak, so there was no chance for him to take control of Arran either.

Arran tried to push onto his hands and knees, but only managed to scoot forward. If those creatures came back, there was no way he could protect Ronnie. That thought kept him moving.

Somehow, he got back on his knees and turned his head to her. She stared wide-eyed at him. How he hated the fear he saw on her face. Didn't she realize he wouldn't hurt her? Didn't she know he'd do anything to keep her safe?

"Willna. Harm. You."

Each word was more difficult to say. The edges of his vision were darkening, and he didn't know how much longer he could stay conscious. He had to get her out of the chamber and to safety, and preferably call Fallon for help.

All he was able to get out was, "Get. Away."

"No." Suddenly she was beside him.

He saw her reaching for him. Arran jerked away, which caused him to topple sideways. Dirt ground into the bite marks and rubbed against the creatures' blood, burning him for a second time.

"Nay. Ronnie. Leave."

Ronnie licked her lips and looked down at the man who had fought so valiantly to save them both. He'd been far outnumbered and wounded. Yet he hadn't given up. He had stopped that monster from touching her.

Bite marks peppered Arran's bare torso, arms, neck, and even his face. She had to help him somehow, and leaving him wasn't an option.

"What do I do, Arran? Tell me," she urged.

She was afraid to touch him, not because his skin was as white as new-fallen snow, but because he was in such pain. When he opened his eyes and she saw they were solid white from corner to corner, she could only stare.

They were the same eyes she'd seen in her dream. The

man who wound her body so tight with desire did indeed have a secret as great as her own.

His eyes shut and his hands fisted. She swallowed when she saw the long white claws. Ronnie looked around, trying to find some way to help him. She could call for help, but what would they do when they saw Arran?

She wouldn't do that to him. Whatever he was, he kept it secret—and now, so would she. Ronnie rushed out of the chamber and saw a large bottle of water that had been left by someone. She grabbed it and ran back to Arran.

All the bites had to be cleaned before an infection began. Hesitantly she dribbled water onto a wound near his shoulder. The water ran down and smeared blood on his biceps.

A sigh left him.

"Better?" she asked.

He gave a single nod. Ronnie began to clean off the bites, but it didn't take her long to realize it wasn't the bites that hurt him, it was the blood.

She then worked diligently to remove the creatures' blood from Arran's chest, arms, and face. Only then did she turn him over so that his head rested on her legs and she had access to his back.

"What are you?" she asked, now that his breathing had evened out.

"A Warrior."

"Of course you're a warrior."

"Nay, Ronnie. A Warrior. Remember the story that old man told you about the Celts?"

She stilled, her hand holding the bottle above his back, ready to pour. "Yes."

"Tell me what he told you."

"I think I'd rather you tell me."

He winced when she touched a spot with the dried blood. "I'm sorry."

He squeezed her leg with his hand, a hand that had so tenderly held her hours ago while they kissed. A hand that was pierced with bite marks and that had claws he kept carefully away from her. "Doona fash yourself. I've withstood worse kinds of pain."

"That's hard to believe after seeing you like this."

"It's true. Ronnie, I'm immortal."

"Okay." She wasn't sure what a person was supposed to say when given a statement like that. She continued to wash the blood off his back. Her hands were soft as she barely touched his skin. But she was sure there had been more bite marks on his back the last time she looked.

"Nay, I really am. The story the old man told you is true. Long ago, when Rome came to Britain, they couldna conquer the Celts. But no matter how hard the Celts fought, they couldna make the Romans leave."

"What happened?" she asked, and began to work on cleaning his hands.

"There is magic in this land I love. It's in the water, in the verra air we breathe."

"And the ground?"

"Aye," he said. "Magic is here because of the Druids. As with anything, there were the good Druids, *mies,* and the evil ones, the *droughs.*"

"What's the difference between them? The choices they make?"

She felt rather than saw his smile. "Somewhat. The *mies* magic is the pure form they were born with. They use it for good, to teach, or to help. The *droughs,* however, give their soul to Satan in order to have black magic. A single *drough* against a single *mie* will win against the *mie* every time. But gather a group of *mies* together, and the *drough* doesna stand a chance."

Ronnie was enthralled with his story and how easily he spoke of magic and Druids. Her hands had gone from stroking his shoulders to playing with his hair. She chided herself and poured more water on the bites.

Only to discover there weren't so many as before.

"So the Celts went to the Druids for help," she said.

Arran nodded. "The *mies* wouldna help them, but the *droughs* would. The *droughs* called up gods long forgotten and locked in Hell. The strongest warriors from each family stepped forward to host a god."

"That doesn't sound like a good idea."

"They were desperate to rid their land of the Romans. So the warriors accepted the gods, and in the process became unbeatable in battle. They attacked Rome again and again. It wasna long before Rome left Britain altogether."

Ronnie twisted her lips. "That's not what Rome says happened, but then again, I know all about how countries in power decide what will be written in history."

"Aye. With the Romans gone, the warriors began to turn on each other and anyone else they encountered. The *droughs* had expected to be able to pull the gods out of the men once their mission was finished, but it didna go as planned. Nothing the *droughs* did stopped the gods. So they went to the *mies* for help."

"That took some guts."

Arran shifted his back, the muscles moving as fluidly as water. "It did. It also took the *droughs* and the *mies* working together to bind the gods inside these warriors. It was the first, and last, time the two sects worked together."

"So the gods were bound. What happened to the men?"

"They remembered nothing of what they'd done since the gods entered their body. The gods were bound, passing through the bloodline and going to the strongest warrior each time. The gods were never again supposed to be unbound. But there was a *drough* who wanted to rule the world. She found a way to unbind the gods."

Ronnie looked across the chamber at the vacant wall and thought back to the old man's story. "The MacLeods. The old man mentioned the MacLeods."

"That's where Deirdre began her run for power. She used her black magic to make herself immortal and spent centuries looking for the MacLeod who was the key. She found out it wasn't just one MacLeod, but brothers. Three brothers, in fact."

"This Deirdre didn't really murder the entire MacLeod clan?"

"She did," Arran said, and sat back on his heels. His skin was still white, and his claws still visible as well. Claws . . .

They accounted for the marks she found in the dirt after Arran had saved her, when the ground caved in. He'd used his claws to secure himself. Now it was all beginning to make sense.

Ronnie took one of his hands in hers again and inspected the long, curved white talon. "Did Deirdre find the Mac-Leods she needed?"

"Aye, and she unbound their god. The three brothers shared a god because they were equal in battle. They were the first of us, and the ones who were lucky enough to escape Deirdre. It didna deter her, though. She set out, finding more of us and unbinding our gods."

"This white skin, the claws, and your . . . your eyes," she said, and paused to swallow. "They are what make you a Warrior?"

"Doona forget these," he said, and peeled back his lips for her to see his fangs.

"Are you trying to scare me?"

"I want you to know me." He glanced away. "Ronnie, the form you see me in now is what happens when I allow my god to rise up. I have control over him, but no' every Warrior does. The gods are strong. They want battle and blood and death."

"As strong as you Warriors are, did you not go after Deirdre?"

He smiled and looked at the ceiling. "That's a verra long story, but we did. And we beat her as well as her successor, Declan Wallace."

"Declan," she said in awe. "Interesting. Does Saffron know what you are?"

"Of course."

He said it so matter-of-factly, and it was a moment before she realized why. "Because her husband, Camdyn, is also a Warrior."

"Precisely."

She looked at his chest in time to see one of the bites heal.

A quick glance showed her all but a few of the bites were now gone.

"You really are immortal. Can you not be killed?"

"Aye. Take our heads, or put *drough* blood in our wounds."

"Lovely," she murmured, and stood. She dusted off her hands and looked around the chamber. "Those creatures. What were they?"

"I've no idea. I've never seen the like in all my years."

"And just how many years are we talking about?"

He grinned and got to his feet. "Six hundred and forty-six."

"Six . . . ," she said, and then lost her ability to talk.

Arran shrugged. "There's a story as to how we were leap-frogged through time, but that is going to have to wait. You didna know you were a Druid. How then did you know how to use your magic?"

"I didn't," she said with a shrug. "At least, I didn't do it on purpose at first. I just thought I was lucky. Then I realized that I could hear the artifacts singing to me. And only I could hear their song."

"Pete doesna know?"

"No. No one but you. I love what I do, Arran. I know it's wrong how I come about the relics, but I have to find them."

"There's nothing wrong with what you do, Ronnie. Each Druid has a special gift of magic to use. You've chosen to use yours in your work, and you doona harm anyone in the process."

"Until today," she whispered.

"Why did you open the box?"

Ronnie shrugged. "It's what I came down here to do, but then I changed my mind. I was going to take the box to my tent and open it later. But the overpowering urge to open it took me. I couldn't stop myself. By the way, I think you need to add those creatures' blood to your list of things that can hurt you."

She could feel his eyes on her, his white eyes. Gone was the golden gaze she'd come to enjoy so much. As if he were reading her mind, his white skin faded away. His claws disappeared, the fangs vanished, and his golden eyes returned.

"We need to look at everything in this chamber." He walked to the nearest item and inspected it. That's when it dawned on her he was looking for something.

"You came to this dig for a reason."

Arran's head slowly lifted, and he looked at her. "Aye. There is a spell I'm looking for. This spell will bind our gods once more and allow the Warriors who are married to live normal, mortal lives. They doona wish to bring children into this world while they're immortal."

"Saffron and Camdyn did."

"And that was an accident. The Druids at the castle have been preventing pregnancy, but somehow with Saffron and Camdyn, the spell didna work."

"Druids? At the castle?" she repeated.

He winced. "Ah . . . aye. There are Druids."

"And you think I'm one?"

"I know you're one. As a Warrior, I feel magic. Yours, Ronnie, is *mie* magic," he said, and turned to face her. "Help us. Help me find the spell. It was taken in one of three shipments from Edinburgh hundreds of years ago. Two of the shipments, one by land and one by sea, made it to London. The third shipment went by land on the most difficult route. We believe this dig is part of the shipment."

"Shipment of what?"

"Magical items."

After the monsters she'd just seen and learning about Arran, she didn't hesitate to believe him. And after what she'd just released into the world, she needed to do something to make things right. "What am I looking for?"

CHAPTER SIXTEEN

Arran shrugged. "I've no idea. It could be anything. At one time it was a scroll, but it had since been changed."

"That's not a lot to go on."

"I know," he said, and picked up a dagger. "It's all we have."

"Don't you need light?" Ronnie asked, and reached for her flashlight.

He inspected the hilt when he found knotwork. "Nay. I can see as well in the dark as in the light. Anything that looks suspicious, let me know. This involves magic, so it could be anything."

"Not anything, surely. I mean, it's a spell that was on a scroll. It's not like it could magically become dirt or something."

Arran set aside the dagger once he was sure the knotwork on the hilt and blade were not the scroll. "Larena, who is our only female Warrior, has a ring. Inside the ring is a list of all the families who had a Warrior step forward so long ago. With just a few words, that list disappears into the stone on Larena's ring."

"Well. Now that I know," Ronnie said, and went back to looking.

Arran smiled and moved to the next object. It was a scroll. He cautiously touched the edges to see how it had barely begun to be affected by time. It couldn't be that easy, to find the spell on a scroll.

Could it?

He gently took it in his hands and unrolled it. With a sigh, he closed his eyes. It was a spell—but not the one he needed.

After he carefully rolled up the scroll, Arran returned it to its spot and stood there. The spell on the scroll could be harmless. Or it could change everything.

"None of these artifacts can see the light of day."

"Why?" Ronnie asked as she picked at a small rock and put it in the beam of her flashlight.

"Each one of them is magical in some way. Some hold magic, like the box, and some *are* magic, like the scroll I just found that has a spell. There are still Druids out there, both good and bad, and it would be better for everyone if no one knew of these items."

Ronnie walked to him and touched his arm. "What about those pieces that did reach London. Where are they?"

"Carefully guarded."

"How would you know?" she asked with a chuckle.

Arran ran a hand over his chin. "Larena's power as a Warrior is to become invisible. She saw for herself just what was under lock and key in the royal palace in London."

"Shit."

"Larena's power has come in handy on many occasions. She helped us defeat Declan and free another Druid, she found Saffron originally, and—"

"Wait. Found Saffron?" Ronnie asked. "What do you mean?"

"It's no' my story to tell, but I'll say Declan kidnapped Saffron and kept her locked in a dungeon below his house."

Ronnie shook her head in surprise. "Dear God. Why would he want Saffron?"

He hesitated, unsure of how much to tell her since it was Saffron's story.

"Or is she a Druid you spoke about?" Ronnie asked. Her eyes widened when he didn't deny it. "Saffron is a Druid? What was it about her that Declan wanted?"

"Declan was a *drough*, Ronnie. Saffron is a *mie*, but she's also a Seer."

Ronnie shrugged and asked, "What does that mean exactly?"

"Seers are the ones who see bits of the future. Saffron will get glimpses of people's futures. Sometimes events will change those visions, and sometimes they willna. There have been a few instances when we've been able to help those involved if we knew them."

Ronnie rubbed at her cheek that was smudged with dirt. "I can't believe Warriors are out there, and that I'm a Druid. A Druid! What else is there?"

"These new creatures now, and to be honest, there probably is more."

"I don't know whether to be excited or frightened."

"Probably a wee bit of both." He moved to the next item and saw Ronnie staring at the box she'd opened.

Arran walked around her and grabbed it. It was completely smooth, with no markings on it anywhere.

"There's nothing," Ronnie said.

"Aye, there is. I can feel the magic. I knew as soon as I arrived at your dig that magic was here. The problem is that I can no' do magic, so this will take a Druid who knows what to look for to look at it and tell me what's being hidden."

Ronnie turned around and put the light on the object behind her. "It's another scroll."

Arran set aside the box and reached for the scroll. He unrolled it to find a manifest of items taken from Edinburgh. He let out a whoop and smiled at her.

"You found the manifest. Now all we need to do is locate every item on here."

"How can you read that?" she asked with a frown as she rose up on her tiptoes to see.

He shrugged. "It's Gaelic. I can read it. Now, let's begin."

"Gaelic. I read a little, but badly. I found a stone before I opened the box. It appeared to have a prophecy."

A muscle ticced in his jaw. "Show me."

Ronnie took him to the broken tablet and watched him

study it. For long moments, silence reigned and she grew uncomfortable. Arran, as usual, was calm and to the point, but she knew just what she had done.

She had nearly killed the both of them by releasing the creatures from the box. Her magic, which had always been used to dig up harmless relics, had been used for evil. For those beasts were evil. She didn't have to be a Warrior to know that.

It oozed from them, choking her with the foulness of it. And now they were out in the world. They had to be stopped.

"This is a prophecy," Arran said as he ran a finger down one broken side of the stone tablet. "One that was put into words long, long ago."

"What does it say?"

He met her gaze. "Why do you want to know?"

She was about to tell him she didn't know when she paused and knew she owed him the truth. "I can't explain it, but I think it's about me."

"It says, 'The one with untapped magic / Will free those trapped by the magic-wielders / She will unknowingly bring about destruction and death.'"

"I got most of that. What does it mean?"

"It would be difficult to know without the rest."

Ronnie grabbed hold of the table to keep herself steady. "There's more?"

"Aye. It's along the sides."

"What does it say?"

The female Druid will be the bringer of doom
Only to be ended by a man-god.
The new darkness will join forces with the Druid
And it will be the end of all.

"Tell me that's not about me," she asked.

Arran took her hand. "It could be about anyone."

"Let's see. I'm a Druid who had untapped magic, and I released those creatures who had been locked away. If that doesn't tell you it's about me, then I don't know what does."

"Easy, Ronnie," he said softly.

And to her amazement, the fear that had its iron grip on her lessened. She knew with him by her side, she'd be able to face anything. He was a Warrior. Immortal and powerful.

And she, apparently, was a Druid.

Arran released her long enough to take a picture of the tablet and send it to someone through his phone. He pulled her away from the tablet.

"Who is the 'new darkness'?"

His eyes grew hard at her words. "I've a feeling we're going to find out verra soon. We'd thought to have defeated them, but I've long had a belief there was something out there waiting to make its move."

"Like what?"

"Someone like Deirdre or Declan. A *drough,* Ronnie. It's been my viewpoint that this new 'darkness' was amassing itself and waiting for the right move. We've no idea who it could be."

"And I just helped it, didn't I?"

He turned to her, halting her. "Nay. If that prophecy is about you, then we'll deal with it."

"You don't have to spell it out for me, Arran. I get that it'll be you, or another Warrior, who will have to kill me before I can do more harm."

He grabbed her arms and pulled her to him. Instantly her body came alive. He drew in a ragged breath and forced his gaze up from her mouth.

"Then let's find out who this new darkness is."

She nodded and didn't pull away when he tugged her head onto his chest. Ronnie leaned on him, with not just her body, but her troubles as well. It was as if he took the weight of her problems onto his very wide shoulders, giving her a boost.

"Come. Let's see what else we can find," he urged.

Ronnie didn't want to leave the safety and comfort of his hold, but she steadied herself and squared her shoulders. There was a spell to find, monsters to kill, and a prophecy to stop. The time for wallowing in pity or guilt was over.

For the next hour, they meticulously went through and matched every item on the list save one.

"Why is just the one gone?" Ronnie asked.

"Verra good question. I've a feeling it's exactly what I'm looking for, too. It says on the manifest that it's a necklace. There are long sections of knotwork connected together and then to the chains of the necklace. There appears to be more, but whoever wrote this didna finish the sentence."

Arran rolled the parchment and sighed. "Bloody hell."

"What do we do?"

"I doona think we can destroy these items, but neither can they be allowed to sit in a museum or chance being stolen. I need to get them out of here."

Ronnie blocked his way when he started to walk off and shone her flashlight on his face. "How do I know you aren't doing all this just to get the relics?"

He grinned and pulled out his iPhone from his back pocket. The screen was cracked, but it still worked. "Call Saffron."

Ronnie took his phone and looked deep into his golden eyes. Would she be able to tell a lie from the truth? Especially when she wanted Arran so desperately? And she did want him, even after seeing what he'd become.

She'd been afraid, but that fear hadn't lasted. He'd had plenty of opportunities to kill her if that's what he wanted. Instead, he'd saved her.

Trust had been an issue with her since Max, but there was going to have to be a time in her life when she did trust once more. She might get it wrong again, as she had with Max, or she might get it right.

She unlocked the phone and found Saffron's number. While the phone rang, she resumed staring at Arran. By the third ring, there was a feminine hello.

"Arran?" Saffron asked over the phone when Ronnie didn't immediately answer.

"No, it's Ronnie."

"Did something happen to Arran?" Saffron asked quickly, her voice low and urgent.

Ronnie cleared her throat. "No, he's standing right here. He wanted me to call you to ask about . . . Well, I need to know if he was sent to take what we found."

There was a moment of silence and then a click as the phone was put on speaker, and Ronnie could hear a man's voice. She'd never met Camdyn, but she'd heard he could be a difficult man to take at times.

"What has Arran told you?" Saffron asked.

Arran jerked his chin and took the phone from Ronnie so he could put it on speaker. At her questioning look, he grinned and said, "Enhanced senses are part of the package."

Ronnie should've guessed.

"Saffron, she knows what I am. She also knows about you and the other Druids."

"Why?" was Saffron's only response.

Arran licked his lips and gave a slight shake of his head to Ronnie. "There's been a wee problem. I'm going to need to talk to Fallon, so Camdyn, get your arse to the castle. It's going to take all the Warriors."

"Shite," came a male voice.

A baby cried, the sound getting closer over the phone. Ronnie could hear Saffron shushing the infant as Camdyn told her good-bye.

"All right," Saffron said a moment later. "Ronnie, everything Arran told you is the truth. All of it. I know it may seem . . . odd, but that's our lives."

"Hers as well," Arran stated.

There was a slight gasp over the phone. "So you are a Druid. Somehow, Ronnie, I'm not surprised."

Ronnie heard the excitement and acceptance in Saffron's voice, which made her grin. "We found the manifest of the magical items lost in the shipment from Edinburgh. There appears to be a necklace missing, and Arran thinks that could be the spell."

Saffron let out a breath. "Thank God."

"I've told Ronnie that the objects here can no' be found by anyone else. There is magic everywhere, Saffron. I even found a scroll with another spell on it," Arran said.

"I wonder what that other spell does. Regardless, he's right, Ronnie," Saffron said. "If you'd battled the evil we had, you wouldn't think twice about making sure those items are never found again."

Ronnie glanced at the door. "That's why this place was built, wasn't it?" she asked Arran. "It's why the door was barred? No one was supposed to find this place or be able to get into it."

Arran gave a single nod, his golden eyes holding a hint of worry.

"I want to know more, but for the moment, trust us," Saffron said. "Please, Ronnie. If not for me, then for the innocents like my baby girl and everyone else out in the world."

Ronnie licked her lips, her mind made up. "What do we do with the objects?"

"I'll handle that," Arran said.

They disconnected the call, and Arran began to gather up items in his arms.

"There's no way you'll be able to get up the rope with all of that."

He smiled and said, "Watch."

Ronnie took the rest of the items, including the manifest, before picking up her flashlight and following Arran. As soon as they walked out, the door slammed shut. The boom of the door was loud and final.

She shivered as something ominous snaked down her spine. When she looked back, it was just in time to see Arran bend his legs before he leapt to the top and over the side of earth.

"Well, hell," she muttered.

It was just a few seconds later that Arran jumped down from the top, his arms now empty. "Everyone still sleeps. Are you ready?"

"I guess," she said.

The words had barely passed her lips before the wind whooshed around her and she was staring at the food tent. Ronnie looked around to make sure they weren't seen and handed the items to Arran.

"Don't get caught. I won't be able to help you if you're seen with these."

"Doona worry. They'll be gone within the hour."

Ronnie glanced down at the arch and door. She could have died in there, and probably should have. She'd unleashed who knew what out into the world, but Arran was still beside her, still helping her.

"What now?" she asked.

"Get to your tent and try to rest. I've got to call Fallon."

"Fallon?"

"MacLeod."

She blinked. "One of *the* MacLeods?"

"Aye. He'll come for the items."

Ronnie laughed. "Not within the hour, depending on how far away he is."

Arran began to walk, and she hurried to catch up with him.

"Remember when I told you each Warrior has a special power given to them by their god?"

"Ah, no, not really."

"I might have left that part out. Well, we do. Fallon's power is teleportation, as you call it. We say jumping."

She rubbed her eyes with her thumb and forefinger as she took it all in. There was an entire world out there she hadn't known about. Now that she'd gotten a taste of it, she was curious to know more.

Though she might be frightened, she knew knowledge was power. And she needed that knowledge.

"And what is your power?"

"I have control over ice and snow."

A glance showed he wasn't joking. "Wow. And all of you are white when you release your gods?"

"Nay. We each have a different color favored by our gods."

When he stopped walking, Ronnie found she was in front of her tent. She was beyond exhausted, and her mind was full of everything she'd learned.

"Get inside, Ronnie," Arran urged softly. "Nothing will happen to you while I'm near."

And strangely, she believed him.

CHAPTER
SEVENTEEN

Arran waited until Ronnie was inside her tent before he continued to his. He dropped the items he'd taken from Ronnie onto his cot with the others and dialed Fallon.

"About bloody time," Fallon said as he answered the phone.

Arran rubbed his jaw. His body was still drained from what he'd gone through, but he was recovering. "I had to get Ronnie safe."

"What happened?"

"She opened the door, and just as I expected, the chamber was full of magical items. I convinced her to allow me to give them to you."

"There's something else. I can hear it in your voice. And you told Camdyn to get here."

Arran dreaded this part. He looked at the box on the bed and clenched his jaw. "Ronnie opened a box. There were . . . creatures that came out of it."

"What kind of creatures?"

"I've no idea, Fallon. I've never seen the like. I didna get to Ronnie in time to stop her from opening the box, and as soon as these things were out, they attacked."

There was a slight pause before Fallon asked, "Did you kill them?"

"I killed some. Or I thought I did. They're immortal."

"Damn. Were you injured?"

Arran frowned and tried to think of how to answer. He didn't want Fallon to worry, but he didn't want to lie to his friend either.

"Answer me," Fallon demanded as he appeared in Arran's tent.

"Shite!" Arran jumped back when Fallon, along with his brother Lucan, materialized in front of him. "Doona do that!"

Fallon pocketed his phone and stared at Arran with intelligent green eyes. "You took too long to answer. Tell me what happened."

Lucan glanced around the tent before his gaze turned to the cot. "Did you find the spell?"

"One thing at a time," Arran said, and raked a hand through his hair as he turned away from the brothers.

He turned back to them with his hands on his hips. "The first thing you should know is that these creatures are verra tall and bony. They have stringy white hair and fangs longer than ours. Their skin is the color of ash, and their blood burns when it comes in contact with our skin. At least it did with mine."

"Just ours or anyone's?" Lucan asked, his brow furrowed.

Arran shrugged. "That I doona know. They're fast, too. But the worst part is . . . they bit me and drank my blood."

"Like a damned vampire?" Fallon asked in surprise.

"I guess, but these things were more, Fallon. They were strong, verra strong. I beheaded a few, but even more got out before I could stop them."

Lucan tugged on one of the small braids at his temple that he'd worn since before his god was unbound. "That means they're out in the world. Who knows what kind of havoc they can wreak."

"I'm sorry." Arran shook his head, angry at himself for not watching Ronnie more closely. "I knew something bad was in that chamber, and I should've known Ronnie would try to get in herself."

Fallon clamped a hand on his shoulder. "You are no' to blame, my friend. You did all that you could."

"Aye, you saved Ronnie," Lucan said.

It should have been enough, but it wasn't. Arran had said

he could handle this mission alone. He'd failed, and by doing so, he'd failed to stop an unknown evil from getting out into the world.

"I know I'm no' the only Warrior looking for something to kill," Lucan said with a grin. "Hayden is one who'll be especially excited we have something to hunt."

Fallon shook his head with a grin. Then he turned to Arran. "I gather Ronnie now knows what you are?"

"Aye," Arran answered. "She had no idea she was a Druid. I've told her the story, but she has questions."

Fallon nodded. "Is she afraid of you?"

"A little. She blames herself for the creatures getting out. They targeted her, Fallon. They knew she would open the box."

Lucan's green eyes narrowed. "Why are you so sure of that?"

"The prophecy she found." Arran pulled up the picture with his phone and showed it to the brothers.

Lucan ground his teeth together as Fallon let out a string of curses.

"Ronnie is sure it's about her," Arran said. "I agree, but I didna want to worry her."

"It says she'll bring about the destruction of the world and that a Warrior must stop her." Lucan rubbed the back of his neck. "But I'm concerned with the 'new darkness' mentioned."

Fallon put his hands on his hips and stared at the ground. "We were fooled for a year. We thought the evil was gone. Tara was right all along. There can no' be good without evil."

"Then who is this new darkness?" Lucan asked.

Arran crossed his arms over his chest. "Ronnie and I will try to find out, just as I'm going to discover what these creatures are."

"How?" Fallon asked. "You doona even know what to look for."

"Nay, but we have to start somewhere. I'm no longer needed here. The spell is gone."

Lucan raised a dark brow. "And Ronnie? Are you willing to leave her?"

Arran met the green gaze of the middle MacLeod brother. "Nay. I doona believe I could even if I wanted to. I'll have to convince her to come with me. Though that might be difficult with the dig still in progress."

Arran picked up the hated box and examined it again. "Ronnie said it was like it made her open it. She had planned to take it back to her tent, but before she could, she said it was like she had no control over herself. She saw herself opening it, and then the white dust swirled around her. That dust turned into those creatures."

"We're going to have a tough mission on our hands if these things can turn to dust at will," Lucan said as he rubbed his hand over his jaw.

"There's magic in the box. We need to know what kind," Arran said.

Fallon took the box and gathered a few other items. "We'll inspect each and every one of these objects. As soon as I know about the magic of the box, I'll call you."

Arran had known Fallon held off asking about the spell. Saffron must have told him. "Here's the manifest," he said, and handed the scroll to Lucan. "Everything was in the chamber save one item. A necklace. The description is written. I believe that's where the scroll is."

"Why take only one object?" Lucan asked.

Fallon grunted. "Why hide the rest beneath the ground?"

Lucan eyed the artifacts before he filled his arms. "I doona think we should take these back to the castle."

"Agreed," Fallon said. "I was thinking of putting them in one of the cottages in the village. Close and still hidden beneath Isla's shield, but no' in the castle with us."

"A good idea," Arran said. "We can always move them later if need be."

Fallon turned those green eyes on Arran again. "By the way, Charon has some information on Max. It seems he worked for a conglomerate."

"Its true identity is a secret," Lucan said.

Fallon shrugged. "It appears Ronnie was just a job for Max."

Arran suddenly felt the need to find Max and give him a beating he wouldn't soon forget. "Interesting. I'd hoped he really liked Ronnie, but it looks like I was wrong."

He had to assure both brothers he was all right once more before they said their farewells and the brothers were gone. Fallon's teleportation definitely came in handy, but then again, Lucan's ability to call the darkness and shadows did as well.

All the powers of the Warriors had aided them in battle every time.

Arran sank onto his bed and dropped his head into his hands. He knew he had to find the creatures and put a stop to them. It was the only way he could make up for his mistake and help Ronnie prove the prophecy wrong.

It meant his time with her wasn't up, and that made him very happy. He clenched his hands as he remembered holding her in the chamber. She'd trembled, and for the first time, she looked frail and scared.

Arran never wanted to see her that way again, and no matter what he had to do, he'd ensure she never did.

He made a quick call to Gwynn to see if she could search the Internet for anything regarding the beings. He gave her a full description, and she promised to call as soon as any of her alerts came up.

Arran ended the call and glanced out his tent to find that people were beginning to stir. As a Warrior, he could go without sleep for days. Sleep was welcome, but he could do without.

Ronnie, however, couldn't. He was going to have to keep a close eye on her.

Jason Wallace adjusted the painting in the corridor for a third time before he stepped back to inspect it. There was a sound behind him, and then Harry cleared his throat.

"Sir, your man has returned."

Jason smiled. Harry had no idea the men were actually Warriors. He knew they were different, but Harry had never been too smart.

"That'll be all, Harry," he said as he turned on his heel and strode to his private office below the house.

He found the Warrior sitting at the table. "Well. I hope you have news?"

"Aye," Dale said, and leaned his forearms on his thighs. "Something happened at the dig site last night. It seems Dr. Reid opened whatever it was she'd been digging around."

"You doona know what it is?"

Dale shook his head. "I couldna get that close. They are watchful of who is around."

"Go on," Jason said. He was irritated that Dale didn't know more about the dig, but he was glad he'd sent a Warrior to watch.

"There was magic, lots of it," the Warrior said. "It felt . . . old. And it was no' too long before this cloud of ash came out of the ground where Reid and the Warrior went."

"So Arran was with Dr. Reid?"

"No' at first. He must have felt the magic when I did, because he ran to her. I could hear what sounded like fighting, but when MacCarrick and Reid came up, neither looked injured."

Jason leaned back against the wall and crossed his arms over his chest. "What else did you see?"

"They were holding different things when they emerged from the place she'd been digging."

"What kind of things?"

"Scrolls, weapons, a wee chest. Different things."

Jason frowned. "Why take them out? Reid is an archeologist. She'd want her finds documented so she could get credit. The only reason they'd take them before anyone could know they'd been found was because they were trying to hide something."

"Could be."

"Find out what it was they took," Jason demanded.

Dale slowly got to his feet. He stood tall and straight like a soldier, but then again, that's what he had been before Jason found him. "I run the risk of getting caught."

"You heard my order. Find why they took the items."

"And if MacCarrick realizes what I am?"

Jason chuckled. "Oh, I imagine he'll be too engrossed with Dr. Reid to pay attention. By the way, is Reid a Druid?"

"There is magic at the site, but there is too much of it to know if she is part of it."

"I'll do some investigating into Reid," Jason said. "I've got the other Warriors nearly ready to be introduced into the world. I'm going to need you to make sure they stay in line."

"You know you can count on me."

Jason smiled. Dale had been his first Warrior, and he hadn't disappointed. There had been a few failures, and the men had had to be killed because they were out of control.

But the spell Jason had discovered in Declan's book, which gave just enough control to the god so the men could turn into Warriors, was pure brilliance. He'd love to thank whatever Druid came up with it, because Declan hadn't been that smart.

"How long do I stay at the site?" Dale asked.

Jason pushed off the wall with his shoulder and dropped his arms. He reached into his pocket and took out a mobile phone. He tossed it to the Warrior, who caught it with one hand.

"Call me on that when you discover what I want to know. We'll go from there. But whatever you do, doona leave MacCarrick. I want him watched at all times. Wherever he goes, you go."

"Understood."

"Good. Get moving."

Jason remained in his office long after Dale left. His mind was going over why Reid and MacCarrick had taken the items out of the dig site.

What was it they'd found? It had to be important. And what had the MacLeod Warrior said to Reid to convince her to go against everything she was and hide the objects?

Jason wouldn't give up until he had the answers. And he knew those answers were going to benefit him greatly.

CHAPTER
EIGHTEEN

He hadn't even kissed her. Ronnie couldn't seem to stop thinking about it. Arran had deposited her at her tent. And then just . . . left.

She'd tried to sleep, but the image of those monsters wouldn't leave her. How tall and grotesque they were. How fast they moved.

How terrifyingly easily they had brought down Arran.

As always, her attention then turned to Arran. She let her mind roll over all he'd told her of Druids and Warriors. Ronnie had seen the proof of what Arran was. There was no denying it now or pretending it hadn't happened.

He was immortal. Immortal! A Warrior with a primeval god inside him. And powers, if she could believe that. Why shouldn't she? She'd seen his skin and eyes change. She'd seen the claws and fangs.

She'd also seen how fast he moved. Not to mention his strength. How he'd thrown off those eight monsters she didn't know, but she'd been impressed even as she'd been frightened.

Was it because he was a Warrior that made her want him? Had her body instinctively known he was something more than a mere man?

There was definitely a connection between them. The attraction and the kiss had proved that. But it went deeper.

Ronnie hadn't wanted to admit it, much less think about it, but she couldn't deny it now.

Arran was part of a world she now belonged to. She'd been right when she guessed that he understood her like no other, because he had. He could feel her magic.

She rubbed her thumb over the pads of her fingers. It was magic that ran through her, helping her find the items she dug for. Was it her magic that brought her desire to such frenzied heights when it came to Arran?

It didn't matter. Nothing mattered but the need, the heart-pounding, soul-stirring passion she felt whenever he was near.

And when she was in his arms, a sigh left her. In his arms the world fell away. All that remained were the two of them. Now she comprehended why the depth of the desire frightened her.

She'd never experienced anything like it before. It was new and glorious and breathtaking. And it was waiting for her to take that leap, to accept Arran's invitation and all the ecstasy he promised.

Ronnie stared blankly at the computer screen, where an email from Pete reminding her about the fund-raiser had been open for over an hour.

She looked at the clothes she'd stripped off that showed evidence of the attack and her being in the chamber. With a click, she opened a new window on the screen and did a search for "immortal Highlanders."

There was nothing other than what had been in the movies and TV.

Then she did a search for "Warriors" and added "Scotland." Again, just movies and TV shows until she happened to go to the next page and found a link that looked interesting.

Imagine her surprise when the page opened and there was an account very similar to what Arran had told her. The story of Rome's departure was even written. Of course, below it were comments by detractors who said the author of the blog had no idea what he or she was talking about.

But Ronnie knew the person did. Who was it? How did they know? And better yet, did Arran and the others know of this blog and its author?

Ronnie read more, looking to see if the author knew the Warriors still existed. One entry did state that the author expected the Warriors to be around, but keeping a low profile.

The author then mentioned something about wyrran, and even posted a picture. Ronnie remembered when those creatures were spotted around Britain, but she'd thought it was a hoax. Now she wasn't so sure.

She made a mental note to ask Arran about the wyrran the next time she saw him. Unable to turn away, Ronnie read more entries and looked at more pictures.

There was a picture of Cairn Toul Mountain, where the author said an evil Druid had lived. Ronnie sat back and stared at the picture.

Arran had said something about being locked in Deirdre's mountain. Could that be it? What horrors had he experienced there?

It was hard not to believe it after she'd seen the monsters and Arran just a few hours earlier. Yet it seemed so farfetched, like a story someone had made up.

There was no denying Arran's skin had been white. It wasn't makeup either. She'd touched it, stroked his warm skin. It had been all him.

Every wonderful, astonishing inch of him.

She'd even seen the white fade away to reveal his normal tanned skin again. There was no way to fake something like that.

Ronnie tapped her fingers absently on the keyboard before she did another search. This one for Druids. After about thirty minutes, her eyes were crossing from all the references she found.

And every reference said something different. What was truth and what was real? She could ask Arran, but she had hoped to find something out herself.

Magic.

He'd said there was magic all through Britain. Is that what was helping her find the items she dug up? It had to be more than that, since she'd had success in more countries besides Britain.

There wasn't a place she had gone to dig that she hadn't found something. And each time, it had been that feeling inside her that led her to the items.

Ronnie leaned back in the chair and sighed. Her eyes burned from lack of sleep. To make matters worse, a stress headache had begun at the base of her neck.

"Just what I need," she mumbled.

"What? Food?"

Ronnie turned to find Andy bent over at the waist and half inside her tent. She returned his smile. "No, I was talking to myself."

"They say that's the first sign that you're losing it," he said as he came into her tent and placed a paper plate full of biscuits, sausage, and scrambled eggs in front of her.

"Eggs," she said. "We haven't had that in a while."

Andy shrugged. "I'm not going to complain. It was something different. You look like shit, by the way."

"Gee, thanks." Ronnie's stomach growled, and she began to eat.

"Just being honest, boss. What's wrong with Arran?"

Ronnie paused in chewing to look at Andy. "What do you mean?"

"He's acting weird. I mean weirder than usual," he amended, and slid his glasses up his nose as he sat on the edge of the cot. "He seems tense and keeps looking in the distance as well as walking around the site as if he's checking the perimeter or something like that."

She shrugged and swallowed her bite. "I suspect he has some kind of military or police training. At least that's my thought. I'm sure he's just checking things over, and he's done it every day and you haven't noticed."

"Still. There's something different about him this morning. About you as well, now that I think on it."

Ronnie's appetite disappeared. She shoved the plate away. "My problem is the fund-raiser coming up," she lied.

"Ah, yes. Speaking of that, I've got the hotel all taken care of."

"Where is this being held again?"

"The same place you're staying, for once." Andy winked and said, "It's the Sheraton Grand Hotel and Spa. It's really gorgeous. And I booked you a suite."

Ronnie rolled her eyes. "Sounds good. No time for the spa, though. Besides, it's money I don't need to spend. I'm already spending enough on a dress."

"Are you going to wear your typical black?"

"Well, I was. And what do you mean typical?"

"It's all you ever wear when it comes to these things. It's almost like you're going to a funeral."

She crossed her arms over her chest and glared. "I'll have you know that basic black is the epitome of elegant when it comes to formal or after-five affairs."

Andy threw up his hands with a grin. "If you say so. I'm no girl, so I wouldn't know."

"Go make yourself useful," she said with a teasing grin.

Andy was more like a brother than a friend. It was a relationship that had begun the instant they'd met. Neither had siblings, and Ronnie wasn't even sure if that's how true siblings acted.

The other foster kids she'd lived with had all been moved around just as much as she, so they all tended to be private and kept to themselves.

She looked at the "Druid" search and closed the tab. If she wanted to know more, she could ask Saffron. But it would have to wait, with everything else she had on her mind.

And she still hadn't found a date to the fund-raiser. Arran had mentioned finding the new darkness as well as more information on the creatures. They couldn't do that at the dig site.

As if he knew she was thinking about him, Arran poked his head in her tent. "Got a moment?"

She nodded and rose to her feet. "Yes."

In all the times she'd been around him, even after the kiss, she'd never been so nervous. She wiped her hands up and down her jeans and tried not to fidget.

"You're scared of me now?"

"No," she hurried to say. The disappointment she heard in his voice made her inwardly wince. "I'm still trying to absorb it all. Really, I'm surprised you're not pissed at me for releasing those things into the world."

"You couldna know what was in the chest, Ronnie."

She glanced away, the need to feel his arms around her, protecting her was so great, she started to take a step toward him.

"I've come to tell you that you need no' worry about the things," he said cryptically. "Fallon and Lucan came for them last night."

It took a second for her to realize he was talking about the items they'd taken from the chamber. "Fallon, as in the one who teleports?"

Just saying it felt weird and made her want to laugh. Never in her life had she thought she'd be saying something like that and actually mean it.

"Aye. He and his brother Lucan were here."

"The MacLeods. I'd have liked to meet them."

Arran's lips tilted in a crooked smile. "I hope you do soon. Do you ever get a holiday?"

"A vacation? Well, sure, but I rarely take it."

"Take it next time. Come out to the castle."

Ronnie opened her mouth to say yes before he'd even finished. It was only at the last moment that she paused. "I don't know when that will be."

"You need to meet the other Druids. I'm sure you have questions they'll be able to answer. Learning more about us Warriors might help you as well."

"I can learn about Warriors from you."

His golden eyes darkened as he took a step closer to her. "Doona tempt me, Ronnie."

"And if I want to tempt you?"

He lifted an arm and gently moved a strand of hair behind her ear that had come loose from the bun. "I should be ashamed to say I'm glad I've got reasons to stay with you, but I'm no'."

Her heart beat erratically in her chest as her stomach fluttered. "Even though you have to stay because you might have to kill me?"

In one step, he closed the distance between them. "You're no' evil," he stated roughly, his voice deep and offering no quarter.

"No, I don't think I could be, not with you beside me."

After her near death experiences, Ronnie was tired of playing it safe. She wanted Arran, needed what he offered.

His hand slid around her neck and pulled her against him. "Ah, lass, you've no idea what you do to me, do you? Your magic feels like a caress, your smile like you're stroking me."

Ronnie splayed her hands on his chest and gazed deep in his eyes. She didn't want to know what life without Arran was like. He'd made his mark, and anyone else would be a poor substitution.

His lips had just touched hers when Andy gave a shout to someone right outside her tent. Arran's mouth curved into a grin, but he didn't release her.

"We are forever interrupted here. Privacy is what we need."

"I have a favor to ask," she said as he reminded her about the fund-raiser. Not only would it get them alone, but it would also afford them time to do some investigating in Edinburgh.

"Name it."

Ronnie grinned nervously. "Don't be so hasty. You might not want to do it."

"I'd do anything you asked."

The honesty shining in his golden eyes made her heart miss a beat. "I have the fund-raiser coming up. I leave tomorrow for Edinburgh."

"You need me to escort you to Edinburgh?" he asked.

"Actually, I was hoping you'd be my date."

His smile was slow, and very male. The gleam in his eyes told her he was thinking about their privacy just as she was.

Never had she asked a man out, and she was anxious. But she also knew the only one she wanted with her was Arran.

"I'd be honored," he said softly, deeply, and let his thumb caress her jaw.

And she felt it all the way to her soul. She had to clear her throat, her emotions were so thick. "I'm glad. Very glad. Do you, ah, do you have a tux?"

"I'll get what I need. Shall we leave together tomorrow then?"

Time alone with Arran? Hell yes she was taking that option. "Yep. Does that work for you?"

"Oh, aye," he said with a wicked grin. "I better leave you alone now. No' sure how long I can keep my hands off you. Or resist stealing another kiss."

And just like that, he was gone.

"He still didn't kiss me," she murmured.

Arran pulled his phone from his pocket as he left Ronnie's and dialed Saffron. If there was one woman at MacLeod Castle who could help him, it was the billionaire.

"I need your help," he told Saffron as soon as she answered.

"As always, I'm happy to help. What do you need?"

"A tux."

There was a choking sound, and then Saffron began to cough.

"Saffron? Are you choking?"

"Yes," she croaked, and coughed some more. After a moment she said, "Are you serious? Arran, you were one of the ones who didn't want to learn so many of the modern things like dancing and such. Why would you need a tux?"

"Ronnie asked me to go with her to her fund-raiser. I said aye. It'll give us some time to search for the creatures."

"Interesting."

He rubbed the back of his neck. "Can you help me? She

asked if I had a tux and I said aye, but I doona even know what that is."

Saffron snorted. "You've lived in our time for over a year and you don't know what a tux is? Don't you remember what Camdyn was in a few months ago when we went to that dinner in London?"

Arran held back a groan as he remembered the black jacket and white shirt Camdyn had worn. The only saving grace was the kilt that had been with it. "Aye."

"I'll take care of everything. What hotel are you staying in?"

"I doona know."

"Never mind," she said hurriedly. "I'll have Gwynn find out. Are you riding with Ronnie to Edinburgh?"

Arran flattened his lips. "Of course."

"Just like a damned Warrior."

"What's that supposed to mean?"

Saffron laughed through the phone. "Oh, Arran, I think you're in for a surprise. A nice surprise, but a surprise nonetheless."

The phone went dead and he pulled it away from his face to look at it. He hadn't liked Saffron's parting words. What could she mean?

He forgot all about it as someone motioned for him to help move another rock they'd found in the ground. No matter how hard he pushed his body, his mind was full of Ronnie.

Of her erotic magic, her seductive smile, and her beautiful eyes.

CHAPTER
NINETEEN

Somewhere deep in the Highlands

Malcolm sat with his eyes closed and simply listened to the sound of the wind as it whistled through the mountains. It had taken him a while, but he'd finally managed to find a place where he was utterly alone for miles and miles.

The air was cooler and thinner at the top of the mountain where he sat. He could see the mountains all around him, the grass swaying in the wind sometimes showing green, sometimes a beautiful purple.

The cries of peregrine falcons brought a smile to his face. The sun had risen and set numerous times as he'd sat. Through sun and rain, cloud-filled nights that hid the moon, and days where the sky had been the most beautiful, vibrant blue.

These were the things that made him happy when he'd been mortal. The things he'd looked forward to. He'd come up to the top of the mountain to try to see if there was any part of that man left inside him.

He hadn't been surprised to find there wasn't.

Malcolm could easily blame Deirdre for turning him into the man he was. But the simple truth was that the fault lay solely with him.

His phone vibrated on the rock beside him. It was the sixth call in less than four hours. Even though he saw Larena's name show up as the caller, Malcolm still wouldn't answer it.

He wasn't worried that it was something important either, because if it was, Broc could easily find him with his powers.

No, it was better if Malcolm remained just as he was. The only company he was fit for was his own, and even that was questionable.

Technically, he hadn't been a Warrior for too long, if he didn't count being time-traveled forward by four centuries. Despite that, he could barely remember the part of his life before he was a Warrior.

He vaguely remembered there might have been a woman he was interested in, but, apparently, she wasn't so special because he couldn't remember her face, much less her name.

Malcolm looked down at his right arm and the scars that ran the length of it and disappeared beneath his shirt. But he couldn't hide the scars on his face and neck so easily. People stared at him wherever he went. He'd seen his reflection in the mirror and knew how horrible he looked.

At least when Deirdre was alive, her magic had hidden his ugliness.

"Is this what life holds for me?" he asked.

Silence greeted his words, but it was that same silence that let him breathe easier. He wasn't the type of man who wanted to be around others.

He was better by himself.

If only Larena would realize that. But his cousin could be very stubborn.

Ronnie didn't know how she'd gotten through the day before. It had been long and excruciating. Not because of the dig or the fact that she had to lie to everyone and tell them that there was nothing in the chamber, but because she was aware of Arran's every move, every smile.

She must have been too upset over the attack to realize Arran had removed any evidence of artifacts in the chamber. Confirming her lie to everyone.

Just one more thing she needed to thank him for.

She wanted to warn them all of the creatures, but she wasn't sure they'd believe her. Arran had told her to wait. Apparently, there was a Druid named Gwynn at MacLeod Castle who was good on the computer, and until she heard about the creatures being spotted somewhere else, they were to remain quiet about them.

That was fine until Ronnie stood in the chamber and remembered the sight of the monsters and the way they had nearly brought Arran down. But Arran had come to her rescue despite the pain he was in.

How could she ever have doubted him? How could she ever have compared him to Max? He was nothing like Max.

Dawn had broken an hour ago, and somehow Ronnie managed to eat a few bites of a biscuit and drink three cups of coffee. Her nerves were utterly frazzled.

"He's just a man," she reminded herself.

Then she covered her mouth as she giggled. Well, he wasn't really *just* a man. He was immortal. And had powers. So much more than just a man.

They were to depart at any moment. She was anxious, and her nerves wound so tight, she couldn't keep still.

She rubbed her hands together and stared at her overnight bag and purse that waited for her. Arran was driving, since her car still wasn't fixed.

Alone. For a couple of hours.

With Arran.

His smile, the smoldering way his eyes watched her. His body that defined temptation. His lips that could steal her breath with just a kiss.

He was all that was sexy and sultry, tangible fieriness that made her babble, unable to keep a coherent thought in her head. Just being near him made her heart race and left her winded. Her blood heated when she thought of him kissing her again.

Leisurely. Seductively.

Thoroughly.

She shivered as she recalled being against his rock-hard

frame again. Her breasts swelled and her nipples hardened. His arms had been strong as he'd molded her against the hard length of him.

And, oh, how she wanted more of that.

It had been . . . well, years since she'd been intimate with a man. With Arran around, sex was all she seemed able to think about. Maybe it was the way his eyes always watched her with that dark intensity that made her feel as if thousands of butterflies would take flight in her stomach.

Ronnie couldn't remember the last time she'd spent any time alone with a man who wasn't Peter or Andy. What would she say? How should she act? Better yet, how could she let him know she was interested?

"Ready?"

She jumped and whirled around to find Arran standing inside her tent. Her hands were shaking, so she held them behind her back. "Ah. Yeah."

He lifted a dark brow and grinned. "That didna sound convincing, lass."

"I hate these things," she said.

"That's just one of the reasons I'm going."

She bit back a laugh. "Just one?"

"Oh, aye. Andy told me I'm to fend off your horde of admirers."

This time she did laugh. "I don't have a horde."

"No' according to Andy."

"Is that the only other reason?"

His eyes glowed with desire, with a dark hunger she felt herself. "Nay. Do I need to say it, lass?"

"No," she croaked. "Not now. Not here."

He reached for her bag. "Doona fear, Ronnie. Who better to protect you from your admirers or . . . anything else out there, than me?"

There was a gleam of something in his golden eyes that made her heart miss a beat. His lips tilted slightly at the corners.

"Right. Who better?"

Before she could say another word, he brushed past.

Ronnie reached for her purse and straightened to find Arran holding the tent flap open for her.

Ronnie exited with Arran at her heels. She looked around the site to see that Andy, as usual, had everything running smoothly.

He was waiting for them by Arran's steel gray Range Rover. Andy smiled and held Ronnie's door for her while Arran put her bag in the back with his. Ronnie slid into the front seat and fastened her seat belt.

"I know you hate these things," Andy said, "but they keep me in a job. At least this time you have muscleman there to keep the jerks from putting their hands on you."

"Who puts their hands on her?" Arran asked, his voice deepening with a hard edge as he climbed behind the wheel.

Andy's smile grew, as if he knew by getting Arran riled that Ronnie was sure to be left alone by everyone. "The jerks who think because she's a pretty face and they have money to give that they can touch her any way they want."

"There willna be any touching unless Ronnie wants it," Arran stated.

Ronnie leaned her head back and held in a smile. She should be upset at the two of them, but it showed how much Andy cared that he was willing to deal with her anger if it kept her safe from the vile men at the fund-raiser.

"Thank you," she whispered as she leaned in to hug him. She sat back and looked through the windshield at the site. "Tare care of things as you always do. We'll be back on Sunday."

"Take your time. You need a break," Andy said.

He gave a nod to Arran before he shut her door. Ronnie looked from one to the other. It was as if some unspoken message had been passed between them. And she was afraid it involved her.

Arran started the SUV, and then they were driving away. Ronnie inhaled and slowly released her breath.

"You doona have to be nervous around me."

She smiled and looked down at her hands. "I don't spend a lot of time in the company of men."

"Andy and Pete doona count as men?"

Ronnie busted out laughing, which helped to calm her nerves. "They're men, but different. Pete has always been like a father, and Andy, he's the brother I never had."

"You were raised alone?"

She cut her eyes to him. "I know how well you know Saffron, and Saffron did her own investigating of me before she gave me any funds. Which means, you know of my past."

He kept his gaze on the road, but shrugged. "I didna want to upset you."

"I appreciate that, but I'd rather you be honest. How much do you know?"

Arran glanced at her, his golden eyes soft, warm. "I know you were raised in a foster home."

"Yeah. My foster parents were decent, hardworking people. There were five others besides me. Two girls and three boys. All three of us girls shared a room, as did the boys. But even then, we kept to ourselves."

"Why?"

She adjusted herself in the leather seat to get more comfortable and watched the passing scenery. "I'd been moved around some, but others had been to several more families than I. Even in that tiny bedroom with two sets of bunk beds, there were invisible lines drawn that no one crossed. Our boundaries, as it were, that each of us knew not to violate."

"I doona understand."

"It's difficult to explain. You don't have much when you're in the system. You only have what your current foster family gives you. Clothes we had to share as long as we could wear the same sizes. Shoes were the same. But our beds, our spaces were ours. We didn't share what we didn't have to."

"I gather the parents didna have much money? Why take in so many kids, then?" Arran asked.

"The government gives them money for each child. That money is supposed to be used to feed and clothe us. My foster parents did the best they could. There weren't unkind, but it wasn't the type of family some of my other friends had with their parents."

"So you had all those siblings, but none of them you felt were your brothers or sisters?"

She shrugged. "It's difficult. Yes, we were close while we were together. We stood up for each other, but as soon as we reached eighteen and were out on our own, no one ever came back."

"You either?"

"I didn't go back, but I kept in touch with my foster parents through cards and phone calls while in college. They hadn't taken in any more children after us six, and when the last one left, they wanted some time alone. Six months later, my foster mother died of a heart attack. My foster dad died a year later."

"I'm sorry."

"It was a long time ago," she said, and cleared her throat. She hadn't thought of her foster parents in years. "They were the only family I remember."

"At least you were no' alone."

"No. What about you? What was your family like?"

Arran grinned and chuckled. "Like most Highland families. My da was a hard man. Hard living, hard loving, and hard fighting. But he and me mum loved each other fiercely."

"Did you have any brothers or sisters?"

Several long minutes went by where Arran didn't say anything. A muscle ticced in his jaw. "I had a sister," he finally said.

"Younger?"

"Aye. She was a bonny lass. So full of laughter and innocence. I was five years older than Shelley, but that didna stop us from being close."

The way he spoke—softly, almost as if he were afraid even to be discussing it—caused a pang in her chest. "I'm sorry. It must have been hard for you to outlive them all."

"I outlived them, but no' in the way you think."

She shouldn't pry, but she was curious about everything in Arran's life. "This is obviously painful. Let's change the subject."

"Deirdre discovered my family was one of the original

Warriors, you see," Arran said. "What she'd do is send her wyrran after men who she thought might have a god bound inside them."

"Wyrran?" Ronnie turned in her seat to face him. "I read about them on the Internet yesterday. What were they?"

"Read about them?" he asked as he glanced at her.

"Yes. I did a search on Druids. A Cairn Toul Mountain came up in the search, as did wyrran."

"Cairn Toul is where Deirdre lived. Her magic was the ability to communicate with rock. She was able to construct a fortress inside the mountain. It was her home, and the rocks obeyed her."

Ronnie shivered just thinking about it. "That's where she held you? Cairn Toul?"

He gave a single nod.

"For how long?"

"I lost track of time. Decades. She tortured and tried to turn me to her side. I never gave in."

She reached over and put her hand atop his, which rested on the center console. As always, a current passed through them. "I'm sorry, Arran."

"I survived," he said, never taking his eyes off the road. "It made me stronger, made me learn to control my god that much sooner."

"How did the wyrran factor into this? Where did they come from?"

"Deirdre. She created them with her black magic. They were small, hairless yellow creatures with shrieks that would burst eardrums."

"I saw pictures on the Net. A year ago, they were seen in Scotland. I thought it was a hoax."

"No hoax. They were here because Deirdre was here. Declan brought her forward in time to combine their magic. But Deirdre didna work with anyone. She wanted no one to get in the way of her ruling the world."

Ronnie licked her lips as she tried to put everything in some kind of time line in her head to keep it straight. "Were you still in her mountain when she was brought forward?"

"Nay. Fallon and Lucan had mounted an attack with the other Warriors to free Quinn, whom Deirdre had captured. That's how I came to be involved with the MacLeods. Quinn and I became friends in that cursed mountain, so when he asked me to return with him to the castle, I didna think twice about it. I'd have a place to live and get to fight Deirdre."

"A win-win situation," Ronnie said with a smile.

Arran laughed. "Something like that."

"I gather your family was already dead by then?"

His smile slipped and a shadow flitted over his face. "My family was killed when Deirdre sent the wyrran after me. Shelley was literally torn to pieces before my eyes. I can still hear her screams. And I couldna do anything to help her, since the wyrran held me."

"This seems so inadequate to say, but . . . I'm sorry, Arran."

She looked out the window, suddenly realizing how good her life had been compared to his. He'd had his family taken from him, and he'd been thrown into evil.

Yet he had survived, just as she had. They had that in common.

As well as coming from a world of magic, a world very few knew about.

CHAPTER
TWENTY

Arran gave the Range Rover keys to the valet when they reached the hotel. Their bags were taken by an attendant, and Arran had no choice but to follow Ronnie inside.

With his hand on her lower back, they walked inside. He noticed the way men looked at Ronnie. She was in jeans, boots, and another plaid shirt with her hair in a bun and no makeup, and still men ogled her.

Arran caught the eyes of several of the men watching her and stared them down until they looked away. He might not have an official claim to her, but she was under his protection.

And in his eyes, she was his for the time being.

They walked onto the lift, and he kept his hand on her back as she pushed the number of their floor. She glanced at him. The last hour of their drive had been quiet as their desire rose with each mile that passed beneath the tires. Knowing he was going to have her to himself made his cock hard with anticipation.

He still couldn't believe he'd told her about his sister. Only Quinn had known about her. But even Quinn didn't know the entire story.

"Ready?" Ronnie asked when the bell rung and the lift doors opened. She then handed him what looked like a credit card.

There were still times Arran was amazed at how the world

had changed in four hundred years. He took the room key and followed her into the hallway.

"It seems the hotel is pretty booked. We're going to have to share a room."

Arran bit back a groan as he thought about sharing a room with Ronnie, of climbing into the same bed with her and wrapping his body around hers.

Of finally seeing her wheat-colored hair down and about her shoulders.

He grimaced as his aching rod strained against his jeans.

"Since Andy booked your room yesterday and the hotel messed up, I was able to get us a two-bedroom suite."

Two rooms. Damn. But it didn't dissuade him from finally taking her in his arms again. He knew she felt the same craving, the same driving hunger that was within him.

It had been pure hell not kissing her again. He couldn't look at her without remembering the feel of her soft curves against him. Or how she moaned when their tongues had first touched.

He wanted that and so much more. Her skin, bared of every stitch of clothing. He wanted to pull the pins from her hair and sink his fingers into her locks. He'd been fantasizing about spreading her hair out on the pillow after he'd divested her of her clothes.

Oh, yes, he wanted her kisses, but he had plans for much, much more.

Arran cleared his throat when he saw her staring at him. What had she said? It took him a moment to remember. "I could've paid for my own. I'll gladly pay for the entire suite."

"There's no need."

But Arran was going to make sure of it.

He smiled as his gaze fastened on her hips swaying side to side. "Jeans or a ball gown," he murmured with a grin.

"What?" she asked over her shoulder.

Arran's grin widened. "Nothing."

He watched as she stopped at their door and slid the slim key into the lock. When the light turned green, Arran reached around her and opened the door.

She looked up at him, their faces inches apart. The world halted as he looked down at her mouth. He remembered the taste of her all too well, the softness of her lips and the silkiness of her skin.

He leaned closer, closing the gap between them. He dragged his gaze from her lips and looked deep into her hazel eyes. His balls tightened, and it grew difficult to breathe when he saw the desire there.

She wasn't trying to hide it. In fact, it was as if she wanted him to know. He gripped the door handle harder as he fought not to throw her over his shoulder and find the first bed he came to.

Ronnie deserved to be wooed, which meant he had to get himself under control. He might want her, but he refused to be a brute about it.

She inhaled, her chest rising as her breasts pushed against the material of the shirt. Yearning came off her in waves. It nearly broke through the control Arran had on his own passion.

He craved her. Desperately.

Her passion matched his, and he knew she wanted him as well. There was no one else watching them, no one to interfere.

She was the one who molded her body against his. Her head tilted up, the invitation clear in her hazel eyes. He wasn't about to ignore it.

With a groan, he slanted his mouth over hers. She wrapped her arms around him and parted her lips. Their tongues touched as he deepened the kiss until she was bent over his arms, her fingers threaded through his hair.

He maneuvered them inside the suite and turned so that he pressed her against the door. His body was engulfed with longing, with need stark and fierce.

Ronnie moaned as their kiss turned fiery, the desire no longer contained. Whatever restraint he had vanished when she came to him.

He was reaching for the pins in her hair, intent on seeing just how long it was, when his phone rang.

Ronnie chuckled as she ended the kiss. Arran put his hands on the door on either side of her head and squeezed his eyes closed. He wanted to toss the phone away, to pick her up in his arms and find the nearest bed. He'd shut out the world and everyone in it for a few private hours with her.

His phone rang again. It reminded him that he couldn't shut out the world, that there were dangers out there Ronnie needed protection from, and creatures that had to be stopped.

"What?" he answered brusquely.

There was a snicker before Ramsey said, "I didna interrupt anything, did I?"

A growl rumbled in Arran's chest. He didn't care that his words were clipped as he asked, "What do you want?"

"To see how things were going? Fallon tells me you're in Edinburgh with the pretty Dr. Reid. Are you her bodyguard or her date?"

Arran watched Ronnie walk around the suite inspecting things, and he caught sight of her kiss-swollen lips. "Both."

"As I figured." Ramsey's voice deepened as he grew more serious. "Listen, Arran, I wanted to give you a heads-up that Camdyn and Saffron are going to be there tonight."

"Did Saffron have a vision?"

"Nay. It's more of a precaution, with those creatures on the loose."

"And the new darkness that was spoken about in the prophecy."

"Aye. That as well. Gwynn has been searching, and there's nothing definitive that says Ronnie is the one spoken about in the prophecy."

"There are too many coincidences for it no' to be her," he whispered.

"Unfortunately, my friend, I agree. Until we know anything, we'll err on the side of caution."

Arran ran a hand through his hair and leaned back against the door. "I'm no' going to lie and say I'm angry Camdyn and Saffron will be here."

"That's what I figured after what happened with those new monsters out on the loose. And there's no update there, by the way. Logan had to physically remove Gwynn from the computer yesterday because she spent so much time searching. The fact nothing has been seen or heard has worried everyone."

"It worries me as well. Something isna right."

"Aye."

"What are they waiting on?"

Ramsey huffed. "I wish I knew."

"Any other news?" Arran asked, hoping they had either proved or disproved that another *drough* had taken Declan's place.

Ramsey's long pause was answer enough.

"What is it?" Arran demanded.

"Declan had an heir. It seems a distant cousin came into the wealth of the Wallaces."

"That doesna mean anything."

"Nay," Ramsey said. "We took all the books on magic from the house. Even if this Jason Wallace does have magic in his blood, he willna know what to do about it."

Arran pushed away from the door and walked into the living area to see Ronnie head into the room on the left. "A *drough* is a *drough,* Ramsey," he whispered. "We need to be sure."

"Already being done. Like most men of wealth, he'll have security cameras on the property. He's rebuilt the Wallace mansion, and from the specs, it's exactly the same. Gwynn is going to hack into the cameras on the property so we can see what's going on."

"She can no' do it all alone."

"Oh, she's no'. She's got Tara, Logan, and even Cara and Marcail helping her."

Arran smiled as he thought of Lucan's wife, Cara, and Quinn's wife, Marcail, helping hack into computers. Cara had been the first Druid at MacLeod Castle, over seven centuries earlier.

"I know," Ramsey said, though Arran hadn't spoken. "All Lucan and Quinn can do is watch as their wives become expert hackers."

Arran snorted. Ramsey was half Druid, and though that gave his powers as a god added strength, Arran always thought Ramsey could do more than he said, some of which had been proved when Ramsey killed Declan. "Admit it, old friend, your magic allows you to see me, does it no'?"

"Nay. I just know you too well. Besides, it's the look every-one at the castle wears while they watch Cara and Marcail. Now Reaghan and Sonya want to learn, no' that Galen or Broc will have any say. My Tara is picking things up a little too easily."

"I could be needed," came Tara's voice through the phone.

Ramsey laughed. "You're always needed, love. As much as what Gwynn does is illegal at times, it definitely comes in handy."

"I think I may want to learn more than I have," Arran admitted.

"I think all of us need to. We rely on Gwynn too much, and put too much on her. I've seen how anxious Logan is at the amount of time she spends on the computer."

After more small talk, Arran ended the call and walked to the door that led to his bedroom. He spotted the large bed and couldn't help but think of Ronnie in it with him. Her wheat hair spread around her, and her body bared to him.

He could just imagine pulling her shirt off and unhook-ing her bra. He'd unbutton her jeans next, then slide them over her hips before hooking his fingers in her knickers. It would be difficult, but he wouldn't cut her panties off with his claws.

No, he'd take his time and remove her pants and knickers while he kissed down those long legs of hers. Then he'd kiss back up them, over her hips and to her breasts.

"I have to go out."

He was pulled harshly out of his daydream by her voice, but it was the anxiety he heard in it that concerned him. He turned as she came back into the living area. "Out?"

"Yes. I need to find a dress, and hopefully if there's time, get some girl stuff done."

He frowned. So much for his hours of making love to her. "What is 'girl stuff'?"

"Hair. Nails. That kind of thing. I may not want to be here, but it isn't because I don't like dressing up. I don't get to do this often, so when I do, I take absolute full advantage of it," she said with a big grin.

"So you do like dressing up in the formal gowns and such?"

"Well. I hate the panty hose, and if I can help it, I don't wear them. The rest, yes, I love. I guess it's the little girl in me that still remembers dressing up and pretending I'm a princess." She giggled and then twirled around the room.

Arran grinned as he watched her. This was a different Ronnie, but one he liked just as much as the other. Here she was more carefree, more open.

She stopped spinning and pinned him with a look that didn't quite work because of her smile. "And if you tell anyone, I'll kill you. Or stab you, since you'll heal," she said with a laugh.

She reached for her purse and started for the door when Arran comprehended that she was going alone.

"Ronnie—"

"I'll be fine," she said as grabbed the door handle and turned to look at him. "The boutique I use for my dresses is three blocks away. The salon is another half block. But I warn you, I'll be gone most of the day."

"Then I'll see you at dinner?"

She opened the door and lowered her gaze. "Ah . . . not alone, I'm sorry. I'm supposed to meet Pete and another man from the Edinburgh museum. You can come, though."

Arran thought about joining them, but he realized he could do a lot of research in Edinburgh while he was there. After dinner, however, he planned to have his way with her. No more interruptions. "I'll be fine. Go have fun."

"I'll see you later, then," she said with another smile, and departed.

Arran looked around the suite once was she gone. It was going to be a long day. He left the suite and got directions from the Sheraton to the nearest computer store.

There he bought a laptop, but before he went back to the hotel, he had some things to see and do about the city.

Ronnie stared at her reflection clad in a body-hugging, strapless black dress. It was gorgeous, but Andy's words still haunted her. Maybe she should try something else besides black.

"Tabitha, how about another color?" she called from the dressing room.

The young owner of the boutique stuck her head of spiky blond hair with pink tips around the door, her dark eyes wide. "Really? You mean, you want color? Actual color?"

"Yes," Ronnie said with a laugh. "Why is that so odd?"

"You've never wanted to before. May I ask what's changed?"

A lot, but it wasn't as if Ronnie could tell her.

"Ah," Tabitha said. "A man."

Ronnie shrugged. "It's part of it, plus it's been brought to my attention that I always wear black."

"Everyone looks good in black, but I think color would be nice. I'll be right back."

Ronnie got out of the black dress and hung it up. Tabitha's shop was pricey, but she had an eye for simple, elegant designs that Ronnie preferred.

She'd never gone to another designer since finding Tabitha five years ago. Even when Ronnie was in another country, she'd call Tabitha up and have a dress shipped. Tabitha never failed to give Ronnie something that was perfect.

"How about this?" Tabitha asked as she walked in with a deep red dress that had an A-line skirt.

"I like it. Let's see."

For the next hour, Ronnie tried on gown after gown. There were many she liked, but she hadn't found the one she was looking for. Which was difficult since she didn't know what that dress might look like. Only that she'd know when she saw it.

After a light lunch, Tabitha brought Ronnie back into the

dressing room and said, "I have two more dresses I've put in the back. One isn't quite finished. I actually had you in mind when making it, but never thought you'd like it."

"Let me see them."

Excitement ran through her mostly because of the way Tabitha had spoken of the dresses. Somehow, Ronnie knew one of the dresses was going to be *the* one.

"Here's the first," Tabitha said, and brought in a hunter green gown with a plunging vee down the front.

Ronnie was quick to get into it. She loved the feel of it, but mostly she liked how it showed off her body. Her breasts weren't big, but the dress made them look bigger.

"I love it," Tabitha whispered happily. "But not as much as I think I'll love this on you."

Ronnie turned around and took one look at the gown. "That's it. That's the gown I want."

Tabitha beamed. "I knew it. Let's get you into it so I can finish hemming it for tomorrow night."

Once the gown was on, Ronnie reached behind her and let her hair down.

"My God, girl. You have no idea how beautiful you are, do you?" Tabitha asked, her voice full of awe. "Wear that glorious hair of yours down. No jewelry either."

Ronnie touched her trinity knot. "None?"

"None," Tabitha said, and pointedly looked at the necklace. "Especially not that. I do have some earrings that are just the thing to complement the gown. And the shoes. I've got those as well. I'm tempted to go to this thing and give you all my money just to see you."

"You already get all my money. It's fair I get yours," Ronnie said with a laugh.

But she looked in the mirror and saw someone different. With her hair down, and in the gown, Ronnie was the person she wanted Arran to see.

The one he wouldn't be able to take his eyes off of.

"He won't be able to," Tabitha said in agreement.

Ronnie hadn't even realized she'd said that out loud.

CHAPTER
TWENTY-ONE

Arran rubbed his eyes as he let himself back into the suite. He'd managed to discover some information about the magical items that had been taken from Edinburgh. Determining how much of the information was truth was going to be the problem.

He listened to the quiet of the suite and hated that Ronnie wasn't there. It wasn't like he could just barge in on her dinner.

"Well, I could," he said to himself with the beginnings of a grin.

He could, but Ronnie wouldn't be pleased. She was with Pete, and that had to be enough for Arran. As much as he loathed the thought, he had to accept it.

Arran turned and walked to his room, where he found a long bag hanging from the door of his closet. He flipped open the paper attached to find Saffron's note that said: *Hope you like it!*

He unzipped the bag and sighed as he looked at the black jacket and bow tie that hung from the hanger. The jacket was short and had a black vest to go underneath it and on top of the white shirt.

It wasn't until Arran removed the jacket, vest, and shirt that he saw the kilt. For the first time that evening, he truly smiled.

"It's no' a true kilt as I was hoping, Saffron, but this'll do, lass. This'll do."

He ran his fingers over the MacCarrick plaid and thought about his family, of his life before he'd become a Warrior. How simply he'd lived and loved.

Nothing had turned out as he'd expected, yet somehow fate had given him something larger than he could have imagined. It had given him a family with the others at Mac-Leod Castle. It had given him brothers and sisters, even if they weren't blood.

The bonds that held them all together were stronger than any other. They were bonds that could never be broken.

Arran reached for his phone to call Saffron and thank her when he got a text from a shop dealer that specialized in antiques. The old man had hardly been able to stand because he was so frail, and he hadn't wanted to talk to Arran at first.

But Arran managed to win over the old man's nephew with his knowledge. Now, the text from the nephew said the old man wanted to see him.

Arran glanced out his door to Ronnie's. He'd wanted to be here when she got back. All day he'd waited to take her in his arms and kiss her, and he wasn't going to let another opportunity pass. Not with a woman like Ronnie.

Yet the idea of discovering something regarding the items they'd found and what the monsters were was too important to pass up.

"Damn," Arran mumbled as he hastily answered the text, promising to be there in ten minutes.

Before he departed the suite, he left Ronnie a quick note letting her know where he was.

Ronnie was so tired, she could scarcely hold her eyes open, but when the elevator doors opened to her floor, excitement chased away her exhaustion. She stepped out of the elevator and lengthened her strides so that she was almost running to her door.

Arran awaited her. There was no way she was going to allow another night to pass without kissing him again.

And . . . if something else happened, she wasn't going to stop it.

All she'd thought about all evening was Arran. Pete had gotten irritated with her, but she couldn't help it. She should have invited Arran regardless of what the others thought.

Arran was . . . Well, she didn't know what Arran meant to her, only that she wanted him next to her. It wasn't just because she felt safe with him near. It was more than that. So much more.

Words couldn't begin to describe how he made her feel, what he made her dream of. His mere presence soothed her even as it scorched her with desire from the inside out. A smile from him could make her heart skip a beat.

And his touch . . . Well, she could forget everything when he touched her.

It took her three tries to get the key into the door to unlock it so she could enter. She was winded, a smile on her face as she let the door slam behind her and she walked into the living room.

"Arran?" she called.

The smile slipped when she saw the note on the table in front of her. She set down her purse next to the note and swallowed her disappointment. Then she went to take a long, hot bath. She started the water and kicked off her shoes before she grabbed a nightgown and a book she'd brought with her from the dig.

She loved reading, but there were many nights she didn't get to immerse herself between the pages of a good romance. The fact she was alone in such a beautiful suite without the man she'd been thinking of all evening made it a night perfect for a romance novel.

Ronnie removed her clothes and tested the water with her toe. She sighed as she stepped into the water and leaned back against the large tub. Steam drifted around her, and just as she'd hoped, her muscles began to relax.

She let herself unwind for a moment with her eyes closed and the water soothing her before she reached for the book.

* * *

Dale leaned against the lamppost and covertly watched the Warrior, Arran MacCarrick. He'd been following MacCarrick for over three hours.

The first thing MacCarrick had done was purchase a laptop. He'd then spent an hour at a café on the computer, but Dale couldn't get close enough to figure out what MacCarrick was doing.

After that, MacCarrick began visiting antique shops. Some he was hardly through the door before he would turn and leave. Others he would stay for several minutes.

Dale was able to see through most of the shops' windows, so he saw MacCarrick talking to the owners. What he was saying Dale didn't know, and that wasn't going to earn him any points with Jason.

"Bloody damned Wallace," he murmured as he thought about Jason.

He should have called Jason as soon as he realized what MacCarrick was doing, but Dale wasn't suicidal. He quite enjoyed the power and immortality he had.

Though he hadn't seen MacCarrick fight, he knew the Warrior was centuries older than he, which meant MacCarrick would probably kick his arse.

Jason would have Dale get closer to MacCarrick, and that would alert the Warrior he was being followed. So, for the time being, Dale was going to keep his distance.

He clenched his jaw as he saw MacCarrick exit the latest antiques shop and turn his way. There was nowhere for Dale to go, nothing he could do but stay absolutely still.

MacCarrick passed so close, their shoulders brushed. Dale kept his head down as MacCarrick mumbled an apology. Thankfully, a group of tourists was coming from the opposite direction, which would help Dale hide.

Since they were atop a hill, it was easy for Dale to keep his eyes on MacCarrick. Until MacCarrick turned a corner.

"Fuck," Dale muttered, and shoved his way through the tourists.

He kept a steady pace instead of running after his quarry.

The closer he got to MacCarrick, the better—but he had to be smart about it.

Dale caught sight of him four blocks later just as Mac-Carrick was entering another store. This time, Dale set up in the shadows of an alley. Warriors had amazing eyesight that allowed them to see even in the dark, but if MacCarrick didn't know to look, the chances were he wouldn't see Dale.

A few short minutes later, MacCarrick walked out of the store. He stood on the sidewalk for a moment and looked first one way and then the next before he turned to his left and continued walking.

Dale was tired of following him, but he had no choice. Jason would have his head—literally—if he didn't do as ordered.

He trailed MacCarrick for six blocks before turning left and heading toward Edinburgh Castle. Several times, Mac-Carrick stopped and looked at shop fronts, but he didn't go inside any more.

The climb was steep as they headed toward the castle, and the tourists in the area were standing in crowds of several dozen as they disembarked off tour buses.

Dale felt his fangs fill his mouth as one of the tourists, a man weighing at least three hundred pounds, ran into him. The tourist was trying in vain to make it up the hill.

In all the confusion, Dale lost sight of MacCarrick. After searching for almost fifteen minutes, Dale still couldn't locate him.

He was pulling out his phone to call Jason when he felt a tingle along his skin. Magic.

Dale smiled as he followed the trail of magic. That had to be where MacCarrick was, and even if it wasn't, Jason would want to know about this magic.

The trail of magic was faint, but Dale was still able to track it. And imagine his surprise when it led to yet another antiques store.

With none other than Arran MacCarrick inside.

Dale quickly dialed Jason's number.

"I hope you're calling because you found something," Jason said.

Dale flattened his lips, the urge to growl his irritation over-powering. "Of course."

"What is it?"

"I've been following MacCarrick."

"MacCarrick," Jason repeated. "Is he still at the dig site?"

"Nay."

Through the phone, Dale heard what sounded like Jason flipping through pages.

"My wonderful cousin Declan does have MacCarrick listed as one of the Warriors from MacLeod Castle but doesna have much on him. I hope you have more, Dale."

"I've been watching him go into antique stores all over Edinburgh. And I found a trace of magic."

Jason made a pleased sound. "I gather that's where Mac-Carrick is?"

"Aye. He's been in there awhile."

"I want to know what he's looking for. Find it, or doona bother coming back."

Dale gripped the phone so tightly, he heard it crack. "MacCarrick and Reid are staying in Edinburgh another night. There's some kind of event tonight."

"Then get in the event, Dale. Do I have to think of every-thing?"

"These Warriors are smart, Jason. If I get too close, I could compromise your plans."

Jason laughed. "If you compromise my plans, then I sug-gest you allow MacCarrick to kill you because if he does no', I guarantee what I have planned for you is much worse."

The call ended.

Dale stuffed the phone back into his pocket and fisted his hands. How he hated Jason sometimes. The bastard might have given him untold power along with immortality, but Jason also ruled him.

At least the Warriors at MacLeod Castle were free. Free to do whatever they wanted, whenever they wanted.

Was Dale's freedom worth immortality? He'd thought so at first, though it wasn't as if Jason gave him much of a choice. Dale's life hadn't been worth much to begin with.

Jason had given him a second chance, and with it a nice house he could live in when Jason allowed it. And Jason's money.

Dale flattened himself against the wall of a building, in the alley, as MacCarrick walked out of the store. He didn't look happy as he began walking back in the direction of his hotel.

For just a moment, Dale contemplated going into the store, but he could do that later. MacCarrick was after something, and eventually Dale would be led to it.

Until then, he'd keep following MacCarrick.

CHAPTER
TWENTY-TWO

Arran couldn't wait to tell Ronnie what he'd learned from the old man at the antiques store. Arran had known the man knew more than he was letting on, and the old man hadn't disappointed.

Unfortunately, getting the information had meant that Arran stayed out the entire night, listening to the old man's stories, going through any books at the store, and then doing more research.

But when Arran walked into the suite, it was to once more find it empty.

He saw her note, written on the back of his from the night before.

Arran—

Andy called late last night to let me know they had discovered more artifacts at the dig. It wasn't from the same section we'd been digging at, but another. I don't know how long I'll be gone, since I'm doing a video conference with him so I can see what's been found.

Pete is on his way back to the site to double-check everything for me so I can remain here. I hope to make it back by the time the fund-raiser begins. If not, I'll meet you at the party.

Ronnie

Arran tapped the table with his fingers for a moment. He was surprised Ronnie hadn't immediately returned to the dig site. Every find was important to her. Why, then, was she remaining in Edinburgh?

Did she need money that badly to fund her digs? If that was the case, maybe Arran could talk Saffron into giving a little more.

Arran wasn't completely destitute either. He had money aplenty, thanks to the others' setting up an account while he'd been leapfrogging through time. He'd give Ronnie money himself, if need be.

She hated the fund-raisers, and if she didn't have to go, then she could remain at her digs, where she wanted to be.

He ran a hand down his face. The only thing that had kept him going through the night was knowing Ronnie would be here waiting for him.

It was hours until the party. He had time to do more investigating on the creatures. Arran walked around a couch and sat down. Then he called Fallon.

"Are you no' supposed to be with the lovely Ronnie?" Fallon asked.

"Aye. She's doing some business. Listen, I think I might have found something regarding my newest enemies."

"Ah," Fallon said, drawing out the word. "The new creatures."

"Since I was in Edinburgh, I thought I'd do a wee bit of looking around to see what I could find. About four blocks from Edinburgh Castle is this tiny antiques shop. There was something about it that drew me in."

"Did you figure out what it was?"

"Magic," Arran answered. "It was faint, but it was coming from the shop. Once I was inside, I found what I'd felt. It was a chalice."

"A chalice?"

"A verra old chalice, and the magic wasna as strong as it should be. But that's no' the interesting part. The owner is an old man who doesna have many days left. His nephew runs the business, but the old man happened to be there when I walked in. I asked a couple of questions to see how much he knew."

"Was that wise, Arran?"

"I had a hunch, as Gwynn often says. As close as the shop is to the castle, and as old as the shop is, I suspect whoever owned it was around when the artifacts were taken from Edinburgh Castle."

"Did the man know anything?"

"He did, but he wouldna tell me at first. Later, they asked me to come back, and the old man admitted that the shop had been in the family for many generations. It's always passed down through the family."

Fallon chuckled. "So your hunch paid off."

"Aye. The monsters from the box, Fallon, they were no' created as Deirdre created the wyrran."

There was a pause before Fallon said, "I doona think that's good news."

"It gets worse. The creatures are called selmyr. The old man showed me a book from ancient Mesopotamia that speaks of these beings. They were greatly feared throughout the land."

"Shite."

Arran leaned back on the couch and looked at the ceiling. He hated to tell the rest, but they needed to be prepared. "They like to hunt other beings of magic. They feed off our blood. It's our blood that sustains them."

"And the humans?" Fallon asked.

"If they get in the way, the selmyr will kill them. If it's a Druid, they are in as much danger as us."

Fallon let out a long string of curses. "Magic against magic again. Can we stand against them? Can the Druids?"

"I know what the blood of those things felt like on my skin. I've also had the misfortune of having *drough* blood in me as well. The selmyr's is much, much worse, Fallon. And when they bit me, it was as if they were draining my god as well. My power diminished, even the sound of Memphaea weakened."

"And we have a massive signal of magic shouting

throughout the world in the form of Isla's shield. Fuck!" Fallon shouted.

Arran knew the frustration Fallon felt, because Arran had felt it, too. "No one will see the selmyr coming. They vanish like dust on the wind. In fact, that's how they travel."

"That helps," Fallon said softly. "But no' enough. We have to figure out something that will repel the effect of their blood. Especially if it just requires contact with our skin. At least with *drough* blood, it had to be inside us for it to hurt."

"The story I was told says that the selmyr were contained by a group of *mie*. Somehow they got the selmyr in the box. I doona know how, nor did the old man. But if it could be done once, it can be done again."

Fallon released a long breath. "That is good news at least. Did the old man say where the Druids were from? Maybe there are still some around?"

"He didna know. He and his nephew were going to do some more digging through their archives after I left. It appears that every member of his family who owned the shop cataloged every item that was brought in and where it came from as well as who bought it. But they also made note of any strange happenings of the time."

"You mean like the sightings of the wyrran last year."

"Aye." Arran laughed. "The old man had the nerve to ask me what I knew of the wyrran."

"What did you tell him?"

"The truth. They were created by a *drough* who wanted to rule the world. When he said the wyrran were mentioned four hundred years earlier, he asked if they were the same."

"I gather you told him the truth."

"I did. He isna afraid of magic, nor is his nephew. I've made us some friends, Fallon. If we ever need them, we simply need to go to them again."

"Good work. I'll have Gwynn and the others see what they can discover online about these selmyr. When will you and Ronnie return to the dig?"

"Tomorrow."

"And when will you return home?"

Arran looked out the window, considering his options. "That isna so simple."

"Nay, my friend, it never is when women are involved."

CHAPTER
TWENTY-THREE

Arran glanced around the ballroom and barely held in his exasperation. He ordered another whisky from the bar and looked down at the dark green, black, and yellow of his kilt. It hadn't been that long since he gave up his kilt for the modern clothes, but he'd missed it nonetheless.

It felt natural to be in a kilt again, even if it was only half a kilt as he thought of it.

"You look almost as good as me," said a voice beside Arran.

He turned to find Camdyn dressed just as he was and wearing a cocky smile. "What are you doing here?"

"We thought you could use a friend or two," Saffron said as she stood between them. She rose up on her toes and kissed Arran's cheek. "Besides, I haven't seen Ronnie in a while, and I wanted to visit."

"That's shite," Arran said, not hiding his grin. "You wanted to check up on me."

Camdyn shrugged. "That as well."

Arran ordered a French martini for Saffron and a whisky for Camdyn. "It's damned crowded."

Saffron sipped her martini as she looked around. "These things always are when the person is someone like Ronnie. Everyone knows if they invest their money with her, the payback is worth it. She always finds what she sets out for."

"Of course she does," Camdyn said with a wink.

"Speaking of these fund-raisers," Arran said as he turned toward them, leaning his forearm on the bar. "She hates these things. She is missing out on the dig because she has to be here. I'm going to be giving her some of my funds."

"And you think Saffron should give more, aye?" Camdyn asked, his brow raised.

Arran lifted one shoulder. "Is Ronnie no' more valuable in the field than at these parties?" He noticed how Saffron was looking at him with a small smile and a knowing look on her face. "What?" Arran asked.

"Nothing," Saffron said, and turned away.

They moved off to a corner near one of the opened glass doors that led to a balcony. Most of the men were in similar dress to Arran and Camdyn, but there were a few who opted for a "regular tux," as Saffron put it.

The women were dressed in an array of colors, though Saffron had chosen a midnight blue gown that Camdyn couldn't stop staring at.

Arran grinned as he watched them. It was obvious they were completely devoted to each other, but then, that was the way it was with all the couples at MacLeod Castle.

He'd never envied them. Arran thought his friends daft for adding more worry atop their lives by finding a woman. He hadn't understood it before, but he did now.

All too well.

As it was, he kept looking around the room for some sign of Ronnie. It was well past the time she was supposed to arrive. No one seemed worried though.

Food was being walked around on silver trays, and the liquor flowed freely. Music had filled the large room since Arran arrived, and many guests were already on the dance floor.

"Don't worry," Saffron said. "She'll be here. And Pete is with her."

"Nay, Pete went back to the dig to help Andy with their new finds."

"Still. She'll be all right, Arran."

At that moment, Arran felt something shift in the air, a fissure of magic that caressed him, enveloped him. Covered him. It caused his blood to sing and his cock to harden.

Ronnie.

He gripped his glass so tightly, he heard it crack. When he was able, he dragged in a rough breath. He knew exactly where she was by the wash of her magic. He hadn't realized how much he missed the feel of it until just then.

Slowly, his gaze moved to the stairs that descended into the ballroom. And the world fell away.

Ronnie dazzled in a dress of deep gold that hugged her body from her shoulders to her hips before it flowed freely and sensuously about her legs. It wasn't until she took her first step down the stairs that he noticed the slit in the gown that stopped high up on her thigh and kept giving him views of her toned left leg.

He grinned as he saw her hair was down and draped sophisticatedly over one shoulder. It had taken long enough, but he finally got to see all that amazing hair. It was longer than he'd expected, stopping just past her breast, brushing against the swell with each step until he was even harder, aching for her.

The man next to her was talking, but her eyes were scanning the ballroom. Until their gazes collided.

She smiled, her hazel eyes lighting up, and Arran forgot all about Saffron and Camdyn. He pushed between them and walked toward the stairs as Ronnie continued toward him.

He stopped, one foot on the bottom step while he held out his hand to her. She reached for him, her smile warm and welcoming, the desire palpable and profound. The gold of the dress made her hazel eyes appear brighter, and the black eyeliner and dark eye shadow gave her eyes a teasing, seductive spin that made his blood burn.

"My God, you're beautiful," he said. His fingers itched to drag the dress from her body, but he held himself in check.

There was a slight flush to her cheeks as she glanced down. "And I've never seen a more handsome man. You were made for a kilt, Arran MacCarrick. I always knew you were that ancient Highlander I pictured. You've proved it tonight."

He looked at the sheer, sparkling gold material that covered her shoulders and arms before it dipped between her breasts to show substantial cleavage. The gossamer material gave way to a sparkling concoction of silk that seemed to have been made specifically for Ronnie.

As tempting as the gown was, he found it near impossible not to touch her hair. It was long and thick, the color made more gold by her gown.

"I doona think I'm keen to share you with everyone," Arran whispered as he drew her down the last step.

"Don't tempt me to leave."

"Would it take much?"

"No," she admitted with a breathless laugh.

He loved how her hazel eyes crinkled in the corners when she laughed, but more than that, he loved the feel of her hand in his.

"Saffron and Camdyn are here."

Her eyes widened in surprise. "Where?"

Arran put his hand on her lower back to guide her and nearly swallowed his tongue when he touched warm, bare skin. He let her get a little ahead of him so he could look at the back of her gown.

It was clasped behind her neck in that same sheer material, but the rest of her back was completely bare until the material began again at her very shapely behind.

"Well?" she asked as she looked at him over her shoulder.

He hadn't noticed she stopped, since he'd been taking all of her in. He cleared his throat, trying to tamp down his out-of-control yearning. "The gown is beautiful, as you well know. But you make it a success."

She didn't have time to respond as Saffron and Camdyn joined them. Arran stood beside her as she chatted with Saffron. His gaze never left Ronnie's face.

"Careful. You just might find yourself a woman," Camdyn warned.

Arran grunted. He didn't bother to tell Camdyn he already had. "There's nothing wrong with admiring beauty."

"Nay. But the looks you give other men when they try to approach makes me think you've something else in mind."

"She doesna like being pawed. That's why she brought me."

It was Camdyn's turn to grunt. "That was an excuse. She wants you here as much as you want to be here. Denying what is developing is futile. Trust me. I know."

Arran heard the strings of a new song, and saw how Ronnie's eyes briefly closed in pleasure. For once, he was glad the women at MacLeod Castle had insisted he learn how to dance.

"Shall we?" he asked Ronnie as he held out his hand once more.

"Yes, please."

He walked her out onto the dance floor and took her in his arms. Arran looked down into her stunning face, flabbergasted that such a woman existed. And was with him.

He was used to seeing her without makeup, but what she wore now only added to her beauty instead of distracting from it. There were no jewels other than gold earrings that hung down from her ears with a single diamond on the end.

They moved easily with the music. He could see others looking at them out of the corners of his eyes, but he didn't care. For tonight, Ronnie was his.

He remembered all too well the feel of her against him, the taste of her kisses. And he wanted more of her. All of her.

The pulse at her throat was erratic, and her eyes had darkened as if she knew what he was thinking. The stayed on the floor as one song flowed into another.

"I could stay here all night," she murmured.

He moved her a fraction closer with a slight pull of his hand on her back. "Here?"

"With you."

"How long do you have to stay?"

She glanced away, regret lining her face. "I have to mingle with these people if I'm to get their money."

"And what if I told you you wouldna have to do this anymore? What if I told you the funds would always be there?"

Her gaze jerked back to him, surprise and concern in her depths. "From Saffron?"

"Some of it."

"You?" she asked softly. "Why, Arran?"

"Why no'? You doona want to be here. You want to be in the field."

"For the first time, I want to be here."

It took everything he had not to lift her in his arms and stride from the room. "Ronnie," he whispered.

Her lips parted. How easy it would be to bend down and take them. How desperately he wanted to do just that. But this was a party, and he wouldn't embarrass Ronnie in such a manner.

Even if it put him in pain too.

"I meant for us to spend yesterday and today together," she said.

"We have tonight."

He whirled her around the floor until she was laughing, her smile wide. Arran didn't care that men were looking at Ronnie with desire.

For tonight she was his, and he was hers.

Arran didn't want to think of the morrow or the days after. The night was about her, about making her smile and laugh. Of melding their bodies until he didn't know where he ended and she began.

After the dance, Arran escorted her back to Saffron and Camdyn, but she was soon bombarded with people coming up to her, wanting her to talk about her project and what she would do next.

He knew she needed to walk around the room, but she stayed beside him and let the people come to her. Most offered money to help fund her projects in the hopes their names might be attached to her next big find. Ronnie simply smiled and thanked them.

Occasionally he would take her back onto the floor so they could have some privacy. When a man tried to cut in on the dance, it only took one glare from Arran to send him away.

That seemed to make it clear to everyone else that she was off-limits.

Even as Arran fought against taking Ronnie from the party, he saw what a good time she was having. Her champagne glass was never empty, and when she wasn't talking to prospective funders, she was laughing with Saffron or smiling at him as they danced.

He wanted her to remember this night forever. But it wasn't just for her. It was for him as well. He hadn't admitted it to anyone, but Arran had hated this modern world he found himself in.

There were conveniences like hot running water and the indoor bathrooms, but it wasn't the same. He missed his time. He missed how simple and easy things had been. Now people didn't even look at each other on the street as they passed because they were busy on their mobiles.

But tonight he was more than happy he knew the music to which they danced and, more important how to hold Ronnie and spin her around the floor.

What else was he missing out on by trying to stay in the past?

The last dance ended, and for long moments Arran and Ronnie stayed just as they were. Their gazes were locked, the desire tangible, becoming a living, breathing thing between them.

Each time he held her, he wanted her more. His hunger was growing with every minute that passed. And he knew, deep in his soul, that once he was inside her, he would never have enough.

Ronnie was an extraordinary woman. She was unique, distinctive. Irreplaceable.

She was made for him. He knew it in the very depth of his being. He might not have wanted to find her, but here she was. And now that she was in his arms, he never wanted to let her go.

His hand moved from her back to her side. With the barest of touches, he ran his thumb beneath her breast. She sucked in a breath as her gaze darkened. Even that slight feel of her breast had his body raging out of control.

"Arran," she murmured, and touched his cheek.

The world fell away until it was just the two of them. He pulled her closer until their bodies were touching from shoulder to hips. The pulse at her throat beat rapidly, as rapidly as his heart.

He shifted them until he had one arm wrapped around her and his other was between them. Her lips parted on a sigh when his hand slid beneath her breast and held the weight of it.

In all his years, he'd never encountered a woman like Ronnie. She was beautiful, genuine, driven, and pure of heart. She touched him in ways he hadn't thought possible. With just a look, she had him enthralled, with just a smile, he was smitten.

The inconceivable hunger, the indescribable yearning he had for her couldn't be explained. And he didn't care. It was enough that she was in his arms.

The spell was shattered when someone said her name and touched her shoulder. Arran dropped his hand and moved to the side to allow her to say farewell to the guests.

"We're staying at the hotel," Saffron said as she walked up to him.

Camdyn clapped him on the shoulder. "Fallon filled us in on what you told him earlier. We're just down the hall from you and Ronnie, in case something happens."

"Nothing will happen," Arran said. "If the selmyr were here, we'd have known of it. At any rate, it's nice to have you near."

Camdyn smiled and pulled Saffron against him. "All you need to do is give a shout if you need me. I'll hear you."

And he would with his Warrior senses. Arran didn't think he'd have need of them. The night hadn't been marred by anyone or anything that would disturb Ronnie.

No selmyr, no *droughs*, no attacks from Warriors.

Maybe he had imagined there was a new evil when there

really wasn't. Maybe the prophecy hadn't been about Ronnie. That part of his life was over. He'd turn to locking the selmyr back up.

And Ronnie.

With her, he could almost enjoy the modern world. Because she made him happy.

CHAPTER
TWENTY-FOUR

"Ready to leave?" Arran asked.

Ronnie smiled and nodded. "Very. I can't feel my toes from standing in these shoes all evening. That's what I get from going from boots to stilettos."

Arran grinned, but when he saw her wince as she took a step, he wrapped an arm around her to support her. He was leading her to the stairs when he saw a man leaning against the wall. A man he was sure he recognized.

"What is it?" Ronnie asked when he pulled them to a stop.

A moment later, Camdyn and Saffron walked up.

"Arran?" Camdyn said, a small frown of worry marking his forehead.

Arran glanced at Ronnie. He wanted to take her up to the room and make slow, sweet love to her, but he couldn't do that until he was sure there was no threat. He had to keep her safe.

Saffron smiled and looped her arm through Ronnie's. "I don't know about you, girl, but I'm exhausted. Since the boys obviously need a moment, why don't we go up to our rooms?"

When Ronnie hesitated, Arran gave a nod. Once the women were up the stairs and in the lift, Camdyn stepped into his line of vision.

"Tell me," he demanded.

Arran nodded to the people passing by as he whispered, "The man leaning against the wall behind you. I saw him today."

Camdyn laughed and slapped him on the shoulder as if Arran had told him a joke. As a waiter passed by, Camdyn shifted positions and grabbed a glass of champagne.

He tilted the glass to his lips to act like he was taking a drink and asked, "The one with the shaved head and goatee?"

"The verra one."

"Where?" Camdyn asked.

"On the streets this afternoon. I ran into him."

Camdyn lowered the glass and sighed. "What are the odds he'd be here?"

"With us, I doona believe in coincidence. People with money, and lots of money, were invited. By the jeans and shirt he had on earlier, he has some money, but no' the kind that would get him invited here."

"Want me to question him?"

Arran flexed his hand. "I say we both question him."

"Oh, I like that idea."

Since the ballroom hadn't been cleared of everyone, they had to weave their way through people to reach the far wall. And by the time they got there, the man was gone.

"Damn," Arran said.

"We could go look for him if you think he poses a threat."

Arran thought of Ronnie waiting for him in their suite, of the need still coursing through his blood.

Of the desire he'd seen in her eyes.

He could spend all night searching Edinburgh for the man and still not find him.

"Or you could go up to Ronnie," Camdyn said. "We're used to having something to fight, and we do in the selmyr. But we also need to get used to the idea of there being no Deirdre or Declan with which to battle."

Arran rubbed his hand over his chin. "You're right. Go to your wife."

"And you to Ronnie."

"That was my plan," he said with a smile.

"There's something there. Doona deny it. Everyone saw it tonight."

Arran climbed the steps beside Camdyn. "I know she's nothing like other women I've met. She's . . . different."

"You're besotted. It happens."

"She's been hurt, Camdyn, and she's slow to trust. I doona want to spook her."

They reached the elevator, and Camdyn pressed the up button. "By the way she was staring at you tonight, I doona think you have much to worry about, my friend."

"I hope you're right," he said as they stepped on the lift.

Because Arran knew he couldn't have a life without Ronnie.

CHAPTER
TWENTY-FIVE

It only took two rings for Jason to answer the phone. "What?" he demanded.

Dale sighed and watched MacCarrick leave the fundraiser with another Warrior. "I've found a Druid."

"Have you?" Jason asked, his voice filled with curiosity. "Who?"

"You're no' going to believe it, but it's Dr. Reid."

"Interesting."

"She's a *mie*."

Jason laughed. "Brilliant. Bring her to me. No' only will we learn what was in the chamber she opened, but we can learn more about MacCarrick. And then, of course, we'll convert her to *drough*."

"MacCarrick got to her first. I doona know if she'll break so easily."

"Oh, she'll break, Dale. Leave that to me. Just get me the Druid. Oh, and I've got a surprise coming for you."

The call ended, and Dale put the phone away as he hurried out of the hotel. He didn't know what Jason's surprise was, but he hoped it was something to fight MacCarrick with.

Dale had a surprise of his own. Jason would be thrilled when he arrived with none other than Saffron.

* * *

Ronnie paced her room. She kicked off her shoes, but she'd done nothing else. Tonight had been like a dream. Arran had been the most handsome man there, and he'd never left her side. He was attentive, considerate, and listened raptly to anything she said.

In all, he was magnificently perfect.

She'd never known a man such as Arran existed, and now that she'd found him, she wondered if she could ever let him go. For the first time in her life, she'd felt like the princess she'd pretended to be as a young girl.

He'd danced with her again and again, his hold steady and secure. He'd made her smile and laugh, and if it was possible, she wanted him more than she had the day before.

There were so many sides of Arran. She'd seen his protective side tonight when he kept the men away from her. Some women might not like that, but she did.

She was able to enjoy herself like never before. She was able to talk about her digs, and all she had done as well as what she had planned next without worry of the men coming on to her.

For the first time since she'd been doing the events, she'd been at ease. It must have showed, too, because she'd raised more money than ever before.

What had kept Arran and Camdyn below? Saffron assured her everything would be all right, but Ronnie wasn't so certain. The muscles in Arran's arm had tightened beneath her hand a second before he'd stopped them.

He'd been on alert, every one of his senses trained on someone or something. It must not have been too dangerous or he wouldn't have let her out of his sight.

Ronnie smiled. Funny that she liked how protective he was. She'd been on her own for so long, she hadn't realized what she was missing. Until Arran.

There was no doubt he could get carried away with it, but she might like that just as much as the rest.

She sat on the bench in front of the bed and began to let her mind wander through the amazing night. It had been so easy being in his arms, as if they were meant to be.

The sound of the suite door opening and closing filtered through her bedroom door. Excitement ran through her as she opened her eyes and smiled. She rose and pressed her ear against her door as she tried to listen to what Arran was doing.

She could stay in her room and never take the next step. Never know if making love to him would be as glorious as she thought it could be. She'd never know how his hands felt on her body or the feel of his muscles beneath her hands.

It had made her dizzy with longing. There was even an instant when she'd thought he might kiss her in front of everyone.

And how she wished he would have.

She licked her lips and reached for the handle. Quietly she opened the door and saw Arran standing in the dark of the living room.

He had the glass doors to the balcony open, one hand leaning against the doorframe. The sheer curtains on either side of the door lifted in the evening breeze.

Arran had removed his jacket, bow tie, sporran, and belt. They were placed neatly on the table next to the couch. He stood against the outline of the night as if he belonged, as if he was something out of a Highland legend come to life.

Slowly, he turned his head and spotted her. Half his face was cast in shadows, but the lights from outside allowed her to see his crooked grin.

"Everything all right?" she asked.

"Aye. You?"

She walked toward him, her fingers grazing the back of one couch. He had known her indecision and had given her time. His voice said what his words wouldn't—that she would have to come to him.

"I'd say that was definitely a yes."

"So you had a good night?"

She swallowed, her mouth suddenly dry as she thought of the way he'd held her—firmly, confidently—as they danced. "I had a fabulous night, as you well know. Thank you."

He turned to face her, and she saw he'd unbuttoned his

shirt to expose a section of his tanned throat. He also held a glass in his other hand. She walked around the end table and then closed the distance between them.

Now that she was standing just a foot away from him in front of the open doors, the cool night breeze made her shiver. Until she looked into Arran's golden eyes.

"There's no need to thank me. I have to admit I had a good time as well," he said.

"You didn't think you would?"

He shrugged. "Nay, no' really. The women at MacLeod Castle taught me to dance. Well, me and the others who had traveled through time. I didna want to learn. Now, I'm verra glad I did."

"Me, too. I don't normally dance. Wait. Did you just say 'time-traveled'?"

He grinned. "Aye. I've been in this time just over a year. When Deirdre was pulled forward in time, the Druids helped a few of us do the same to track her."

"So many stories I want to hear. You lead an adventurous life."

"A dangerous one," he cautioned.

She leaned a shoulder against the doorframe. "Are you trying to frighten me off?"

"On the contrary, lass. I verra much want you in my life."

Her stomach jumped into her throat at his words, said in the deep husky brogue. "Do you?"

"Do you pretend no' to know what I want?"

Gone was any fear she had of what would happen with her and Arran. She'd asked for honesty, and that's what he was giving her. It was only fair that she give the same. "I know. I was afraid before."

"No' now?"

She shook her head and grinned. "Not now. Not anymore."

He lifted the short glass to his lips and sipped the amber liquid. "It's scotch whisky. This is from my favorite distillery, Dreagan. They've been around the longest here in Scotland, and make the smoothest whisky you'll ever drink."

"I haven't drunk whisky before."

"Would you like a taste?"

"Yes, I believe I would."

He was turning to the small table filled with liquor. And then, before Ronnie lost her nerve, she took the step separating them and kissed him.

Instantly his arm came around her, holding her securely against his firm body. His arm was like a band of steel, his hand splayed on her back. Ronnie forgot to breathe as she found herself plastered against the rock-hard chest she'd spent days gazing at and hours dreaming about.

His lips parted and his tongue swept into her mouth. The taste of the whisky was on his tongue, and only added to the heart-stopping kiss. He groaned and bent her over his arm. Just as before, Ronnie felt the world fading away. She was floating, gliding.

Soaring.

Dimly she heard a soft clink of glass on wood, and then Arran's other arm closed about her. He turned his head and deepened the kiss.

She might have initiated the kiss, but Arran had quickly taken over. No one had ever kissed her as he did. He wasn't just skilled—he knew exactly what to do to fan the flames of desire until they were spiraling out of control.

His large callused hand was warm as he spread his fingers over her bare lower back. One of his fingers dipped into the edge of her gown where it dropped into a vee just millimeters above her bottom cheeks.

"I love this gown on you," he said between kisses.

Ronnie dropped her head back as his mouth moved down to her neck. "I've never been this daring."

His head lifted so that he could look at her. "In the design of the gown or our kiss?"

"Both," she answered.

His smile was slow and seductive. "Just what I wanted to hear. I've hungered for you since our first kiss."

She clung to his shoulders, her chest rising and falling rapidly as she struggled to get her body under control. But then again, nothing was under control for her when Arran was around.

It was as if he knocked her off center, spun her inner compass in circles. The only thing that kept her upright and focused was him.

"I'm not going to stop you," she said when she realized he was giving her yet another out. "I want this. I want you."

His mouth took hers in a fierce, demanding kiss. It stole her breath, robbed her soul. And she was glad to give it. She'd give everything of herself because of who he was— the man who had wooed her, enticed her.

Seduced her.

She plunged her hands into his long, dark locks. His hair was cool and soft to the touch, and when she scraped her nails softly along his neck, he groaned deep in his chest.

It took her a moment to comprehend he had been backing her up while they kissed, steering her toward his room. Ronnie's heart was pounding with excitement and desire.

She didn't loosen her hold even when the back of her legs bumped against the bed. Arran lifted his head and locked eyes with hers.

His golden gaze smoldered with need. The sight made her stomach flip and her blood burn as it rushed through her body. She trembled, not from the cool air, but because she wanted him so desperately.

He sank his hands into her hair on either side of her head and slowly pulled them out, letting the strands fall between his fingers.

"You've no idea how long I've wanted to do that," he said. "Your hair is glorious."

"It gets in the way when I'm working."

He twirled a strand around his fingers. "Aye, but hair like this should be down, tempting me almost as much as your lips."

"My lips?" she repeated in surprise. What could be tempting about her lips?

"Oh, aye, your lips." He dropped her hair and ran the pad of his thumb along her lower lip. "Your lips tease me with smiles, scold me with that sharp tongue, and arouse me with their sweet taste. Your lips, dear Ronnie, are a temptation I can no' ignore."

"Then don't."

With one hand spread on her back, he leaned forward until she was falling back on the bed. His other hand caught them before she could hit, and he slowly lowered her to the mattress.

"It's no' just your lips that stir me," he whispered in that deep voice that made her quiver, his mouth hovering over hers.

"What else?"

Was her voice really that breathless, that soft? She shouldn't have been surprised. Arran produced all kinds of strange and exhilarating feelings in her. She wanted more. She wanted it to never end.

Which was impossible, since she was mortal and he immortal.

He kissed a spot where her ear met her jaw. "Have you no' guessed?"

"No." She was having trouble concentrating with his big body covering hers and his arousal pressed against her stomach.

"All of you, sweet lass. All of you."

His words, their truth and simplicity, made her want to cry. "Where have you been all my life?"

"I think I've been trying to find you," he whispered.

The words shattered whatever small hold she'd had on her heart to guard against him. With eight words he had taken her heart, and he didn't even know it.

This time when he kissed her, it was slow, rousing. She felt all his need, his yearning. His hunger.

And it matched her own.

He took her arms and moved them up over her head. His wonderful hands caressed her arms until he laced his fingers with hers, never breaking the arousing, soul-stirring kiss.

Ronnie loved the feel of him atop her. She ran her foot

along his bare calf, just now realizing he'd taken off his socks and shoes.

She gasped when he rocked his hips against hers. Her sex clenched in response. It had been so long for her, the need filling her, his kisses stimulating her.

Suddenly, he straddled her and rose up on his knees to jerk off his shirt. Ronnie smiled as she ran her hands from his narrow waist to the rippled sinew of his abdomen and then his muscular chest.

She'd wanted to do that from the first time she saw him shirtless. So many times she'd looked at those muscles, had felt them against her. But now, they were hers to touch, if only for the night.

He grabbed her arm and pulled her up so that he could kiss her. But Ronnie wasn't done touching him yet. She shoved against his shoulder until he fell sideways onto his back.

She lay atop him, and he drew up her gown so that it was her turn to straddle him. "I thought men with muscles like yours were just dumb brutes."

"We are," he said with a grin.

"No, you're so much more," she said as she leaned down and kissed his chest.

He cupped her face on either side and took her mouth in a savage, hungry kiss. Her nipples pebbled against her gown as they rubbed his chest. Her breasts felt swollen, full.

Ronnie clung to him as he sat up and scooted to the end of the bed, where he stood up and turned. Then tenderly set her down on the bed. He ended the kiss so he could kneel in front of her.

She shivered at the possessive, hungry look in his eyes because no man had ever gazed at her with such need. No man had ever looked at her as if she were the center of his world.

Until Arran.

Gently he hooked his thumb in the sheer material at her shoulders and tugged it down one arm before repeating the process on her other. Soon she was free of the gown from the waist up.

"My God," he murmured.

Ronnie's eyes rolled back in her head when he cupped her breasts and ran both thumbs over her aching nipples. Heat and desire ran straight through her body to pool between her legs.

And the night was just beginning.

CHAPTER
TWENTY-SIX

Arran couldn't look his fill of Ronnie, couldn't touch her enough. Her skin was warm and smooth as down. The soft sighs coming from her swollen lips only made him yearn for her more.

He massaged her breasts and watched her pale pink nipples harden. Already he had pushed himself to the limit by holding back with her, he wasn't sure how much longer that control would continue.

Her head rolled to the side, granting him access to her slender neck. Arran wasted no time in kissing along the column of her throat.

With a flick of his hand, he shed his kilt. He rose to his feet and leaned over Ronnie so that she was lying back on the bed.

"I want to see you," she whispered.

"We have all night. Right now, you're mine."

Arran slid his hand beneath her back as he straddled her. Then he gave a tug and scooted her up, and just as he'd hoped, her gown slid off her legs.

He let his gaze run down her body and spied the little strap of lace between her legs.

"I think, lass, you have too many clothes on."

She smiled, her eyes heavy-lidded and her lips swollen. "Don't you like my thong?"

"Thong?" he repeated slowly before turning her onto her side so he could see the strap of material disappear between the globes of her ass. His cock jumped at the sight.

"I take it you like it?" she asked with a knowing smile.

"Is that what you normally wear?"

"Yes." She rolled onto her back and watched him.

He tried to swallow. He'd never be able to look at her again without knowing about the thong. Which was her intention.

"How much do you like this . . . thong?" he asked.

She ran a hand down his chest, stopping just short of touching his hard, aching rod. "They're just panties"

"Good."

He held out a hand and let one white claw extend from his finger. She gasped, but there was no fear in her hazel eyes. Her gaze never wavered as she followed his hand down to her hip, where Arran slid the long claw beneath the material and sliced. With barely a pause, he repeated it on the other hip and watched the thong fall away.

Her hand was suddenly over his while one of her fingers ran along the top edge of his claw.

"Careful," he cautioned. His claws were sharp, and he didn't want to cut her.

Her eyes met his with determination and need, and what little restraint Arran had snapped. He kissed her hard and fast, his desire riding him relentlessly. Tenaciously.

Ruthlessly.

He held himself up by one elbow while his other hand ran down her body. Arran had gotten a look at her lithe form in the gold gown, but it was nothing like touching her.

He caressed down her side to the hollow of her waist, and then over the soft swell of her hips down to her toned legs.

Those gorgeous legs parted so that she was open to him, the pale gold curls hiding her sex from him. He cupped her, a growl sounding deep in his throat when he found her wet and ready for him.

Her fingers dug into his back as she sucked in a quick

breath. He watched her face and every emotion that passed over it. She held nothing back, kept nothing from him.

For the first time, Arran believed that a woman was giving all of herself to him. And something strange happened in his chest, almost as if something moved.

He thought no more about it as he delved a finger inside her. Her hips rocked against his hand. How he wanted to thrust inside her, to feel her walls hold him.

But Arran wasn't ready for this to be over anytime soon.

He held himself in check and leaned down to wrap his lips around a turgid nipple. His tongue swirled around the bud before he suckled.

A cry wrung from Ronnie's lips, her body stiffening for an instant before she arched her back. He smiled and moved to the other breast.

The way her body reacted to his every touch only made Arran want to give her more. He wanted her screaming his name, her body flushed and languid.

He kissed down her stomach and around her navel until his mouth hovered over her wheat-colored curls. He added a second finger to the one inside her and kept the slow pace of his fingers sliding in and out of her.

With a shift of his shoulders, he put them between her thighs that spread even more. He licked her slowly, sensuously.

Her hands fisted in the bedspread and her legs stiffened against him. But he was just beginning. He put his mouth against her sex and flicked his tongue back and forth over her clitoris.

The sound of her cries grew louder, longer, the more he continued to tease her. She said his name, her head moving from side to side.

He felt her body tightening, knew she was close. And just before the climax took her, he pulled back. She gave a frustrated cry that brought a smile to his lips.

A few seconds later, he resumed his teasing. He loved the taste of her in his mouth, loved the feel of her sex contracting around his fingers as he once more brought her to the brink.

It took no time at all to have her body trembling with need, her chest rising and falling rapidly. But this time he didn't stop.

Not when he felt her legs squeeze him. Not when her body stiffened. Not when her back arched off the bed.

A strangled cry tore from her throat as the walls of her sex clenched around his fingers. He pumped his hand faster as his tongue continued to lick.

He prolonged her climax until she was languid on the bed, her chest heaving. Only then did he rise over her, hooking one arm beneath her knee as he did.

Her eyes fluttered open and looked at him. She ran her hands up his arms and over his shoulders before pulling him down for a kiss.

Arran jerked when she wrapped her fingers around his cock and slowly caressed up and down the length. He groaned, rocking his hips in time with her rhythm.

He broke the kiss and clenched his jaw to keep from spilling. It would be so easy to give in, to let her take him there. But he held back. Somehow.

Her grip tightened a fraction, causing him to moan with pleasure. "Ronnie," he warned.

Only then did she guide him to her entrance. His chest tightened at the first feel of her hot, slick walls. She was incredibly tight, and he eased his way into her until she finally took all of him.

Her legs wrapped around his waist as her arms draped over his neck. He slowly pulled out of her and held himself still for a moment. And then he thrust hard inside her.

Her lips parted with a moan. He set up a steady pace, plunging faster and harder each time. Their eyes met, their bodies moving in harmony.

No words were needed. Everything was being said through touch, through their joining.

Suddenly, Ronnie's magic began to surround them. Arran might not be able to see it, but he could feel it through every inch of his body. It heightened his passion, driving him on-ward.

Ronnie clung to him as he propelled her higher and higher. The sound of skin meeting skin mixed with their harsh breathing. She couldn't look away from Arran, and didn't want to.

In his golden gaze was some deep, primordial emotion she couldn't quite name. In his every move he claimed her, body and soul.

And she eagerly, willingly gave it to him.

Sweat glistened along their bodies. She could feel her desire tensing low in her belly once more, winding tighter and tighter.

Arran's muscles bunched and shifted beneath her hands with each movement. Her skin felt too tight around her. Her nerves were stretched taut as she rose toward the climax.

As if Arran knew what was happening, he angled him-self so that his arousal drove deeper, harder into her body. He was ruthless, unrelenting in his drive to bring her plea-sure.

Her short nails dug into his skin as she felt the orgasm coming. There was no holding it back, no stopping it.

Just when she didn't think she could stand it anymore, she was swept away on a surge of bliss so profound, so in-tense, she was blinded by it.

She gripped Arran's arms in an attempt to hold on as the most powerful climax of her life ran through her body. It spun her, tossed her.

Consumed her.

And all the time, her gaze was locked with Arran's. That connected them deeper than before. As if the invisible bond between them strengthened, intensified.

And when he gave one final thrust as his orgasm took him, her breath rushed from her body at the emotion she saw swimming in his golden eyes.

Feelings, strong and powerful, flowed through her and around them. They were sealed in a cocoon of passionate sen-sation that would forever alter them.

As if their souls had been marked somehow.

After several minutes, Arran rolled to his side and wrapped his arms around her. She tried to comprehend what had just happened, but she couldn't find the words.

They stayed locked in each other's arms, content in the quiet of the room and the peace in their hearts.

CHAPTER
TWENTY-SEVEN

Arran looked at the ceiling as he ran his hands up and down Ronnie's back. They'd lain just as they were for over an hour, and he wasn't yet ready to move.

"Did it hurt when Deirdre unbound your god?" Ronnie asked quietly in the darkness.

He released a long breath. "Verra. It isna just the pain. It's the god itself. Suddenly you have another voice in your head, and his demands are difficult to ignore."

"But you did it."

"Aye, and for every Warrior who does, four more doesna. You have to be strong, no' just physically, but mentally, to take control of the god."

She rubbed her cheek against his chest. "It sounds risky."

"It is, but it isna like we had a choice. Deirdre didna give us one. One day we're men, and the next, we're Warriors."

"Are you sure Larena is the only female Warrior?"

Arran grinned. "Nay. But she has a goddess, no' a god."

"I'm surprised there aren't more goddesses."

"Hmm. I wouldna be surprised to learn that there are." Arran tucked a strand of hair behind her ear. "The goddess isna the only difference with Larena. We all turn a certain color, as I've told you, but with Larena, she turns almost iridescent."

"I want to meet her."

"I want you to meet her and the others."

"Aren't you afraid I'll tell someone about you?" she asked as she folded her hands on his chest and rested her chin on them.

"Nay."

"Very trusting of you," she said with a grin. "What does this mean for me, being a Druid?"

"It means you're special."

"I mean, I don't know the first thing about being a Druid."

"There's nothing to it. You already know what your magic is."

Ronnie laughed and ran her hand up his spine as he flipped her onto her back. "That I do. So that means you won't be leaving anytime soon?"

"Nay."

How one little word could make her so joyous, Ronnie didn't know—nor did she care. She'd been prepared, and afraid, for Arran to depart from her life.

"You thought I was leaving?"

She shrugged and lifted her head to kiss his shoulder.

"I'm no' done with you yet, Dr. Reid," he said with a heart-stopping smile. "No' nearly."

She groaned in need when she felt his hot, hard arousal against her. He smiled slyly before he kissed her.

His hand skimmed down her side as he ground his hips against her. She gasped as he suddenly flipped her onto her stomach.

Ronnie's eyes closed, her blood heating so that it sizzled as it flowed through her. Arran's breath was warm on her neck, an instant before he placed hot, wet kisses along her shoulder.

All thought halted. She couldn't think, couldn't do anything but feel Arran's hands and mouth on her body. His caress incited her, catapulted her into another world, a world where only the two of them existed.

He whispered her name, the sound its own caress as it sank into her skin and through her bones, into her very essence. In Arran's arms, she became the woman she had only ever dreamed she was.

Ronnie didn't stop the wanton from rising within her. She reached for it, embraced it.

Welcomed it.

Her breasts ached for his touch as he shifted and pulled her up on her knees. A deep fiery need pulsed within her. For Arran. For the passion he wrung from her.

From the yearning only he could quench.

Arran had never known anyone so passionate, so fervent in her lovemaking. The urgency within him to take her once more, to mark her as his, burned inside him.

It was all-consuming, this wild, untamed need to have her. It was a new experience for him. But one he couldn't turn back from.

He buried his face in her neck and inhaled the sweet scent of her hair as she pushed back against him.

With breaths coming in panting gasps, her body shook with need. He plunged inside her, her scalding wetness clutching him, holding him.

It was as if he hadn't just taken her an hour before. He realized then it wouldn't matter how many times he was with Ronnie—it would never be enough.

Her magic felt like bliss, but it was more than that. It was her. Her smile, her laughter, her tenacity, and her kind heart.

She had gotten into his psyche without him even knowing it. Or maybe he had known it, and didn't care. None of that mattered now, though. Not when she was in his arms.

Arran withdrew and thrust again. He drove into her deeper, harder, faster. Her soft cries only pushed him onward. He wanted to hear her scream her climax again.

He needed to feel her sheath clamping around him.

With his hands on her hips, he held her as he pounded into her relentlessly.

Ronnie couldn't breathe, couldn't move because of the desire coiling through her. She wanted to tell him to stop, to wait because she wasn't ready to peak yet, but Arran didn't give her a chance. He drove her higher, the passion consuming her.

With his name on her lips, Ronnie shattered.

Every sense had been crushed, every thought splintered. Into a blinding cascade of ecstasy.

Arran smiled when he felt Ronnie's climax. Her body had stiffened, and her scream had been glorious to his ears. The roar of his blood grew until release swept him. Once more finding the contentment in Ronnie's arms.

He pulled out of her and took her in his arms as he fell onto his back. She nestled against him, her eyes already closed.

Arran stayed awake long after she'd drifted off to sleep. He stared at the wall, his thoughts filled with Ronnie. He wasn't sure what was between them, but it was powerful.

Did he even want to know what it was? Because once he went down that road, there was no turning back.

He thought of Camdyn and Saffron and their baby girl. He thought of Fallon and Larena and their desire for a child. He thought of all his friends who had found love through their years of battle.

Arran had never expected to find anyone who suited him as Ronnie did. The intensity of his need for her frightened him.

But the thought of not having her in his life left him feeling ill. If he had his way, Ronnie would never leave. They were connected, joined.

Bonded.

Ronnie smiled as she came awake to the feel of Arran's hand on her breast, slowly rolling her nipple between his fingers. "What a way to be woken."

"I should let you sleep."

"I can sleep tomorrow," she whispered, and wrapped her arms around his neck.

His lips had just touched hers when he suddenly leapt off the bed. Ronnie pushed up on her elbows to find Arran standing on the side of the bed, his legs bent and his gaze focused on the living area.

"Arran?"

He held up a hand to stop her. Several tense minutes passed before Arran turned and motioned her toward him. She eagerly went to him, only to have him shove her behind him as he hastily dressed in a pair of jeans discarded on a nearby chair.

"We have company," he mouthed as he looked at her over his shoulder.

Ronnie's eyes jerked to the doorway as her ears strained to hear anything. She was looking down at her gold dress and torn panties when a shirt hit her in the chest.

She hastily slid Arran's tee over her head. A glance down showed that it barely covered her ass. But at least she wasn't naked.

Arran moved so that his mouth was by her ear. "We need to leave."

She frowned, hoping he understood she needed to know why.

"They're coming in through the window," he whispered. "We can no' stay."

In other words, he couldn't stay and fight because of her. If only she'd known she was a Druid before, maybe she could do some kind of magic to help him. Did Druids even do that?

Another question to ask Saffron.

"Stay behind me," Arran cautioned.

She still hadn't heard anything when, all of a sudden, a light green Warrior filled the doorway. Ronnie gasped as Arran growled, his skin instantly turning white as his claws sprouted.

The Warrior smiled at Arran, showing his fangs. Arran simply growled louder before letting out a loud whistle. Ronnie stepped backwards and ran into a chair.

With a glance at the chair, she moved around it and backed herself in the corner, and then slowly slid down to her haunches. Her heart was hammering sickeningly, her blood like ice in her veins.

Who was this Warrior, and what was he doing there? Obviously he wasn't a friend, which meant what exactly?

Ronnie bit back a scream as the Warrior attacked Arran. Or at least she thought he was attacking Arran. He only swiped his claws across Arran's chest and tried to run past him.

To her.

Arran didn't let him take one step before he wrapped his arms around the Warrior and pulled him to a stop. Arran let loose a loud roar and sank his claws in the Warrior.

The Warrior let out his own snarl and elbowed Arran in the face. He tried to repeat the move, but Arran ducked in time. Then, with his claws still sunk in the Warrior's abdomen, Arran jerked his hand upward.

The bellow from the Warrior made Ronnie cover her ears. Arran continued to move his claws around. To a mortal, it would have been fatal, but to a Warrior, the damage was minimal since they healed so quickly.

Ronnie looked around the room for some kind of weapon, but there was nothing. Her only defense was Arran.

There was a loud crash as the Warrior propelled them backwards and slammed Arran into a small table. Wood splintered, and the lamp toppled to the floor.

The two continued to wrestle as the Warrior tried to dislodge Arran. Finally, he succeeded and turned to face Arran.

The light green Warrior had blood running down his chest while it covered Arran's hands and arms and splattered his body. And by the looks of things, the fight was far from over.

Ronnie could only watch in fascination as the two attacked at the same time, their bodies slamming into each other. The sound of claws sinking into flesh was overshadowed by the growls.

It was hard to determine who was winning. Several times Arran got the upper hand, and then the Warrior would get in a good move.

Ronnie wondered if she could get to the living room so she could get Camdyn when a loud boom sounded from the entrance of the suite.

A moment later and Camdyn filled the doorway, his Warrior skin a deep brown the color of the soil. It took barely a moment for the light green Warrior to realize he was outnumbered.

Arran tried to hold him, but desperation made the Warrior have the advantage for a brief second. That second was all it took for him to get free of Arran and run toward the window.

Ronnie heard Arran's shout and covered her face a millisecond before the Warrior crashed into the window and glass went flying.

"Ronnie? Are you hurt?" Arran asked, his hands gentle as they touched her.

She lowered her arms and looked at the window. "What happened?"

"I scared him," Camdyn said, his tone dead serious.

Arran nodded. "Aye. He had no intentions of leaving until Camdyn arrived. Apparently, the bastard had no idea I wasna alone."

Ronnie looked at Camdyn to find his Warrior form gone, as was Arran's. Thankfully, all of Arran's wounds were healed. She looked around the room and saw the destruction and the claw marks along the wall and even scouring the sheets on the bed they'd just been in.

"We need to go," Arran said as he scooped her up in his arms. He looked at Camdyn. "He was after her."

"Get Ronnie out of here. Saffron and I will gather your belongings and bring them," Camdyn said as he followed Arran.

Arran set Ronnie in her room. "Can you be ready to leave in two minutes?"

She nodded numbly, and then turned to grab some clothes. As she dressed, she could hear Camdyn and Arran discussing something in mumbled tones, but she couldn't make out what it was.

"We're going back to the dig site," Arran said when he returned to her room.

He'd put on a shirt and shoes as well as cleaned the blood from himself. She slid her feet into her boots and grabbed her purse.

"I'm ready."

"I still think you should go to the castle," Camdyn said.

Arran took Ronnie's hand and walked her to the door. "We are, but first we need to see if there's anything else in the chamber about the selmyr."

She looked at him. "The what?"

"The monsters from the box."

"Look, I've never been attacked like that, Arran. I don't even know what he wants, but—"

"I do," Arran interrupted her. "It's the same man I saw at the fund-raiser that I saw earlier in the day. He felt your magic, Ronnie. That's why he wants you. And if he's coming for you, that means there's someone out there searching for Druids."

Camdyn sighed. "He's no' a Warrior we've seen, which means you were right, Arran. The evil isna gone."

"And Druids are in danger again," Arran said with a nod.

Ronnie rubbed her temple over her right eye. "You're making my head hurt. Should I be afraid?"

"Aye," they said in unison.

Ronnie rolled her eyes. "Great. I'm not ready to die."

"I willna allow that to happen," Arran promised.

Camdyn crossed his arms over his chest. "Then tell me why the dig site versus a castle no one stands a chance of getting to."

Arran looked from Camdyn to Ronnie. "Because we willna be alone. Camdyn, call Fallon and the others. I want the site surrounded by Warriors by the time we arrive. Keep them hidden, though."

"And Druids?" Camdyn asked.

"Nay. Whoever is after Ronnie will sense their magic. It's better to keep it to just the Warriors."

Camdyn's lips twisted in a frown. "Now I have to tell my wife that."

"Tell me what?" Saffron asked from the doorway.

"What the hell are you doing here?" Camdyn demanded as he went to her.

Saffron opened her mouth to answer when Ronnie saw her eyes go milky and begin to swirl. Camdyn cursed and caught Saffron before she fell as she tipped sideways.

A few moments later, Saffron blinked her eyes, once more the tawny hue Ronnie knew.

"What did you see?" Arran asked.

Saffron looked at Camdyn, her eyes sad, before she turned to Ronnie and Arran. "I saw Declan's mansion."

CHAPTER
TWENTY-EIGHT

Ronnie was still reeling from watching Saffron have a vision. She hadn't had time to process what Saffron said when the sound of glass shattering made her duck and cover her head with both arms.

It was as if time slowed to a crawl. Ronnie turned her head to see Arran and Camdyn release their gods at the same instant. Arran's roar was long and loud, his gaze intent on something behind her.

And Ronnie had a feeling she knew who it was.

The pale green Warrior.

Arran put his hand on her shoulder, his claws careful never to touch her, and gave her a slight shove to put her behind him. That shove sent her toppling over, but she didn't take her eyes off him.

Camdyn and Arran stood like a wall between her and Saffron and the Warrior. Ronnie barely felt Saffron grab her hand she was so focused on Arran.

"We have to leave!" Saffron shouted.

Ronnie knew Arran could be killed, and even though the intruder was outnumbered, the fact he had returned didn't bode well.

In the next instant, two more Warriors joined the pale green one.

Ronnie's stomach fell to her feet like lead as the tables

turned on Arran and Camdyn. But neither man seemed affected by the shifting odds.

Arran took a deep breath, his chest expanding while his gaze was riveted on the Warriors. His hands flexed, and his knees bent slightly.

Ronnie saw how Arran's weight was evenly distributed so he could move in any direction in a split second. Camdyn's stance was much the same.

Unlike the other three Warriors, who stood straight, amusement in their eyes. Even Ronnie, newly initiated into this world of magic, could tell these three Warriors weren't battle-hardened.

That was the difference between Arran and Camdyn—who had battled for hundreds of years—and newly made Warriors. Still, Ronnie couldn't help her fear that somehow Arran might be killed despite his prowess and superiority.

Saffron was still trying to get her out of the suite when the Warriors attacked Arran and Camdyn. Ronnie wasn't surprised when Arran shifted to keep the fight as far from her as possible.

"Ronnie! Move!" Saffron yelled.

Ronnie ducked in time as a vase careened toward her. It jerked her out of her trance. She turned to Saffron and nodded.

They both got to their feet and pivoted to the door to find another Warrior. He smirked menacingly as he took a step toward them.

Before the Warrior had finished that step, he gasped, blood bubbling through his lips. Ronnie's eyes widened as she saw a copper-colored hand punch through the Warrior from behind, to emerge holding a heart.

Ronnie watched the Warrior topple to the floor. Her gaze moved to the man who had saved them. By the dark copper of his skin, he was obviously a Warrior. However, he also had thick copper-colored horns protruding from his head near his temples and curling around to his forehead.

But whose side was he on?

"Charon, thank God," Saffron said with a sigh.

Charon tossed aside the heart and stepped over the fallen Warrior to sever his head. He stood, his dark hair held back in a queue, and glanced inside the suite.

"Help them," Ronnie urged him.

Charon took a step inside the suite. Arran happened to turn in their direction. He locked eyes with Charon and barked, "Get them out now!"

Charon didn't need to be told twice. Saffron was already running toward the elevator when Charon took Ronnie's arm and pulled her behind him.

Ronnie looked over her shoulder, the suite growing more distant with every step she took.

"He'll be fine," Charon told her as he looked in the elevator when the door opened, and then promptly shoved her inside.

Ronnie moved to the back while Charon stood before the doors like a sentry. He had tamped down his god, but that didn't hide his threatening demeanor or the warning in his dark eyes.

"How did you know?" Saffron asked.

Charon didn't even look at her as he said, "Camdyn asked that I stay near just in case. No' long after his call, I got one from Arran."

"Arran called you?" Saffron asked, disbelief written on her face.

Charon gave a single nod.

"We can't leave them," Ronnie said, uncaring—for the moment—why Saffron seemed so surprised that Arran had called this new Warrior. "They need help."

Charon chuckled. "Nay, Druid, they do no'. They'll be fine."

The elevator dinged, and the door opened to the lobby of the hotel. Police were swarming inside while everyone else rushed out of the hotel. No one noticed the three of them as Charon ushered them out through a side door of the hotel and into an alley.

Ronnie walked on wooden legs. Outside she could hear

the roars of the Warriors. Was it Arran? Had he gotten the upper hand? She stopped and looked up at the hotel.

"He'll be all right," Charon said tenderly. "Now that he knows you're safe, he'll be able to do what he must."

Ronnie looked into Charon's brown eyes. The kindness and intelligence gave her a measure of assurance she needed to go on without Arran. "And what is it that he needs to do exactly?"

"Kill the bastards," he answered with a sly smile.

Ronnie nodded, perfectly in tune with Charon's assessment. She turned to the sleek black Mercedes CLS two-door to find Charon had already moved the driver's seat and was waiting for her to climb in.

It wasn't until they were all in the car and Charon drove away that her hands began to shake. Adrenaline was playing havoc with her body.

Ronnie leaned her head back and closed her eyes. Which was a dreadful mistake, since she kept seeing the pale green Warrior attack Arran.

"Where are we going?" Ronnie asked a short time later, once her heart had stopped pounding.

Charon looked at her through the rearview mirror. "I have explicit instructions to get you to the dig site. No detours or stops allowed."

"Arran's orders?" Saffron asked.

"Oh, aye," Charon said dryly.

Arran made sure Charon had Ronnie and Saffron in the lift, and then he and Camdyn let loose the rage and violence they had been holding back.

He wanted to kill all three Warriors, but the smart thing to do would be to keep at least one alive so they could get some answers.

Arran was battling two. He ducked a claw, only to release a bellow of pain as the second Warrior sank his claws into Arran's sides.

He elbowed the Warrior to try to get free while the first

growled as he lifted his hand again and readied to take Arran's head.

"No!" someone shouted.

Arran caught a glimpse of Camdyn standing over the decapitated body of his opponent. He and Camdyn shared a smile.

"What are you smiling about?" the Warrior who had his claws in Arran asked.

Arran propelled them backwards until the Warrior crashed through the wall that separated the living room from Ronnie's bedroom. With the Warrior dazed, Arran jumped up and faced his adversary.

"I'm smiling because you lost the moment you tried to attack us."

The Warrior attempted to rise, but Arran rammed him against the far wall and put his claws to his throat. "Twitch wrong, and I'll take your head."

"Dale!" the Warrior yelled to the light green Warrior.

It took only a glance to see that Camdyn was gaining the upper hand with Dale, but as soon as Dale saw Arran had his comrade, he leapt out the window.

"Seems like Dale isna going to help you," Arran said.

Camdyn kicked a part of the broken couch out of his way as he stormed to the Warrior. "The only way to save yourself is to tell us what we want to know."

The Warrior looked from Arran to Camdyn and back to Arran. "I'm newly made."

"Aye, that's obvious," Arran said flatly.

The Warrior flinched at Arran's claws at his throat and swallowed. "What do you want to know? Ask, and I'll tell you."

"Who sent you?" Camdyn asked.

The Warrior shook his head. "Ask anything but that."

"That's what we want to know," Arran said. "Tell us, or we kill you."

"I tell you, and I die," the Warrior said.

Camdyn frowned. "How newly made are you?"

"A few weeks."

Arran looked at Camdyn and jerked his head back to the Warrior. "A few weeks? And you have control of your god?"

The Warrior's forehead furrowed deeply. "I doona know what you mean. The god inside me has never tried to gain control."

"Fuck," Camdyn ground out, and punched the wall, his hand sinking through the plaster.

Arran leaned close to the Warrior. "I doona know who it was that released your god, but I'll find out. Make it easy on yourself and tell me."

"I can no'."

"Then tell me why you were after Ronnie."

The Warrior shrugged and leaned his head back against the wall to try to get away from Arran's claws. "Dale is our leader. He knows why. I was simply told to attack and kill you."

Camdyn crossed his arms over his chest. "Why? Why come after us?"

"This one," the Warrior said, and jerked his chin to Arran, "has been followed for some time. They've been at the dig site, watching."

"So you know of the magic there?" Arran asked.

The Warrior nodded. "We do."

"So you want what's there." Arran made a sound in the back of his throat and shook his head. "Did you think you could just walk in and take it?"

"After Ronnie was ours and you were dead, aye."

"You didna count on me though, did you?" Camdyn asked.

The Warrior's lips flattened. "Nay."

"Dale failed in his mission," Arran said. "I doona think your leader will be pleased. Tell me, will they kill you if we let you go? After you've given us all this information?"

The Warrior glanced at Camdyn but didn't utter a word.

Arran didn't give up though. "How much trouble has this master of yours gone to in finding and creating Warriors? A lot, I would think."

"How many new Warriors have been created?" Camdyn asked.

"None of that should matter to you," the Warrior said with a satisfied smile.

Arran shared a look with Camdyn right as he saw the red laser dot on Camdyn's chest. "Duck!" Arran shouted as bullets began to fly.

He jumped sideways, stretching himself out horizontally as he dived for the door. A bullet grazed his thigh and another slammed into the wood near his head.

Arran landed hard on his side and quickly rolled behind a chair that was barely standing. Camdyn crawled out of the room on one arm while the other gripped his forearm and blood seeped through his fingers.

"Shite," Arran murmured.

The bullets had yet to stop, and at this rate it was simply a matter of time before he got hit. And by the pallor of Camdyn's skin, those bullets were the hated X90s—bullets filled with *drough* blood, which Declan had used against them.

Arran reached for his phone in his back pocket to find it busted from the fight. He showed the phone to Camdyn, who had managed to find shelter behind the portion of couch he had kicked earlier.

Camdyn shrugged, letting Arran know he didn't have his phone either. With no way to call for backup, they were well and truly screwed.

Arran thought of Ronnie, of how sweet she had tasted, how wonderful she had felt in his arms. How *right* it was to be with her.

He wanted more of her, needed more of her. He hadn't realized how much he longed for her until she came into his life.

There was no way he was going to die now. Not after just finding her.

"I've got an idea!" he hollered to Camdyn over the bullets ricocheting around the room, and looked at the open window.

Camdyn shook his head. "You'll be hit before you make it."

Maybe, but it was a chance Arran was going to have to take. At least Ronnie was safe now. Regardless of what happened to him, Ronnie would always be safe. His brethren would see to that.

Arran shifted so that he was squatting, his hands on the floor keeping him steady. The men atop the building across the street stopped to reload.

He measured the distance from the window to the roof. It was going to be close, but all he had to do was time it perfectly.

Arran waited until the next round of bullets paused as the men reloaded again. And then he stood up. Using all the speed and power of his god, he ran to the open window and leapt across the wide street to land atop the roof where the men were.

He landed and rolled before he come to his feet with a little slide. Then he turned to the men. "You missed."

CHAPTER
TWENTY-NINE

Ronnie woke up just as Charon pulled to a stop at the dig site. She rubbed her eyes, wincing at the sandpaper feel as she did so.

"You need to rest," Saffron told her.

Ronnie sat up so she was leaning between the two front seats. "What time is it?"

"Six in the morning," Charon answered.

She leaned her forehead on the seat back. "I've already missed two days from work. Not to mention some artifacts were found yesterday, so I need to get in there."

"You won't be doing anyone any good if you fall asleep on your feet," Saffron said.

Ronnie smiled as she looked at Saffron. "That's what I've always loved about you. You tell it like it is."

"It's a trait that has to grow on people."

They shared a laugh as Charon sat with his hands on the steering wheel, looking around the site with the same meticulous gaze that reminded her of Arran.

"There is so much magic here I can no' tell if it's Druids or something else," he said.

"Arran said the same thing," Ronnie said. Her smile slipped at the thought of him. "When will he get here?"

Saffron covered Ronnie's hand with hers. "As soon as he can. He was parted from you only for your safety."

Charon opened his door and stepped out of the car, unfurling his tall body clad in jeans and a dark blood-covered tee. He helped Ronnie out but didn't release her hand when she began to walk away.

"You willna see us, but we'll be here," he whispered.

"Thank you. For getting us out of there . . . and for this."

He gave a nod, and then got back in the car. Saffron waved at her before Charon drove them away.

Ronnie watched them, unsure what to do. She should go back to work, but how could she concentrate on anything if her mind was filled with worry for Arran?

Then there was the knowledge that someone wanted her. "The new darkness," she murmured. Without a doubt, she knew that's who was after her.

Did this new darkness know that she had let loose the monsters? Or was there another reason the evil wanted her?

Did it really matter? Evil was evil, and no matter the reason, she refused to side with it. Arran had told her he didn't believe she would bring about the destruction of their world.

She would hold that in her heart and carry it with her in the dark times. For she knew dark times were coming. They had already arrived.

Right on the heels of the best night of her life. It was cruel, but fate was rarely kind.

Saffron believed Arran and Camdyn would make it out alive, as did Charon. Ronnie had no other recourse than to believe the same. If she didn't, if she allowed herself to think that he was gone, she wouldn't be able to face the day.

"There you are," Andy said as he walked up and hugged her. "We missed you. How was the fund-raiser?"

Ronnie forced a shaky smile as she thought of the event and how she'd spent it in Arran's arms. It had been a night of magic, a night to be cherished. "Wonderful."

"Wonderful?" Andy repeated as he looked at her suspiciously. "That didn't happen to have anything to do with Mr. Tall, Dark, and Dangerous, did it?"

Ronnie allowed him to lead her to her tent. She knew Andy realized something was wrong, but he kept her talking, kept her thinking of anything other than what was wrong. "It might have. All right, it definitely did."

Andy let out a whoop and pumped his fist in the air. "About damn time. You deserve someone good, Ronnie."

She nodded, because he was right. She did deserve Arran. "We received several donations, too. So it looks like we'll be digging at least five more years."

Andy lifted her tent flap and smiled. "It's Christmas and my birthday all come early. That's awesome news."

"It is." She stood in her tent and looked around. It seemed so barren without Arran. All the reasons to smile went out the door. She couldn't pretend she was fine, couldn't feign happiness when all she could do was worry whether Arran was alive.

"Then tell me why you seem so sad? And where the hell is Arran?"

How she wanted to tell Andy everything, every amazing, scary detail. Instead, she faced her friend and said, "He'll be along soon. He had some business in Edinburgh that held him there for a bit."

Andy's gaze probed hers. "There's more to this story you aren't telling me."

Ronnie didn't deny or agree.

After a moment Andy said, "Just tell me if he's really coming back."

Ronnie blinked away tears. "Yes, he's coming back."

"Good. I was thinking I might have to unload a can of Andy whup-ass on him."

She laughed along with Andy, but she knew he was deadly serious. That's what family did for each other. He was her family, just as Pete was.

How she hated lying to them, but the deception was for their safety.

She took a deep breath and realized she had two choices. She could sit on her cot, catatonic until she heard from Arran, or she could dive into work to help pass the dreadfully long hours she knew were ahead.

Ronnie pulled back her hair and wound it into a bun before placing a couple of pins to hold it in place. Her body was sore from the incredible lovemaking she'd experienced at Arran's loving hands.

The soreness made her miss him all the more. There was an ache in her chest that would only be filled when she saw him again.

"Show me what was dug up yesterday. Seeing it on the screen was one thing. I need to hold it."

Andy ducked out of her tent and said, "I've already started to get everything logged and categorized, just as you like it."

"Good."

She followed him to where several long tables had been covered with white material and set under a specialized tent with four sides, all of which could be rolled up as necessary.

Ronnie was impressed with how Andy had gotten everything going. "Great job, Andy. You're one of the few I can trust."

"Anything for you," he said with a wink.

She ran her hand over a piece of rock about the size of a sheet of paper that looked as if it had been broken off a larger piece. The knotwork was extraordinary as it interlaced around the edges.

It reminded her—eerily—of the prophecy she had found in the chamber: *The female Druid will be the bringer of doom. Only to be ended by a man-god.*

She was the bringer of doom. Those ash-colored monsters weren't just hideous, they were lethal and quick.

"Pretty, isn't it?" Andy asked regarding the rock.

Ronnie pulled herself from her thoughts. "I'd love to see the rest of this."

"We all would," Andy said. "I'd hoped to find it already, but we haven't."

"It's all right," she said, and straightened from the table. "It gives me something to do today."

Ronnie let her gaze look over the pieces on the table one

more time before she headed out to the dig. She couldn't be idle, not now. Not today.

Arran found a mobile phone from one of the dead men at his feet and called Fallon. Fallon teleported to the hotel room and got Camdyn out right as the police came charging into the room from the opposite roof.

Arran kept to the shadows on the rooftop and watched the police while they looked through the room. Ronnie's stuff was still in there, and the room had been in her name, so they would be contacting her.

Unless someone spoke to them first.

He waited until the police had their backs to him, and then Arran jumped across the distance to the hotel, landing quietly on the balcony. He hurried to sit down, his back against the wall and his eyes closed.

It didn't take long for the police to find him. He opened his eyes, making sure he looked dazed for their benefit.

"What happened, sir?" someone asked.

He looked around. "We were attacked. Tell me Ronnie got out of here all right?"

The police began to talk amongst themselves, and it wasn't but a moment later that they came back to him.

"The only people here are men. Why did they attack you?"

"They thought she had the money on her," he lied. "The fund-raiser, it was for Ronnie. Dr. Veronica Reid."

"Ah," one of the men said. "I've read about her. She's an archeologist, and a damned fine one at that."

"So, the men thought you had the money she raised from the event?" another asked.

Arran dutifully nodded his head. He let one claw lengthen to slice his side. Blood spilled through his fingers. "I'm hurt. Can I get to hospital, please?"

"We have someone who needs medical attention!" one of the police shouted.

The next thing Arran knew, Ramsey and Galen were beside him.

"It's all right," Galen told the police. "We'll take our friend to hospital."

Arran clenched his jaw. "I need Ronnie's necklace first."

"Already swiped it," Ramsey whispered.

"Good. Now we need to find the bastards who did this."

The three exchanged looks, and just as Arran was about to get to his feet, a man took a step toward them.

"We need to find Dr. Reid," a policeman said.

Galan clapped the policeman on the shoulder and exerted his power to control minds. "She's with us. She got out and called us to help."

Arran was pulled to his feet and they rushed out of the suite.

"Are you really injured?" Ramsey whispered.

"Nay," Arran answered. "It was for show."

As soon as they were in the lift, Galen tossed a backpack at Arran. Arran caught it and quickly shed his blood-soaked clothes for new ones. He wiped the blood from his face, arms, and hair with a damp towel.

By the time the lift opened on the ground floor, all evidence of an attack had been erased from Arran and stuffed into the backpack he now carried.

"Is Ronnie safe?" he asked as they walked through the lobby.

"Charon just delivered her to the site," Ramsey said.

"And Camdyn?"

Galen punched open the hotel door harder than was needed. "Sonya is still healing him, as far as I know."

Arran didn't say more until they rounded the corner into an alley and he spotted Fallon. "Camdyn?"

"Going to be fine. The X90 didna penetrate his skin far," Fallon said. "What happened, Arran?"

"There were Warriors."

Ramsey raked a hand down his face. "That's what Camdyn said. Three of them?"

"Four," Arran corrected. "The first was the same man I saw yesterday as I walked the city, and then I saw him again at the event. Before I could question him, he was gone. The next time I saw him was when he sneaked into the suite and tried to take Ronnie.

"Camdyn arrived and he left. Before we could get Ronnie and Saffron out, the Warrior came back. With two more. Another came at Ronnie and Saffron as they tried to leave, but Charon was there."

"Charon?" Ramsey asked.

Arran nodded. "I called him."

"I thought you hated him," Galen said.

Arran shrugged. "He got there in time to save the girls, and that's all that matters."

"Tell me you got some information," Fallon said. "Camdyn passed out before we could ask."

Arran glanced around them. "Get me out of here, and I'll tell you."

Fallon placed his hand on Arran's arm, and the next moment he was standing inside the great hall of MacLeod Castle. He'd rather have been at the dig site with Ronnie, but that would have to wait.

"The others are guarding Ronnie," Fallon said as if he knew Arran's thoughts.

Arran sank onto a bench at the table, the same table he had eaten numerous meals at. The same table where there had been laughter and tears, rejoicing and anger.

For a year they'd had peace, but that was gone now. How much more anger and tears would there be before this fight was over?

"Arran?" Galen urged.

He cleared his throat. "The Warrior didna tell me the name of his master, but I did learn they were all newly made."

"So their gods were in control," Ramsey said.

Arran shook his head. "That's just it, they were no'. Apparently, whoever released their gods managed to curb that."

"That's no' good," Galen said, uncertainty lacing his voice. "No' good at all."

Fallon slammed a fist on the table. He closed his eyes for a moment and whispered, "Damn."

"The leader of these new Warriors is pale green. Look

for him. His name is Dale. The other Warrior was too afraid to tell me the name of the person who released his god. He feared his master more than me."

"Yet, it was his master who killed him with X90s," Fallon pointed out.

Ramsey grunted. "This new master must no' be worried about losing so many Warriors in one night."

"One more thing," Arran said. "The Warrior told me that I'd been watched since I arrived at the dig."

"Which means they're watching the castle." Fallon straightened and crossed his arms over his chest. "I doona like being spied upon."

"They know when we leave by car," Galen said.

"But no' when Fallon jumps us," Arran finished with a smile.

"Hey," Dani said from atop the stairs, her silvery hair in a ponytail. "I think you need to see this. Gwynn hacked into the cameras at the Wallace mansion."

"And?" Arran asked.

Dani cut her eyes to him and grinned. "Get up here and find out."

With a snort of laughter, Galen was the first up the stairs, followed by the other three. Arran wanted to know what was going on, but he couldn't stop thinking of Ronnie.

If he'd been watched at the site, that meant whoever watched him also knew all the comings and goings at the dig. They would know when to strike to get Ronnie and when to wait.

Arran paused, struggling to keep his patience and wait before going to Ronnie.

Fallon stopped beside him. "If it makes you feel better, there are ten Warriors watching Ronnie. And Larena is staying by her side, though Ronnie doesna know it."

Arran released a long sigh. The fact that Larena was staying invisible and near Ronnie did help. "Thank you. Wait. Ten? Does that mean you got in touch with Phelan and Malcolm?"

"Charon found Phelan. Malcolm never answered my

calls to his mobile, but Larena texted him and he showed up at the site."

Arran nodded at the news.

"Now come, let's see what Gwynn has found," Fallon said.

He followed Fallon into Gwynn' chamber that she shared with Logan. Gwynn was sitting in the middle of the leather couch with Dani on one side of her and Tara on the other.

"What did you discover?" Fallon asked as he moved behind the couch to see over Gwynn's shoulder.

Gwynn lifted her head of black hair, her violet eyes filled with worry and anger. But her gaze didn't stay on Fallon for long. They moved to Ramsey.

Ramsey raised a black brow, but before he could ask anything, Tara rose and went to her husband.

"Tara, love, you're scaring me."

Arran glanced at Gwynn to see her worry her bottom lip with her teeth.

Tara leaned back and ran her fingers through Ramsey's long black hair. "I thought we got everything."

Ramsey's gray eyes cleared as understanding dawned. His face grew hard and a muscle ticced in his jaw. "What? Tell me now."

"We knew Declan's fortune would go to someone," Dani said.

"And?" Arran urged.

Gwynn tapped her fingers on the keyboard of her laptop. "I already told you his name—Jason Wallace. The more I watch him, the more I'm sure he's doing magic."

"What did we leave behind?" Fallon asked.

"That's just it, I don't know." Gwynn rubbed the back of her neck. "We were so thorough in grabbing every book of magic we found of Declan's."

"No' thorough enough," Ramsey stated angrily.

Arran knew how Ramsey felt. All of them had battled Deirdre, and then Declan. There were many times when it seemed all was lost, but they had won against both Druids.

"It makes sense then," Arran said. "Whatever we left behind has allowed him to control the release of the gods inside the Warriors to his benefit."

Galen nodded. "How do we stop him?"

"First things first, we need to know why he wants Ronnie," Fallon said.

Ramsey slashed his hand through the air. "That's the easy part, Fallon. He wants her because she's a Druid."

Arran rocked back on his heels. "Maybe no', Ramsey. That could be part of it, but Ronnie's magic is that she has the ability to find magical items in the earth. They call to her."

Gwynn cut her eyes to him. "Don't forget the prophecy found in the chamber, Arran. We've all had a look at it, and it's disturbing."

"What's this Jason Wallace looking for that he would need Ronnie?" Galen asked.

"I say we ask him." Arran wanted a fight, and Jason seemed just the bastard to have it with.

Fallon turned to Ramsey. "We'll be back soon."

Ramsey nodded, and then looked at Arran. "Be careful, my friend. It's easy to let emotion get in the way. That's when the ones we care about get hurt."

Arran didn't have a chance to respond as Fallon touched him and teleported them to the dig site.

"What the hell," Fallon muttered.

Arran looked over to find Gwynn had grabbed hold of Fallon just as he jumped them, allowing her to tag along with them.

She lifted her chin and looked Fallon in the eye. "I've heard plenty of times how much magic this place has. No Warrior will even be able to determine I'm here. Besides, you're going to need me."

"She's got a point," Arran interjected before Fallon could talk.

Galen shrugged. "Her communicating with the wind could give us an advantage."

"Fine," Fallon said. "Then you two be the ones to tell Logan why his wife is here."

Arran hid his grin and looked around. They weren't far from the dig site, but not as close as he'd like.

"There's no cover," Logan said as he walked up. "A few trees would be ni—" His voice trailed off as he caught sight of Gwynn. "Baby, what are you doing here?"

She smiled and lifted her face as a gust of wind surrounded her. "Need I say more?"

"Dammit, woman, you're going to be the death of me," Logan said as he pulled her against him for a quick, hard kiss.

Arran knelt in the tall grass and looked out over the land to the dig site. Sound carried well on the wind, and with that added to his enhanced hearing, he deciphered a lot. He heard the sound of metal hitting rock, laughter, and conversations.

When he caught sight of Ronnie he let out a sigh. The viselike grip around his heart released. For now, she was all right. Danger was coming, but his friends had been there, watching out for her.

Logan clamped a hand on his shoulder. "We've had eyes on her since Charon dropped her off."

"What has been going on at the site?" Fallon asked.

Logan pointed to the left. "Nothing much over there. That's where the chamber is, where all the magical items were stored. But over to the right is where everyone is at."

"Andy phoned yesterday to tell her they'd discovered some artifacts," Arran said. "I'm sure she got to work as soon as she got here."

They all turned and faced each other in a tight circle. Logan began pointing to where everyone was set up, and just as Arran had requested, the entire site was encircled with their Warriors.

"Has anyone else been around?" Arran asked.

"No' that we've seen. They may be staying farther off."

Arran scrubbed a hand down his face, his mind running with possibilities. First, he needed to get to Ronnie and try to get her out without anyone seeing.

The problem was, he couldn't do that. Not yet.

Fallon caught his gaze. "Does Ronnie know she's bait?"

"No' yet."

Gwynn tsked and shook her head sadly. "Bad move. You should've told her."

"There was no' time."

"Then tell her now."

Arran looked at the site and saw Ronnie. Her lovely hair was once more pulled back in a bun. She was directing people this way and that, her focus entirely on the dig.

She would be angry about being bait, but she was also the type of woman to assess the best course of action. And this was it.

They needed to know why Jason Wallace wanted her. As soon as they did, Arran would know how to keep her safe.

And keep her from becoming the bringer of doom.

CHAPTER
THIRTY

Aisley sat in the corner of the dimly lit office below the mansion and watched her cousin's face turn red and his nostrils flare as anger took him. At one time Aisley would have laughed. At one time she would have reveled in his torment.

But she'd learned the hard way just how powerful Jason had become.

She touched the scar on her left side through her shirt. That had been an agonizing, grim lesson. But nothing compared to what Jason had done to her mind with his magic.

Or to her parents.

Aisley might be defiant, but there were limits. She'd reached them quickly with Jason. The woman she had been ceased to exist months ago. There were times her past life seemed almost a dream.

She wasn't sure what was worse. Her past. Or her present. She'd been living in hell for so long, she hadn't realized she traded one devil for another in Jason.

"How could you?" Jason bellowed.

Dale's eyes blazed with fury, but he kept his gaze on the floor in submission just as Jason expected. "My men were no match for the others."

"I gave you all you needed to best him," Jason said as he paced the length of the private office he used beneath the house, the heels of his boots hitting the floor hard.

"Arran wasna alone!" Dale paused and said in a calmer voice, "Two more were with him."

Jason paused and lifted his blue eyes to Dale. "Did no one know others had left MacLeod Castle?"

Aisley crossed one leg over the other and tapped a broken nail on the arm of her chair nonchalantly. "It appears not."

Jason's head whipped around to her. He glared and pointed a finger in her direction. "When I want your opinion, I'll ask for it. Now, shut your trap!"

She waited until he'd turned his back before she rolled her eyes.

"We know Charon disappeared from our watch," Jason said.

Dale stroked his goatee. "He's the copper Warrior? He was the one who came in last and took the two Druids."

"You had two Druids within your reach." Jason leaned his hands on his desk and shook his head. "And you didna return with them. How does that happen?"

"You have no' fought those Warriors," Dale said.

Jason straightened and looked at Dale. "No' yet, but I will. Who was the other Druid?"

"Saffron. She was meant to be a surprise."

"You should've told me! I could've been there and gotten both the Druids. Do you have any idea what a Seer could do for me?"

"Aye," Dale said tightly. "Declan used her, remember."

"Exactly. I need Ronnie, Dale. I need to know what was in the chamber, and I suspect her magic has something to do with her being able to find so many artifacts. That could prove verra useful if we need to find something."

"You think you can convert her to a *drough*?" Mindy asked as she caressed a hand down Jason's back.

"I converted you, did I no'?"

Mindy giggled and rubbed her large breasts against him. "You were *very* convincing."

Aisley thought she would throw up if she had to keep watching them. She hated Mindy with a passion that bordered on extreme. One day she and Mindy were going to have it out. The "when" was the question.

"All isna lost," Jason said after a long kiss with Mindy. "I have three more Warriors."

"Three?" Dale repeated. "How did you find them? I thought it was growing more difficult to locate men who had the gods within them."

Jason took a deep breath and slowly released it. "My magic is that great. It's true I had to go to Ireland for one of them, and the other two were . . . no' easy to bring home."

Not easy my ass.

Aisley didn't know how much longer she could sit and listen to Jason go on about his magic. He might have located the men, but she was the one who had persuaded them to come to Scotland.

One she'd had to drug just to get him on the ferry and out of Ireland. He was a crazy bastard. But that volatility was nothing compared to his rage when he awoke to find himself locked in a cell.

He'd promised her and Jason they would pay for what they'd done.

Aisley still shivered when she thought of his warning. Jason hadn't been concerned, not even when he released the god within the Irishman.

But Aisley had seen the promise of retribution in the Irishman's green eyes.

"Did you no', Aisley?"

She jerked her gaze to Jason. "What?"

"I said you did a good job in getting the men here."

He still smiled, but she saw the spark of annoyance in Jason's eyes. "Yes. Thank you."

Jason slapped Mindy on the ass and winked at her as he walked slowly around his office. "Since Mindy has reported that Charon hasna returned to MacLeod Castle with Ronnie and the other Druid, there are only two places he would have taken them. To his village, or the dig site."

"I'll have a look at the village," Dale said.

Jason held up a finger. "Already being taken care of.

There are those who know what I am, those who want to help me in my quest. They may no' have magic, but they're useful. One has reported that Charon isna in his village."

"Then we go to the dig site," Mindy said with a wide, eager smirk.

Aisley frowned. "Wait. I thought only Warriors were going to the site?"

"A little slow today, are we?" Jason asked her, the sarcasm dripping from his voice.

"Apparently."

Jason slid his gaze away from her. "There is enough magic in the area based on what Dale has told us that if there are other Warriors, they willna be able to detect you."

Aisley had an uncomfortable feeling about Jason's new plan. He'd told her a Druid with enough magic could stop a Warrior in his path, but she wasn't sure she had enough magic to do that.

And from all she knew of the MacLeod Warriors, they weren't men to be trifled with.

"In other words, Aisley," Jason continued, unaware of her turmoil, "they willna know you're there until you send them a blast of magic. I just need them detained long enough to get Dr. Reid."

"And when does this plan of yours take place?"

Jason cut his eyes to her. "In a matter of hours. We leave in five minutes. Be ready."

Aisley slowly stood as he and Mindy left the office. She placed a hand on her stomach, which had turned sour at Jason's words.

"Aisley?" Dale whispered.

She looked into his dark eyes and tried to smile. Dale witnessed what Jason had done to her, and it was Dale who had given her the tools to stitch her side—since she'd never been able to use her magic for healing. He'd tried to do it himself, but Jason hadn't allowed it.

"I'm all right."

"You're no' a good liar."

She touched her side, still feeling the blade that had cut

through her skin. "Were the MacLeod Warriors really that good?"

"Better. I doona relish fighting them again."

"They why do it?"

"Because Jason demands it."

"You're a Warrior. You could fight him."

Dale looked away from her gaze. "There are things you doona know, Aisley. I have to do as he orders. And doona ask more. Just leave it as it is."

She looked up the stairs where Jason had gone.

"I'll watch over you," Dale promised. "The MacLeod Warriors willna harm you."

Aisley took his hand and squeezed it. She appreciated his words, but she knew in battle they would be useless. "Thank you."

She knew all she had to do was show Dale the slightest interest and he could be hers. For as long as Jason allowed it. But Aisley didn't want to give Jason anything to use against her.

Aisley released Dale's hand and squared her shoulders before she followed Jason up the stairs.

Ronnie wiped the back of her arm across her forehead and sat back on her heels. It had felt good to get her hands in the ground again and dig.

The activity hadn't completely taken her mind from Arran, but it had helped. Her emotions swung from anxiety and fear about the attack to warmth and protection when she thought of their hours alone.

One minute she knew everything would be all right, and the next she was a bundle of nerves. Each hour that ticked by with no word from Arran took ten years off her life. She'd be lucky if she survived the day.

Several more items had been found in the section she was working. She'd even discovered a bowl with amazing knot-work that somehow reminded her of Arran. The bowl had come through the ages faring well, with only a few chips along the rim.

Ronnie held up the bowl and turned it first one way and then the other. It might be one of the items she requested to keep for herself, if the government allowed it.

She handed it off to Andy to be cataloged and numbered along with everything else. Ronnie had started the catalog and numbering system after Max stole from her.

At least now she could account for everything.

Ronnie spent another three hours slowly moving dirt in the hopes of finding something else. She could still feel there was something in the ground, but she could no longer tell exactly where, since her mind wasn't completely in it.

Finally she rose to her feet and looked at the sky. It was well past midday. She'd expected Arran by now. Where was he? And why hadn't he contacted her?

She took off her gloves and shoved them into the back pocket of her jeans as she walked to the tables where everything was laid out.

Andy was there with his clipboard, keeping track of everything. Ronnie couldn't contain her smile. That clipboard was never out of Andy's sight, not even when he ate. She often teased him that he took it in the shower with him.

"Hey," Andy said when he saw her.

"Hey. How's it coming?"

He grinned boyishly and shoved his glasses up on his nose. "It was another good day. I wonder how much more is in that section?"

"More, I hope."

"I wish I knew how you pick the sectors to excavate, Ronnie. It's magic, I swear."

She stilled and slowly looked at him. For long moments she'd didn't breathe until she realized he hadn't meant actual magic.

"What is it?" he asked, his forehead furrowed. "You went white."

"Nothing. Sorry. It's been a long day."

"You look beat. I think you should call it an early day and get some rest."

"Maybe I will." Ronnie ran her hand along the bowl she'd just dug up.

Someone shouted for Andy, and he hurried away. Ronnie didn't mind. She liked being alone with the items she'd dug up, items that hadn't seen the light of day in centuries.

She often wondered what the people who had used the pieces she found had been like. Were their lives good? Bad? Had they loved and been loved? Did they have a family? How had they died?

Her gaze moved slowly over the items displayed on the table. It wasn't until her second look that she realized the large piece of rock carved with amazing detailed knotwork was missing.

There was no empty place on the table, but she knew it had been there. And that wasn't the only piece missing.

A sick feeling filled Ronnie.

"No," she said softly, her stomach curdling as she realized what had occurred. "This can't be happening to me again."

She spun on her heel and went to find Andy. She didn't say a word as she pulled the clipboard from his hand and looked over his inventory.

Ronnie put an asterisk by the pieces she knew were missing. Then she went back to the tent and looked, piece by piece.

"What is it?" Andy asked worriedly as he stood behind her, a frown marking his brow.

Ronnie turned around, barely able to take a breath. "There are six pieces missing."

"What?" he gasped, and took the clipboard from her.

She held her stomach as she tried to keep the little food she had eaten for lunch down.

"I don't believe it," Andy whispered.

Ronnie couldn't either. Nor could she believe Arran would do something like that to her. Arran. The man who had danced with her, kissed her. Made love to her.

The man she had given herself to.

The man she had begun to fall for.

She blinked hastily to stop the threat of tears. Now she

knew why she hadn't heard from Arran, why he hadn't bothered to call. He'd been busy stealing from her while she worried about his safety.

Did that mean Saffron was also in on it? Ronnie hoped that wasn't the case, but at this point, she didn't trust anyone.

She stumbled out of the tent.

Only to lock eyes on Arran as he strolled casually toward her.

CHAPTER
THIRTY-ONE

Arran couldn't keep the pleasure from showing as he looked at Ronnie. He'd waited hours to be able to hold her again, to know that she was all right. How he had missed her.

As he closed the distance between them, all he could think about was having her against him again. Holding her, touching her.

Loving her.

He was nearly to her when he saw how pale she was. The smile dropped and concern took over. Before he could say anything to her, Ronnie turned on her heel and walked away.

Arran lengthened his strides and followed. He glanced at Andy to see him shaking his head as he looked from his clipboard to artifacts arranged on tables. It didn't take a detective to know there was something up.

And Arran suspected more items had been stolen.

No wonder his Ronnie was upset. After the first time, he suspected Ronnie had thought never to have it happen again. Arran would find who had stolen from her and make them pay.

He privately hoped it was Max. He wanted to find the bastard and make him hurt as he'd hurt Ronnie.

Ronnie walked through the dig site until they reached the spot where the tents and caravans were. She suddenly stopped behind her tent and whirled to face him.

Arran was right on her heels, ready to take her in his arms and give her whatever comfort he could. It would be short-lived because of the danger approaching, but he'd take the time.

He saw her arm rise, saw her hand come at his face, but he did nothing to stop the slap. The sound was loud as her hand connected with his face.

He rubbed the spot on his cheek and looked at her. So much for offering comfort. "Care to tell me what that was about?"

"Stop it," she ground out. Her body shook—but with fear or anger, he wasn't sure. Her eyes were bright, as if she held back tears. "Just stop it. I've had enough of the lies and your seduction. Why did you come back? To take more?"

Arran frowned as he struggled to comprehend what she was saying. "What do you mean, why did I come back? Why do you think I came back? I came for you. I promised I'd keep you safe."

She laughed, the sound filled with hurt and indignation. "Oh, you're good. So much better than Max."

And then it dawned on Arran. "You think I stole from you?"

"I know you did!" She closed her mouth and put her hands on her hips as she looked at the ground. "I trusted you."

"The only thing I would have tried to take from you is your heart, lass."

She shook her head slowly. "Stop the act. I've counted six items gone, not including what you convinced me to give you from the chamber. How much have you taken in all?"

Arran grabbed her arms and gave her a little shake. "I. Didna. Steal," he said slowly, enunciating each word.

"Am I expected to believe you? Nothing has been stolen until you arrived. I don't believe in coincidences, Arran."

Neither did he. He dropped his arms and took a step back. How had this happened? More important, why didn't she believe him?

They had a connection, a bond. It hadn't been a figment of his imagination. He'd felt that bond, knew it had strengthened while in Edinburgh. Arran wished now he'd never let her out of his sight.

"Aye, I expect you to believe me. You saw the attack. I've been battling men since Charon took you out of the hotel. I made sure the police knew you were no' involved, and I got information from the Warrior we were able to keep alive for a wee bit. I watched Camdyn get struck by bullets filled with *drough* blood and prayed that I got him out in time so Sonya could save him.

"Fallon jumped us back to MacLeod Castle so Camdyn could get healed and he could tell me what they've found. I returned to you as quick as I could. Tell me what I need to say so you'll believe I didna steal from you."

"Was it all a setup?" she asked as if he hadn't spoken. "The attack, the story about the Warriors and Druids? Was it all some elaborate scheme to get close to me?"

Arran clenched his jaw as he felt his connection with Ronnie unraveling with no way to halt it. "Nay. What I told you was the truth. You've seen me and the others. You know I didna lie about being a Warrior, and you know you're a Druid."

"All I really know is that I've been used." She blew out a shaky breath and put her hand to her forehead. "I want the items returned immediately, and maybe then I won't report you to the authorities. I don't know if anything you've done involves Saffron or not, but either way, I don't want her funding anymore."

"Ronnie, this has to wait." He'd debated on telling her that she was bait after everything she'd said, but she needed to know. "There's an at—"

"An attack," she finished, and dropped her arms to her sides. "Yes, I'm sure there is. Now, get out of my sight, Arran. I don't want to see or hear from you or anyone you're associated with ever again. I hope I'm clear on that. Go away."

Arran watched her walk away. He felt as if he'd been gutted. He was crushed, shattered.

Destroyed.

All by one woman.

He couldn't think straight, couldn't even begin to understand how this had happened. All he kept hearing in his head was her parting words. They echoed in his mind, getting louder and louder until he was deafened by them.

Someone touched his arm, and Arran spun around to find Andy. Only then did Arran realize he had Andy by the throat. He quickly released him. "Sorry, mate."

Andy rubbed his throat and warily looked at him. "I don't think you did it," he said after clearing his throat several times.

"I didna."

"She won't listen to you, though." Andy pushed his glasses up on his nose and gave a shake of his head. He seemed suddenly older than his twenty-something years. "Max really messed her up. There's nothing you can do or say to make her believe it wasn't you."

Arran suddenly grunted. "There's one way. I find the real thief."

"That would work," Andy said with a chuckle. "Where to start, though."

"I begin with you."

Andy held up his hands so quickly, he dropped the clipboard. "I—I wouldn't dream of do-doing that to Ronnie. She's like my si-sister, dude."

There was no mistaking the honesty and distress reflected in Andy's eyes. Arran slapped him on the back. "I believe you."

Andy's shoulders slumped in relief. "Dude, if I had the nerve, I'd hit you for what you just did."

"Hit me anyway," Arran said with a grin he could barely manage. "Besides, I'm doing this for Ronnie."

"True." Andy bent to get the clipboard.

"Who else could have stolen? Do you think Pete would know?"

Andy frowned. "Pete? Why ask him?"

"Because he's here."

"Ah . . . that would be a nope."

Arran's gaze moved around him. "Pete isna here?"

"That's what I said."

"He told Ronnie he had to miss the fund-raiser to help you."

Andy laughed. "Yeah, right. Pete says a lot of things that he doesn't always do."

"Does Ronnie know?"

"No," Andy said, and flattened his lips. "I try to keep those things from her. She's been hurt too many times, and she thinks of Pete as a father."

Arran ran a hand down his face. "Andy, think hard. Have there been things that have gone missing from other digs?"

"No—and I'd know, since I keep track of everything. I make the occasional mistake, but Ronnie forgives me."

"Mistakes how?"

"I'll give an artifact the same number on my spreadsheet, or accidentally put two of something."

Arran looked to the sky as he began to put two and two together. He lowered his gaze to Andy, fury boiling his blood. "You were no' making mistakes. Things were being stolen."

"That's not . . ." He trailed off. "Oh, shit."

"Who is always on the digs? There has to be the same people every time."

Andy scratched his head. "The only ones on every dig who are the same are Ronnie, me, and Pete."

Just as Arran thought. It was Pete. All he had to do was find Pete, get the missing items, and tell Ronnie the man she thought of as a father had been stealing from her.

"Oh, God," Andy said, his devastation at figuring it out showing in his eyes. "It's Pete. This will destroy Ronnie."

It would, and Arran couldn't have that. She'd been through enough already. "Andy, I need you to keep this between us. I'm going to find Pete and get the artifacts. I'll make sure he doesna dare to steal from Ronnie again, but I need a couple of things from you."

"Name it."

"Doona tell Ronnie any of this. And second . . . if anything is suspicious again, you tell her immediately. And then call me."

Andy jabbed his pencil behind his ear. "You're a good man, Arran. I wish you'd tell Ronnie what you're doing so she wouldn't let you go. You'd be good for her."

"I'll keep watch over her from afar. She needs the man she thinks of as a father more than she does me."

"I think you're wrong, but I'll do as you ask."

Arran grabbed Andy's arm when he began to walk away. "One more thing. There are some men after Ronnie. They tried to get her last night in Edinburgh. It's why I wasna with her when she returned. I've taken care of them, but there could be more coming back. Matter of fact, I'm sure of it."

"What do you want me to do?"

Arran liked Andy, and knew he could count on him. "Regardless of what Ronnie said, I'm no' leaving. No' yet. I'm going to be near, but I need you stay beside her at all times until this thing is over."

"Should we tell her about the men coming back?"

"I tried. I'm also no' sure exactly when they'll attack, but I think it'll be soon."

"What do these men want?"

Arran knew he couldn't tell Andy the truth. Instead he told Andy what he'd told the police. "They think Ronnie has the money from the fund-raiser. They doona understand the funds are transferred to an account. Or maybe they do and they want access to that account. Either way, they want Ronnie, and I'm no' letting them near her."

Andy gave a firm nod. "I'll stay by her."

Arran didn't move once Andy left. All Arran could think about was Ronnie. He'd seen the desolation on her face when she thought he was the one who'd stolen from her. He couldn't imagine how she'd react if she discovered it was Pete.

"But she willna learn that," Arran murmured.

He closed his eyes and concentrated on Ronnie. It took no time for him to discern her magic easily through all the rest.

It was the same brilliant, thrilling magic he'd felt when

he first arrived, but it was stronger now, more potent. He still felt the magic of the chamber, and there was a trace of more magic. But Ronnie's was prominent in his mind.

Once he located where she was, Arran put himself on the opposite side of the site and began to patrol. Most people knew him and spoke with him. It gave Arran the reason he needed to stop and talk to others and determine how long they'd been at the site.

Almost two hours later, everyone had been accounted for. There were no Warriors waiting in surprise among the volunteers and workers.

Arran made sure Ronnie was well away from her tent before he went inside. He looked at the cot she slept in. His body heated as he recalled how wonderful she'd felt in his arms, how responsive her body had been to his touch.

How fitting, how suited they were for each other.

He pulled her necklace from the front pocket of his jeans and held it in front of him. The gold trinity knot twirled before him, its magic making a dull hum in his mind.

Slowly, he lowered the necklace until it rested on the table next to some papers. As much as it hurt him to do so, Arran would stay away from her as she'd asked.

That is, unless the Warriors went for her, as he knew they would. Then he would be near her, and only to save her.

He could fight for her. He could tell her about Pete and all the thefts, but to do so would be to wreck her. Ronnie meant too much to him to do that.

She reminded him so much of his sister. Shelley would've liked Ronnie. Just as Shelley had been beautiful and good and so brilliant, it hurt to look at her, Ronnie was the same.

Ronnie deserved a good life, a life he'd not been able to give his sister. He was a Warrior now. He could—and would—ensure that Ronnie got what had been denied his sister.

Arran jerked as he felt Ronnie's magic drawing closer. He hurried out of her tent, and just managed to duck behind a caravan when she came into view.

He wanted to watch her find the necklace, or at least see

her with it on once more. Arran waited for her to go inside, but someone called out to her, drawing her away from the tent.

The new mobile phone in Arran's back pocket vibrated. He pulled it out and answered it.

"Why are you no' with Ronnie?" Gwynn asked.

Arran squeezed his eyes closed. "Some artifacts were stolen, and she believes it was me."

"It wasn't you."

Her indignation made him smile. "I know."

There was a pause before Gwynn said, "You know who did it."

It wasn't a question.

Arran walked from Ronnie's tent toward the parking area. "I do. None of that matters now. Nothing has changed."

"I know."

"Good. Has anyone seen anything?"

"Nothing so far."

Arran looked at the sky and the rolling landscape before him. "They'll come tonight when it's the darkest. Be ready."

He ended the call and continued to make his rounds, continually keeping out of sight of Ronnie.

But he always knew where she was.

The afternoon progressed into evening and then into night without incident. When everyone found their beds, Arran set up watch so he could see Ronnie's tent and a vast area of the site.

And just as Andy promised, he stayed near Ronnie. He was outside Ronnie's tent in a chair, dozing.

Arran smiled inwardly, impressed by how far Andy was taking his pledge. Ronnie had done well to put her faith and trust in Andy.

The sounds of the evening filled the air as midnight approached. The summer sun ducked behind the mountains, giving Scotland its few hours of darkness in the summer.

Headlights occasionally could be seen on the distant road as cars weaved around the curves and up and down the hills. But none approached the dig site.

It was around 2 A.M. when something in the air caused Arran to sit straighter. It didn't take him long to realize it was danger.

And it was approaching fast.

Arran shifted from sitting so that he was squatting with his hands braced on the ground. With his enhanced vision, he could see something moving in the tall grass.

It would have been easy for one of his brethren to take out the Warrior coming for Ronnie, but a trap had been set. And a trap they would close.

Arran crept closer to Ronnie's tent. He knew the feel of her magic, but the Warriors attacking would be disoriented and not know for sure. It would take them time to get to her, and Arran would use that to his advantage.

Andy was sound asleep when Arran reached him. He covered Andy's mouth so he wouldn't cry out upon waking.

"It's me," Arran whispered. "Is there a way to alert everyone?"

Andy nodded, and Arran removed his hand. Andy looked around and then turned in the chair to Arran. Arran put his finger to his mouth to quiet him.

"I have a bullhorn," Andy whispered back.

Arran saw the shapes of Warriors coming closer. These weren't his friends, these were enemies who needed to be killed.

"When you see the signal, use the bullhorn. Until then, keep out of sight," Arran said, and pulled him to his feet.

Once Andy was away and in his own tent, Arran melded into the shadows. Hiding didn't do much good around Warriors, but hopefully they had no idea he awaited them.

One, then two came into the center of the site. They had their gods released, and Arran recognized the light green Warrior as Dale. The other was a rust color.

The two turned one way, then the other, trying to decipher where Ronnie was.

Arran flexed his hands as he released his god. Fangs filled his mouth, and claws extended from his fingers. Memphaea roared with the need for battle, for blood.

For death.

And for the first time in a long time, Arran was in agreement.

When a third Warrior joined the other two, Arran readied himself. They would soon sense magic coming from Ronnie's tent.

And just as he expected, Dale turned in the direction of Ronnie's tent, his head cocked to the side. He stared at it a moment before he searched the area.

Arran waited to be spotted, but the Warriors were more interested in the magic they felt than in any attack that might happen. They were overconfident, which would work to his benefit.

Dale took one step, then two toward Ronnie's tent. When he had taken a half dozen more, Arran moved out of the shadows. There was no way anyone would get near Ronnie. Not while he guarded her.

Dale bared his fangs and growled. Arran smirked and motioned the Warrior toward him.

The battle was about to begin.

CHAPTER
THIRTY-TWO

Arran watched Dale approach, but he kept the other three in his sights as well. They would attack at once. It was their only course if they wanted to be rid of him. And it might work except for one thing.

He was protecting Ronnie.

They had no idea that she was his very existence, his everything. He would give up his own life if it meant Ronnie would be safe.

And a Warrior who loved was a Warrior on a mission.

Dale growled long and low, which brought a smile to Arran's face. The Warrior was still angry over being defeated in Edinburgh.

"Best get used to it, lad," Arran said. "You're about to be beaten again."

"Never," Dale stated.

"You've no idea what you've walked into. Be smart. Leave."

"Are we going to talk all night or fight?" Dale asked, his lip turned up in a sneer.

Arran had killed enough to last an eternity. He was tired of killing, especially Warriors. These Warriors were different from those Deirdre had unbound. These Warriors had control of their gods, and had they been with the MacLeods, they would be serving on the side of good.

But they were serving dark forces. Nothing and no one could change them from that course. It was there in their eyes, in the way they looked at Ronnie's tent.

If Arran was going to keep Ronnie from harm, he would have to kill these Warriors. And as many as kept coming for her.

Arran spread his arms wide as he drew air into his lungs. Memphaea bellowed with pleasure at the idea of a battle—as well as protecting Ronnie. And in his mind, Memphaea was showing Arran ways to hurt his enemy.

He wasn't the god of malice for nothing.

Dale leaned his head back and let out a loud roar. Soon the other three Warriors did the same, and Arran simply waited. His enemy thought he'd come alone. They thought they could get rid of him and have all they'd come for.

How wrong they were.

And then Arran felt a tingle of magic, nasty and vile. *Droughs.*

So the Warriors hadn't come alone either. The question was, did Fallon and the others sense the *droughs*? Could they detect the dark magic from the other magic of the area? Arran prayed they could, or things could turn in favor of his enemies.

"Never," he whispered as he heard Andy use the bullhorn once, twice urging everyone to run.

Arran's arms slowly lowered to his side. He bent his legs, ready to spring. His chin tilted lower so that he could watch the four Warriors more clearly.

Suddenly, Dale's roar cut off and he jumped forward, his claws extended as he came at Arran. Arran spun to the side and extended his claws so that they raked across Dale's back when he landed.

Dale growled and snapped his fangs. Arran enjoyed the feel of blood on his claws. He wanted more of it, needed more of it.

Craved it like never before.

Something cracked inside Arran, something he'd kept locked deep inside. But Ronnie had found it somehow. No matter what he had to do—or become—Arran wouldn't hesitate.

For her.

Dale circled him as the other three Warriors came closer. Arran didn't move. He watched Dale with his eyes, tracking him as the Warrior drew closer and closer.

Arran didn't utter a sound when Dale's claws scoured his back from shoulder to waist. He didn't move when Dale sank his claws into Arran's side.

Dale was close enough that Arran turned his head to him and watched his brow furrow with confusion.

"There's nothing you can do to me that will stop me from killing you," Arran said.

"We can take your head," said one of the other three.

Arran kept his gaze locked with Dale's. But he sensed when another Warrior decided to attack. Arran ducked and spun toward the approaching Warrior.

He straightened, and both his claws plunged deep in the Warrior's stomach. He jerked his claws up, satisfaction filling him when he heard the Warrior gurgle with pain.

"I could kill you now," Arran whispered. "I could take your head with one swipe of my claws."

The Warrior laughed as blood fell from his lips. "We're no' alone, fool."

Arran pulled out his claws, reared back his hand, and effortlessly took the Warrior's head. The body fell at his feet, and he slowly turned his gaze to look at Dale.

Arran prayed the Warriors stayed tuned to what he'd just done and didn't realize that Andy was getting everyone out of the dig site.

He swore silently when one of the Warriors lifted his head and growled.

"The people are leaving!" he shouted.

Dale's nostrils flared in anger as he glared at Arran. "A nice diversion."

"I've had centuries of practice," Arran said.

Another Warrior took a step toward Arran. "Let's dance, you bastard."

Arran had brawn and years of fighting with swords on his side, but this Warrior was quick and agile. He moved with lightning speed and used his feet and legs more than his claws. Arran had seen enough movies to know the Warrior was using martial arts. But the moves wouldn't save him.

He let the Warrior believe he was making headway and defeating him. Arran continued to move away from him, but always kept near Ronnie's tent.

Of a sudden, the Warrior let out a yell and leapt into the air. Arran saw Dale begin to head to Ronnie's tent and went to stop him, so he never saw the attacking Warrior's claws coming.

Arran grunted as the claws sank into the top of his shoulder near his neck. The Warrior then wrapped his legs around Arran and jerked back, sending both of them to the ground.

He elbowed the Warrior twice in the face and heard bone crunch. Yet he never took his gaze off Dale. Just before Dale reached Ronnie's tent, Charon came around it and grinned.

"My turn," Charon said.

Arran roared as the Warrior twisted his claws into the wound, sending more blood gushing down his body. The Warrior's other hand hooked onto Arran's face, and his claws tore open Arran's cheek, nearly getting his eye.

The dig site become a place of chaos and panic. People screamed as Andy desperately tried to get them to safety, though Andy himself wasn't the calmest of the bunch. The Warriors of MacLeod Castle had begun to show themselves, but a few stayed hidden.

Arran was satisfied that Dale wouldn't get to Ronnie, thanks to Charon. And when Arran rolled to his stomach, the damned Warrior remained on his back. When he got to his hands and knees, he saw that Phelan had the third Warrior locked in battle.

It took great effort for Arran to get to his feet while the Warrior continued to slice open his face as he tried to get to Arran's eyes.

Arran's shout of rage surpassed that of Memphaea inside

him. Arran reached behind him and stabbed his claws into the Warrior's sides.

He continued to slash and stab over and over as he weakened the Warrior. Madness took him. He saw nothing and no one but the Warrior he fought.

He liked the feel of battle, wanted the smell of death. It went beyond craving to *need*.

They were after Ronnie—his Ronnie. He had to keep her safe. It was the only thought that kept running through his mind.

It took Arran a moment to realize he had not only gotten the Warrior off his back, but had him pinned to the ground. He blinked when his claws struck bone. Only then did he see he had completely gutted the Warrior, who even now lay gasping for breath.

Arran threw back his head and roared his pleasure and anger at losing such control. Never in all his years had he done so, but he didn't regret letting loose. Not when it was for his Ronnie.

He looked at the Warrior, and then leaned close to him. "I told you you'd never get her."

The Warrior sneered, and it was all it took for Arran to sever his head from his body.

Arran climbed to his feet and ripped off his tattered shirt, which hung on his body by threads. He blinked the blood out of his eyes and looked around to find that Charon and Phelan had subdued the other Warriors and were watching Arran cautiously.

They weren't the only ones. Fallon, Quinn, Hayden, Ian, and Camdyn looked at him as if they didn't know him. The only one who seemed to understand was Malcolm, who simply gave a nod.

Arran turned to walk away, and then stopped dead in his tracks when his gaze locked on Ronnie. Her hazel eyes were wide, her lips parted in dismay.

He took a step toward her only to have her take a step back. He'd let loose something terrible inside him to save her, but he'd lost her forever in the process.

Whatever chance he might have had to win her back vanished as she'd watched him kill the Warrior. All he could do was watch her walk away.

"Larena is with her," Fallon said as he came to stand beside Arran.

Arran inhaled and walked to where Charon held Dale. "Why did you come for Ronnie?"

"I doona know. I simply follow orders."

"My arse," Arran barked. "You thought four of you could come and take her?"

That's when Dale grinned and then began to laugh. As Dale's laughter echoed around the site, Arran looked at Charon to see him frown.

And then all hell broke loose.

Black magic ripped through the site, slicing the caravans in half and crumbling tents. Arran drew his arm back to take Dale's head when a blast of *drough* magic tossed him several feet away.

The magic pounded against him, causing his god to scream in pain and fury. Arran grabbed his head with both hands. It took him three tries before he was able to get to his feet.

He looked up to find his friends all in the same kind of pain. Dale and the other Warrior were gone.

Arran winced as his god grew louder, but he pushed the screaming aside as he searched for Ronnie. It was a feat in itself that he was on his feet from the *drough* magic directed at them. If they were hurting, it was most likely affecting Larena as well. Which meant Ronnie was in danger.

He tried to walk, but only fell to the ground again. Arran gritted his teeth and pushed himself to his hands and knees. He thought of Ronnie's smile, of her hazel eyes that looked at the world unlike anyone he'd ever known.

He thought of her soft touch, her kisses, her welcoming embrace. He thought of her laughter, her . . . love.

And he got to his feet with a growl.

Arran took a small step, and then another. He kept going in the direction he'd seen Ronnie leave. He had no idea how many *droughs* were there, and it didn't matter. He had to find them and kill them, or Ronnie would be in the hands of evil.

Lightning streaked across the sky, and for just a moment, the *drough* magic ceased. Arran looked over to find Malcolm with his arm raised to the sky and lightning forking from his fingers.

In those few seconds, Arran was able to see most everyone had gotten away from the site. He could see them running away. But he was also able to see five *droughs* as they stood around the site in a large circle.

Malcolm sent another round of lightning, this time directed at the *droughs*. They used their magic to counter his attack, but in doing so, it freed Arran and the others from their magic.

Hayden threw a ball of fire at one *drough,* while Lucan called the darkness around him and faded into shadows. A moment later, and he had killed one of the *droughs*.

Malcolm had given them the opportunity to turn the tide. The *droughs* now had to protect themselves in order to stay alive.

Arran left the *droughs* to his brethren and concentrated on Ronnie's magic. He found her almost instantly, but the fear mixed into her magic sent him into a rage.

He used his speed and raced after her. Dale was nowhere to be seen, but the Warrior who held Ronnie never saw Arran coming.

Arran wrapped an arm around the Warrior's neck and yanked him away from Ronnie and to the ground. Just as Arran was about to take his head, a hand locked around his wrist, halting him.

He looked up to find Phelan beside him.

"We need him," Phelan said.

Arran couldn't get the sight of the Warrior holding Ronnie out of his head, couldn't forget the fear in her magic.

"We'll gain more by sparing him. For now," Phelan added.

Arran peeled back his lips and growled at the Warrior on the ground. "I'm going to kill you for touching her."

The Warrior simply laughed in response. Then his head jerked to the side as if he'd been punched, and he fell unconscious.

"I was sick of hearing him," Larena's disembodied voice said from Arran's other side. "Take him to Fallon. I'll keep watch over Ronnie."

Phelan released Arran and lifted the Warrior so that he draped over his shoulder. With a nod, Phelan made his way to Fallon.

Arran looked to Ronnie, but her gaze was focused on her arm, where she held a hand over a cut that bled viciously.

"Go, Arran," Larena said. "I'll take care of her."

Arran didn't want to leave, but he didn't know what to say to Ronnie. What could he say? He swallowed and turned to follow Phelan. Each step he took from Ronnie was like a little piece of him dying.

Whatever had begun to grow in him with meeting Ronnie was dying a swift death. And he wanted to follow it. The world would be a gray, lonely place without Ronnie by his side.

He was about halfway back to the site when he felt a wave of *drough* magic. Arran spun to find the Druid, but before he could get to her, a gust of wind whirled around the Druid and tossed her into the air.

Gwynn let out a laugh as she stood in the tall grass about twenty paces from him. "Damn. That felt good. Don't tell Logan, though. He's protective enough that he'll get mad knowing I endangered myself."

Arran nodded in understanding. "You shouldna have gotten so far from Logan. Anything could happen to you out here."

"Arran, please. Y'all keep forgetting that I can hear the wind. It alerts me when danger is near. I'm safer than any of y'all."

"Come on," he said as he took her arm. He might have lost his woman, but Logan wouldn't lose his. "I'm taking you to your husband."

* * *

Aisley lay as still as stone on her stomach in the grass as Arran walked right past her. Dale lay on top of her, urging her to keep quiet and still.

He was the one who found her after the first lightning strike and pulled her to the ground, effectively cutting off her spell to halt the other Warriors.

She'd tried to ask what he was doing, but he simply held a finger to her lips. Aisley stayed quiet and listened as Arran had not only found Ronnie and the Warrior, but was stopped from killing him by someone else.

Someone with a voice that made her skin prickle with awareness. The voice was smooth, and deliciously deep. She wanted to see the face that went with such an amazing voice, but Dale wouldn't let her move.

She then heard a female voice that wasn't Ronnie's. It was someone watching over Ronnie, but Aisley hadn't seen a woman near their target.

And then there was the Druid who had taken out one of their *droughs*. With wind.

Wind!

Aisley couldn't believe the *mie* had the ability to communicate with the wind, and if she could, why didn't the *mie* know of her and Dale's presence?

Several moments passed after Arran walked away before Dale rolled off her. Aisley rose up on her elbows. "What now?"

"They have Jordan," Dale said.

"Will he talk?"

Dale shrugged and stayed on his back with his gaze to the sky. "I knew there would be other Warriors from Mac-Leod Castle here, but I didna expect so many."

"You and Jason keep underestimating them. It'll get you both killed."

Dale turned his head to look at her. "You as well when they discover who you are. And you know it's just a matter of time before they do."

"So why save me?"

"Because I like you," he said with a shrug.

Aisley rose up to hesitantly look over the grass. "They have Jordan surrounded. It looks like they're questioning him."

"Where is Ronnie and the other female?"

"I don't see either."

"She's no' far," Dale said after a moment. "We have one more shot to get her."

"I saw what Arran did to one of you tonight. Do you want him to do the same to you? Because he will. He'll do that to anyone who threatens Ronnie."

"What's so special about her?" Dale asked, confusion marring his face.

Aisley picked a piece of grass from Dale's goatee. "He's in love with her."

"You can hide her from him."

Aisley looked at her hands and felt the magic within her. It had always been powerful, but that was nothing compared to what flowed within her now.

Black magic. Dark magic.

Either way, it was evil.

And so was she.

"Jason will kill you if we fail. We have no choice but to get her," she said.

Dale gave a nod and got to his feet. "We're far enough away from the magic of the dig that I should be able to locate Ronnie."

Aisley closed her eyes as Dale moved away. Every day her soul grew blacker and blacker. She wasn't sure why she continued to fight it. She was bound for Hell anyway after performing the *drough* ceremony.

But she hated who she was, despised who she had become. All because she'd been too weak to say no.

CHAPTER
THIRTY-THREE

Ronnie was in shock. She knew it, but couldn't pull herself out of it.

She'd woken out of a troubled sleep to the sound of a roar. A Warrior's roar. It had been joined by others, and she had instinctively known it hadn't been Arran or his friends.

For long moments she'd sat on her cot and listened to the sounds of battle. It wasn't until she heard Arran's bellow of pain that she'd rushed out of her tent.

She'd stared in fascination, and a fair amount of fear, as the man who had made such sweet love to her literally tore apart the other Warrior.

When Arran coldly cut off the Warrior's head, she found herself glad he did. She inwardly rejoiced, and that made her sick at herself. What kind of person was she that she'd cheered another's death?

It's not the person she was, or was it? Was that what happened to someone who had their life threatened? Did a person forget who they really were when evil tracked them?

Or was this new person she'd become always there and she hadn't known it?

Ronnie hadn't been able to look Arran in the eye. Not because of what he'd done, but because of what she'd done. He had been protecting her, just as he'd vowed to do.

The joy inside her at the death of a man, even an evil man, made her realize she didn't know who she was. And if she didn't know who she was, how could Arran?

So she'd walked away from him.

Ronnie had seen Andy quickly getting everyone away from the site, and so she followed him. She hadn't gotten far before a Warrior found her.

His hold had been so tight and powerful that no amount of wiggling or punching affected him. Arran had that kind of power, but never once had he used it on her. He'd been kind and gentle, even when she opened the chamber and released something deadly into the world.

Or when she told him to leave.

He had stolen from her, but she wasn't angry about the thefts. She was hurt that he would do that to her.

It didn't take her long to realize that the Warrior who had her wasn't going to let her go. And since she'd walked away from Arran, no one knew what had become of her.

And then, suddenly, Arran was there.

He spun the Warrior away from her and tossed him to the ground as if he were nothing more than a bag of leaves. Pain ripped up her arm, and Ronnie looked down to see a gash that ran the length of her forearm.

She hastily put pressure on it, dimly aware that another Warrior had joined Arran. Soft hands touched Ronnie's shoulder, but she was so close to passing out from the alarm and pain that she couldn't focus her eyes.

There was so much she wanted to say to Arran. And she wanted to feel his arms around her again. She wanted his comfort, his steady hands to soothe her and tell her everything was going to be all right. No matter how she tried to get the words past her lips, nothing worked.

"I'm Larena," said a woman near her.

Ronnie swayed, but arms she couldn't see caught her.

"Oh, my. Maybe I shouldn't have sent the men away. Ronnie, you need to listen carefully."

Ronnie swallowed and struggled to keep her breathing even. She could no longer feel her fingers, and even though she kept pressure on the wound, blood still flowed thick down her arm to drip from her fingers.

"I'm Larena," the woman repeated. "I'm a female Warrior."

The invisible one. Ronnie tried to say the words, but it was too difficult.

"I'm invisible right now because of my power," Larena whispered, and turned Ronnie toward the vehicles. "Can you get to the cars? Any car?"

Ronnie took a hesitant step, and then another. She managed two more before her legs gave out.

"I've got you," Larena said, catching her before she hit the ground.

Suddenly, Ronnie was picked up and carried. She closed her eyes since it was too difficult to keep them open. No longer could she hear the sounds of battle.

"Arran," she whispered.

Was it over? Was she safe again?

No sooner had that thought gone through her mind than Larena cried out. And then Ronnie was falling.

She landed hard on the ground with a rock jabbing into her side. Ronnie forced her eyes to open and saw the pale green Warrior punching what looked like air. But his hands were landing against something solid.

Larena.

He extended his claws and was swinging them downward when a shot fired. Something fell in the grass beside Ronnie. A moment later, and she saw Larena's nude body lying on her side with a bullet in her back.

"Why did you do that?" Dale demanded of someone.

"The X90 will kill her just as surely as you beheading her," said a woman.

Ronnie grabbed a handful of grass and tried to pull herself away. They had killed Larena. All because Larena had been helping her.

A pair of boots stepped in front of Ronnie's face.

"We've finally got you," said the woman.

Ronnie looked up to see a woman with cold eyes and black hair pulled back in a ponytail before she passed out.

CHAPTER
THIRTY-FOUR

Arran's patience deserted him when the Warriors had thought to come for Ronnie again. The fact that the Warrior they captured refused to tell them anything only made Arran's frustration grow.

"Easy," Fallon said. "We need information from him."

Logan stood off to the side with Gwynn behind him. Logan made sure to keep between Gwynn and the unwelcome Warrior. Not that Arran blamed him. Logan was protecting his woman.

The only other one there who had someone to worry about was Fallon, but everyone knew Larena could take care of herself. With her power of invisibility, she was the one least likely to be injured.

"Just tell us what we want to know," Quinn told the Warrior.

Arran still hadn't tamped down his god. Malcolm and Phelan also kept their gods unbound, but no one seemed surprised. Arran wanted to be the one to hold the Warrior along with Ian, but Fallon had Hayden do the honors instead.

The talking wasn't enough for Arran. He needed answers, answers the Warrior wasn't providing them.

Lucan narrowed his gaze on Arran. Arran knew his anger was there for all to see. It was a living, breathing thing inside him, but there was nothing he could do to shut it off.

He feared it would never shut off again until Ronnie was in his arms once more.

"I'm no' telling you anything," the Warrior said to Quinn. "I couldna even if I wanted to."

"What do you mean?" Galen asked.

The Warrior cackled. "It was made clear that if I told anyone who unbound my god, something awful would happen."

Broc snorted. "You're a Warrior. You have power, strength, and speed. Why are you answering to anyone but yourself?"

"You answer to the MacLeod."

Broc crossed his arms over his chest and glanced at Fallon. "He might be leader of us, but in the end, I answer to myself. I stay with the MacLeods because they are family."

"Say what you want." The Warrior smirked and turned his gaze to Arran. "There's nothing you can do that will keep us from getting the Druid. Nothing."

Arran had heard enough. He lunged for the Warrior, only to be brought up short by Lucan and Charon, who held him back.

"This willna solve anything," Lucan said.

Arran growled, his anger festering the longer his enemy continued to smile. "I willna allow them near her."

"There's another way," Charon whispered.

Arran paused and looked at the man he had hated for so long. There was a calculating gleam in Charon's dark gaze, one that Arran recognized all too well.

He relaxed, and they released him. Arran turned his attention to the prisoner.

"Whoever made you must have great power," Charon said to the Warrior.

The Warrior shrugged as best he could, considering Hayden and Ian held him by his arms. "Oh, aye. He does."

"He," Logan said with a sly grin.

The Warrior's grin faded. "What of it?"

Charon walked in front of the Warrior and then turned and did it again. "Does this Druid have many Warriors?"

"Some."

"Some," Charon repeated, and glanced at Arran. "This Druid considers himself verra powerful, does he no'?"

"Oh, aye. Verra. He is. I've seen his magic."

"Do you know there are two different kinds of Druids?"

Arran bit back his sneer as he realized Charon was putting the Warrior at ease answering mundane questions.

The Warrior gave a quick shake of his head. "I recall something about that. No' that it matters."

"It should, but we'll get back to that later. Did this Druid tell you the story of how the first Warriors were created?"

"I doona give a shit about that. Look at me! I'm a god!"

Charon paused in his pacing and raised a dark brow. Strands of his hair had come loose from the queue, and anyone who didn't know him might not see the anger simmering just below the surface as he smiled easily. "You have a god inside you. It's two different things."

"No' to my way of thinking."

"This Druid who unleashed your god, has he shared his plans with you?"

The Warrior shook his head. "Nay. He tells us some, but I doona ask a lot of questions."

"Where does he conduct his magic and unbind the gods? A warehouse in Glasgow maybe?"

"His home, of course."

Arran had to keep still as Charon got more information than any before him. There was no denying Charon's skill. It made Arran rethink how he'd always thought Charon foolish for returning to the village he'd grown up in.

"How many Druids does he have?" Charon asked.

The Warrior hooted. "More than ever come around the house. There are a couple I'd like to warm my bed."

"I'm sure," Charon said, his lips flattening. "So, does Jason Wallace have a specific interest in Ronnie? Or does he want her just because she's a Druid?"

"Jason told us that he needs her because there's a possibility she can find magical artifacts." As soon as the words left the Warrior's mouth, he gave a great roar and tried to yank free. "You bastard!"

Charon smiled coldly. "Intelligence is clearly something you need to master."

Arran took a step toward the Warrior when he screamed in pain. Arran stopped and watched as the Warrior's chest suddenly split open and his heart erupted for all to see.

Hayden released the now dead Warrior to watch him fall to the ground. "Fascinating."

"You could say that," Fallon said.

Arran looked around. "I need to make sure Ronnie is all right."

"Larena is with her," Quinn said.

But Arran ignored him. "Broc, can you find Larena and make sure she and Ronnie are all right?"

With a nod, Broc closed his eyes and used the power of his god to locate Ronnie. It took just a few seconds before his eyes snapped open. "Ronnie is with a *drough* and a Warrior."

Fallon pushed past his brothers and stood before Broc, panic in his green eyes. "Where is Larena? Where is my wife, Broc?"

Once more Broc searched, and this time when he opened his eyes, there was sadness there. "She's here, but injured. Follow me."

Logan and Hayden stayed behind to guard Gwynn while the rest of them raced after Broc. Arran came to a halt as Fallon let out a bellow and fell to his knees beside Larena's unmoving form.

Fallon said not a word to any of them as he gathered Larena in his arms and teleported to the castle.

Arran had seen the bullet hole in Larena's back. There wasn't much blood, but there didn't need to be if the bullets used were X90s.

How long had Larena been lying here injured? How long had Ronnie been gone?

Arran turned to Lucan and Quinn. "Your brother is going to need you. Go to him."

"What are you going to do?" Lucan asked.

Arran looked into the distance, a great, voracious hole opening in his chest where his heart had once been, knowing Ronnie was in enemy hands. "I'm going to find Ronnie."

"No' without me," Charon said.

Phelan nodded with a cruel twist of his lips. "It's been too long since I've had a good fight. I'll go. Besides, you arses will no doubt need the power of my god."

"I'm going, too," Ian said.

Malcolm gave a nod, and that's all Arran needed to know he could count on the Warrior.

"We'll need Ramsey," Ian said. "If Jason is anything like Declan, Ramsey will be a huge boon."

Arran wanted Jason dead by any means necessary. And if it meant allowing one of his friends to kill the bastard, then Arran would do it.

"Call Ramsey and see if he's in," Arran said, and started toward the parking area.

A form suddenly blocked his way. He looked into the green eyes of Quinn MacLeod.

"You had my back in the bowels of Deirdre's mountain, Arran. I'll no' desert you now."

Arran was honored by Quinn's words. "I know if I asked, you'd come."

"You doona have to ask."

"Your brother is going to need you. Larena didna look good. We can handle Jason."

Broc sighed loudly. "I agree with him, Quinn. You and Lucan need to go to Fallon. The rest of us will go after Jason."

Arran looked at Broc, Galen, and Camdyn. Before he could say anything, Logan, Gwynn, and Hayden walked up.

"Count me and Logan in," Hayden said.

Arran looked at each of the men who had become brothers to him. "Thank you."

"We're family. Did you think we wouldna be here for you?" Ian said, and punched him in the arm.

Broc's lips tightened for a moment before he and said, "Ronnie is with Dale. They're on the road going north."

"To Wallace's mansion, no doubt," Logan said with a growl.

Arran saw how Gwynn took Logan's hand. Both she and Logan had barely come out of the Wallace mansion alive. That was before they'd killed Declan.

It was time to kill another evil.

And Arran was more than looking forward to it.

"Hold on, Ronnie. I'm coming," Arran whispered.

CHAPTER
THIRTY-FIVE

Fallon teleported to his and Larena's bedroom, bellowing for Sonya as soon as he arrived at the castle. Larena's motionless form reminded him all too vividly of holding her four hundred years earlier, after she'd been stabbed with *drough* blood and nearly died.

It was a much more massive amount of *drough* blood in her then, which was the only reason he hadn't totally lost his calm.

Yet, he wasn't ready to release her when Sonya threw open the heavy oak door and gasped.

"What happened?" Sonya asked as she hurried toward them.

Fallon briefly noticed the other Druids venturing into his chamber. He swallowed and looked at Larena's pale face. "She's been shot in the back."

There was no need to tell Sonya the bullet fired was an X90. The fact Larena wasn't moving proved the situation was critical.

"Lay her down, Fallon."

Sonya's voice was soft, her amber eyes patient as she waited for him to do as she asked. Fallon could feel how slow Larena's breathing was. He was afraid to let go of her.

"I can no' lose her."

Ramsey touched his arm. "Then let Sonya do what she can."

Fallon had watched Sonya use her magic to heal many of them struck down with *drough* blood, including Larena.

He gently laid his wife on the bed before turning her onto her stomach so Sonya could get to the wound. Fallon moved a strand of Larena's golden hair out of her face and noticed the blood that stained his hands.

"Here," Tara said.

Fallon looked to find a damp towel held out to him. He absently took it, and quickly turned to watch Sonya. She smoothed back her red curls and took a deep breath. Then her hands were held palm down over Larena's wound as she whispered words as ancient as the Druids themselves.

Sweat beaded Sonya's brow and dampened her hair as she continued to pour magic into Larena, yet the bullet hadn't exited her body. Marcail, Cara, Isla, and Reaghan soon joined their magic with Sonya's.

Though they didn't have healing magic, their magic could boost Sonya's. It wasn't long before Dani, Saffron, Tara, and Ramsey also combined their magic with the others'.

And still the bullet wouldn't be removed.

"It's lodged in her spine," Sonya said, though she didn't open her eyes.

Fallon dropped to his knees and took Larena's hand. "Fight," he whispered near her ear. "Fight to live, Larena. You've survived this once. You can again."

His heart pounded like a drum in his chest. His blood was like ice in his veins. He'd always thought himself lucky because he never had to worry about Larena dying.

She was a Warrior, immortal and powerful just as he was.

Yet, here he was, on his knees praying God would hear him and spare his wife. He prayed the Druids' magic would be strong enough to help, because he couldn't live without her.

"This bullet is different," Isla said, her ice blue eyes filled with unease.

Fallon squeezed Larena's hand. "Come on, baby. Come

back to me. We're supposed to start a family soon, remember. I promised you. And I never go back on my promises."

Sonya sighed and dropped her arms. Her eyes opened and a tear fell down her cheek. "The X90 has to come out or it'll continue to leak *drough* blood inside her."

"I know," Fallon said roughly. "What are you waiting for?"

"My magic isn't affecting it. I'm going to have to go in and get it out myself."

Fallon shook his head. "Nay. I'll do it."

He rose to his feet and sank onto the bed beside Larena. Her wound had begun to turn black at the edges. Fallon lengthened his claws and sliced her back so that the injury was larger.

Then he used his claws to tenderly pull apart her skin until he could see the bullet. It was lodged among her vertebrae, just as Isla had said.

If he could get the X90 out, then Larena had a chance for her goddess to heal her. Twice he scraped the bullet with his claws, but he couldn't get a hold of it.

"Use these," Cara said as she handed him tweezers.

They were small, and his large fingers had a hard time controlling them. But he gave them a try. Once his claws retreated, he managed to get the tweezers around the bullet.

After four attempts, he was about to give up when Isla put a hand on his arm.

"Give it one more try," she said.

Fallon glanced at her before he inhaled deeply. He focused on the bullet and waited until he had the tweezers firmly around it before he moved his hand slowly side to side, dislodging the cartridge.

He blinked away the sweat that fell into his eyes. Even when the bullet began to move, he didn't smile with joy. He wouldn't smile again until Larena opened her smoky blue eyes and looked at him.

The tweezers began to slide off the bullet, so Fallon eased his grip and tried again. It was a painstaking process, and the longer he took, the closer to death Larena got.

"She's not breathing," Dani said.

Fallon's heart fell to his feet. He growled and tossed the tweezers aside. "Forgive me, my love," he whispered before he pushed his hand into Larena's wound and grasped the bullet with his fingers.

He got a good hold of it, and with a snarl, yanked the offensive object out. Fallon threw it to the floor, and with blinding speed extended a black claw and sliced open his arm. He let blood pour from his wound into the hole in Larena's back left by the bullet.

"We're going to need more," Sonya said softly.

Ramsey didn't say a word as he cut his arm and gave his blood. He nodded to Fallon.

Fallon didn't want to take the time to get his brothers, even if it was just a few seconds. He also didn't want to leave Larena. But if he didn't do something to save his wife, she would be gone forever.

He clenched his hands and waited until the last bit of his blood fell into her wound before his cut healed. Without a word, he jumped to the dig site.

Quinn, Lucan, and Gwynn stood in a small huddle as the rain drenched them. Fallon didn't give them time to ask questions as he teleported them back to the castle and into his chamber.

"Holy hell," Quinn said as he took sight of Larena.

Fallon went back to his spot by the bed and cut his arm once more for his wife. Lucan moved beside him and slashed his arm and let the blood fill Larena's wound.

Quinn took the other side of the bed near Marcail and Ramsey and did the same. Again and again the four Warriors gave their blood to Larena.

Each second that ticked by on the clock with Larena still not stirring made Fallon's gut clench with dread.

Even the Druids had taken their places around the bed once more, their magic filling the chamber until it fairly hummed.

And still nothing.

Fallon's throat closed as he stared at Larena's lifeless body.

"Nay!" he shouted, and gathered her close. He ignored the arms that grabbed him, and held her even tighter.

"Please," he whispered. "Larena, live. Please, live."

He cradled the back of her head in his hands and rocked her. Memories flashed through his mind of their four hundred years together. The laughter, the tears, the fights, the teasing, and even the battles they'd fought to save the world.

At every turn, Larena had been there with him. She'd encouraged him, loved him. Made him a better man.

The thought of not having her in his life seemed . . . wrong.

"I can no' lose you," he said through his tears.

Quinn leaned his head back against the stones of the corridor and sighed. Fallon had been alone in his chamber with Larena for over two hours.

"I doona understand," Lucan said.

Quinn looked at his brother, who was squatting across the hall from him, his head in his hands.

"What was different about these X90s that could cause such damage?" Lucan lifted his head, his green eyes troubled.

Isla held up the crushed metal bullet. "The amount of *drough* blood that was contained doesn't seem to be different. It appears that it's the bullet itself. Or, rather, the magic surrounding it."

Ramsey grunted. "It's the magic."

"The only one who used those damned bullets was Declan. It makes sense that Jason could've altered them," Quinn said.

Lucan stood and pulled Cara into his arms. He ran his hands down Cara's chestnut tresses. "We've always gone into battle knowing *drough* blood could kill us. We battled Declan and his mercenaries, and won."

"You aren't going to give up, Lucan MacLeod," Cara said as she looked up at him. Her mahogany eyes, filled with love and concern, were locked on him. "You're a Warrior. For whatever reason, Fate gifted you with a god inside you. If it wasn't for you and the other Warriors, Deirdre would've ruled the world long ago."

Marcail nodded her head of sable hair and threaded her fingers with Quinn's. "Cara's right. Aye, I fear every time you leave for battle that it might be the last time I see you. As much as I'd love to keep you beside me always, if it wasn't for you Warriors, I wouldn't have a world to live in."

Tara didn't say anything as she rested her head on Ramsey's chest. They'd been through it all just the year before.

"After all that happened when I lost my magic," Sonya said with a shake of her head as she swiped at her eyes. "Even the combined magic of all of us couldn't save Larena."

Isla picked at a fingernail. "Arran and the others are going to need all three of you MacLeod brothers as well as Ramsey."

Quinn glanced at the door leading into Fallon's room. "Fallon willna leave Larena. He pulled himself out of the despair after Deirdre unbound our god, but I fear this time we'll lose him forever."

"I refuse to even consider that," Lucan said. "Every one of us here—Warrior and Druid alike—needs Fallon. We're a family, and we'll do what a family has to."

Quinn glanced at his brother as he recalled it had been Lucan who held the brothers together during their darkest hours. "We hold strong."

"We hold strong," Lucan repeated through the sadness that had descended over the castle.

Gwynn cleared her throat, her arms crossed over her chest. Her violet eyes touched on each of them. "Fallon lost Larena. If y'all don't get him to the Wallace mansion, he won't be the only Warrior to lose the woman he loves."

"She's right," Saffron agreed. "Ronnie and Arran are meant to be together, even if they don't know it yet."

Quinn kissed the top of Marcail's head. "He'll know it soon. Sometimes it takes almost losing our women to make us realize we need them."

"If Fallon doesna come out, we must leave immediately

to get to the mansion in time," Ramsey said, and ran a hand through his long black hair.

With a nod, Quinn and Lucan entered Fallon's chamber and silently closed the door behind them.

The eldest MacLeod—who had overcome being a drunk, who had been trained to lead a clan, who had become a great man—sat upon his bed holding his dead wife.

Quinn blinked away the moisture that filled his eyes. Larena had been special, not because she was the only female Warrior. But because she had been the one to steady Fallon. She'd been the one who stood beside him through it all.

"Damn," Lucan muttered and looked at the floor.

Quinn took a deep breath and tried to find the words to speak. They might have won against Deirdre and Declan, but they had lost people.

Duncan, Ian's twin and a fellow Warrior, had been killed by Deirdre. There was Fiona and Braden, two Druids who had come to the castle with Reaghan. But none had ever lost a spouse.

Until now.

"Fallon—," Lucan began.

The eldest MacLeod lifted his dark green eyes, and the stark grief in them made Quinn take a step back.

"Arran and Ronnie need us," Lucan said.

Fallon nodded. "I know. I doona want anyone else to lose their mate. Too much blood has been spilled already."

Quinn cocked his head at the strange inflection in his brother's voice. He'd at first thought it was just grief, but as Fallon laid Larena on the bed and rose to face them, Quinn saw Fallon's eyes.

"Oh, fuck," Lucan mumbled.

CHAPTER
THIRTY-SIX

Aisley pulled into the drive of the Wallace mansion. As a child, the few occasions she'd been to the mansion had been ones of great happiness. She'd get lost playing in the maze of hedges in the back.

There she'd been able to pretend she was a magician, a superhero, and any number of things that had crossed her mind at the time. Then, she'd been able to do and be anything she'd wanted.

Funny how life never turned out the way a child dreamed.

Aisley put the car in park and looked in the rearview mirror to see Dale. "Is she still out?"

"She started to come to about an hour ago. I gave her a little tap to keep her unconscious."

Aisley jerked around in the seat to gawk at him. "Have you lost your mind? You don't know your own strength."

"Give me some credit, lass. I didna hurt her."

Aisley gave a snort and turned to reach for the door handle, only to have her door yanked opened for her.

"It's about time," Mindy said, her foot tapping on the small stones lining the drive and her red lips puckered in a pout.

Aisley pushed Mindy aside and got out of the car. "Get over yourself."

"Where have you been?" Jason demanded from the front steps.

Aisley wanted to tell him to go screw himself. Instead, she opened the back passenger door and looked down at the unconscious Druid.

"We made it here, didn't we?" Aisley said.

Dale stepped out of the car on the other side and gave a nod to Jason. "Ronnie and Arran were no' alone."

"I expected they might bring a few friends," Jason said with a smile.

Aisley barely kept her lips from lifting upward in a grin as she said, "Oh, they brought a few, all right. They brought all of them. And a Druid."

Just as she thought, Jason's smile vanished. His gaze jerked to Dale. "Where are my *droughs*?"

"You ordered me to get Ronnie back here as soon as I could. That's what I did. I'm no' sure if any of your *droughs* are still alive, no' after what those Warriors did."

Jason stomped down the steps and got in Aisley's face. "How? How did the Warriors get an upper hand? They should've been powerless with the force of you Druids."

"They were. For a moment. There was one there, a maroon Warrior, who didn't seem to be affected. He used his power of lightning to strike us."

"You seem to have come away unaffected," Jason said with scorn as he looked her up and down.

Aisley wasn't going to tell him that it was Dale who had saved her. It would only cause Dale to get a dose of Jason's wrath. "I'm a Wallace, remember, Cousin? We seem to have a knack for staying alive."

Her explanation sufficed, because Jason turned away without another word. Aisley shifted her gaze to Mindy, who still stared at her with hatred burning in her eyes.

"Go on like a good doggie, and follow your master," Aisley said with fake sweetness dripping from her words. "Be a good bitch."

Mindy took the two steps separating them and rammed her finger in Aisley's shoulder. Aisley felt a blast of magic hit her, but she managed to keep the pain from her face. A trick she had learned quickly while under Jason's roof.

"One of these days, Jason is going to give me leave to kill you."

Aisley turned her lips up in a mocking smirk. "I look forward to the day you try."

It was only after Mindy had gone into the house that Aisley touched the spot where the magic had entered her. She shifted the collar of her shirt and saw the burned skin.

"Does it hurt?"

She jerked her head up to stare at Dale. She'd completely forgotten he was there. Aisley shrugged and released her collar. "It's nothing I can't handle."

"I didna ask that. I asked if it hurt."

Dale had protected her from the Warrior's lightning. He'd also done small things over the months to keep Jason's ire off her. Dale liked her, she knew. But was it enough that she could trust him?

The big man frowned and swiped a hand over his shaved head. "You doona trust me."

"I don't trust anyone."

"Aye. That's probably a wise move. Though you may no' believe it, Aisley, you can trust me."

Dale bent inside the car, and when he stood, he had Ronnie in his arms. Aisley shut her door and then walked around to the other side of the car and shut that one as well.

She followed Dale up the front steps, but stopped before entering the house. Her gaze moved to the tall gate that kept out unwanted guests.

Yet nothing would keep out the Warriors from MacLeod Castle. Aisley had no doubt they would come. Especially Arran. The Warrior would come for Ronnie.

The problem was, did she want them to win? They'd kill her on the spot for her involvement with Jason and the fact she was a *drough*.

Because unlike the others in Jason's little clan, she had done her research on the Druids.

Either with the MacLeods winning or Jason winning, Aisley knew she wasn't long for this world. And that didn't bother her. Death was more acceptable than the life she led.

Even if that death meant she went to Hell.

Ronnie came awake slowly. The first thing she felt was the ache in her jaw, and then the raw, excruciating pain of her left forearm. The events of before came rushing back to her like a tidal wave.

"No!" she screamed and bolted upright in a cot so similar to the one in her tent that for a moment she thought that's where she was.

She tried to turn, only to be jerked to a stop by something on her right arm. Confused, Ronnie looked down at the large iron manacle around her wrist to the thick, heavy chain that fell to the floor and all the way up the wall behind her where the chain was bolted.

"So glad you're finally awake."

The cold, eerie male voice made Ronnie's skin itch. She turned her head to find herself looking through a row of metal bars. It took her a moment to realize she was locked in a prison.

The man banged his fist against the metal. His blond hair was cut short, making his hawkish face and long neck appear more angular. "It's stout. This dungeon survived even the fire. Declan used magic to make the cells strong, and then I added my magic on top of it."

Ronnie parted her lips to breathe through her mouth as her stomach began to grow queasy. She glanced down at her injured arm to see that it was wrapped in gauze.

"You look confused," the man said with a sly smile.

Her gaze turned to him. The glee on his face at her predicament only made her more ill.

"I guess I should introduce myself. I'm Jason Wallace."

Ronnie lifted her chin and looked him in the eye. "Should I be impressed?"

Jason clapped his hands together once and threw back his head and laughed. "Brilliant. Just brilliant."

"Where am I? Why have you taken me from my dig site?" Ronnie thought by appearing ignorant of Jason's identity and scheming, she might be freed. She should have known better.

"Oh, please. Is that the best you can do?" he asked with a frown. He rolled his eyes. "You can stop with the act, Dr. Reid. You know all about Druids and Warriors and magic. It's an amazing world we Druids live in, is it no'?"

"It would be without people like you."

One side of his lips lifted in a grin. "There's that spirit I've heard so much about. But, lass, you know as well as I that good can no' exist without evil. There is no such thing as Utopia. The idea of a place where everyone gets along and loves one another makes me twitchy, because it isna real."

"And the world where you dominate all doesn't make you twitchy?"

"Actually, it makes me all warm and fuzzy inside."

Ronnie made a sound in the back of her throat. "You don't see what you're doing as wrong?"

"Wrong? Of course no'. I'm doing the world a favor, darling. Right now, everything is complete chaos out there. No one can trust anyone. The media in every country is lying to the public to keep their fears down. Every country is arming themselves with nuclear and biological weapons. People are stealing, raping, murdering. I'll put a stop to it all."

"While you lie, steal, rape, and murder?"

He shrugged. "I'll do what I must to get things where they need to be."

"Isn't that the Utopia you just vilified?"

"You're a smart one," Jason said as he leaned a shoulder against the metal. "I'm no' stupid or naïve enough to believe everyone will be happy in the world I create. But they will answer to me. There willna be a threat of nuclear war."

"No, just the fear that you won't like what they're wearing so you strike them down with your magic?"

"Oh, there will be fear, Ronnie. I never said there wouldna

be. There will be order, though. Order out of chaos. Does that no' appeal to you?"

She didn't want to admit that the thought of no more wars sounded good, but to reach that state, everyone would lose their basic human rights.

There wasn't a doubt in her mind that Jason Wallace was the "new darkness" spoken of in the prophecy. She was more frightened than at any other time in her life, but she refused to allow him to see it.

"You can no' lie, nor can you bring yourself to tell me the truth." Jason tsked. "It's all right. I'm no' giving up on you yet."

"Just what do you want with me?"

He pushed away from the bars with his shoulder. "Originally I wanted you for your magic. There are thousands of magical items buried throughout Britain. I want to find them, and you're going to help me do it."

She thought over all she'd learned about Jason's predecessors, Declan and Deirdre. Arran had made them sound like monsters, but as she stared at Jason, all she saw was a man. A demented man, but just a man. He might have magic, but so did she. Did that make her evil?

Even if he were malevolent, Ronnie wouldn't help him in anything.

"No."

Jason's eyes watched her carefully. "I thought you'd say that."

"You said originally. Did you change your mind?"

"No' exactly. What none of you realize yet is just how powerful my magic is. While you slept, sweet Ronnie, I searched your mind. The mind is an amazing place. So many corridors and rooms. There was one room that was right in the front of your thoughts."

She fisted her good arm and thought of Arran. If Jason hurt him . . . she didn't know what she would do, but she would do something.

Jason suddenly smirked like a Cheshire cat. "Ah. You

think I'm speaking of your Warrior. I'll get to him in good time, Dr. Reid. Nay, I speak of something else."

The only other thing she'd been worried about was the . . . prophecy.

"The one with untapped magic will free those trapped by the magic-wielders. She will unknowingly bring about destruction and death. The female Druid will be the bringer of doom. Only to be ended by a man-god. The new darkness will join forces with the Druid. And it will be the end of all."

It was all Ronnie could do not to cover her ears and sing at the top of her lungs. Those words were branded in her mind, a constant companion as she wondered if Arran would have to kill her or if, as Arran said, she was strong enough to withstand the evil.

"I see those words are familiar," Jason said as he put his hands in his pockets and regarded her. "Of all the things I imagined finding inside that mind of yours, a prophecy wasn't one of them. And you think it's about you."

"It might not be."

"You believe it is, though," he said with a cocky wink. "Is that why Arran stays so close to you? Is he the one charged with ending you if you bring about the doom?"

Ronnie refused to answer him. She lifted her chin, letting him think whatever he wanted.

"Then maybe you'd like to tell me what it was you released in the chamber you found."

She swallowed and looked away. "I didn't release anything."

"You're a verra bad liar, Dr. Reid. I tried this the easy way, but you want to do it the hard way. Which is fine by me. You see, I brought along a little insurance to assure you comply with my every question and demand."

Her shoulders slumped as Andy was shoved into sight. Dried blood coated the left side of his face from his forehead down to his neck. His glasses were gone, and it looked like his nose was broken. His hands were tied behind him, and he landed heavily on his shoulder. She winced as his head banged against the concrete.

With a wave of Jason's hand, someone in the shadows grabbed Andy and lifted him to his feet.

"This," Jason said as he motioned to Andy and took a step back that put him in shadows, "is what I like to call incentive. You do as I ask, and your friend lives. I know how much he means to you, based on what my intel has told me. I know he's no' your lover, but I think he'll do."

"Ronnie?" Andy said thickly, and squinted to try to see her.

Ronnie swallowed past the lump in her throat. "I'm here, Andy. Everything is going to be fine."

"Who are these men?" Andy asked.

She didn't get a chance to answer, as he was quickly led from the room. Ronnie wanted to scream her frustration at Andy's capture, her imprisonment, and the pain in her body.

It was her fault she was here. She'd sent Arran away. Not just that, but he'd tried to warn her they would come for her again, and she hadn't listened. She was utterly alone in this.

Even if she had her cell phone, who would she call? Pete? He'd never believe such a wild tale. Saffron? After all Ronnie had done, would Saffron believe her? Arran?

Ronnie's heart ached just thinking about him. She could still see his amazing golden eyes fill with hurt when she'd sent him away.

Arran would come, but then what? Another battle? It was a moot point anyway, since she didn't have any means to contact him.

No, she was explicitly, keenly alone. The only one able to help Andy was her. Arran had told her she could use her magic to defend herself, but she didn't have the first clue how to do that.

Jason knew how to control and use his magic, and he had many people to keep watch over her. Which left her with just one choice since escape was out of the question.

She would have to do as Jason asked.

Ronnie turned her gaze to him. "Do I have your word that as long as I do as you say, Andy will be left unharmed—by humans, Warriors, and Druids alike? That no magic will touch him ever?"

"You have my word."

She clenched her jaw, blood drumming in her ears. "I want to see your face clearly. Come into the light."

There was a click of boot heels as Jason went into the light. "Better?"

"Give me your word."

"I give it. No magic will harm Andy."

Still she didn't believe him, but what choice did she have? "I want you to swear it on your magic. Vow to me that Andy will not only remain unharmed, but you'll also treat his injuries, and once I do as you ask, you'll let him go."

"Why would I release him? He'll keep you doing what I want."

Ronnie swung her legs over the side of the cot and stood. She tested the heavy chain holding her and made her way to the wall separating her and Jason. She looked at him through the bars. "I give you my word that I won't try to escape. Just let Andy go."

For long minutes, Jason simply stared at her. "I'll keep Andy around for a few weeks, but I'll release him as long as I can trust you."

Then Jason held out his hand, palm up, and a ball of dark purple light formed in his hand. His blue gaze caught hers. "I, Jason Wallace, do vow that no Druid, Warrior, or human shall harm Andy while he's under my protection."

The ball of light grew and the purple darkened until it was completely black before the ball lengthened and first wrapped around Jason's hand and then Ronnie's. A moment later, it disappeared.

"There," Jason said. "I've given you my promise, and even set it in magic. Are you ready to give me what I want?"

Ronnie thought of Arran and how his eyes had looked at her so lovingly while he made love to her, how she'd felt loved, needed, and protected. He might find her, but there was no way he or any of the Warriors could win against magic like Jason's.

"Yes."

The door to her prison unlocked and swung open the same instant the manacle around her wrist fell to the ground with a hard thud, the metal clanking on itself. Jason smirked as she stepped out of her cell and stopped beside him.

"That was much easier than I thought you'd make it."

She turned her head away. "You didn't give me a choice."

"Now you know what kind of ruler I'll be for mankind. I'm the parent everyone needs or else the children of the world will run amok, as they've done for ages."

"With all your magic, you should be able to find the magical items you seek."

"Verra true, sweet Ronnie. But I want you for much more."

"Like what?"

"You're going to tell me what you and MacCarrick took out of the chamber. And eventually, you're going to become a *drough*. Because, you see, I'm going to make sure the prophecy you fear so greatly comes to pass."

He walked past her, but Ronnie couldn't make her legs move. She knew she'd done the right thing in order to save Andy, but all she could think about was Arran.

And the awful future in front of her.

"Come along, Dr. Reid. We've work to do," Jason's voice said from the doorway where he waited.

"Forgive me, Arran," she whispered.

CHAPTER
THIRTY-SEVEN

Arran once more stood outside Wallace mansion. It was over a year ago that he'd been there with the others to defeat Declan. That night had been horrendous. Not just from the battle, but also because they lost two Druids, and Ramsey nearly died.

Ramsey had risked his life in order to save Tara. Yet it was Tara's unbalanced magic that had saved Ramsey after he conquered Declan.

The mansion was burned to the ground. Arran had been one of the ones who looked through the house to retrieve anything remotely magical. And all Declan's books.

He looked at the mansion, and it seemed the year before had been nothing more than a dream. The house looked exactly the same, right down to the yellow rosebush on each of the front corners of the house.

"I'd thought it was over," Camdyn said wearily as they stood hidden from the road and the house.

"We missed something," Arran said. "We have to accept that, but that doesna mean we give up."

Logan slapped Arran on the back, his smile tight. "My thoughts exactly."

"How should we proceed?" Charon asked.

Broc squatted outside the ten-foot iron gate and peered

through the thick hedges. "Jason kept quiet for a year. I suspect he's building his magic."

"As well as unbinding gods to make Warriors," Hayden added.

Broc nodded, and turned his head to look at Arran. "It's your woman in there."

Arran wanted to tell him Ronnie wasn't his. She had turned him away. He'd told her nothing but the truth, even when he feared how she'd react. And she hadn't believed he wouldn't steal from her.

"Arran?" Galen prodded.

He looked back at the imposing sight of the mansion. "Aye. Ronnie."

"Do you have a plan?" Broc asked.

Arran grinned as he released his god. "Ah. I kill the bastard."

"Sounds good to me," Hayden said as his skin shifted to the red of his god.

Phelan moved to stand on Arran's other side. "We each have powers that could aid us and give us an advantage."

"Need I remind you what the Druids did to us at the dig site?" Ian asked.

Galen released a long breath. "This would be easier with the MacLeods. And Larena."

It grew quiet as their thoughts turned to Larena. Arran didn't know if she lived, but he'd seen Sonya and the other Druids do amazing things with their magic.

Logan had been all but dead after being riddled with the X90s, but Sonya had saved him. Surely she could save Larena, who had just one bullet in her.

"We can do this," Arran said. He clenched his jaw as his gaze moved over the outside of the mansion. "We know the layout of the house. It's obvious Jason hasna changed a thing."

Camdyn gave a nod. "There's just one way in and out of the dungeons. That's probably where Ronnie is being kept."

"So, underground." Arran turned his head to Camdyn. "That shouldna be a problem for you."

Camdyn's smile grew the longer he stared at Arran. "I'm liking this plan already."

"While Camdyn attacks from below, I'll attack from above," Broc said. His dark eyes clashed with Arran's as he released his god. Indigo skin covered him, and massive, leathery indigo wings sprouted from his back.

Galen clicked his dark green claws together. "Attack from above and below. I take it we're striking from the sides?"

"Hmm. This is going to be good," Hayden said, and rubbed his hands together, fire surrounding his fingers before he extinguished it.

Arran looked at Logan and Hayden. "You two take the west side. Galen, you and Ian take the back. Charon and Malcolm can take the east side."

"And where am I?" Phelan asked.

Arran glanced at the door of the mansion. "I want you with me. I'm going through the front."

"Sounds like a suitable plan," said a voice behind them.

They all spun around to find Lucan. He smiled, but it didn't reach his eyes as he stepped out of the shadows. Quinn gave a nod as he followed. And then they spotted Fallon.

Arran couldn't believe the man before him. Fallon was a shell, his green eyes blazing with hatred and the necessity for vengeance.

Ramsey brought up the rear, his gaze locked on the Wallace mansion. "I'd hoped never to return."

"All of us did," Quinn said.

Arran couldn't stop looking at Fallon. It was obvious by the stiff way he held himself and the muscle working in his jaw that Larena wasn't doing well.

"I need to kill something," Fallon stated flatly. "Tell me where you want me, Arran."

The raw anguish in Fallon's voice made Arran turn his gaze away from his leader. Larena wasn't hurt. She was dead. The knowledge rippled through them like lightning.

"Nay," Malcolm whispered from the back.

Fallon turned and looked at Larena's cousin. A lone tear

traced slowly down Fallon's cheek. There were no words between them, but Fallon's eyes said it all.

For the first time in months, Malcolm showed emotion.

And it was rage.

Arran almost felt sorry for the ones inside the mansion. Almost. Then he remembered Ronnie. Fallon had lost Larena. Arran knew he'd lost Ronnie as well, but it wouldn't be to death.

"Lucan, can you get to the roof and aid Broc?" Arran asked.

One side of Lucan's mouth tilted in a grin. "I'm looking forward to it."

"I'll go with Camdyn," Quinn offered.

Arran nodded and looked to Ramsey and Fallon. "Ramsey, can you use your Druid magic again?"

"What's your plan?" Ramsey asked, interest sparking in his silver eyes.

Arran glanced at the house and then to Fallon. "There are spells guarding the house. If you can lower them long enough for Fallon to teleport in and out, he can do all kinds of damage."

"Consider it done," Ramsey stated.

Arran had formed the plan on the drive to the mansion. He had the Warriors paired to use their powers to the fullest. But everything hinged on getting through the spells protecting the house.

Declan had used layer upon layer of spells. Would Jason do the same?

"Do we wait for the darkness?" Charon asked.

"Nay." Arran wasn't about to delay that long.

Fallon faced the mansion once more. "I agree."

"There are cameras everywhere," Ian said.

Arran shrugged. "Stay out of sight until it's time to attack."

"And the signal to attack?" Quinn asked.

Arran looked at Malcolm. "Lightning."

Everyone split up then, going in teams as they surrounded the house. Camdyn found the best place in which to use his power of moving the earth so he could strike from below the house, and hopefully find Ronnie in the dungeons.

Arran, Phelan, Malcolm, Fallon, Ramsey, and Charon stayed where they were. Phelan had gone to make sure no one could enter or leave through the gates on the drive, and Charon was scouting the east side.

Fallon moved off away from them, letting everyone know he had no wish to talk. Ramsey was concentrating on the spells to see just how many Jason had put up.

Arran silently rejoiced. He'd always known having a Warrior that was part Druid would come in handy.

Malcolm was quiet as he kept his attention on the mansion. Arran found it difficult to wait. He had to give everyone time to reach their spots, and to be sure that Ramsey could get through the spells.

"How did you do it?" Arran asked Malcolm.

Malcolm blinked slowly, but didn't look at him. "Do what?"

"Withstand the Druids' magic at the dig site. I couldna move."

"There is much that doesna affect a person when there is no feeling within them."

Arran snorted. "There's feeling within you, Malcolm. I saw it when you learned of Larena."

Malcolm's head jerked to him, his blue eyes flashing with fury and the scars on his face standing out more than usual. In an instant, he released his god, maroon coloring his skin and eyes. "I did everything for Larena, to keep her safe. I became what Deirdre wanted so Larena could have a happy life. I did . . . I had to shut off my feelings or I'd never have survived."

"You betrayed Deirdre and killed her. That should've set you free."

Malcolm looked back at the house. "Should have doesna always equal what happens. I'm dead inside, Arran. The only thing that kept me connected to the MacLeods and all of you was Larena. She's been taken."

"So you'll exact your revenge, then disappear."

Malcolm's silence was answer enough.

Arran couldn't begrudge him. What had happened to Malcolm was wrong. From the first, when Deirdre's Warriors had attacked him and left him for dead.

Sonya had saved Malcolm, but even then he hadn't woken the same man. And then Deirdre had captured him and released his god, a god he didn't know he had.

It was a secret Larena and Fallon had kept from Malcolm in the hopes that he could handle the knowledge one day. They never got the chance to tell him.

And once Malcolm was in Deirdre's hands, he had become the one Warrior who did as she'd demanded without question. It was Malcolm, after all, who had taken Duncan's head on Deirdre's order.

Arran wasn't sure if he were in Ian's shoes, that he could forgive someone, even a friend such as Malcolm, for killing his twin.

Duncan, Ian, and Quinn had been all that kept Arran sane and in control of his god while stuck in Deirdre's Pit deep in Cairn Toul Mountain.

They had fought together, watched each other's backs, and escaped together. They were the first Warriors Arran had dared to trust.

That trust had led him down the road he was currently on, and he didn't regret one minute of it.

His gaze slid to Charon as he walked up. There had been a time Arran wanted to kill Charon for things Deirdre had made him do. It took a while, but Arran finally saw that a man did what he had to do to survive.

"Are you all right?" Charon asked as he ran a finger along one of his horns.

Arran gave a small nod. "Did you take care of the gate?"

Charon chuckled and elbowed Ramsey in the ribs. "Oh, aye. No one is getting in or out, no matter how much magic they use."

Ramsey cut Charon a nasty glare. "It looks as if Jason doesna use half the spells Declan did."

"You should sound happier about that," Phelan said as he joined them.

Ramsey sat back on his heels. "Unlike Deirdre and Declan, Jason has the house full of *droughs*. That's more dangerous than all the spells."

"How many *droughs*?" Fallon asked.

"I count seven, no' including Jason, but there could be
more. And then there's Ronnie."

Arran fisted his hands. "I feel her magic, but I can no'
locate her, because of the spells."

"She could be anywhere in that massive house," Charon
said.

"Get me inside, and I'll find her," Arran vowed.

Fallon leaned his head back, and in an instant he had released his god. Black covered his skin, and onyx claws extended from his fingers. His eyes were black from corner
to corner, and he lifted his upper lip to growl, revealing his
fangs.

Arran had already called forth his god, but he smiled as
the rest released theirs.

"It's time for Jason Wallace to die," Fallon said.

Arran rotated his shoulders as Charon and Malcolm took
their positions.

The only one inside the Wallace mansion who was going
to survive was Ronnie.

CHAPTER
THIRTY-EIGHT

Aisley leaned against the corner of Jason's office, the one he showed visitors. Mindy was sitting on the edge of his dark cherry desk, running her fingers across Jason's shoulders as he leaned back in his chair.

The office was covered in expensive layer paneling, and on the walls hung paintings she knew cost more than her car. Rugs of various sizes and colors were placed haphazardly on the floor.

There were two dark leather Chesterfield couches facing each other with a coffee table between them. Near one set of large windows sat two chairs.

Behind Jason's desk were bookshelves stocked with first editions she would bet her soul he'd never read, much less opened.

He'd been on his mobile for a good ten minutes already. And with every minute that passed, his delight increased. Aisley knew whoever was on the other end of the phone couldn't be good for the MacLeods.

"Are you sure?" Jason asked the caller.

Jason's smile was that of a cat who'd just gotten into the cream, and it left Aisley cold. She knew that smile. It was the one he gave her when she'd begun the *drough* ceremony. The same one when she had given her blood and soul to the Devil.

"Perfect. She's lonely, so you should get in easily," Jason continued.

Aisley wondered who Jason was talking to, but more important, who were they talking about? Not that Aisley could do anything about it.

Knowing only makes it worse.

It was the truth, and even when she knew she was better off not knowing, she couldn't help but find out. Just more sins heaped onto her black soul—a soul destined for the fieriest pits of Hell.

"So he's no' in his village now?"

Aisley looked down at her chipped nails when Mindy glanced her way. There was much Jason had going on that Aisley didn't know about. He'd alluded to something the day before that would surprise everyone.

And knowing Jason, that could be anything.

"Keep at her then," Jason said. "Do whatever it takes. She's close to him, so we'll get him one way or another."

A few moments later and Jason ended the call. No one had moved in his office since he got there. Dale and another Warrior Aisley hadn't bothered to get a name from stood on either side of the door as sentinels.

Two female *droughs,* sisters who Aisley couldn't tolerate being near, sat in the overstuffed chairs by the window.

And on the sofa was none other than Dr. Ronnie Reid.

Aisley looked at her from beneath her lashes. Ronnie was pale, and though she tried to hide it, her hands shook. From pain or fear?

Though Aisley wished it were otherwise, Ronnie was right to be afraid of Jason. Aisley had been foolish for not realizing just how much magic her cousin wielded. Until it was too late.

Ronnie sat with her back straight and one leg crossed over the other. Her left arm was heavily bandaged, and she held it close to her body.

She had a wealth of wheat-colored hair that fell to her waist, though it was in desperate need of a good brushing to get the grass and debris out from when she'd fallen.

Aisley thought of the female Warrior she'd stopped Dale from killing. Why had she done that? If Jason discovered what she'd done, he'd torture her, making every second feel like an eternity.

Aisley thought it amazing that the female's power was invisibility. There was something about the Warrior that Aisley couldn't allow to be killed. She didn't know what it was, but she didn't want the female's death on her conscience.

It brought a smile to her face, wondering if Jason knew that she had kept a Warrior alive. He had a little red book that listed the Warriors from MacLeod Castle and their powers, but was the list complete? Jason thought it was, but she wasn't so sure.

Aisley hadn't seen it, but if Jason knew there was a female Warrior and she had the power to turn invisible, he'd have alerted them.

She hated that the female had been shot. But at least Aisley gave the Warrior a chance, though it was a slim one. She'd had a choice once and made the wrong decision.

But like many things, that decision had altered the course of her life. She was on a course she couldn't veer from, one that was destroying her a day at a time.

She turned her head and looked up to find Dale watching her. The hulking Warrior gave a nod that barely moved his shaved head, but it was enough for her to know he was watching over her.

Odd, for someone who had always relished her independence, she liked knowing Dale was there. A friend— somewhat—in the viper's nest.

"So," Jason said as he rose from his chair and walked around his desk to lean against the front of it. He crossed his ankles and stared at Ronnie. "Are you ready to begin?"

Ronnie's brows rose. "Now?"

"No time like the present, my sweet archeologist."

Jason's sneer was cold and calculating, just as he was. It sent a shiver down Aisley's spine.

"You don't seem to understand how this works," Ronnie said.

Jason placed his hands on the desk next to his hips. "En-lighten me."

"I don't hear the artifacts until I'm near them. So I can't simply point west and say there's something there while sit-ting here."

Aisley liked Ronnie's harsh tone, but it wouldn't serve her well. Something Ronnie would learn soon enough. Right now Jason was being lenient because he needed her cooper-ation. If only Ronnie knew Jason didn't have the leverage she thought he did.

"How close do you need to be?" Mindy demanded as she came to stand beside Jason.

"Within a few miles."

Mindy rolled her eyes. "You're a Druid, bitch. Use your magic."

Aisley bit the inside of her mouth to keep from smiling when she saw Ronnie narrow her eyes on Mindy.

"If you think you can do better, why don't you go find them?" Ronnie retorted icily. "Oh. Wait. That's because you can't."

Aisley coughed to hide her laughter, but Mindy heard it just the same. Mindy pushed off the desk, her high heels clicking on the wood as she stormed over to Ronnie.

"I'd advise you not to mess with me," Mindy stated.

Ronnie slowly stood until she was eye to eye with Mindy. "What are you going to do, tell your boyfriend?"

Mindy let out a rage-filled scream and jerked her hand back as she readied to strike. Aisley straightened the same time Jason lifted his hand. With that simple movement, he effectively halted anything Mindy tried to do.

Aisley's hated enemy stood frozen, her hands clawing at her throat as Jason cut off her airflow. "It's a good look for Mindy. I vote you leave her like that."

Jason sighed dramatically, and Mindy suddenly bent at the waist, choking and gasping for air after Jason lifted his magic.

"Too bad," Aisley mumbled.

When she looked at Mindy, it was to find Ronnie watching her. Aisley lifted a shoulder in a shrug, and went back to leaning in the corner.

Ronnie wasn't sure what to make of the *drough* in the corner. There was animosity between her and Mindy that seemed to go deep.

Even if Ronnie's eyes were closed, she'd know the sound of the *drough*'s voice. It was the one who had stopped Dale from taking Larena's head. But it was also the voice that belonged to the person responsible for shooting Larena with the X90.

Was Larena dead? And if the *drough* was going to kill Larena anyway, why not have Dale take her head?

"I apologize," Jason said.

Ronnie swiveled her head to him. He hadn't so much as twitched from his position other than raising a hand. Mindy now glared at Ronnie as she did the *drough*.

"I'd think as leader you'd have better control of your . . . team," Ronnie said.

Jason smiled. "They get a wee bit heated at times, but I control them."

"So I see. Is this how you'll control the world?"

"Of course."

Ronnie was careful not to hit her injured arm as she lowered herself back to the couch. "You're only one man. How do you figure to rule the entire world? You can't be everywhere at once."

"My faithful companions, of course."

"Of course." Ronnie knew she was pushing her luck, but the longer she put off whatever he wanted the better. "Tell me, how well do you think your lover will do keeping everyone in line? She likes to hurt people. I can see it in her eyes."

"She willna be ruling anyone," Jason said.

Mindy whirled around to him. "What? That's not what you promised me!"

"I promised you'd have a position of power, my sweet. I never said what that position was," Jason said calmly.

Ronnie tsked. "Should've gotten it in writing, Mindy."

Mindy looked from Ronnie to Jason. "You know I'm loyal, Jason. Why are you doing this to me?"

It was a dangerous game Ronnie played, and by the anger burning in Jason's eyes, she'd all but crossed a boundary.

Jason pushed off from his desk and walked slowly to Mindy. He cupped her face in his hands and said, "Because you, darling, I was going to give the position of Punisher."

"What?" Mindy asked, her eyes nearly glowing with excitement. "Really?"

"I said 'was.' Keep up," Jason said flatly before he released her and turned away. He looked at Ronnie. "Happy now?"

"I'm getting there."

"What's your point in doing this?" Jason asked. "To prolong not doing as I asked? Do you forget that you and I made a pact? I gave you a promise bound in magic, but in order for that promise to be effective, you have to keep your end of the bargain."

Ronnie held his gaze when all she wanted to do was look away. She was scared to the point of falling apart. The only reason she was able to hold it together was because of Andy. Somehow she had to get the both of them away from Wallace. "Point taken."

"Good. Now, where do you suppose we begin? Is there anything else at this dig site of yours?"

"You mean the one you tore to shreds? Nothing magical. That was found already."

Jason resumed his position of leaning against the front of his desk and tapped his fingers on its dark wood. "And where are those items now?"

"The MacLeods took them. I have no idea where they're at." And she prayed Jason wouldn't make her go find them. She'd never be able to look Arran in the eye, knowing she was betraying all that they had been fighting for. Not to mention she didn't know how she wouldn't start crying and beg for his help.

Arran had an inherent nobility that would make him help her, but would it be enough before Wallace killed Andy?

Did she dare to try something so reckless on the off chance Andy would be saved with her?

She didn't want to die, nor did she want to help Jason in any way. But Andy was a brother she never had. How could she leave him to Jason' devices?

Ronnie inwardly screamed in defeat. She didn't have a choice. Jason had made sure of that. If only she hadn't turned Arran away, if only she hadn't run from him.

But she had, and she was royally screwed.

Jason stared at her for long, silent minutes. Her heart pounded so loud in her chest, she was sure everyone could hear it. All the while she silently prayed that he wouldn't ask her to go to the MacLeods.

"I'll get those lost items soon enough. I've a feeling there is something important among them, which is why MacCarrick was so hasty to remove them. So. Tell me what was in the chamber."

Ronnie racked her brain for an answer that would lead him away from the MacLeods. She finally decided on as much truth as she thought he'd accept. "There was a dagger, several bowls, a small wooden chest, and other items like that."

"I can no' help but think you're leaving something out. I want to know every item, Dr. Reid."

"It's not like I haven't been running for my life or anything," she replied before she could stop herself. "You try doing it and tell me if you remember every little detail from one night almost a week ago."

Jason silently stared at her for several minutes. "We'll move on for now. But understand, I will get the information. Now, why don't you tell me what it was you released?"

"I didn't release anything."

"That's not what the prophecy says."

Ronnie knew everything counted on her next words. She'd failed drama class in school, but then again, her life hadn't been on the line. "I found the prophecy, which you know. I haven't released anything yet."

"Yet." Jason drew in a long breath, his persistent, smug

smile grating on her nerves. "But you will. I'm going to make sure of it. Where is it you would've gone to dig next?"

Ronnie nearly collapsed with relief, but she had to keep it in check. She had lied, but if he went in her mind again, would he discover that? She hoped not.

That wasn't all she was afraid he'd find. If Jason ever learned just how much she cared about Arran, Saffron, and the rest, he would use it against her.

"Ronnie," Jason urged when she didn't immediately answer.

She swallowed and looked at the floor. There were two places, but one she knew had many legends of magic surrounding it—the Isle of Skye.

And the other place was a small town northwest of Inverness.

"Redcastle."

Jason looked at Dale. "Ready the cars. We leave in thirty minutes."

Ronnie closed her eyes, unable to believe what she was about to do. She was thinking how she could get to Andy and rescue him when there was a loud boom that shook the mansion.

And then all hell broke loose.

CHAPTER
THIRTY-NINE

Arran closed his eyes and concentrated on Ronnie. He hated that Jason's spells had prevented him from zeroing in on her magic as he normally could have done.

The fact that he could discern Ronnie's magic from any other Druid's wasn't something Arran wanted to look at deeper. He wasn't a fool. He'd heard the other Warriors who were married talk about how their wives' magic was different than the rest.

Arran inhaled deeply when he felt a rush of Ronnie's magic. It was tinged in fear, and that only made him angrier. Only made his god howl louder for blood and death.

"There will be blood," Arran whispered.

Lots of it. The only one immune from his wrath in the mansion was Ronnie. Everyone else was fair game.

Arran opened his eyes. He glanced at Malcolm, who stood with Charon on the left side of the house. They had already jumped the fence, thanks to Ramsey using his magic.

All Arran was doing was waiting for Ramsey to make it back to him. There was a flap of wings from above. Broc had been flying around the mansion, testing to see how far the spells surrounded the house.

"Everyone is in place," Ramsey said as he silently moved to stand between Fallon and Arran.

"Let's get inside," Arran said. "I want to make a grand entrance."

Fallon growled low in his throat. "Aye. A grand entrance."

Arran watched in amazement as Ramsey, with the bronze skin of his god showing, used the potent magic he held as the only half-Druid, half-Warrior. It was a secret he'd kept from everyone, even Deirdre, until recently.

Ramsey was able to tear a rift in Jason's magic that allowed them to get over the tall gate. The rift was so slight that Jason would never feel his magic had been tampered with.

"He's too bloody cocky," Phelan said with a growl.

Arran grunted in agreement. "I count just six guards patrolling the front. The bastard underestimates us."

"Better make that five guards," Fallon said, his gaze lifted to the roof.

Arran looked up just in time to see shadows overtake a guard. A moment later, a woman fell to the ground. "Lucan strikes again."

"That's a damned *drough*," Phelan murmured.

Fallon snorted in disgust. "Declan used mercenaries. Jason uses Druids."

"That could be a problem for all of us," Arran said.

Phelan looked at Fallon, then Arran. "Each of us knew what we were attacking. Whether it was Deirdre, Declan, or this new asshole, evil is evil. I'm no' afraid to die."

Arran wasn't either, but he also wasn't ready to die. He wanted to hold Ronnie in his arms one last time.

He squatted and put his hand on the ground. With his acute hearing, he could detect Camdyn moving the earth and getting closer and closer to the mansion.

Every Warrior there was able to call forth his power at will. Everyone except Arran. He was only able to use his power if there was snow or ice around him. It would be just his luck the battle had to occur in summer.

"What is it?" Phelan asked.

Arran gave a vicious shake of his head. Even without snow or ice, Arran was still a Warrior. He had speed and strength. He'd use those to defeat Jason.

With a glance to Malcolm who stood waiting off to the right, Arran nodded. Malcolm raised his hands above his head, and lightning streaked from his fingers.

All around them lightning erupted. Streaks zigzagged and forked across the sky in a majestic display, shooting from seemingly out of nowhere to hit the ground one after another. It was an impressive sight.

And then Malcolm turned his hands toward the mansion. The lightning began to strike it, blasting windows and doors with a magnificent exhibition of power.

Arran stood and walked to the front door. He didn't need to look above to know Broc and Lucan were making their way into the house from the roof. He didn't need to look to know that Camdyn and Quinn would attack from the dungeon up. Nor did Arran need to check to make sure the others were attacking from each side.

That's what happened when men fought side by side through battle after battle.

"Careful," Phelan said from behind Arran.

Phelan and Fallon were staying hidden for the time being, but it wouldn't be for long.

Arran jogged to the front steps and bounded to the top in one leap. He delighted at the shattered double doors that had splintered upon a lightning strike.

He didn't bother to duck as Malcolm continued to strike the house. Lightning would hurt, but it wouldn't kill a Warrior. It was effective, however, in causing the Druids to be more interested in avoiding it than seeing who attacked.

"Who is it?" Jason yelled from somewhere to Arran's left.

Arran stepped over a dead Druid who had a long piece of wood from the door stuck in her chest. Now that he was inside the mansion, he could locate Ronnie with ease.

And somehow he wasn't surprised to find Jason had her with him.

Arran's claws itched to sink into Jason's flesh. He yearned to see Jason's blood seeping from his body. He needed to see the life drain from Jason's eyes.

And he would. If it was the last thing he ever did, he would see it done.

Arran spotted the set of doors that were caved inward, but still on their hinges. Jason's voice—and Ronnie's magic—were through the doors.

He'd taken two steps toward them when the doors suddenly flew at him. Arran raised an arm and knocked one of them away before it could hit him.

Dale's large form filled the doorway. A second later, another Warrior joined him.

"Oh, good. Someone else to play with," Arran said with a smile.

There was a feminine scream from inside the room, and Arran could only guess that was Fallon teleporting in and attacking.

"Use your magic!" Jason barked to the Druids above the screams.

Arran could detect several *droughs* in the room, but just as he'd hoped, there was too much disarray for them to gather their black magic and use it.

"Have you come to be killed?" Dale asked.

Arran chuckled. Damned if he didn't like the Warrior's attitude. "You left the last battle early. I actually came to finish what I was meant to do."

"Interesting." Dale kicked at a piece of broken door and stepped out of the room. "Is that all you came for?"

"Nothing else you need to worry about."

"You'll never get to her. Jason will make sure of it."

Arran shrugged while the screams escalated as Fallon teleported in again and killed a *drough*. "We'll see."

"She's working for us now. She and Jason made a pact."

For a moment Arran couldn't breathe, then he realized Ronnie had to have been under some kind of duress. No matter what the prophecy had said, he knew she wasn't evil. "What did he use against her?"

It was Dale's turn to grin. "Nothing."

No. Arran refused to believe it. He knew Ronnie. He'd felt the goodness of her magic and her heart. She knew how dangerous Jason was, and she would never side with him. Never.

Arran flexed his fingers. Dale lowered his head as he prepared to attack. Before he could, the second Warrior roared and came at Arran.

Camdyn broke through the ground into the dungeon. He and Quinn both jumped out of the ground and onto the floor. It was quiet. Too quiet.

"Camdyn," Quinn whispered.

They held their claws at the ready as they scanned the darkness.

"Quinn!" Camdyn yelled as he detected a *drough* hiding in the shadows.

He barely got the word out before a blast of magic hit him.

Hayden grabbed the top of the windowsill as he swung inside the second-floor window. His feet planted against a Warrior, who went flying backwards to crash into the opposite wall.

Hayden landed smoothly in the room and held out his hand as a ball of fire formed.

"My wife wouldna want to hear it, but I've missed battle," he said.

The Warrior shook his head to clear it as he slowly gained his feet. He looked at Hayden's fireball and showed his fangs.

"Ah, how I've forgotten how stupid baby Warriors are."

The Warrior charged Hayden, but he launched four fireballs in quick succession, setting his attacker ablaze. Hayden then jabbed him in the gut so the Warrior bent over.

And with one clean slice, he took the Warrior's head.

Hayden knew Logan was in a room down the hall. He stepped into the corridor and drew up short as *drough* magic slammed into him, pinning him roughly against a wall.

Ian and Galen stormed into the first-story window only to find the room empty. With a silent look, they crept from the small room into the hall.

All around them, lightning continued to strike and screams could be heard throughout the house. But neither let their guard down.

A woman turned the corner and started to race past them, her gaze continually looking over her shoulder. Ian caught the *drough* by the shoulders and held her as Galen put his hand on her head.

He looked deep into her eyes and said, "You're never to return here. You willna ever see or talk to Jason again. If he contacts you, you'll run."

Galen dropped his hand, and Ian watched the *drough* rush from the house.

"Will it work?"

Galen turned his head to Ian. "Aye. I couldna bring myself to kill a Druid, even though she's *drough*."

"I know," Ian said. "We're probably going to regret it."

They jerked as they felt more *drough* magic. Both turned toward the source to find three *droughs,* who quickly lashed out at them with magic.

Ian gave a bellow of fury as he was brought to his knees by the pain in his head. He glanced up to see they had Galen frozen in place as one of the *droughs* came up to him.

"Finally," Phelan said as he strode around the house near where Malcolm and the vicious lightning were.

Phelan stepped through a broken window, his boots crunching on glass. All the lights flickered and then went out throughout the house.

No doubt thanks to Malcolm.

Phelan walked from the dining room, which housed a table that could easily seat twenty. The sliding door that had sectioned off the room was all but gone.

He walked out of the dining room and found two *droughs* on the floor. "Fried extra crispy," he said of their blackened, smoking skin.

With barely a thought, he used his power to manipulate reality so no one would see him. They might have lost Larena and her power of invisibility, but his was the next best thing.

Phelan heard a grunt toward the back of the house that was unmistakably Warrior. After a quick look around a corner, Phelan saw Arran locked in battle against two Warriors, and Fallon was making quick work of the Druids inside the office.

He turned and nearly ran into Charon, who was coming toward him. Phelan eased his magic down so Charon would see him. Charon slid to a halt, his bronze Warrior eyes filled with the bloodlust that often took them.

"I heard Warriors."

Phelan gave a nod. "Me as well. I was just going to check it out. Arran and Fallon are doing all right for the moment."

"Then what are we waiting for?"

Phelan lifted a brow and replaced his power. Charon quickly took off toward the stairs, and Phelan ran to the back of the house.

When he saw the *droughs* torturing Galen and Ian with their magic, memories of his time in Deirdre's mountain swarmed him. Phelan forgot all about his power to manipulate reality.

His only thought was to kill the *droughs*.

CHAPTER
FORTY

Ronnie launched herself over the back of the couch and crouched on the floor next to it when the lightning began. Jason was yelling, people were screaming.

She hadn't moved when the windows blew out around her. She hadn't made a sound when the doors were knocked off their hinges and shattered to bits.

Ronnie covered her ears, her eyes squeezed closed as the force of the impacts about the house flew around her while the mansion literally shook on its foundation.

And then she heard Arran's voice.

Her entire body trembled, but Ronnie lifted her head to make sure she wasn't dreaming. Arran's voice, calm and deep, with a hint of arrogance and a mocking bite.

He was like a beacon in the dark. His presence gave her courage, mettle she hadn't known she had. She had to get to him, to tell him everything Jason had planned. Arran would know how to rescue Andy.

Arran would have all the answers. She wasn't sure when she'd come to rely on him as she had, she just knew she had.

Ronnie looked around her to find debris everywhere. She rose up carefully on her knees and saw Jason standing in the middle of the office and staring out the blown doors with his hands waist high, as if he were holding an invisible ball.

The two Warriors were at the door, both staring out.

Arran's voice reached her again, and she knew that's who the Warriors were talking with.

Aisley was no longer in the corner. She was lying on the floor, unconscious or dead, Ronnie didn't know or care.

There was a flash of something out of the corner of her eyes, and she spotted Fallon for a split second before he disappeared. With one of the *droughs*.

Ronnie got to her feet, thankful that no more glass could come at her despite the lightning continuing to hit the house.

There was a loud roar, and one of the Warriors attacked Arran. Ronnie wasn't sure what to do. Did she try to leave, did she find Andy, or did she kill Jason?

Her hands squeezed the back of the couch as her mind struggled to make a decision. She glanced out one of the windows and saw she had a clear shot.

Jason was occupied, as was everyone else. It was the perfect time to escape. But if she did, Andy would die.

She happened to look down at the spot on the couch where she'd been sitting to see a large chunk of glass the size of a dinner plate stuck in the back cushion.

Ronnie shuddered. She desperately wanted to get to Arran, but how could she? There wasn't just Jason to contend with, but also the two Warriors Arran fought.

Maybe if she could get outside there was another way into the house where she could find Andy. Her mind set, Ronnie made a dash for the opened window.

Her heart pounded in her chest, and adrenaline pumped through her, giving her a little extra speed. Just as she was about to hurdle over the windowsill, a hand grabbed her arm and spun her around.

"Jason."

He leered viciously, his blue eyes alight with anger. "Did you forget our pact? Because, if you leave, I'll kill Andy with a mere thought."

Ronnie wasn't willing to bet Andy's life on the hopes that Jason was bluffing. Arran had come for her. He'd promised to keep her safe. And she knew he would continue to try to free her.

She stopped trying to pull away, her decision made.

"That's what I thought. Now, this is what we're going to do. You're going to march to the door so Arran can see you, and you're going to tell him to stop."

Ronnie wanted to scream that she wouldn't do it, but what choice did she have? Jason knew better than to threaten Arran, he was a Warrior. And Jason must have realized bullying Ronnie herself would do no good either.

He'd managed to pick one of the two people she would have done anything for. At least Pete was far enough away that he was safe.

"Arran doesn't need to see me," she said.

Jason's smile was evil and conniving. "Oh, but he does, darling. Now, move!" he shouted in her ear.

Each step toward Arran was like a knife in her heart. Her feet seemed to be made of lead. Would Arran know she lied? Would he realize she did it to save someone? After all she'd said to him, would he believe the worst about her?

Ronnie knew that he probably would. At every turn, Arran had been there for her, even when she hadn't wanted him to be. So he took a few items. Was that so much to worry over after everything he'd done?

She could hardly take in a breath by the time she reached the doorway. Ronnie watched as Arran fought both Dale and the second Warrior effortlessly.

It was almost as if he were playing with them. He moved elegantly, fluidly. His claws and hits lethal. Even when he sustained an injury, he barely gave notice to it.

He was a magnificent fighter, a majestic warrior. And for a time, he'd been hers.

Those few precious hours made all the heartache she'd ever endured worth it. And if she had to do it all over again, she would. In a heartbeat.

When she thought of those wasted days with Arran, she wanted to scream. Somehow, someway she would get away from Jason and she would do her damnedest to make it all up to Arran.

If he doesn't kill you first.

Ronnie inwardly flinched at the reminder of the prophecy. She watched as he elbowed Dale before he spun and ducked the second Warrior's claws.

She could have watched him all day. The slight smile on his face when he landed a good hit, the way his white eyes sparkled with challenge. The way his muscles moved with fluid grace beneath the white skin of his Warrior form.

Ronnie's inspection halted when she found Arran's gaze fastened on her. For a few moments he increased his attack. Then he saw Jason standing beside her.

She wanted to cry when she spotted the brief flare of pain and betrayal that burned in his gaze. But somehow she held back the tears.

It wasn't just her own life she was playing for. It was Andy's and Arran's and everyone's in the entire world. For she wouldn't be the bringer of doom. She wouldn't align with evil. Not now, not ever.

But first, she had to make Jason think she was.

"Tell him," Jason said, his tone brooking no argument.

Ronnie fisted her hands at her sides, her soul withering in her chest. "Arran. Stop."

Malcolm rarely gave in to his power as he did in that moment. It felt . . . right . . . to release the lightning, to hurtle it toward his enemy. Each strike released the pain he kept locked, bound within him.

For his scars. For being a Warrior. For killing Duncan.

For losing Larena.

He squeezed his eyes closed at the thought of his cousin gone from his life for good. She'd been the only one he let in after Deirdre and Declan had been vanquished.

Larena had a way of making him listen even when he hadn't wanted to. What was he going to do now that she was gone?

Malcolm's eyes flew open, his lightning ceasing instantly. He tried to release a breath, only to have agony streak through his body.

The pain was blinding, the suffering growing tenfold with

each second. His blood burned like fire, and his lungs seized as they struggled for breath.

"Not so powerful now, are you, Warrior?" asked a female voice behind him.

Malcolm looked down to find the head of a spear showing through his stomach. But the weakening of his body told him his end was near.

Because the spear was coated with *drough* blood.

Phelan took off running, intending to impale the first *drough* he encountered with his claws until something barreled into him from the side and knocked him into a small room.

He banged his head against something hard, and looked over to find a toilet. Phelan growled and brushed aside the blood that began running down his temple. He turned his head to find Charon at the door with his back to Phelan and peering around the corner.

"What did you do?"

"Saved your bloody arse, you idiot," Charon whispered over his shoulder.

Phelan jumped to his feet. "Explain yourself."

Charon softly closed the door and leaned back against it. "I found Hayden and Logan. Both were being tortured by *droughs*. I knew I was going to need your help, so I came to find you."

"What you did was stop me from killing a *drough*."

"What I did, you arse, was keep you from being discovered."

Phelan frowned. "I was using my power. They wouldna have seen me."

"Then how did I?"

"What do you mean?"

Charon dropped his chin to his chest. "What I mean is that you had stopped using your power. They would've seen you before you could have done anything for Ian or Galen."

"Fuck me." Phelan prowled the small bathroom. "Have the *droughs* cornered everyone?"

"No' Malcolm."

As soon as the words were out of Charon's mouth, the lightning ceased.

The two Warriors looked at each other. In order for any of them to get out alive, it was now up to Phelan and Charon.

"They'll try and bring us all together," Charon said.

Phelan leaned back against the sink. "How do you know?"

"It's what I'd do. Plus, that gives Jason the means to kill all of us at once."

"No' bloody likely."

Charon smiled. "As if I'd allow that. Now. Here's the plan."

Arran's world was spinning out of control, and at its center, looking pale and withdrawn, was Ronnie. His beautiful, bright Ronnie.

Her hazel gaze met his, but the warmth, laughter, and honesty he was so used to were gone. As if they'd never been. This wasn't the same woman he'd made love to, the woman he'd spent the evening dancing with. This woman was . . . different.

She'd asked him to stop fighting. She stood beside Jason without being held or threatened. Had she really joined the other side?

He'd have bet his life that nothing could make Ronnie join evil. His instincts had never been wrong before. How could he have been so mistaken with the one person who had his heart?

Arran wished he knew Jason Wallace better to determine just how he'd gotten Ronnie. Because Arran wasn't sure he could fulfill the prophecy and kill her.

Even if it meant saving the world.

"I think he's in shock," Jason said to Ronnie and leaned over, a smirk on his face.

Arran released the hold he'd had on the Warrior, and didn't even bother to look at Dale. Fury unlike anything Arran had ever experienced consumed him.

Inside him, Memphaea was screaming with outrage. And

Arran let him, because his god was doing what he couldn't. Yet, as Memphaea's frenzy grew, so did the need for blood and death.

It was all Arran could do to hold himself back, to keep the craze, or bloodlust, from taking him. But how he wanted to give in.

He accepted the fury and glowered at Jason. "You look nothing like Declan. Declan must have gotten all the good looks, talent, and brains in the family."

Arran's lips lifted slightly when Jason's face mottled red. So, he'd hit a nerve. Good.

"Declan was a buffoon!" Jason screamed.

Arran's brows rose at Jason's tone. "There's some history there, I think. Was Declan no' so nice to you? Did he get the fine clothes and you didna? Was it his hair, or maybe Declan's strong jaw? Those seemed to have skipped you, but you did get the weak chin."

Jason started to say something, but suddenly stopped and glanced at Ronnie. "It doesna matter where I was before this. I'm here now. I have the power and position to do everything Declan imagined. My first order of business is killing every Warrior and Druid from MacLeod Castle."

"Good luck with that," Arran said.

"Oh, I'm no' worried. After all, I have many people at my disposal," Jason said as he slowly walked around Ronnie. "You know my newest one. Intimately, I'm told."

Arran fisted his hands and let his claws sink into his palms, anything to keep his calm and not attack Jason. Yet. "You'll never touch anyone at the castle."

"Is that so? Did you really think you could get past my spells without me knowing it?"

"Aye," Arran answered confidently.

The way Jason's eyes narrowed proved he had been right.

"I knew you'd come for Dr. Reid," Jason said. "Dale told me how close the two of you have gotten, how you watched her so . . . tenderly. I wasna sure when you'd come for her, but I knew you would. And I made sure I was prepared."

There was something in his words that gave Arran pause.

It wasn't that Jason might have been expecting him, it was the thought that they could have very well walked into a trap.

"Doona fight," Dale whispered from behind him. "There's nothing you can do."

Arran looked over his shoulder at the Warrior, and that's when he saw his friends being herded into the large foyer by *droughs*.

"As I said. I was prepared," Jason said, laughing at his own remark.

Arran looked back at Ronnie, but she wouldn't meet his gaze. And that's when he knew they had lost.

CHAPTER
FORTY-ONE

Fallon was about to teleport into Jason's office and kill the
son of a bitch when *drough* magic sizzled along his skin. He
turned his head to the right just in time to see the Druid
skewer Malcolm.

"Nay," Fallon ground out.

He'd lost Larena. He wasn't going to allow her cousin to
die along with her.

Fallon teleported directly behind the *drough* and, with
one vicious swipe of his claw, took her head. He didn't even
wait for her body to hit the ground before he grabbed Malcolm and teleported him to the castle.

As soon as they arrived in the middle of the great hall,
Fallon bellowed for Sonya. Fallon stared at the spear sticking through Malcolm's back, his fellow Warrior desperately
trying to take in air.

"Hold on, my friend. Sonya is coming."

Malcolm grasped Fallon's arm, his blue eyes filled with
pain and grief.

Fallon knew Malcolm would want to talk about Larena,
and he wasn't ready to do that. Not even if it was Malcolm's
dying breath.

He yanked the spear from Malcolm and tossed it aside.
Malcolm listed to the side, and Fallon easily caught him.

"You're no' going to die. Do you hear me? You're no' going to die."

"Fallon," Malcolm rasped.

"Nay. Save your words." Fallon looked up to find Sonya rushing down the stairs with Larena's blood still on her jeans and white shirt.

"Not another one," she said, and jumped down the last few stairs to run to them.

Fallon tightened his grip on Malcolm as he looked at Sonya. "Save him. I've got to return to the others."

"Fallon, wait!" Sonya called.

But Fallon laid Malcolm on one of the long benches used for seating at the table, and then jumped back to the Wallace mansion.

Arran never took his gaze off Jason as the bastard paced slowly in front of them. It had been a kick in the balls for Arran to see his fellow Warriors being led into the foyer by *droughs*. Their magic was nauseating, heavy.

And none of it touched him as of yet.

"I told you I was prepared," Jason said with a satisfied laugh as he walked into the foyer. He stopped to smooth down his dress shirt in the mirror. "I'm always prepared."

"One day, you willna be able to say that."

Wallace threw back his head and laughed. "You willna be around to see it." He halted in front of Arran. "Because I'm taking every one of your heads tonight. There will no longer be Warriors at MacLeod Castle."

"There will always be Warriors at MacLeod Castle." Arran readied, his claws itching to thrust into Jason's chest and rip out his heart. With his speed, and with as close to Jason as he was, it would be a simple thing.

Just as Arran was about to do it, Jason took two quick steps back.

"Do none of you wonder how I was able to keep myself hidden from you for a year?" Jason asked.

Since Arran was the only one who could speak because

there was no *drough* magic halting him, he shrugged. "We didna suspect you or anyone. We didna look."

"Exactly!" Jason put his hands in the front pocket of his dress pants and looked down at his once shiny black shoes. "I spent the year no' just restoring this beautiful house, but in building my army."

"So you worked fast. Shall I give you a golf clap?"

Jason ignored him and continued. "It's amazing what can be accomplished with unlimited funds. I used to never care for expensive clothing, and certainly never suits and ties. But," he said, and stopped in front of a cracked mirror hanging on the wall for a second time. "I make this suit look good."

Arran raked his gaze over Jason. The man might be tall and slim, he might have a head full of blond hair, but that was all Arran could say. He was the exact opposite of Declan and his fine looks.

Jason wore the expensive suit, but it didn't improve his looks. If anything, it only brought to attention how unsuited he was to wearing it.

"You no more make that suit look good than you know what you're doing with magic. You don the suit because that's what Declan did. But Declan knew how to wear it. Same for the magic."

Jason turned to Arran. His blue eyes were cold with fury and malice. "I know all about Declan and Deirdre. He had a book he kept hidden between walls. It told about Deirdre and what he'd done to achieve his magic."

With a calculating smile, Jason once more stood in front of Arran but out of reach. "The book also described each Warrior living at MacLeod Castle as well as a few of the Druids. So you see, MacCarrick, I know much more than any of you ever realized."

On either side and behind Arran were his friends, all silently listening to his conversation. Ronnie had taken a seat as far from him as she could, her gaze on the floor. She hadn't moved or uttered a single sound since she'd sat.

Arran might be free to move, but there was no way he

could kill Jason or best the *droughs* holding his friends and not be killed himself.

For the first time since he'd woken imprisoned in the deep bowels of Deirdre's mountain, he felt beaten. Defeated.

Conquered.

And for a Warrior it was a feeling he never wanted to experience. For all his power and strength, Arran was helpless to do anything.

Much as he'd been watching Shelley killed before him.

He'd vowed to never be in that position again. And yet, here he was. Fate really was a bitch.

Arran kept his face devoid of expression as he watched Jason. "And I suppose you're as unoriginal as Declan and want to rule the world as Deirdre tried to do?"

"I do. But whereas Declan and Deirdre made a crucial mistake, I've learned from them."

"And what might be that mistake?" Arran knew he wasn't going to live to use the information, but maybe, just maybe, Ronnie would realize her error and take the information for herself.

He had faith in Ronnie, faith that the goodness inside her would keep her from turning evil and damning the world.

"Deirdre slaughtered the Druids, and Declan didna trust them. Neither realized that having the Druids as allies would have shifted the balance in their favor."

"You obviously never had an encounter with a wyrran," Arran said with a snort.

Jason shuddered with revulsion. "Those nasty yellow creatures Deirdre made from magic? They might have been many, but they didna have the ability to use magic as my army does."

Arran hated to admit Jason had made a good move. There were few things that could stop a Warrior, but a Druid with strong enough magic could do it.

"Before I kill you, I'll give you one chance," Jason said. "Each of you gets an opportunity to move to my side in this war. I'll spare you, and in return, I want your complete and total loyalty."

Arran knew his answer, but he didn't have a wife or children as the others did. He turned to look at each of his brethren, their answers written all over their faces.

It was then that Arran realized two Warriors were missing. Fallon and Malcolm. There was still a way for them to get out of this—or at least some of them.

Arran turned to Jason. "The answer is nay. For all of us."

Even if each of them died, Fallon and Malcolm, along with the Druids, would have a chance against Jason. At least then the world wouldn't be at the mercy of Jason Wallace.

"A pity," Jason said. "At least then you'd have been with the lovely Dr. Reid. I've no doubt there will be someone who will warm her bed soon enough."

Arran growled, low and long, at the thought of anyone touching his woman. Jason could threaten him all he wanted, but not Ronnie.

A slow grin spread over Jason's face. "I see I struck a nerve. It's a pity I need Ronnie, or I'd love to torture her in front of you. Maybe I'll keep you alive long enough to see it done."

"I'd advise you to take my head now, because the first opportunity I get, I'm killing you," Arran said between clenched teeth.

No longer did he hide his anger. He let it rise up within him, let it fill the air as his growls grew. He let loose the monster inside him, welcomed him with open arms.

He glanced at Ronnie to find her watching him. For just an instant, a millisecond of time, he saw the old Ronnie. But that's all he needed.

Arran took a step toward Jason, only to be brought to his knees by the pain slicing through him. Arran threw back his head and bellowed with rage as the *drough* magic surrounded him, choking him.

The agony doubled, then tripled as more and more magic pummeled him. Arran wouldn't bend though. He was a Warrior. He would die defending the people he cared about.

It took several tries, but he got to his feet, his gaze locked on Jason. Jason's lip curled in a sneer as he threw more magic at Arran.

Arran braced himself, but the magic was so strong, so penetrating he had to take a step back just to stay upright.

There was a crash behind him, but Arran refused to take his eyes off Jason. Wallace was his target, and he wasn't going to stop until he had his hands around the bastard's neck.

Arran leaned forward and bared his fangs as he fought against the unimaginable agony in his head. It was near impossible to think beyond the torture, but Arran kept just one thought in his mind: *Kill Jason.*

It seemed an eternity had passed as he took two more steps. Jason's confidence began to wane by evidence of his widening eyes and hesitant step backwards.

Arran kept moving. Just one foot in front of the other.

There was a shimmer out of the corner of Arran's eye, and he heard the high-pitched scream of a woman, but still he didn't see what was going on.

Jason, however, wasn't so single-minded in his focus. He looked over Arran's shoulder, and it was all the time Arran needed to launch himself.

Arran's claws sank into the left side of Jason's jaw and scoured across his neck. Arran raised his other hand to repeat his attack when something toppled Jason.

The *drough* magic surrounding Arran was suddenly gone. He caught himself before he could fall, and looked to find Ronnie on top of Jason, punching him in the face with her one good fist.

Arran started for her when he heard a Warrior growl from behind. He turned to find that somehow, his brethren had gotten the upper hand on the *droughs*. Several Druids had already been killed, and Dale was getting the others away.

And then Fallon was there. He glanced at Arran before he put his hand on Ronnie and they both disappeared.

Arran approached Jason with the intent to end everything right then. Blood coated the front of Jason's suit he'd been so proud of, and by the looks of it, Ronnie had broken his nose.

"A fitting end for such a pig," Arran said as he lifted his hand, and to his surprise, a long shard of ice formed. That had never happened before, but it was perfect timing. Arran grinned and started to hurl it at Jason.

"Arran!" Charon yelled from behind him.

Arran turned in time to see a Druid come at him with a dagger coated in *drough* blood. She threw the dagger, the blade going end over end and aiming right for Arran's heart the same time he threw the shard of ice. The shard embedded deep in her throat, killing her instantly.

Before Arran could dodge the weapon, Charon was suddenly in front of him. Arran could only stare in horror as the blade sank into Charon's chest.

Charon landed hard on the floor. And didn't move.

Arran whirled around to Jason, but the bastard was gone.

"Damn," Arran mumbled.

He squatted next to Charon and yanked out the dagger. Charon's eyes were closed, his breathing labored as Arran tossed aside the blade and hefted the Warrior over his shoulder.

When he stood, it was to find his brethren had taken back control of the mansion.

"They're all gone," Lucan said, breathing hard as blood coated him.

Hayden grunted. "Where's Fallon? I want the hell out of here."

Phelan moved the bodies of several *droughs* and shook his head as he stared down at Fallon. "We're going to have to find another way."

"Is he—?" Quinn couldn't even finish the sentence.

Phelan knelt and touched Fallon. He shook his head. "Nay. I saw a Druid fighting him. He took her down, but when he did, he hit his head. He's just unconscious."

"We need to hurry back to the castle," Arran said as he sprinted past them and out of the mansion. "Charon's been wounded by *drough* blood."

Seconds later, they were loaded up in three vehicles and speeding down the Wallace drive.

All Arran could think about was getting to Charon healed. And holding Ronnie.

CHAPTER
FORTY-TWO

Ronnie stared aghast at the emptiness of her dig site. She'd begged Fallon to take her back to find Andy, but he hadn't believed her.

He'd assumed the worst and believed she was with Jason now. Not that she could blame him after what she'd made everyone believe. If only she could talk to Arran.

Had he gotten the silent message she'd sent him? Did he understand her part was all a ruse? She prayed he did. If not, she was prepared to do all sorts of begging until he listened to her.

He had to know she wasn't evil.

She walked aimlessly around the site. There had been something different about Fallon. In the midst of the battle at the mansion, her focus had been on Arran and Jason, but it hadn't taken her long to see Fallon for what he was.

A man possessed.

Ronnie hadn't stayed close to him because he frightened her. His skin of jet-black, his claws coated with blood, but it had been his eyes that glistened like obsidian death that made her shiver with anxiety.

Those eyes were now lifeless and cold. Dead.

Ronnie hadn't dared ask about Larena, but then she didn't need to. The answer was in Fallon's eyes. Larena was deceased.

She swiped at her hair that kept flying in her face because of the wind. If only she'd had a few minutes to convince him of what Jason had done to her, but Fallon had teleported away.

There was nowhere Ronnie could run, nowhere she could hide that Jason or the Warriors couldn't find her. She didn't know who would win the battle, but she suspected it would be Arran.

All she could do now was pray that Fallon believed her hastily told explanation about Andy and find him. Otherwise, she suspected Fallon might just kill her for her supposed siding with Jason Wallace.

She released a pent-up breath, and her legs folded beneath her. She dropped her head in her hands and let the tears come. All the fear, all the worry. All the death.

And still, she was alone.

The eerie quiet of the site made her skin crawl. The only sound was the wind whistling through the tall grass and the carnage of her site.

Ronnie wiped her eyes and lifted her head. It broke her heart to see her dig in such shambles, but more than that, her soul ached for all those who had died.

She slowly rose to her feet not caring that it was the middle of the night and the sun was just setting into the horizon. Her gaze roamed the area, from cars that looked crushed in half to the RVs that were broken into pieces.

Ronnie ambled around the site looking at broken pottery that she had dug up just hours before. Pottery that had been almost completely intact.

At one time she would have cried for the loss, and though she hated that the artifact was ruined, she, at least, had her life.

"Andy. Please be all right," she whispered when she came to stand in front of his RV.

She smiled as she recalled how he'd refused to call it a caravan as they did in the UK. It had been his RV, and he'd been especially proud of it.

There wasn't much left other than a portion of the back

wall and his world map, where he'd put in thumbtacks to every place they'd been.

Her thoughts soon turned to Arran. Before she knew it, she was standing in the area where his tent had been. There was nothing left, not even his cot.

She recalled the day they first met and how even then the attraction had been fierce and undeniable. Her fear kept her from having Arran sooner. Her apprehension had nearly cost her the most amazing man she'd ever met.

A laugh bubbled through her tears as she remembered how affronted he'd been when she compared him to other men. Now she knew why. He was in a class all his own.

Arran was a true Highlander, an ancient warrior from a bygone era. He was proud, loyal, and honorable. He put himself between her and danger without a second thought.

He'd recognized her for what she was—a Druid—and helped her to accept the new world she'd been thrust into. He'd smiled and charmed his way into her heart.

And he'd seduced his way into her soul.

For now and always, she would carry him in her heart. No longer would her work simply be digging up relics of the past. She would use her magic to hunt the things Jason Wallace might use against the Warriors and Druids of MacLeod Castle.

She would prove to them by her actions that she wasn't evil. It would take her learning more about her magic, because she would need to ensure she was protected against Wallace.

Pete would have to be told the truth. And Andy. She sighed. If she ever got Andy back, he would need to be told as well. They were the only two outside of Arran she could fully trust. Everyone else was a potential enemy.

Ronnie glanced at her tent, and though it still stood, it was the last place she wanted to be. She walked to the area where they'd dug around the chamber and sat, her legs dangling over the side cut from the ground.

Memories of how Arran had been there helping her unearth the vault filled her mind. She could recall in vivid detail his smile and laughter, his muscles and sun-kissed flesh as he worked without his shirt.

She remembered how he'd been there to save her from the selmyr, and how he'd almost died in the process. Then there was the fund-raiser. She'd felt like Cinderella, and though the dress had been spectacular, that wasn't the reason.

It had been Arran.

His smile, his touch. The way he held her. The way his golden eyes had filled with desire and yearning.

"Oh, God," she said as fresh tears coursed down her face. "I love him."

Arran sped around corners and passed untold number of cars as he raced to get Charon to MacLeod Castle and Sonya. Some ways back, Broc had left the black SUV and flown to the castle in full view of anyone who dared to look up.

The dire situation called for such drastic measures. It was a chance they all took, because Charon's life depended upon it.

Arran glanced in the backseat as Ian stared gloomily at Charon.

"We're no' going to make it," Ian said.

Arran jerked the wheel to miss a dog that trotted onto the road and noticed his skin was still white. The others had already tamped down their gods. With a sigh, Arran did as well. "Then use your blood."

"We have been."

Phelan cut his arm. "Let me. My blood will heal him instantly."

It was the first time any of them had spoke since leaving the mansion. Arran glanced in the rearview mirror to see Phelan cutting his arm deep to let his blood flow into Charon's wound.

"What happened at the mansion?" Arran asked. "How did everyone get free of the *droughs*?"

Phelan shrugged, his face lined with worry. "Charon and I discovered the Druids had gotten the upper hand. We hid as they were herded into the foyer and then into Jason's office."

"No one noticed you?" Ian asked in surprise.

Phelan said, "Nay. Amazing as that is. Too many *droughs* to know who was doing what. We slipped right in the foyer and watched as we waited for the appropriate time to attack."

A cold chill ran down Arran's spine just thinking about it.

"And then you and Jason were having words," Phelan said. "I waited until the opportune time so you could get as much information as you could out of him. And then, I used my power to alter reality a wee bit."

Ian made a sound in the back of his throat. "He made the *droughs* think dozens of *mies* had flooded the mansion."

"Too bad I missed that," Arran said while trying to form some semblance of a grin. He would have loved to see the *droughs* turn in fear.

Phelan's face was grim. "All but a few *droughs* were so frightened they dropped their magic and tried to run. That's when we began to attack."

"I almost killed Wallace," Arran said with a shake of his head.

Phelan briefly put his hand on his shoulder. "I know. I saw. I also saw what Charon did."

Arran swallowed past the lump of emotion in his throat. "He can no' die. Especially no' for me."

"What happened to Ronnie?" Ian asked as he watched Phelan cut his arm once more.

Arran didn't let off the accelerator as he came to one of the numerous one-lane stone bridges, even though there was a car coming at him. He wasn't going to be the one to slow. Fortunately, the other car slammed on its brakes and turned into the grass to miss Arran.

"Close one," Phelan said grimly.

Arran gripped the steering wheel. "Fallon took Ronnie. I pray she's at the castle with the others."

"Where else would he have taken her?" Ian asked. "The castle is where we've always taken Druids who needed protection."

"She broke Wallace's nose," Arran said. "She faked it all. The problem is, I need to know why. He had to have used something against her."

Ian nodded with approval. "Good for her for hitting him. Wish I could've."

"You didna hear her asking me to stop as she stood beside him. I want to believe she lied, but I'm no' sure."

Phelan cleared his throat. "A lot could've happened at the mansion before we arrived. Remember that."

"Deirdre was inventive when it came to getting people to do what she wanted," Ian said. "Declan was as well. What would make Jason any different?"

Arran did a quick glance over his shoulder at Charon. "How is he?"

"My blood seems to be helping. A little. It's no' healing him as it should, but it's doing something. I just doona know for how long."

Phelan paused as he cut his arm again to use more of his blood in Charon's wound. His lips were in a tight line and worry lines bracketed his mouth. That in itself made Arran push the car to greater limits. Phelan's blood always healed instantly. Just what was going on with this *drough* blood?

First Larena was killed, and now Phelan's blood couldn't stop it. Unease churned in Arran's stomach.

"I've been thinking," Phelan said. "If the evil bastards we keep fighting can have ways to hurt us like the X90s or anything with *drough* blood, why could we no' have something as well?"

"Or something that could counter the effects of the *drough* blood," Ian said thoughtfully. "That's a good question."

Arran weaved his way between cars. His friends were trying to take their minds off the fact Phelan's blood wasn't working on Charon.

He sighed and tried to stay calm. Charon couldn't die. No more Warriors could be lost, no matter what Arran thought of him. "Aye, but one no' easily answered. We have no idea what it is about *drough* blood that affects us, nor why the blood of another Warrior helps to counter it."

"True," Ian said. "And blood type doesna matter when it comes to us."

Phelan shrugged, never taking his eyes off Charon. "We're Warriors. There isna much that does pertain to us as it does mortals."

They fell into silence as the miles passed. Night had finally fallen, but it wouldn't last for long. At this time of night the roads were nearly deserted, which allowed Arran and the others to travel as fast as they wanted.

Several times Phelan phoned Lucan and Quinn to see if Fallon had woken. The fact Fallon hadn't began to worry everyone. First Duncan, and then Larena. Arran was still wrapping his head around Larena's death. To lose Charon and possibly Fallon as well made Arran want to tear Wallace in half.

They were about an hour from the castle when Broc phoned to say he'd arrived at the castle and was going to bring Sonya to meet them.

Arran was determining the best place to go when Ian's phone rang, and he motioned for Arran to pull over.

"Fallon's awake," Ian said.

Arran put the car in park once he came to a stop. "Stay there," he told Broc before he disconnected his phone.

A second later, Phelan opened the passenger door as Fallon strode up. Fallon didn't say a word to any of them as he hefted Charon over his shoulder and was gone in a blink.

Arran got out of the car and walked to the hood where he placed his hands on the metal and hung his head. With Charon now being cared for by the Druids, there was a chance of his survival.

"We need to get back to the castle," Phelan said.

Arran lifted his head to look at him from across the car as the others walked up. "I have somewhere else to be."

"Aye, you do," Fallon said from behind him.

Arran whirled around to find Fallon and Broc. "What do you mean?"

"Ronnie told me she agreed to help Jason because he had Andy."

Arran slammed his hand against the hood of the car. "I knew Jason used something against her."

"There was no one in the dungeon," Camdyn said as he walked up. "No one other than the *droughs* waiting for us."

Ian and Galen exchanged looks before Ian said, "We didna get to look in every room, but I didna see anyone other than the *droughs*."

"Same here," Lucan said.

Arran turned to Broc. "Can you find Andy for me?"

Broc closed his eyes, and a few moments later opened them. "Andy is in Glasgow. He's safe, and trying to find Ronnie."

"Why did Ronnie think it was Andy?" Arran asked, more to himself than anyone else.

Quinn leaned his hip against the car. "We underestimated Wallace. We thought he would be like Declan and Deirdre. He's proven he isna. Which means, we have no idea what kind of magic he has, or what that magic is capable of."

"If he can make someone believe they're looking at someone else, we're fucked," Hayden said.

Logan nodded. "We'll never know what's real and what isna."

"Malcolm was injured as well," Fallon said into the silence. "Sonya was still healing him when I dropped off Charon. She said there's something different about this *drough* blood being used now."

Phelan crossed his arms over his chest. "I already figured that out."

"If Jason didna have Andy, then at least we doona have that to worry about," Ramsey said.

Lucan said, "And Ronnie is free of Jason. How is she faring with the others at the castle, Fallon?"

"She's no' at the castle."

Arran stilled as Fallon's gaze turned to him. "What do you mean she's no' at the castle." Fallon was his leader, the man he trusted, but when it came to Ronnie, none of that mattered.

"I had to know she wasna working with Jason. Until I

did, I wasna going to take her to the castle to possibly harm any of the Druids."

Arran moved to stand nose to nose with Fallon. He felt the others tense, ready to tear them apart.

"Where. Is. She?" Arran demanded.

Fallon didn't so much as flinch. His dark green gaze held steady, no emotion showing. "At her dig site. Now can we go?"

Arran caught Broc's eyes. "Nay, but there is something else I have to do."

"What is it you need?" Broc asked.

Arran clenched a fist and said, "I need you to find Pete Thornton."

CHAPTER
FORTY-THREE

Arran somehow wasn't surprised when Broc located Pete in Edinburgh. Fallon jumped them to a secluded alley they often used when coming to the city.

"Where is he?" Arran asked Broc.

Broc's head turned to the right. "He's in a warehouse no' far from here."

Arran halted the others as they started to follow him. "Pete is mine."

"Understood," Phelan said. Then he grinned, but it was full of cruelty and viciousness. "But if he tries to escape, he's fair game."

Arran shook his head. "He's fair game to catch. But I deal with him."

He said no more as he started jogging in the direction Broc had looked. Broc kept a little in front to lead the way. A few blocks later, Broc pointed to the warehouse, and the group split into different directions.

Arran and Broc continued straight on to the warehouse. Once they reached it, Arran came to a halt near the entrance.

"He's alone," Broc said before Arran could ask who else was in the building.

Arran looked at the door. "What floor?"

"Ground level."

Arran's god wanted to be released, and it was only by a

thin thread of restraint that Arran held him back. He grasped the doorknob, and with one twist, broke it off. He then shoved his shoulder into the door to break past the dead bolt.

"That's one way of doing it," Broc said from behind him.

He probably should have been quieter about his entrance, but Arran didn't want to chance losing control of Memphaea. Not when he needed to confront Pete with a clear head.

Ronnie had to get in touch with Arran somehow so she could tell him she had to find Andy. Surely Arran would help her in that.

She spent almost two hours scouring the debris of the site, looking for a cell phone. It wasn't until she went to the vehicles that she got lucky.

Breaking into a car looked a lot easier on television than it actually was. She finally found a large rock and smashed it into the window to get to the phone.

She was punching in Arran's numbers when she paused. Something told her to try calling Andy. She dialed his phone and licked her lips as it rang.

It was on its sixth ring, and she was just about to hang up when she heard, "Hello."

"Andy?" she asked breathlessly.

"Ronnie. Oh, my God. Is that really you? Are you all right?"

Ronnie slumped against the car and slid to the ground. "Are you with Jason?"

"Jason? Jason who? Never mind. I'm in Glasgow at a pub, wondering why the hell Arran won't answer his phone."

She closed her eyes and sighed in relief. "Jason told me he had you. I saw you, Andy. I saw you beat up with all the blood over your face."

"I've got a few scrapes from running away. And I think I might have broken my hand while I was helping this really gorgeous girl get away."

Ronnie chuckled and leaned her head back against the

car. Only Andy would think of women in a time like this. "I hope this chick at least gave you a kiss for such a valiant display."

"Oh, she did. And much more."

"I don't need to know any more," she hastily told him, but couldn't hold back her laughter. As her smile faded, anger welled inside her. Jason had tricked her.

She'd given her word and betrayed Arran because of magic. It was then Ronnie knew she had to learn all there was to know of magic quickly.

"Andy, I need you to stay in Glasgow. I'll contact you as soon as I can. I've got a lot I need to fill you in on. Some you won't believe."

"Is Arran with you?"

"No."

Andy sighed. "He told me he'd keep you safe. Did he?"

"Without a doubt," she whispered.

Arran stepped into the warehouse to see rows and rows of wide shelving stacked high above them. There was a soft sound, and Arran saw movement at the very top.

Camdyn squatted behind a large wooden crate and peered down at him and Broc.

"To the right," Broc whispered.

Arran ran on silent feet toward the right. He'd gotten halfway down the huge warehouse when his enhanced hearing picked up a sound. Arran lengthened his strides as he gave a burst of speed and came around a row of shelving to catch a glimpse of Pete between crates stacked haphazardly on the ground.

Fury ripped through Arran. He slowed to a walk, his footsteps as quiet as a ghost's. As he approached, he saw Pete had a crate open and was sifting through the packing material used to stuff the crate.

Arran still held out hope he was wrong about Pete, even when he knew in his gut he wasn't. But when Pete held up a cracked trencher to the light behind him, Arran's suspicions were confirmed.

He stood half in the shadows, half in the light, and simply watched Pete check the contents of the crate. Arran was glad Ronnie wasn't there to see this. She'd be devastated.

It wasn't until Pete began to repack the box that Arran said, "Going somewhere?"

Pete's head snapped up, his eyes searching the darkness in the direction Arran stood. "Who's there?"

"What amazes me is that you actually thought you could get away with it."

"Who's there?" Pete shouted again.

Arran inwardly cheered when he noted the perspiration dotting Pete's brow and the way his nervousness grew the longer Arran held his silence.

"Dammit. Show yourself!" Pete yelled, and took a step back from the crate to a table behind him.

Arran slowly moved into the light.

Pete's eyes grew large. "*You*. What are you doing here? How did you find me?"

"I have certain . . . friends," Arran said. "I came to retrieve what's Ronnie's."

"She'll never miss this stuff. I've been taking little things from her from the very beginning. If that fool Max had not gotten greedy, Ronnie would've never known."

"She's always known," Arran stated calmly. "Always."

That gave Pete pause, but then his apprehension doubled. "Did Ronnie send you?"

"Does it matter? Make things easy on yourself and return the items. Doona make me take them from you, because you'll regret it."

Pete's arm swung around, and Arran found himself staring down the barrel of a pistol.

"I don't think so," Pete said. "I need this money. So I've taken a few things. Big deal. Ronnie gets the glory and moves on to another dig."

"So jealousy prompted this?"

"Not at first. But when my funding dried up and I was being told the money was going to her, what was I supposed to do? Archeology is my life."

The tide of rage Arran had been holding back broke through. "And you were like a father to her!" He took a step toward Pete. "How could you? How did you even look her in the eye?"

"A man has to do what he has to do," Pete said, the gun never wavering.

Arran jerked his chin at the weapon. "Go ahead. Shoot. I guarantee you willna leave here alive."

"You're not alone?" Pete asked, his brow furrowing.

Arran simply grinned. "Oh, Pete. There is much about me you doona know, but you're about to find out."

All around him, Arran could hear the others taking up position. They wouldn't show themselves unless Arran asked them to. They were there to watch his back.

Arran took another step, quickly closing the distance between him and Pete.

"Stay back," Pete warned.

He sneered at the gun. "There isna much in this world I fear, and your weapon is certainly no' one of them. Put it down and walk away."

"You'd allow me to walk away."

"Aye. Give me the items you've stolen and keep away from Ronnie. Stay away from any archeological dig site, and you'll never see me again."

Pete frowned. "You're not here to arrest me?"

"I can if it would make you feel better. Make your decision, but quickly, because my patience is running out."

"Who are you?" Pete demanded.

Arran glanced at the floor. "I'm of no consequence. Unfortunately, you hurt someone I care about, and I can no' let you get away with it."

Pete seemed to consider his words. He looked at the crate and then back at Arran. "I've got debts. I have to sell these for the money or I'm dead."

Arran allowed his god to poke through enough to change his eyes to complete white. "If you doona do as I say, I'll kill you myself."

"Holy mother of God," Pete said, and stumbled backwards, his eyes widened in horror. "What are you?"

"Your worst nightmare. Walk away now, Pete. It's the last time I give you this offer."

Pete began to lower his gun, but just as Arran thought he would turn away, Pete raised his arm and fired the weapon. Arran leaned to the side and easily dodged the bullet.

He turned his head to Pete and growled, the sound rumbling deep within him and echoing around the warehouse. He was still full of rage from the battle at Wallace mansion. Knowing Ronnie had been tricked only notched his anger up by degrees.

There was a soft swish as someone jumped from the top of the shelves to the ground. The next thing Arran knew, Ian and Quinn stood on either side of him.

Pete gave an alarmed cry and dropped his gun as he turned and ran. He was slow and clumsy because of his size and age, but the fact he was leaving was good enough for Arran.

Arran saw a shadow move as it followed Pete. And he knew Lucan was making sure Pete didn't return.

"What now?" Ian asked.

Arran walked to the crate and set his hands on the side. "Now, I return these to Ronnie. And all of you go home."

"Are you going to tell Ronnie who took the items?" Camdyn asked.

Arran turned his head to look at Fallon. "Take them home, and check on Malcolm and Charon."

"Wait!" Ian said, but Fallon had already put his hand on him.

Arran let out a breath once he was alone. He dropped his chin to his chest and briefly squeezed his eyes closed. The first part was done. Now all he needed to do was get the artifacts back to Ronnie without her seeing him.

She'd made her wishes regarding him clear, and though a part of him wanted to fight her and make her listen to him, he knew that would only make things worse.

By making sure Pete stayed away, he was already taking away her father figure. At least she had Andy.

Arran remembered the way Ronnie's body had reacted to his touch, how her passion had erupted when they came together. After having her, how would he get through eternity without her?

"You look how I feel."

Arran's head snapped up to find Fallon standing in front of him on the other side of the crate. "What are you doing here?"

"I can no' stay at the castle. There are too many memories of Larena. The women keep trying to get me to stay, and I know it's because Larena has to be buried and they want me to grieve."

"What are you going to do?"

Fallon shrugged. "I can no longer think of the future. I'll get through today, and then think about tomorrow when it comes."

"The men need you."

"Nay," Fallon said with a slow shake of his head. "None of you need me to lead. All of you do it yourselves just fine."

Arran wanted to argue with him, yet he understood exactly how Fallon felt.

"Are you going to talk to her?" Fallon asked.

He shook his head and pushed off the crate. "It's better if I doona."

"I think you're wrong there. I think you should talk to Ronnie, tell her what happened. Make her see it was Pete who stole, no' you."

"Nay. I willna hurt her that way."

"So you'll allow her to think the worst of you? That doesna sound like the Arran I knew."

Arran smiled wryly. "That's because I'm no longer that man."

"You care deeply for her."

It wasn't a question. "Deeply."

"Do you love her?"

Arran looked away from Fallon as he faced a question he

hadn't been able to ask himself. But it was out there, and now he had to face it. Yet suddenly, it didn't frighten him as he expected. "Aye. More than anything."

"You're allowing your pride to keep you away, then?"

"She asked that I never speak to her again. I'm granting her wish."

"And making yourself miserable in the process."

Arran slid his gaze to meet Fallon's. "You didna see her face. You didna see the anguish in her eyes, or hear it in her voice. She's hurt profoundly, Fallon, and there is nothing I can say that will reach her. Even if I tell her it was Pete who stole, she willna believe me."

"Aye." Fallon inhaled deeply. "I see your point. Maybe you should've brought her here to see it was Pete."

"It would've killed her. I would no' do that to her. I was in a position to save her that pain, and that's what I did. I didna mean anything to her. Let her despise me, no' the man she thinks of as a father."

Fallon walked around the crate and clapped Arran on the shoulder. "You're a good man. But I think you're wrong in thinking you didna mean anything to her. You forget, my friend, I watched her as well at Wallace's. She had eyes only for you. There was worry—and pride—as she watched you fight."

Arran had no words in response. He didn't want to be a good man. He wanted Ronnie, but in order to have her, he had to destroy her world. What kind of man did that to the woman he loved?

"Let me take you to her," Fallon said. "We'll leave the artifacts, and then you can see if you want to talk to her."

Arran opened his mouth to answer, and in the next instant Fallon had jumped them from the warehouse to Ronnie's tent at the dig site.

"Shite," Arran muttered as he stepped away from Fallon. He could feel Ronnie's magic.

It surrounded him like a blanket, soft, comforting. Powerful. Alluring and erotic. His cock swelled with need and his hands clenched air, wishing it was her.

He wanted to go to her, to pull her into his arms and kiss her for hours. He wanted to lay her down and make love to her in a thousand different ways. He wanted to tell her of his love, of the way he wanted her in his life.

He wanted so many things, but the time for them had come and gone. After all the many years of his life, he'd finally found the woman for him. And he'd lost her.

"Take me home," he begged.

Fallon said not a word as he touched his arm and they teleported away.

Just before Ronnie entered her tent.

Ronnie rushed into her tent because she'd heard Arran's voice. Her stomach fell to her feet when she found her tent empty save for the large crate.

"Oh, Arran," she whispered as she pulled out an artifact.

He hadn't stayed because she'd said she never wanted to see him again. But she did want to see him. She wanted to see him, to talk to him.

To hold him.

God, how she missed his touch. She'd thought she could go through life without needing someone, but she'd been proved wrong so effortlessly.

Her artifacts were returned, but she'd rather have her Warrior beside her. If only she'd gotten to her tent sooner. If only she'd never said those cruel words to him. She hastily blinked to keep the tears at bay.

Ronnie moved aside the straw and saw something among the packing material. She reached down and pulled out a cell phone. Her heart pounded with dread as she recognized the beat-up old phone she'd seen countless times.

She flipped open the phone and saw Pete's name carved crudely above the numbers. Her world began to spin as realization crashed upon her.

It wasn't Arran who had stolen. It was Pete. Arran had known, but he hadn't told her. Not that she'd given him the chance, or believed him when he swore he hadn't taken anything.

Ronnie tossed down the phone and grabbed the keys to the Range Rover Arran had driven. She ran to the SUV and climbed inside.

She might not know how to find MacLeod Castle, but she knew where to start looking—MacLeod land.

CHAPTER
FORTY-FOUR

Arran stood in the great hall of MacLeod Castle and briefly watched the Druids still embracing their husbands after their return.

He'd never felt more out of place than he did at that moment, because all he could think of was how right it would have been for Ronnie to be among the Druids.

How right it would have been to walk into her arms after battle and simply hold her.

The knowledge that it would never happen was what made him start for the door. Until everyone caught sight of Fallon.

It was all the women talking at once that made Arran turn around and find out what was going on. Fallon was soon surrounded, but even with enhanced hearing, it was difficult for Arran to discern what the women were trying to say.

Fallon closed his eyes as if it pained him too much to even be in the castle. Arran understood the discomfort of his friend. He might not have had Ronnie for over four hundred years, but the little time they'd had together left a mark that would forever alter him.

Arran was turning to leave when something moved on the stairs out of the corner of his eye. He turned and saw Larena. She was staring at Fallon, her smoky blue eyes filled with tears.

As one, the Druids grew quiet. Only then did Fallon open his eyes. And he caught sight of Larena. He slowly pushed his way out of the Druids as Larena descended the stairs.

For several minutes they simply stared at each other, and then Fallon pulled her against him, his told tight as he buried his head in her blond hair.

Arran was happy for his friend, but it made his heart ache even more. He left the hall quietly and shut the door behind him. The sun had once more claimed the sky though it was only four in the morning.

He walked down the stairs and across the bailey to the gatehouse. The gates of MacLeod Castle stayed open now, but there had been a time when Arran and the others had them bolted and they patrolled the battlements waiting for an attack from Deirdre.

Though he didn't miss the attacks, he missed how simple life had been. It had been easy to hide who they were. It had also been easy to keep people away from the castle.

Arran let out a long sigh and walked beneath the gatehouse where he paused for just a moment trying to decide where he would go. To the cottages that had once been a small village a little ways from the castle? Or to the cliffs?

It was the call of the water, the smell of the sea that pulled at Arran. He turned right and made his way to the cliffs.

He'd come here often through his time at the castle. The first time he'd seen the castle sitting at the edge of the cliffs he'd been in awe at the sheer magnificence of it, the beauty that had held him spellbound even before he'd felt the touch of magic.

The stones had been weathered by wind and rain, but the castle was built to last, and MacLeod Castle showed that best of all. It had survived many battles, and even being burned by Deirdre. It had seen untold number of deaths, but instead of being a place to stay away from, it offered hope to any who sought it.

He stood at the edge of the cliff and looked down to the beach below. Huge boulders rose from the water like giants reaching for the sun. Those same boulders had been used by each of them to cast nets into the water for fishing.

During the summer there was hardly a day they hadn't been down at the beach, sitting in the sun or swimming. Arran peered over the side to look at the hollowed-out sections in the cliffs. Several of them were caves, and one had been used to hide the Druids during an attack by Deirdre.

Arran inhaled, the salt thick in the air. The sea was in constant motion, the waves white-capping as far as the eye could see.

It was effortless for him to allow his thoughts to wander as he looked at the ebb and flow of the tides. They made it easy for Arran to stop thinking of what to do and give in to the memories of centuries prior, and days past.

The crunch of a boot on the grass broke through his thoughts. He turned his head slightly to find Fallon walking toward him.

It was good to see him happy again. Arran wondered if he would ever find happiness again. How could he stay away from Ronnie when he wanted her so that his chest hurt from it.

"I worried you left as Malcolm did that fateful day so long ago," Fallon said.

Arran bent and picked up a small rock by his foot. The day Fallon referred to was the day Deirdre had captured Malcolm and released his god. Malcolm had left the castle during an attack, and no one had known it until it was too late.

"I'd say good-bye if I was leaving."

Fallon held out his hand for the stone. "So you are no' leaving?"

"I doona know what I'm going to do. All I can think about is her. All I want is her."

"Then go get her."

Arran wished it were that easy. He handed Fallon the stone and crossed his arms over his chest. "I'm happy to see Larena is all right. What happened?"

"Sonya isna sure. Maybe it takes longer for the magic to work against this new *drough* blood being used."

"That's no' a good sign. How are Malcolm and Charon?"

Fallon tossed the stone in the air and easily caught it. "They're recovering. Slowly. Larena has been with Malcolm since I brought him in. And that was a good try in changing the subject."

"It was a try," Arran said with a sigh. He didn't want to talk about Ronnie, because it only made him miss her even more. If that was possible.

"You didna know me before Larena, but I was no' a man you would've wanted to be around."

Arran glanced at him. "Quinn told me how you turned to drinking because of what Deirdre had done."

"It wasna just the killing of our clan. It was the fact I considered myself a monster. It wasna until Larena that I began to imagine we could use what I thought of as a curse to help save people."

"We are monsters," Arran said softly. "We hide the castle from the world so they willna find us. Do you know what they would do with us if they ever learned what we are?"

"I doona want to even think about it. My point, Arran, is that Larena made me a better man. She made me want to be the person I had always thought I would be. I had to fight for her, and there were times I wondered if I should. But then I would think of life without her and I knew I'd do whatever it took to have her as my own."

Arran turned his head to him. "Even if she had said she never wanted to see you again."

"Even then. I knew from the first moment I touched her that she was the other half of my soul. I would've walked to Hell and back if it meant I could have Larena."

Maybe Fallon was right. Maybe Arran needed to fight for Ronnie. He didn't have to tell her it was Pete who had stolen from her.

Fallon reared back his hand and let the stone soar over the water and travel far into the horizon before it skipped four times and sank beneath the waves. "I see by your look you're actually contemplating how to get her back."

"I doona want to live without her. No' even for one second."

And once the words were said aloud, Arran comprehended just how far he would go to get her back.

"Do you need me to jump you to her?" Fallon offered.

Arran turned on his heel and started walking. "Nay," he said over his shoulder.

He'd use the time it took to get to Ronnie to figure out all he wanted to say to her.

Ronnie pulled off the road and put the SUV in park as she stared at the trees. She was officially on MacLeod land, and had been for a few miles. But she had no idea where to go. She'd asked Arran nothing about the castle or where it was located.

Sure it was hidden by a shield of magic, but MacLeod land was massive, with the one road going through it. Did she look toward the sea, or did she look the other way?

Ronnie put the Range Rover in drive and eased her way along the trees. Arran had driven to her site, which meant there had to be some kind of drive or hidden road. If she could find it.

She looked on both sides of the road, and fortunately for her, there were few people on the road at this time of night.

"Morning," she corrected herself.

It was very early morning, and exhaustion was beginning to wear on her. She needed rest, but she didn't want to stop looking. Not until she was forced to.

Ronnie had to halt and pull fully off the road as a car came at her. She looked in the rearview mirror to make sure the car passed safely, and that's when she saw the unmistakable ruts from a vehicle.

She threw the SUV in reverse and backed up. Her heart was thundering in her chest as she turned off the road.

"Please let this be right. Please let this be the place."

She kept chanting that over and over as she slowly drove the vehicle through the dense trees following the obvious path that was used as a road. Suddenly the trees stopped to an openness that stretched endlessly before her.

The bright green grass then gave way to the deep waters of the ocean that met the sky on the horizon.

"Wow," she whispered.

Ronnie kept having the disturbing feeling that she needed to turn around and leave, but it was that feeling that kept her foot on the accelerator. The feeling grew intensely until she drove through what felt like an invisible wall. And then she saw the castle.

"Oh, shit."

She stopped the Range Rover and put it in park before she hesitantly got out. The castle rose like a stone giant from the cliffs, large, beautiful, and imposing. Six turrets like large beacons stood against the sky while the gray stones seemed to welcome her.

Ronnie looked around to see a smattering of cottages. Those same cottages hid some of the castle from view. She glanced at the drive that led around the cottages, but decided to proceed down the narrow road through what looked like a village.

The cottages were devoid of people from what Ronnie could see, but she spotted furniture through open shutters.

Once she was through the village, she got a good look at the castle. And it took her breath away. It looked like a classic castle, only without a moat or drawbridge.

A massive gatehouse stood sentry and connected the battlements that ran around the castle. She could well imagine the views the towers offered.

This was where Arran and the others lived. Now she understood why it meant so much to him. It wasn't just because the castle was striking in the setting of the green of the grass and the different blues of sea and sky against the stark gray stones.

The castle projected magic even she could feel.

Ronnie stuck her hands in her back pockets and tried to imagine what life would have been like for Arran before he'd been thrown into the future.

Now that she was here, she wondered if he would even

want to see her. Fallon hadn't believed her at first, and she wasn't even sure if he did now. He hadn't come back for her. Maybe that was because they were still looking for Andy.

Ronnie had left a message on Saffron's phone about Andy, but Saffron had yet to return her call.

She turned her head to the side and froze as she caught sight of Arran. He stood about two hundred yards from her and just stared.

Minutes ticked by as neither moved. Ronnie knew she had to take the first step. After all, she'd been the one to send him away.

She started toward him, but still he didn't move. The closer she drew to him, the more she wondered if he would acknowledge her.

Ronnie stopped when she was ten paces away. "Jason never had Andy."

"We know."

She'd hoped for more than two words as a response. "I swear it was him. I'd never have agreed to help Jason if I'd known he had tricked me."

"I know."

Another two words. She was about to scream, she was so frustrated. "You found the stolen artifacts."

He gave a single nod.

Ronnie rapidly blinked to hold back the tears. She had really screwed things up. The one man she could have been happy with, and she might have ruined it all. "I came . . . I came to tell you . . ."

"Aye?" he urged, and took a step toward her.

"I came to say . . . I love you."

He moved so fast she didn't see him until he was right before her, and pulling her into his arms. "What did you say?" he whispered.

Ronnie looked deep into his golden eyes. All the hopes and dreams she had of their life together she let reflect in her eyes. "I love you."

"Say it again."

This time she smiled, her heart pounding. "I love you."

He closed his eyes as his arms tightened their hold. "I could only hope you'd feel it." His lids lifted and desire darkened his gaze. "I was coming for you. I was going to make you listen to me, no matter how long it took."

"Why?" she asked excitedly.

His smile was slow, seductive. Hungry. "Because I love you."

Nothing else existed beyond that. All Ronnie felt was Arran's wonderfully solid muscle against her, his insistent lips as he kissed her.

The kiss robbed her of all her fears as he slid his tongue past her lips and into her mouth. He groaned and deepened the kiss. Her arms wound around his neck while her fingers plunged in the cool silkiness of his dark locks.

Within Arran's embrace she felt safe and sheltered. Loved. It was a feeling she'd never had before, and one she would do anything to keep.

She ended the kiss despite his growl of frustration. Ronnie tried to get her breathing under control as he rested his forehead against hers.

"I'm sorry for thinking you stole from me. I should've listened to you."

His body tensed beneath her hands for a moment, and then he began to relax. "How do you know it wasna me?"

"I found Pete's phone in the crate. Why didn't you tell me it was him?"

"You thought of him as a father. I didna want to hurt you."

"So you allowed me to think it was you." She gave him a soft punch in the side that resulted in his grunt. "Don't ever do that again."

He grinned boyishly. "Promise."

"Where is Pete?"

"Long gone. He willna steal from you again. That I vow."

Ronnie rested her head against his chest. "What now?"

"Now I take you to my bed."

She laughed, but quickly grew serious. "I meant about Jason."

"I knew what you meant. I'd hoped to avoid that for a wee

bit. We've hurt him, but it's far from over. If our battles with Deirdre and Declan were any indication, I think Jason will come at us hard."

Ronnie leaned back to look at him. "He wanted me to find magical objects for him. He'll be looking for them. Maybe that's what I should concentrate on. I want to help. I want to be able to use my magic to defend myself, not to just find artifacts in the ground. I want to be a part of this war."

"You need to learn to use your magic, but I'm no' sure I want you a part of the war."

"Too bad. I am a part of it. I'll be safer with you."

He slid a hand around her neck into her hair. "You know I'll always protect you."

"There's one thing, though. Jason and I made a pact through magic. He swore he wouldn't hurt Andy if I did as he asked. Does that pact still apply?"

Arran's shrugged and turned her toward the castle. "I doubt it, since he used magic to make you think Andy was there. But that's a worry for another day. This day is ours."

"Just this day?" she asked with a teasing smile.

When he looked down at her, the love shining in his eyes brought tears to hers. "Nay. I want you beside me forever."

"I don't think I can live here, Arran. The thought appeals to me because the magic of Isla's shield would stop my aging. But I'm an archeologist. I move around."

He winked at her before sweeping his arm across the land. "This has been untouched for over seven hundred years. There was a mighty clan here once, and a thriving village. I wonder what you could find."

The thought of looking over virgin land intrigued her. "Do you think the MacLeods would allow it?"

"I'm certain they'd make a concession for my wife."

She jerked her gaze to him, her heart in her throat. "Your wife?"

"Aye," he said softly. "Would you marry me, Dr. Reid?"

She threw her arms around his neck. Her heart was about to burst from her chest, she was so happy. "Yes. Oh, yes!"

CHAPTER
FORTY-FIVE

Jason gripped the arms of his chair, the wood cracking beneath his hold. His clothes were soaked with blood. His blood.

The plan he'd formulated so carefully in his mind had gone to shit all too easily. There was no way the Warriors should have been able to break the hold of his Druids. Their black magic was powerful.

Yet, that's exactly what the Warriors had done.

"Oww," Jason yelped as Aisley cleaned his wound.

Her eyes were dilated and her face pale. Dale had said she had a concussion, but Jason didn't care. If she'd been conscious and using her magic, the Warriors wouldn't have gotten free.

"Be still," Aisley said. "If you keep moving, it's going to keep hurting."

"Let me slice open your jaw and throat with five gashes and tell me if it doesna hurt to breathe," he said between clenched teeth.

Dale walked into the house. "The area is secure. The Druids we managed to save are setting up spells to keep everyone out."

Jason was glad he had discovered the hunting lodge that belonged to the Wallaces. It hadn't been used in decades, but he'd seen a place he could hide if need be, so he'd promptly had it made ready.

And a good thing that he had.

"I need to find a Druid who's a healer like the one the MacLeods have," Jason said as he watched Aisley thread the needle she was going to use to stitch him.

Dale leaned against the huge stone hearth. "That would have saved two of the *droughs* who died on the way here. I'm sure there were others we left behind that were wounded and could've been saved."

"Then they should have followed us. And where is Mindy?"

"She'll be here soon, I'm sure," Aisley said.

Jason narrowed his gaze on Aisley. "And how did you manage to get out since you were unconscious?"

"I carried her," Dale answered.

Jason looked from Aisley to Dale and back to Aisley. "Is there something going on between the two of you?"

"No," Dale said. "She's your family. I grabbed her because I didna think you wanted family left behind."

Jason studied the Warrior. Dale could be telling the truth, or there could very well be something going on between his cousin and Dale. "Then I offer my gratitude."

Dale gave a slight bow of his head. "Two of the Druids went for food and medicine to help dull your pain. They should return shortly."

"My magic will dull my pain." Jason waited until Dale was gone before he said, "You owe him your life, cousin."

"I know," Aisley replied softly, and poured rubbing alcohol on the needle before sticking it over the flame of a candle.

It grated his nerves that as great as his magic was, he couldn't heal the wounds made by a Warrior. "Do you care for Dale?"

Aisley met his gaze, her dark eyes emotionless. "He did what he was supposed to do. What is there to care about?"

"That's my girl," Jason said with a half smile that ended in a cringe.

He didn't want Aisley to be indebted to anyone but him. If she was, then that would change everything.

"Ready?" she asked.

Jason took a deep breath and slowly released it as he gave

a nod. The first prick of the needle in his skin was nothing compared to the slide of the thread through the wound.

When he found Arran and the rest of the Warriors, he was going to put them through pain unlike anything they had experienced before. But he would have something special for Arran and Ronnie.

He'd mark Ronnie's body as Arran had scarred him. And then he would make Arran watch as his Warriors took Ronnie again and again. There were ways he could extend Arran's pain for years.

And that's exactly what he was going to do.

"What's our next move?" Aisley asked.

Jason cackled. "Oh, my dear, it was put into place days ago. They'll never see it coming."

CHAPTER
FORTY-SIX

Arran leaned against the Range Rover as he watched Ronnie stand in the middle of the dig site. It had taken him and the others a few hours to clean things up, thanks to Andy's help directing them.

Now, Ronnie stood with her eyes closed and her magic swirling around her. It made his cock hard to feel her magic run over his skin like silk. She had no idea of her allure or her beauty, which made her all the more beautiful and special.

They'd barely had an hour at the castle, and then only fifteen minutes alone. But they'd made the most of those fifteen in the cottage he'd claimed as his.

There hadn't been a need for a bed. There had been no slow hands, or soft kisses. Their lovemaking had been needy. Frantic.

Fierce.

He smiled every time he thought about how he'd pushed her against the wall and wrapped her legs around his waist. And then he'd sunk into her wet heat.

Their need had been too overwhelming and hungry to be denied. It had come at them quickly, and there had been no putting off their climaxes.

"Do you think Ronnie will ever stop blushing from you having to come to the castle to get her more clothes?" Ian asked.

Arran rubbed his chin as he thought of Ronnie. None of her clothes had survived his hands as he'd torn them off her. Ronnie had been mortified that he'd gotten her more clothes, but she'd asked how soon they could get back to the cottage.

"Where will she look for artifacts next?" Galen asked.

Arran pushed off the SUV when he felt a change in Ronnie's magic. "I've no' asked."

"What is it?"

Arran shrugged. "There's something wrong."

Suddenly Ronnie's gaze turned to him. She mouthed his name and he was by her side in an instant.

"What's wrong?"

"I feel something. Here," she said, and pointed to the ground below her feet.

Arran waved Camdyn over. "Ronnie feels something in the ground. Can you bring it up for us?"

Camdyn grinned. "Of course."

Ronnie slid her hand into Arran's as they waited while Camdyn used his power to shift the earth until a piece of stone the size of Arran's palm was revealed.

He gazed at it while Ronnie took it, turning it one way and then the other. The stone looked familiar, as if Arran had seen it recently.

"It looks like it's from a piece of something."

Arran shouted for Fallon before he turned to her and Camdyn and said, "Because it is."

Ronnie grew nervous when Arran ran to Fallon and spoke quietly before he rushed back to her. "What is it?"

"Just wait," Arran said.

"I'm not a patient woman."

"That, lass, I learned early on."

They shared a knowing look when Fallon suddenly appeared beside them, the stone that had the prophecy chiseled on it in his hands.

She took a step back, but it was Arran's hand on her back that halted her.

"Trust me," he urged.

Ronnie didn't need to be told twice. She forced herself to

look at the prophecy that had changed her life. "This new piece looks as if it belongs, but there's nowhere on the stone that shows it had been broken off."

Fallon narrowed his gaze. "I'd agree with Ronnie, but there's something about this stone."

"Aye," Camdyn said quietly.

Arran took the two broken pieces from Fallon and held them in front of Ronnie. "Hold the broken piece over them. I think that somehow you're involved with this. If this prophecy is about you, then the piece you have belongs with it."

Ronnie looked at the knotwork on the small piece in her hand. "Granted, it is the same workmanship, but I just don't see—"

"Magic, lass," Arran whispered. "Trust in it."

Ronnie had questioned him before and paid a steep price. She wasn't going to question him again.

She licked her lips and held the piece over the stone tablet. Something warm and electric zinged through the arm that held the broken piece.

Her gaze flashed to Arran's to see he'd felt the magic as well. Fallon took a step back while Camdyn peered closer at it.

"Arran . . ."

"Trust it."

She closed her eyes then and gave herself up to the magic that was calling her. Something strong and magical surged from the stone in a flood of light as bright as the sun and in a rainbow of colors. It rose straight to the clouds before doubling back on itself and slamming into Ronnie.

She sucked in a breath at the sweet sound of chanting and drums she heard as if from far, far away. She tried to reach out to them, but she couldn't get close enough.

As suddenly as it had come, it was gone.

Ronnie opened her eyes to find the stone in her hand gone. She looked at the tablet to see it melding all three parts together.

"I'll be damned," Camdyn murmured.

Arran turned the now solid piece of the tablet around. "There's more to the prophecy now."

"Well?" Ronnie urged.

"It says," he paused to read. Then his gaze locked with hers.

"Arran," she said, another queasy feeling beginning in her stomach. "Did I do something bad again?"

Camdyn took the tablet and read. "Nay, Ronnie. It appears as if you've ended the prophecy. It says here that the Druid, with the love of a man-god, has the strength to stand firm against the new darkness."

Fallon lifted one shoulder in a shrug. "It seems, Ronnie, that by finding this missing section, you have indeed ended the prophecy."

"Thank God," she said as Arran enfolded her in his arms.

They stayed that way for several minutes until a thought took root. Ronnie pulled out of his arms and asked, "Does it say how Jason can be ended once and for all?"

"Nay," Camdyn said. "That it doesna. Have faith, though. We killed Deirdre and Declan. We'll get Jason as well."

With a grin, Fallon walked away, Camdyn on his heels, the tablet tucked beneath his arms.

"That's a load off my shoulders," she said.

"I knew there was more magic I felt. I'm glad we came back. Now you can concentrate on becoming my wife."

Ronnie forgot all about the tablet and prophecy as her mind turned to her upcoming wedding and being in the arms of the man of her dreams.

"Fallon!" Arran called.

She barely had time to look at the dig site one last time before she was inside MacLeod Castle.

"Arran, you got a call from some old man from Edinburgh. He said you'd know what it was about!" Reaghan shouted from the kitchen.

Arran kissed Ronnie quickly on the forehead and rushed to the kitchen. "Did he leave a message?" he asked Reaghan.

"He did," she said, and shoved a strand of auburn hair from her face. "He said the Druids you need to be looking for came from the Isle of Skye."

Galen slapped him on the back. "You were right about the old man. He's going to be a good resource, I think."

Ronnie shoved past them and started talking to the women about what had happened at the dig site.

"There's been no sightings that I've found of the selmyr," Gwynn said as she came into the kitchen from the outside herb garden.

"That's good news, right?" Cara asked.

Arran traded looks with Hayden. "It could be," he answered.

"Oh," Gwynn said. "But I did do some research into that Web site Ronnie found regarding the story of the Celts and Warriors. The owner hid her information well, but not well enough. Her name is Evangeline Walker, and she lives in Britain somewhere."

The information settled in Arran's head, but before he could talk more about it, the women took Ronnie and they disappeared out of the castle.

"Doona try to go after them," Ian said with a laugh. "Dani has spoken of nothing but the wedding since you announced it."

A wedding. His wedding.

Arran smiled and looked to the men who he considered his brothers. "I'm getting married!"

"No' for another couple of days," Lucan said as he took Arran's shoulders. "The women have their things to do. And so do we."

There was shouting all around him, and Arran had time to look out the kitchen window to find Ronnie staring at him before Fallon jumped the women from the castle.

EPILOGUE

Arran couldn't stop smiling. It had been a glorious week. Not only had the Druids welcomed Ronnie with open arms, as he'd known they would, they had also quickly shown her how to harness her magic.

As great as it had been to have Ronnie with him, it was nothing compared to making her his wife. The wedding had been hastily thrown together, and no matter how many times Arran offered to give her a lavish wedding, Ronnie had insisted she wanted something small and private.

So they had exchanged vows at the chapel in the castle with everyone from the castle and Andy. Thankfully, the preacher had welcomed the donation to his parish in exchange for being blindfolded and brought to the castle.

Ronnie had never looked so gorgeous as in her off white gown, which had hugged her curves. The gown looked even lovelier puddled on the floor by the bed.

"What are you grinning at?" Ronnie asked as she rolled over to lay on his chest.

"Ah, I'm just remembering how nice you'd looked in your wedding gown, but I much preferred getting you out of it."

She lightly nipped his shoulder. "Just like a man."

He rolled her to her back and leaned over her. "Nay. Like your husband."

"Well, husband," she said softly, "are we going to talk all night?"

Arran bent to kiss his wife, his cock hardening at the thought of claiming her again. Ronnie was his. Now and forever, their souls melded together.

But ever in the back of his mind was Wallace. They could only hide away so long before the next battle began.

"No dark thoughts," she mumbled between his kisses.

"Nay. Only thoughts of you."

"Of us," she corrected.

Arran claimed her mouth and let all the worries and dark thoughts leave him while he was in Ronnie's arms. There would be time enough to face the new evil.

Until then, he was going to love his wife over and over.

"I love you," he whispered as he thrust inside her.

Her answering kiss was all he needed.

Coming soon . . .

Don't miss the next Dark Warrior novel by
Donna Grant

MIDNIGHT'S CAPTIVE

Available in July 2013 from St. Martin's Paperbacks